THE HUNTRESS

SARAH DRIVER

EGMONT

To my readers, for a dazzle-bright debut year.

Heart-thanks for crewing up with me and Mouse!

May the sea-gods always swim close to you.

EGMONT
We bring stories to life

First published in Great Britain 2018

by Egmont UK Limited

The Yellow Building, 1 Nicholas Road, London W11 4AN

Text copyright © Sarah Driver 2018
Illustrations copyright © Ray Tierney 2018
Map illustration copyright © Joe McLaren 2018

Additional illustrations first published in 2017 in the titles *The Huntress: Sea* and
The Huntress: Sky written by Sarah Driver and published by
Egmont UK Limited, The Yellow Building, 1 Nicholas Road, London, W11 4AN.
Additional illustrations copyright © Joe McLaren 2017
Additional interior illustrations by Janene Spencer.

The moral rights of Sarah Driver, Ray Tierney and Joe McLaren have been asserted.

ISBN 9781405284691

65150/1

A CIP catalogue record for this title is available

from the British Library

Typeset by Avon DataSet Ltd, Bidford on Avon, Warwickshire
Printed and bound in Great Britain by the CPI Group

Stay safe online. Any website addresses listed in this book are correct at the time
of going to print. However, Egmont is not responsible for content hosted by third
parties. Please be aware that online content can be subject to change and websites
can contain content that is unsuitable for children. We advise that all children
are supervised when using the internet.

Egmont takes its responsibility to the planet and its inhabitants very seriously.
All the papers we use are from well-managed forests run by responsible suppliers.

THE HUNTRESS

STORM

SARAH DRIVER

EGMONT

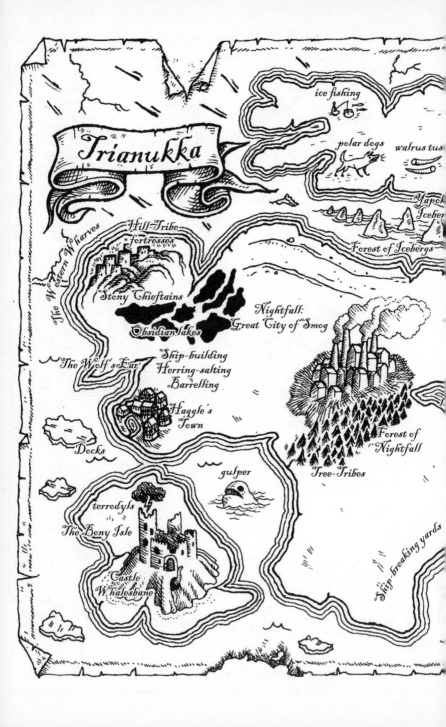

Contents

The Spidermaster's Lair

1. Door to shop
2. Counter
3. Tickets, timetables, shelves
4. Spider Kennels
5. Cauldrons on stove
6. Fly pies
7. Kitchen table
8. Buckets of frogs, birds, woodlice and millipides (for the spiders)
9. Holes to sewers

Full fathom five thy father lies;
Of his bones are coral made;
Those are pearls that were his eyes:
Nothing of him that doth fade,
But doth suffer a sea-change
Into something rich and strange

– William Shakespeare, *The Tempest*

Excerpt from *The Sharkskin Scripts, Volume I: The Great Trianukkan Tribes*

Dating back three thousand years, this ancient manuscript now resides in the Skybrary high in the Iceberg Forest of the Wildersea, under the care of the Skybrarian and his apprentice, a young Wilderwitch boy named Yapok.

We, the gathered Sea-Tribe captains, scratch these runes into skin with ink, tears and blood-truth.

In troubled times, dark forces rise. This is known. Long ago, the land of Trianukka was ravaged by unending war. In this dark time of blood and iron, a great evil rooted into our world. The evil grew, then spread. It bled into the minds of many, becoming a movement known as the

We must never forget the darkness wielded by this movement. We must make sure it never befalls our world again.

This dawn, at a ceremony on the highest peak, the Kings of Sea, Sky and Land have set three Storm-Opals in a golden crown, weaving the Tribes together in peace. Each sacred stone has been instilled with a sliver of the elements: a foam of sea, a fragment of sky and a fracture of earth. The jewels are to be guarded by a king of the giants. It is foretold that if the Opals are ever separated, evil will rise once more, and the land will be torn apart.

PART 1

The Hunted Child

1
The Withering

*Hackles. Ancient stronghold of the Sky-Tribe of the
draggle-riders. One full moon's turn after a Fangtooth hunted
me through the snow.*

Stark eyes glint all around me, peering from the depths of fur
hoods. I sniff the air. Fear-stink. *Everywhere.* The long-hall is
packed with scarred and bandaged folk. Outsiders seeking
refuge in this Sky realm of thick grey walls. Their murmurs
clot together and rise into the air, crowding it with questions.
Some are Sea-Tribe, and looking at them makes me wonder
about my ship, and the rest of my own crew.

I'm huddled on a bench, ice-bitten and swamped in a
heavy cloak of goatskin, listening to storms pummel the
mountain fortress with daggers of ice.

I try to stop the fright in the air from seeping through
my skin. But the walls are smeared with silver streaks that
tighten my belly into knots. Moonsprites are dying, cos no
moonlight can pierce the frozen clouds.

'You alright, Little-Bones?' Da whispers. He's sitting next

3

to me, grey-skinned and pretending he's got no pain. He still ent recovered proper from being kept a prisoner of the mystiks. With food grown scarce, the flesh is slow to gather on his bones, and his jaws grip his teeth too tight. 'You don't have to be here for this, you know.'

'I ent no little 'un,' I hiss, rolling my eyes at my crew-mate Crow, who's sat on the other side of me. The former ship-wrecker boy gifts me a grin.

A door bangs and we turn to stare as Leopard – seven hundred and seventy-seventh in a great line of Protectors of the Mountain – leads five Sky Elders through the crowd. Leo looks worn to rags by exhaustion, but she's wearing her goat headdress and a cloak of gold-dipped feathers, and she's standing arrow-straight.

I straighten my own spine at the sight of her, and in the corner of my eye catch Lunda scowling at me. The pale-haired Spearsister – one of the Protector's best trained warriors – still don't like outsiders. She throws the spear of her fright even surer than her spear of iron.

The Elders are a mix of draggle-riders and Wilderwitches – enemies until one full moon's turn ago, when I freed Leo from the possession that Stag and the mystiks were wielding to control her and her territory. The Wilder-King remains our enemy, swearing fealty to Stag even though storms have been trying to throw his iceberg forest flat and Hackles would be safer for his people. But some Wilderwitches fled to Hackles and Leo welcomed them heartily.

I watch as the Elders tread behind Leo. They're draped

4

in flowing sky-blue robes spun from ice worm silk and sewn with berg owl feathers. Orca teeth hang from their hems.

They carry offerings to the Sky gods – in their cupped palms sit crystal jars filled with tiny forests, dragonflies and spark-spluttering miniature storm clouds. They reach the dais and turn to face the benches.

Silence drops. The might of Hackles presses down on us – seems like even the ancient stronghold is straining to listen. Everyone says the Elders only utter a squeak when their pipes have seriousness to spill. And folks are proper desperate for them to gift words of certainty while chaos is sweeping through the world.

Chaos like how the trees can't summon their life-blood from the sealed earth, and winter won't thaw. Like how the land has erupted into riots, since the fires lit by Stag destroyed the Icy Marshes. Famine has seen more tribes joining Stag's side, or taking to crimes that have long been outlawed – raiding and slave-trading. Others are divided, like the Wilderwitches, and fighting amongst themselves.

Leo addresses the hall. 'Unity is our aim. Let us remember – our mountain was born from the sea, and the wind carved the rocks. *Here* is the birth of a mountain!'

'And here is the birth of an iceberg!' drone the Wilderwitches.

'May swift feathers bear your Sky-Tribe glad tidings,' I mutter along with the rest of them.

'Let us hear the latest reports from the Sneakings,' says Leo grimly.

Shoulders sag, mutters rise, boots stamp the floor impatiently. 'Can't we just hear the Elders, and get it over with?' someone whispers behind me.

The Sneakings. Leo's draggle patrols that slip into the world when no one's looking. Leo promised I can join the next one, and I'm counting every beat until we fly cos the next Sneaking will be for a Tribe-Meet. Besides, it's too long since I roved.

'We have flown to the furthest corners of the land, Protector,' says a lean woman with wind-burned cheeks. 'The whole of Trianukka is blotted in the shadow of frozen cloud. Winter will not end. Fangtooths are leaving the Frozen Wastes and spilling across the ice, terrorising all in their path. They have raided the Bay of Thunder and the fishing villages along the Black Coast.'

Another rider stands. 'Our spies have heard that the creeping ice has already spread as far south as the Giant's Backbone; a stack of hovels teetering twenty deep upon an ancient ribcage, on the edge of Nightfall.'

Crow turns his head and our startled eyes meet.

As the reports go on, the despairing news weighs heavy on my spine and I feel my chest grow tight.

After the final report has rung through the hall, the Elders creak to their feet. Thick silence plunges once again.

Leopard nods to the Elders, then sits at the edge of the dais, opposite me. She twists her thin hands in her lap. Her lips move, and I can just hear her prayers. '*Wakening's Dawn, please come to us, please melt this ice and wake the sun.*'

The Elders hook a cauldron over a fire, then pinch powder inside and feed lumps of resin to the flames. Sparks race each other into the air. The Elders make a circle, linking hands.

Steam noses over the edge of the cauldron, coiling up to the damp cavern that yawns over our heads. The Elders crane their necks to see the shapes made by the steam.

I scrunch my toes inside my boots.

'A darkness spreads across all the sea, sky and land . . . the great wheel of Midwinter has turned, but new life fails to wake in the earth!' croaks an Elder. 'It is as we feared. The age of the Withering has befallen us!' She rakes her wide, watery eyes through the crowd. Then she spits. 'Sky-gods save our souls.'

The fire claws at the sides of the cauldron. The steam thickens and writhes.

Draggle-riders are a goat-hardy, wind-sculpted folk. But still their frighted whispers leap into the air like sparks from a stabbed fire.

'My granny always warned of a Withering – why weren't we ready?'

'The fear was lost . . . we turned our backs on the demon!' comes the hissed reply.

'It's the gods that turned *their* backs, on *us*!'

'A Withering means no food, yet we take more stragglers in! Where will it end?'

Pika, the tall, cinnamon-skinned draggle-keeper boy, buries his face in his hands. 'All my life, I've been taught to fear the Withering,' he whispers. 'I can't believe it's here.'

'What is it?' I ask, leaning forwards to see him, sitting on the other side of Crow.

'Death of light,' he answers absently, eyes roaming the hall. 'A long, cold night of dead things. If no life stirs, there'll be a food shortage even worse than the one made by war.'

The Withering. I try to picture it in my mind's eye, but it's hard to imagine a thing so vast. Not long ago – but exactly *when*, no one can agree on – dawn failed good and proper. Now we're stuck in a grainy light, like a nightmare.

The steam from the cauldron twines and shifts, until I see grim faces with stretched eyes pulling upwards and swarming through the air.

One of the Elders throws a jug of water over the fire, smothering the flames. The steam dissolves slowly, the gaunt eyes fading into nothing. Something terrible is coming. Something worse than a Withering. Something even worse than Stag. I can feel it.

Leo stands. 'We must focus our energies on the fight ahead!' she calls. 'A destructive force is gaining power, taking full advantage of the peril of our world – a marching movement of evil, with Stag and the mystiks at its helm. They control the devastated Icy Marshes and have dug their claws into the Frozen Wastes and the city of Nightfall. We must not let them claim further territories.'

Sickening thoughts knuckle my skull. Thoughts about what Stag is to me, now there's a link that I'll never be able

8

to cut. He fathered me. He ent my da but my bones are threaded with his poisoned blood. How could Ma have chosen such a gruesome mate? Was he always the same, or was he different when she met him? I stub my toe against the floor. I *hate* wondering about him!

'You say they take advantage,' says a stout old rider called Coati. 'But Stag is offering shelter to those in need. He has opened Nightfall as a refuge, just as we have here.' A furious clamour rises. My fingers tighten on the bench. 'Hear me,' Coati calls gruffly. 'They say he distributes food in the territories he controls. I am yet to see how we know he intends war.' He sits down, puffing out his ruddy cheeks.

My belly squirms and fury lights my chest. I'm about to gift Coati the truth when Pike, the leader of the homeless Marsh-folk, stands and strikes the floor with his fish spear three times. 'Stag burned our home and drained our marshes. He treated us as though our lives counted for nothing!' His eyes blaze. 'And mark me, Rider. He offers shelter only to certain *breeds* of people – those he and his allies deem *elite*.'

'Aye!' I call out, thumping my chest with my fist.

Coati shrugs. 'I meant no offence,' he says. 'But I have heard the reports with my own ears. People are desperate. They say Stag offers a stability no one else can provide.'

Shouting, cursing and gesturing breaks out, with most folks telling Coati to mind his tongue. But more than a few are voices praising his words. The noise stops when the doors smash open, making every head in the hall turn.

Boots stride along the floor. A hornblower, draped in ice-matted furs, folds back his raindrop cowl. 'Protector! An urgent message, received through the ghostways.' The parchment *rasps* as he unwraps the scroll. 'It is signed with the claw mark of the Wilder-King,' he announces. But then something crescent-shaped – like a small moon, or a shell – slips to the floor. The hornblower stoops to pick it up, mouth slackening. 'It's – an ear,' he stutters.

Folk gasp. Some leap to their feet, others reach for spears.

'Whose ear is that?' I ask Da. Crow leans close to listen.

Da shakes his head. 'I can't be sure, but – the Protector did send an envoy to the Wilder-King, who has not yet returned.'

Leopard stalks towards the hornblower and takes the ear in her hands, gently, as though it's a broken bird. She grips the scroll and scans it quickly. Then her eyes search me out.

Me?

The look in their depths carves a hollow in my gut. I wrap my arms over my chest.

What does that scroll say?

'This meet is dismissed,' says Leo briskly. 'Tribesman Fox, please stay behind.'

The Scarred Girl

I hurry to Leo's side as the hall begins to empty.

She looks from me to Da. 'Sorry Mouse – it's just your father I want to speak to.'

'Anything you got to say to Da, you can say to *me*,' I tell her, jabbing my thumb into my chest. 'Ent that so, Da?'

But he just looks at me like I'm five moons old. 'I think you'd better listen to Leo this time, Bones.'

'For serious?'

'Aye. Get your hide gone and I'll see you soon.'

I want to snatch the letter and gobble every rune on it, right now. I'm sure it's got something to do with me, from the look Leo shone out. But I turn on my heel and shove my way past the stragglers. 'He'll tell me as soon as he gets out of here, anyway!' I yell over my shoulder.

I wait for Da in his chamber. Beats and beats pass, until my belly growls and my nerves are bowstring-tight. When he opens the door, I leap out at him. 'What's that letter gabbing on about, then?'

Da ghosts a smile at me. 'Ah, Little-Bones! Almost stopped my heart, you did.'

'Don't even think of changing the subject. You know that don't work with me.' I lift my chin. 'Well?'

'Well what?'

I swallow a scream. 'The *letter*,' I repeat, ominous-calm.

Finally, he sighs. 'Let's just say, it wasn't anything good.' I gulp a breath but he stops my quiverful of questions with a look. 'But it's nothing we don't already know, either – this world is full perilous, no doubts. So, there's a new rule. You're not to leave Hackles.'

"Til when?'

'Until . . .' He pauses. Shrugs. 'It's safe.'

I snort a messy laugh through my nose. 'It ent never been safe, and won't never be, neither!'

'You know what I mean, Mouse,' he says wearily. 'The world's different, now. Things are – proper crooked.'

I cross my arms. 'But I'll be going to the Tribe-Meet.'

'I don't think so, Bones.'

Which means 'no' in full-grown speak. '*What*? Why?'

He turns to a pouch by his bedside and rummages inside it for his pain medsins. 'Like I said – it's too dangerous.'

But I remember the way Leo looked at me. 'For everyone? Or just me?'

He busies himself with looking around for something. But I know when he's trying to dodge my gaze. 'Da!'

He stills. 'It's naught to fret about, Mouse. It's just something to keep you safe.'

But as he hobbles from the room, my chest feels bruised. I touch the dragonfly brooch on my tunic and when I close my eyes I can smell salt-traced air and see the great black shadows of the *Huntress*'s sails ghosting across her wooden boards. How can Da force me not to rove when I'm so full of fight?

I've got to get my mitts on that letter.

My hand moves to an amulet hanging around my neck, and an idea tingles through me. The amulet is a slim oval of silver, gifted to me by Egret Runesmith and etched with the runes for binding, so I'm safe to dream-dance without having to draw protection runes all the time. My fingers brush my other amulet – the amber Bear gifted me.

Gods, I miss my friends.

I fling myself down on Da's bed and shut my eyes, imagining climbing out of my skin. I gather all the fright in my chest – about the Withering, and the dying moonsprites, and the way Leo looked at me in the long-hall – and use it to hook onto my spirit. I feel the familiar dragging, and push into it, until my spirit *nudges through layers of bone, muscle and skin. I tread the air above my body, blinking slow spirit-eyes. Then I dive through the door and into the corridor outside.*

I drift past Pika, who's kicking draggle dung off his boots at the entrance to the crooked corridor. As I pass, he shudders and glances up, looking through me. Then I startle a warmth-seeking goat that's got lost in the maze of passageways. I turn in the air and dart along another passageway, past a group of Wilderwitches heading for the stone baths, drying-cloaks hung over their arms.

Leo's chamber is a small, plain room at the top of a sweep of stairs, set deep in the rock above the long-hall. I slip through the wooden door and fly around the room, searching.

A small collection of books, bound in red, blue, green and gold, is stacked on her night table. A clothes chest stands at the foot of her bed. There's a set of raindrop armour hanging from a hook, a gathering of stubby candles and a portrait of her and her daughter Kestrel that she had painted before Kes left on her mission to unite the youth of the Tribes. There's no sign of the letter.

Just then, the door whines open and Leo strides in, tension tightening her face. She paces the floor, breathing fast. Then she draws a length of parchment from inside her cloak and yanks it straight. 'How dare he?' she mutters to herself.

I slither through the air and hover behind her shoulder, gulping the black runes burned into the parchment.

'Consider this your first and final warning.' My spirit startles, fracturing around the edges – I can almost hear the Wilder-King's slow purr of a voice. 'Do not imagine that your fortress protects you against the allies I have won. Allies that could be yours, also, if you heed the war cry echoing through Trianukka. The scarred girl is a hunted child. They will not allow her to further damage their cause. Surrender her, for the sake of your people. And surrender any chatterers dwelling amongst you.'

I raise my hand to trace my scar with my fingers, but my spirit edges just whisper against each other. I'm a hunted child. Small wonder Da tried to keep it from me.

The memory barges close – the night just one full moon ago,

when slow, stealthy footsteps creaked through the snow behind me. I half-turned, as a salty hand wrapped around my mouth.

'Fangtooth!' boomed Da's kelp-rich voice, stronger than his weakened body. 'Release my child.' The Protector's spear-warriors surrounded us. Me and my brother were pulled from danger, but not before a blade against my neck nicked a tear in the skin.

Axe-Thrower, Stag's wretched first mate, had hunted through the shadows of the stronghold, trying to get to me and Sparrow. Now she's locked in Leopard's dungeon, a hostage claimed by no one. And as for Da – he's acting guilt-stung that he weren't better at protecting me now we're finally back together. For a while he kept saying sorry that Axe attacked me, like it was his fault.

Now I know the Fangtooth weren't acting alone. That her attack was ordered by someone else. And that the attack ent really over. I keep my eyes on the letter as I read the runes again and again. Then Leo tenses, crumpling the parchment in her fingers, and twists to stare behind her.

I must've drifted too close and touched her – I can see how the skin at the back of her neck's gone goose-pimpled. Suddenly I remember that she's a dream-dancer, too.

'Who's there?' she whispers.

I flick towards the door, squeeze through and soar down the stairs, spirit-heart weighing heavy. Most times, I can find a way to get Da on my side. But this time he's never gonna let me go with the others to the Tribe-Meet. Not in a thousand moons. I stare up at the dark stone roof of the passageway as I fly. I feel like the walls of this stronghold are closing in, and if I ent careful, I'll be buried alive.

3
The Sneaking

Thunder grumbles, restless as a shark. I sit cross-legged on my bed, breathing the storm-stink that's trickling in through the stones of Hackles. Thaw-Wielder breathes it with me, her eyes shining with added wildness.

The stink of a storm is the only thing that makes me feel free, these days. It kindles the flame in my blood. Stormlight flutters against the walls and I feel like I'm underwater with electric eels.

Crow sits in a chair, greasing his boots. 'Could you give it a rest with all the sniffing?'

I tut. *He don't get it, Thaw.*

She shuffles her feathers and spits in his direction. *Soft-shell two-leg notknownotknowthings! Not REAL winged one.*

'And stop talking about me to Thaw! It ain't fair.'

I stick out my lower lip. *The poor bab don't think it's fair!*

Thaw chortles.

Crow gifts me his danger-face.

I raise my brows. 'Alright, don't scorch your lugholes over it!'

The thunder cracks the sky apart, loud as huge iron

drums being thrown around. Crow gasps, but I grin. 'You should try hearing that when you're out at sea.'

He scowls. In the attic rooms above, claws begin to scrabble. The rats are spooked.

Boots clank past my chamber door. I leap off my bed and rush to look – riders march along the passageway, heading to the caves to prepare their draggles to fly to the Tribe-Meet. Other preparations have been happening, too – spear-sharpening and armour-mending and gathering together of things to trade, like pots of squidge ink and stinking draggle furs and wooden snow-goggles and eggs scooped from the bogs. I've been shut out of all of it.

I slam my door and jump back onto my bed. 'I am *proper* blubber-bored! They're leaving for the Tribe-Meet at the morning bell. How can Da force me to stay here?'

'At least someone cares if you live or die!' interrupts Crow, loudly. His tone makes Thaw flap herself into outrage, rasping and spitting, eyes bright.

'Calm your feathers, you stupid bird,' snaps Crow.

Trymakeme, hisses my hawk.

Crow stands up, eyes on his boots. 'Mouse, I mean – can you blame your da, really? How addled would he have to be to let you roam the place now that the Withering's set in *and* there's a hunt for your skin?'

I pull at the loose threads in my blankets. 'But no one gets how bad my bones are itching – itching! – to move, to rove, to do *something*!'

'But maybe you can't do anything, this time,' he says

17

more gently. 'And maybe your da's right – maybe, for once, you don't have to. It ain't your job.'

I shine my fierceness through the grime coating my skin. 'I can't do nothing – that's never been what I do.' *And it never will be!*

'None of this is about you, though, is it?' He picks up the pot of grease he used for his boots and turns away. 'What would you do if you *could* leave Hackles, anyway?'

'Um, let me ponder.' I chew my cheek, pretending to think. 'Go to the Tribe-Meet, then find the Opal, and *save the world*?'

He sighs. 'How about you start by coming to supper?'

'Aye,' I tell him, trying to keep my voice steady. 'See you in the hall.'

Thaw oozes a low hiss at his turned back.

'I heard that, Thaw-Wielder!' he snaps, before leaving the room.

Thaw, I gabble quickly, my mind wheeling. *I HAVE to go to that Tribe-Meet. Cos if I don't prove myself to Da, how's he ever gonna let me do anything, ever again? I've got to remind him what I can do. I'll be back before he can blink, anyway!* Thrills explode in my belly.

Thaw's eyes glow, but her pipes spew tiny doubts. *Two-leg girl danger times . . . hunthunthunt?*

Aye, Thaw. But how's any of them stupid lumberers gonna hunt me if I swap places with a Spearsister – like Pang? She'll swap with me, I know it! And if the riders do a count they won't find anyone extra. I block out a thought about what might happen if anyone needs me to throw a spear. *Anything's better than sitting here, ent it? And I might get to scratch around for snippets of news – or even CLUES – at the Meet.*

She takes to the wing, soaring in circles around me until my hair's stirred into a black cloud. *Wild girl show them all!*

Thaw wakes me before the morning bell. My limbs are stiff and cold-clumsy as I force myself out of bed. I tiptoe through the gloom to the draggle caves, pulling on the eelskin gloves Marshman Pike once gifted me to keep my fingers warm enough to wield weaponry. If I'm to be a Spearsister, I'll have to be able to grip a spear, as well as draggle reins. I wait amongst tangled ropes of orangey draggle fur, huddled in a white goatskin cloak that Pangolin hung with iron storm-weights. Underneath clings the rune-spelled breastplate she loaned me, charged runes flickering across it like worms.

I watched the giant shaggy beasts shuffle their wings in their sleep. When the first riders clamour into the cave, heading to the tack room to don armour and fill saddle bags with supplies, I drift from my hiding place and begin sharpening Pangolin's spear.

Once the whole stronghold is awake, Wilderwitches line the rocks outside. I edge as close as I can to the mouth of the cave and watch them standing, palms held up in front of them, trying to clear a sky-path through the storm. Their weather-magyk battles winds that thrash around like maddened beasts.

A rich smell catches in my nose and I turn to see a cook

with greasy white hair passing cups of bone-broth among the riders. A mug finds its way into my hands, glowing with heat that I am more than heart-glad for. I stare down at myself in the gleaming surface of the broth. My eyes are painted from brows through to cheekbones with the black stripes of a Spearsister, an eagle-feather hood is pulled over my head and a raindrop cowl is moulded to my face.

'Sup your broth and prepare to fly,' commands Leopard. She wears a long black cloak of eelskin, gifted to her by Pike. I drop my eyes while she's talking, in case she knows my stormy greys.

I listen to the bubbling of the broth and the crackling of the flames and the nerve-tense chattering of the draggles.

Huntnohuntnohunt? WhywhywhyHUNGRYwherefoodfly?

I'm half asleep with my chin propped in my hands when the storm dies, gaping breathlessness in its wake, sudden as the *thunk* of a dropped longbow. My chin slips out of my hands and my neck bends painfully as my head lolls. The Wilderwitches' weather-magyk must have finally pushed the storm away from us. Now there's just a deadened stillness.

Leopard pulls a small bronze spyglass from her pocket and presses it to her eye. 'The chief storm has raged west,' she announces. She sighs, tucks away her spyglass and nods to the draggle warden. 'We fly.'

I blow out my held breath and we mount our draggles, Leo taking the lead. I copy the others; holding a spear in one hand and the reins in the other. When Leo raises her hand, the draggles swoop from the mountain.

Rough air bruises my eyeballs. My belly *plunges*, sloshing the broth I glugged. But hidden inside my armour, my lips riot into a grin. Finally, I'm roving.

Below, a group of song-weavers has gathered on the rocks to gift us music as we fly. A little clutch of Sea-Tribe kids – I spot the white shock of Ermine's hair and Squirrel's red braid – bang drums they've painted to look like whale-eyes. Eyes like portals, or knots in wood. I spot Da and Sparrow, singing together, and duck lower in the saddle. A flush of guilt steals across my skin, itching under all my layers.

We pull away from the mountain, dodging the silvery ghostway tubes that cobweb the stronghold so the Sky-Tribes can pulse messages to each other. The tubes quiver with voices.

Across the valley, tangles of lightning sprout like trees, and the sky flickers as though it's blinking. When the lightning branches fade, their ashen ghosts hang in the air. My draggle fights the wind, despair mixing with the ice in her fur. I lean down and mutter heart-strengths to her.

We fly over Hearthstone, where almost all the dwellings have been rebuilt, with Leo's help. But when we reach the Icy Marshes, fury flares in my gut.

Terrodyls swirl through the sky, patrolling to make certain the Marsh-folk never dare to return. All that's left of Pike's home is a field of blackened wooden stumps capped with bulbs of ice.

Refugees wade through the reeds and ford the rivers on their way towards the mountains, seeking higher ground. We hover while a few riders drop to land and tell them how to reach Hearthstone or Hackles.

As we pass into wilder territory that could be more hostile, Leo calls for us to douse our lamps. I lie along my draggle's back and stretch to reach the metal lantern hanging on its pole. The hinges squeak as I fumble the door open, making my draggle flick her ears irritably.

Sorry! That needs oiling, I chatter.

I wet my fingertips and squeeze the life from the flame. As the other lamps blink out, heavy gloomlight thickens around us. We race deeper into the murk. I keep to the rear. We soar over leagues of ice-ridges carved by the storm winds; great blue-white dunes that gift the land the look of the wrinkled skin of a whale. Maybe that's all we are. Whale lice crawling over some giant sea-god.

When Leopard drops back to check we're all well enough to keep going, I dodge but she draws alongside me and leans across to grip my chin, guiding my eyes to meet hers. My heart skitters.

'You really thought I would not realise?' she asks, letting go of me with a sigh. A few Riders twist in their saddles, staring at me with narrowed eyes.

I shrug, cheeks burning. 'Reckoned it were worth a stab.'

To my startlement, Leo's face dimples into a grin. 'I promised your father I would keep you safe – I will deal with this disobedience when we return,' she swears. 'But I do admire your determination.'

I don't dare return her grin, but I let my eyes sing out my wildness.

We reach the sea, where storm-waves have frozen solid, into ice-mountains that rise like great dark fins. Between them, the sea that ent yet frozen bubbles weak as a dying Tribesperson's spit.

Ice-bound ships litter the sea, wounds agape in their flanks. Tears well in my eyes as I think of my ship. *Bear. Frog. Pipistrelle. Vole.* I breathe the names of my Tribe into white ghosts on the air. Where are you? *Where?*

In the distance, a steady drum begins to throb, shattering my thoughts.

The drum beats louder, closer. It rattles my ribs. Riders stare around them, and I feel their nerves tense.

The rider nearest me draws a breath. But then there's a choking sound as the air catches in her throat.

Movement catches my eye from the left. I twist in the saddle. My skin jumps. Smoke puffs in time with the drumbeat I heard. As I stare I realise that it's vapour, that it's something's breath. Something big, to make that much steam. Something with a footstep even bigger, to make a drumbeat that loud.

A dark shape is looming. My heart clangs and hammers.

Through the bleak light stamps a chalk-white giant with a skull bubbled all over in milky sores.

4

Blood on the Stones

Yellowy fluid seeps from sores and trickles down the giant's body. He leans down, opens his cavernous mouth and smashes his tombstone-teeth around a frozen wave. He chews the ice, then bends for another bite.

The giant's blistered flesh sucks any last warmth from the half-frozen clouds and the sluggish sea, which throws up a new tower of ice as he passes.

A long, low groan knocks from the giant's mouth, echoing around the sea of crystal waves. I remember seeing giants like this one in the stories etched in bone that Grandma and Da used to read to us. They were called stogs – the biggest of the Tribe of giants, and the most miserable. They made the seas by weeping, and liked to pluck ships from the waves, crushing them with their bare hands. But the stories said the giants were all sleeping . . .

Not any more.

The stog's face is craggy-glum and his legs are as long as masts. His hot breath knocks the draggles up and down in the air like toy ships. He snaps a hateful glare onto us and roars, a sound that booms through my chest and makes my teeth chatter. Then his fist swipes through the air.

The draggles scatter. Leo calls orders lost as the storm winds begin to whip again. The stog groans, and kicks out against a wave, making icy rubble fall.

I've ended up alone on one side of the giant's flailing arm, the others all watching me from the other side. As I struggle to control the draggle, I lose my grip on Pangolin's spear and it falls, clanging onto the ice below. A Spearsister jerks her face towards me. Wisps of white hair have escaped her hood – Lunda. 'Is that who I think it is?' she spits. 'She's not even meant to be on this patrol!'

I grit my teeth. The stog's breath reeks, even through my raindrop cowl. I guide my draggle lower, trying to dodge underneath the huge arm.

'Mouse!' warns Leo.

The arm sweeps towards the ground but I swoop low and fly past the dank hollow of the armpit, gulping a lungful of a sharp tang that makes my head woozy. The stog snatches me from my draggle. My chest is squeezed until black spots dance in my eyes. There's no air left in my lungs for screaming. My legs swing wildly in the air, and my belly pitches into my mouth . . . and dimly I'm aware of riders yelling before I'm shut inside a huge, clammy fist.

I gulp for breath, heart skittering. I slip on the thick yellow sweat pooled in the stog's palm, clawing at the ridges of his skin. 'Leo!' I yell, but my voice bounces back into my own ears, stabbing painfully into my head.

I'm running out of air. My eyes scan the roof of flesh above my head – there are thin gaps between the fingers. The stog's grip tightens so I push through one of the gaps, kicking, clawing, scratching, wriggling . . .

Finally I squeeze through and leap out of his hand, grabbing hold of a thick brown vine sprouting from his ear – but the vine is slippery, and I can't hold on.

Lunda zooms towards me, one foot planted on her draggle's back, the other on mine. Two sets of reins are bunched in her hands. She hovers as near to me as she can get. 'Jump, fool child!'

The giant roars, thrashing his head around.

I swing myself across the space, miss my own draggle and land with a thump behind Lunda. I grab her waist as I regain my balance. 'Bleeding blood cockles,' I whisper, eyes watering with shame. My palms are coated in stinking, gloopy ear wax.

'Fly on!' calls Leo, and we wing away from the giant.

I wipe my hands on my breeches as we tear away through the sky.

Jealousy nags me. Wish I could be as skilful riding one of these beasts as Lunda is. 'You should stay behind with the other youngsters from now on!' she hisses, holding the reins while I scramble back onto my own draggle. Her hard blue eyes graze my face.

I glare at her while my lungs suck shallow breaths. The stog's distant howls of fury rattle through my chest and make my teeth throb.

In spite of everything, excitement bubbles in my belly when I think about the Tribe-Meet, where my Tribe traded jet and amber for songs, stories for furs and fish. Sometimes Da and Bear traded sailcloth or silver for songs *alone*, and even though magyk could be spun from them, Grandma weren't never too impressed. The last Meet I went to – for Dread's Eve – feels so long ago. And it weren't exactly a normal meet, with Da missing and me almost getting swallowed by a gulper. It's where I lost Sparrow, too, when Stag had him snaffled by wreckers.

The Tribe-Meet for Wakening's Dawn is all about drumming Spring up from her grave. There'll be market stalls and music-makers and acrobats with flaming torches, bakers whose spices dance in the air, traders with bundles of brightly dyed cloth and sword-sharpeners, tanners and tricksters.

'I can't wait to show you your old Sky-Tribe path and gateway stones!' I call to Leo, to gift her good cheer.

She nods. 'I am keen to see these things,' she says. 'But nervous, also. Many suns and moons have risen since any Sky-Tribe attended. How do we know the etiquette, here?'

Lunda's draggle drops closer as the Spearsister tries to listen. Maybe her nerves are tightening, too.

'You approach the circle along your Great-Tribe's path – that's the Sky Path, which you get to through the gateway stones shaped like eagle heads. There's no weapons allowed, so we'll have to leave our spears outside.'

The old rider called Coati, who angered Pike in the long-hall, laughs, face fury-flayed. 'Leave our weapons and we are sitting targets, mark my breath.' He twirls his spear.

Leo rolls her eyes at me, the tension melting off her face. But when we can see the tips of the circle of stones piercing the drifting fog, I sense my draggle wants to bolt.

'This place is eerie,' hisses a rider, a man with two long black braids hanging over his shoulders.

I struggle to steady my draggle, stroking her head, but she hisses.

'They're spooking!' I call. My hands are sweaty on the reins as I jostle to get my balance. The draggles' voices rise in panic.

Suddenly, a young terrodyl flickers up and out of the fog, wings lashing inches from our flock. Black blood drips, fizzing, from a wound in its flank.

'Pull back!' shouts Leo, and the draggles bare their teeth at the terrodyl.

Gold gleams like shattering stars as the riders level their spears as one. But Leo warns them not to shoot. 'You'll burn whoever's down there with black rain!'

Black rain – the weapon wielded by Stag, extracted from the veins of terrodyls, that burns warped, bubbled pits in the flesh. My belly writhes at the thought that he's twisted a beast's own life-blood into a weapon.

The riders hold fire, their spears shining in the depths of the terrodyl's eyes.

Dead things! Ice! the beast screams, wheeling away. *Sad-hearts rotted!*

What's down there, beast? I chatter. *What're you fleeing?*

The terrodyl's panic mingles with the draggles' fright-pangs, gifting me a sore, woozy head. *Troubletroubletrouble HIDEflyflyhideinnest!*

What trouble? I ask, but she's pulling further away and thudding out of sight. *Wait, you're hurt!*

'What is that child doing?' Coati asks Leo, watching me with hard eyes.

What trouble? I call again, threading my beast-chatter through the air to touch the creature's hair-prickled hide.

The terrodyl jerks in the air and her wings carve the sky as she twists around and soars towards me.

'She's brought it back upon us,' gasps Lunda.

'Spears!' declares Leo, flashing me a frighted look.

'No, just trust me for a beat!' I beg.

Lung-stink! snaps the terrodyl, fixing me with her great lantern eyes. *Blood-stink! Spine-shudder bad-taste bled. Life fled, bled, BLED!*

My breath comes quick and tattered. *Life fled? Bloodshed?* That *can't* be what she's saying . . .

Uuuuuughhhhh tongue-tang rot-shadow-HOME! She bolts.

My head fizzes with her fading beast-chatter. *No, you must be wrong!* I chatter after her desperately. *There's never bloodshed at the Stone Circle! It's forbidden!*

The draggles pop up and down in the air. Mine bucks underneath me, half crazed from fright.

Gods. Blood at the *Tribe-Meet?* Grandma must be writhing in her sea-grave!

Leo watches the terrodyl vanish from sight before guiding the flock closer to the Stone Circle.

'Wait!' I shout.

'What is it now, Mouse?' calls Leo, impatience sharpening her tone.

'We can't land,' I plead. 'A proper bad thing's happened.'

Coati gruffs a laugh of steam and bitterness. 'Why does a child ride among us? Someone get her back to the mountain!'

Leo turns away from me, leading the draggles lower.

'Protector!' My urgent use of her title makes Leopard jerk around in her saddle to look at me. I force my voice steady. 'There's bloodshed.' I wipe my palms on my cloak and stare around at the riders. 'At the Stone Circle.' Shock guts my words even as I spill them. *Gods swim close.*

Our flock pauses, beating the air. Leopard's eyes are large and fixed on my face.

Then everything erupts into a tumble of loud babblemaking.

'That's impossible!'

'It's the Fangtooths, isn't it? They're terrorising again!'

'What if there is? Bloodshed does not faze warriors!'

'Mouse, are you certain?' asks Leo. As the words steam from her mouth, a great black talon of smoke stabs the sky in the distant west.

'I'm heart-certain,' I pant, thumping my fist to my chest.

A tide of disappointment floods Leo's face. 'We've come all this way,' she says, through clenched teeth.

'How do you know?' challenges a narrow-eyed

Spearbrother.

'The terrodyl told me.'

Coati watches me darkly. 'You are sheltering a *chatterer*?' He flicks his eyes to Leo.

'*Enough*, Coati,' warns Leo.

The old man snorts rudely. Heat creeps up my neck to sting my cheeks. I remember the Wilder-King's letter. *Surrender any chatterers dwelling amongst you.* 'If it wasn't for me you'd have landed unawares!' I spit, hurling the old man's gift of shame back to him.

Coati's face darkens. But then the draggles begin to scream, borrowing the words of the terrodyl. *Life-stink! Lung-stink! Troubletroubletroubleflee!*

The chatter is like a punch in the brain. Before I can breathe it smacks into me again.

UhhhhhmurkworldreachreachSTRETCH seizecatchslithergulpboness mashsmashdepthscrawlingcreepingdarkdark pushdarkabovedarkbelowreachreachSTRETCH grabuhhhhhhhh . . .

'Mouse?' The Protector's voice breaks through the chaos as she guides her draggle towards mine and touches my shoulder. As I return from the beast-world I taste blood and realise I've clamped my teeth onto my tongue. I gulp a breath, glancing at the faces of the Spearwarriors.

They're gifting me a look of fear. They're frighted of what I *am*.

We've drifted closer to the Stone Circle.

31

While I'm grappling to stay mounted and catch my breath, a sight emerges below that almost makes me plummet to my doom.

Lying across the standing stones is a dead terrodyl.

When the tips of the stones pierce the drifting fog, some are bloodied. Others are dripping with black rain.

A ragged figure darts out from beneath the dead beast's wing, wielding a longbow. An arrow pierces the fog.

'Go!' shrieks Leopard.

As we're wheeling our draggles around to flee, the sight of the blood-splashed Sea gateway stone clangs into my brain and the chatter of the draggles rises to a storm inside my chest.

The world blinks and melts into a frenzy.

Deathridesclosedrowningredsoakedgetawaypointawaygogogofly strongwingfightridersgogogoBOLTgogogoDODGEgogogoRUN gogogoNO!

Dizziness swarms my head. Faces slip in and out of focus.

Noise. Swelled. Everything. Everywhere. Sick bursts up my throat and blurts from my lips. My foot slips from the stirrup.

'Tooth-and-bone storms!' yelps Lunda, pointing.

Great cyclones sweep from gaps in the ice out to sea, packed with shark and whale teeth that tear bites from whatever they touch.

Chatter. Stealing breath. *Stealingthoughtsthoughtsthoughts.*

Stealingbreathbodymindgrowingcuttingsqueezingweare panickingflutteringbreathingironbloodstinkdeathlurksheregreed squatsherenosafetynohome–

I push away the chatter but it presses close again,

32

suffocating like lungfuls of damp fur.

GETAWAY–

Lash of whips–

'Is she *breathing?*'

Falling backwards ice nipping ears blood in nostrils chatter in head.

Everything hurts.

'Who are you?' bellows a deep voice from the ground. 'Are you Sky-Tribe?'

The world fades in and out.

'Show yourselves!' booms Leo.

Black emptiness swarms close.

'We need help!' The voice snips at my memory. My draggle stays close to the others, her muscles squirming with horror and wanting to get back to her cave. We drop lower in the sky, towards the ground.

Chatter squiggles in my blood, setting it alight.

FrightfrightfrightSPARKrawbloodbeatboomboomBOOM!

A tall man garbed in salt-stained boiled leather steps out from behind a blood-splattered standing stone. His face is swamped in a wild tangle of icicled beard.

Then I'm flung into a dream-world of beasts. *Getawaygetawaygetawayspeartipshadowspressingbreathstopping helphelphelpwrongnessnomoonnosunclamouringbuzzingrunning runningnowheretorun. Nowheretohide.*

I'm flying so fast, so far. I'm diving into the shallows, spearing a fish on my claws. Heavy wingbeats slice the air, carrying me so fast the wind slips past me like water.

5
Trouble's hook

Paws and hooves drum the snowy plains. Starlight writhes under us, locked in ancient graves. Bellies sore, bloated-not-with-cubs. Wind-spirits lick our fur. We move. We fight! We hunt! We roar! We face dark burrows, endless night. But we shudder secretly, blood roiling. Our bones click with ice. Life starves, withers. Storms boil.

A shiver brushes my belly as my fur drags in the snow but then a brown-and-white blur streaks into my room and I'm waking up, straining against iron-heavy dreams that drag at the edges of my brain.

My eyes crack open. I'm in my featherbed in my chamber at Hackles, sweating buckets. The room thumps into being around me, full of fuzzy outlines in the half-dark. In the hearth, a fire devours kindling in a spit-crackle frenzy.

Thaw-Wielder soars across the chamber to the messy nest of twigs she's built atop one of my bedposts. My sea-hawk's been thieving kindling from all the hearths in the stronghold to build it, much to the vexation of the cooks. I hear the thud as she drops a fish onto the twigs, and the scratching as it thrashes. *Fillpipesfillboots*, she chatters, jostling her feathers. She squints down at me, stirring a love-pang in the pit of my belly.

A bright droplet of blood falls from her wing onto my pillow. Reckon she must've got scraped flying through the arrow-slit again, cos at just the same moment the skin on my arm burnt and the muscles throbbed. Sometimes when she hurts herself, it's as though I feel it with her.

Thaw gurgles at me, low in her throat, and then the beast-world presses closer to me again, its rich stink clogging my mouth and nose. My skull thuds. I know the hunt Thaw flew. I can taste the fish she speared. I can feel the ice carried by the wind, wrapping around my claws.

A wave of sickness rolls over me. I blink filmy eyes and suddenly *I'm looking down into the nest and my own huge talons, one of my claws still hooked through the flesh of the dying fish.* I gasp, shaking my head, grabbing fistfuls of bedding. What's happening to me? For a beat, I'd swear I was peering through my hawk's eyes. It feels like something inside me is tearing.

There's a movement to my left. I roll blearily towards it. Da sits in a chair by my bed, rubbing his jaw. The stubby hairs make a scratching sound.

'Da,' I croak stupidly. My skull pounds, and a foul, rusty taste clogs my mouth.

I can only see one side of his face, lit by the pale glow of a moon-lamp he's wedged onto a table next to him. He's garbed in a midnight-blue tunic with pearls for buttons and a shaggy black goatskin cloak. His yellow hair is bundled into a messy knot on his head. Behind a tangle of reddish beard, his face is the pale grey of a skimming stone.

'*Bloodshed!*' I blurt, lifting my head from the pillow. The room spins wildly. 'At the Stone Circle!'

'Peace, Mouse,' says Da softly.

I stare at him through great matted clumps of black hair. He's full-vexed at me, so I make ready to charm my way off trouble's hook. 'You *know* the sea is calling me but still you come in here dressed like her, in blue and pearls and gold like the sun on the waves, eh?'

He stares at me evenly. 'A hailstorm broke the skulls of three draggles and two riders. Leo—'

'She's alright, ent she? *Is* she?'

'Let me finish. Leo told us that the rest of the flock spooked, and badly. She managed to shoot a message into a ghostway and called some of the Wilderwitches to her aid. They used weather-magyk to help get the party home. But before they arrived, you passed out.' He clears his throat and looks away.

I know I'm in for the worst earful of my life, so I clutch handfuls of bedding and get ready to beg myself blue. 'Staying still is too hard!' I whine. 'I loathe it here! I miss home! You can't blame me!'

'Are you eight moons old?' he demands.

I flush.

'You of all people should know there are worse places for those without a home. Don't be so guppy-witted.' He reaches over and gives my leg a shake – not hard, but enough to put me in my place. 'Can you picture how it feels to find your child gone, in the middle of a pack of angry storms, in the breath before a war? Because mark me, girl—'

'It weren't my—'

'*That* is what is coming. A *war*! A war that I would *die* before seeing you caught up in!' he yells.

Da's only yelled at me a handful of times my whole life long, but when he does, it's frightful cos normally he sails so easy, and suddenly he's so mad-vexed his face is purple. The odd thing is, the frightfulness of it makes me *laugh*, which don't help matters at all. Grandma used to give in much quicker when fury bit her.

'Banish that smirk or so help me Mouse I will *lock* you in this chamber and you won't even have the run of the stronghold. Then we'll see how trapped you feel.'

I force the corners of my lips down.

'Better.' He sits back, pulls the band from his hair and runs his fingers through it, blue eyes flashing. 'Gift a man a young death, you will.'

'I'm not trying to hurt you, Da. I just can't stay here. I don't know how.'

'You'd better get learning, then, hadn't you?'

I puff up my cheeks and blow all the air out in a rush. 'When are we gonna find the Land-Opal?'

'Mouse.' He folds his arms and leans closer to me. 'What sort of a father would I be if I let you go running off into this perilous world again, when I've only just got you safe?'

I raise my brows. *He* got *me* safe?

He sees my look and narrows his eyes. 'You don't need to fret – I'm going to find the *Huntress* and rescue those of our Tribe who are still aboard. Then I will search for the Opal.'

A howl of hope arrows from my throat. 'And I'll go with you!'

He frowns. 'No. No, you won't.'

'I'll gift you a knowing for nothing,' I hiss, tears sparking in my eyes. 'You're too tall, too full-grown and still *too* slow to be anything but a hindrance on a mission! You stick out like a sore thumb, old man. Any bad-blubber will see your hide coming from a league away.'

Finally, a laugh splutters out of his dry mouth. He grabs for me and musses my tangles into an even worse mess. 'Listen, Bones. I've got a knowing for you, too.' His voice is taut with heart-worry.

An oar-drum booms in my marrow. 'What?'

He drops his voice to a whisper. 'I need you to promise to keep quiet about your beast-chatter.'

Something slithers in my gut when I see the fright stretching his eyes. It's the first time Da's told me to hide anything, and the oddness of it bites like a ray. 'Why?'

'Just . . . trust me. Alright? These folks don't know you like your own Tribe. They may not understand your blood-wildness like we do.'

I frown, thinking back to how Coati looked at me before I fainted on the Sneaking. The way he called me a *chatterer*, like his tongue was wrapped in poison.

Da leans down and presses his forehead to mine. 'Keep

your brother safe 'til my return.'

I chew my tongue to keep from hurling curses. Cos I remember what happened when I parted with Sparrow after a frightful row where I said I hated him. Now I always wanna part with my kin on good terms. So all I do is nod. 'Come back safe, Da. Don't be long.'

'I swear it.'

He limps towards the door, and a rock swells in my throat that I have to fight and fight to swallow down. My mind fills with a picture of him with ice crackling in his yellow brows, his sea-eyes sweeping vast plains of land. *May the sea-gods swim close to you*, I pray, laying my weary head back on my pillow.

I fall into a fitful doze. When I wake in the glow of the dying fire, my brother crouches at the end of my bed, humped like a bowhead whale and draped in a thick grey bed-fur. I croak out a startled yell but he don't look up. His moonsprite Thunderbolt sits in his hair, a paling slip of silver. Sparrow's song is a husked whisper under his sticky, blue-lipped breath. He's staring at something on the blanket. Sparrow lost his sight after the worst shaking fit I ever saw, at the same time as a great storm at sea. Now he can see hazy shapes and colours, and things like Thunderbolt's light help his eyes work better. But in other ways, he sees better than anyone. He glimpses the future in visions that leave him frighted breathless. Sky Elders say he is gifted with True Sight.

Last time Sparrow had a vision was the day Axe-Thrower attacked me. He told it to me after we'd both been taken for healing in the sawbones' nest, and as he spoke I saw that, under his tunic, his muscles still twitched.

'I saw you,' he said, eyes blackened by exhaustion. 'On a carriage pulled by polar dogs, past a beach of white stones in the shape of eggs. A place where–' He started to cry, lightning webbing his fingers. 'Sea-gods die, and there are so many polar dogs, with blood on their teeth. There were doors of ice, covered in reindeer fur. You got shoved through them. Then I woke up.' He shuddered with his whole body, like someone swam over his grave.

Thunderbolt chitters softly at me, bringing me back into the here and now. *Black-Hair better now? Thunderbolt fretful for Black-Hair!*

Heart-thanks, Thunderbolt! Aye. I'm better now.

Her frail voice and thin light make me look at her more closely than I have for a while. Gods! With everything that's been happening, I barely thought that if the other sprites need moonlight, so does she. *Come back with that Opal soon, Da*, I pray.

The middle of my bed is aglow with purple, the light from Sparrow's lightning that webs between his fingers.

'What are you–'

'Shh!' he says, face screwed up with determination.

'Don't you *shh* me!'

He ignores me. He prods something lying on the bedsheets. I step closer. It's a dead frog, stretched out on its back.

I sigh. 'You don't have to fry your own frog for breakfast, too-soon. Things ent that bad.' *Yet.*

'I just made a *thing* happen,' he whines, lightning flaring. 'And now you're distracting me!'

I pull a face. 'What?'

'The frog's leg just moved!'

I roll my eyes. 'That beast's stone dead.'

He shakes his head, still not looking up. 'I ent ready yet – my lightning went into a skinny thread. I want to make it do it again.'

Sparrow reaches down to lift the limp body of the frog. Purple light pulses through it.

He flexes his fingers, dropping a splodge of purple that fizzles on the sheet until I lunge forwards to smother it. Then he flicks a small lightning bolt into the frog's chest. He draws back, breathing hard through his mouth. Then he yells, 'Why won't it do it again?'

I try to distract him. 'Ent you heart-glad I'm better?'

Finally, he looks. 'Aye,' he says doubtfully, with a half-shrug. 'You passed out cold, dint you?'

I press my lips thin. 'I'm strong as ever I was,' I tell him, hating the thought that folks might think me weak.

'Mouse?' calls a bright, hesitant voice outside the door, making my skin jump.

I brush my tangles out of my eyes. It *can't* be. Can it?

6
Visitations

Sparrow slithers off the bed and yanks open the door. Kestrel steps into the chamber, face flooded with concern, coppery hair threaded with firelight. 'How is she, Sparrow?'

I watch them watching me from the doorway. A little spark flares in my belly. 'Aye, and who might *she* be? The ship's cat? The shark's mother?'

'She's as prickly as ever,' announces Sparrow, ducking under Kestrel's arm and marching from the room.

Kes bites the corner of her mouth to keep from laughing as she hurries to my bedside. My heart rolls over in my chest and all in one beat I'm kneeling up, bed-furs and blankets flying, and my arms are wrapped tight around her neck. 'Is it really you? Am I still dreaming? What you doing here?'

'So many questions!' She laughs, returning my hug just as fiercely.

We pull away, checking each other over. She's thinner; her plain garb is slack and her cheekbones jut. Her light brown face looks tired, her freckles are pale and there's no gold paint on her catlike green eyes. But they glow with more heart-strength than ever.

'You have grown, sea-sister!' she says. 'And your scar continues to heal well – I wonder who stitched it so finely?' Her lips quirk into a grin.

I laugh, more loud and pure than I feel like I have in an age. Thaw thuds onto my pillow, stretching out her long neck to peer at Kes, blood glistening in the feathers beneath her hooked beak. *Hoodwink-high two-leg girl home?*

Aye, Thaw!

A strange look crosses Kestrel's features, seabird-swift, but she blinks and the look melts away and then she's clasping my hands. 'So, to answer you. Yes, it is really me. No, you're not dreaming. And I came to meet with Mother, to reassure her all is well and beg more provisions – not that there are many to be had. I hear more goats have frozen to death, so now Butter and Bone rule the hearth-sides, hogging the heat.'

Butter and Bone are the oldest goats on the mountain – two sisters who do as they please and bite anyone who challenges them. Cantankerous bleaters, both, and forever underfoot. I nod. 'But how is your mission working? Have you reached many of the Trianukkan youth yet?'

Her face grows flushed, burning with a look of hope and excitement. 'We've been camped with the Tree-Tribes at the edge of Nightfall, sneaking into the colleges when we can. Staying safe and hidden takes so much of our energy, and I tire of hiding,' she tells me with a small smile. 'But we've left scrolls full of our writings for folk to find, spreading word that the draggle-riders have returned and are seeking unity, not war. Also, about how women should be permitted to study, and about what Stag and the Wilder-King have been doing. We have met with young ones fleeing the city, helping them escape slavery, teaching them medsin and rune skills. And we've met with poor people on the outskirts, teaching them to read runic script. But it's all so much harder than I had thought! I must have been so naïve,' she says, burying her face in her hands. 'Our words have been discovered by angry, powerful people. I believe—' She pauses, studying her lap. 'They have begun to search for us.'

'Have you told your ma?' I ask, dread tumbling in my belly.

She shakes her head. 'And I beg you, please don't tell her! She would keep me here, and even if I were willing to stay for her sake, I could never leave Egret.'

I nod, slowly, the breath turned to iron in my lungs.

'You know, Mouse,' she says, like a conspirator. 'Even when you're stuck in one place, you can still make waves. Think of all the allies you have, right under your nose.'

She's misread my look – for once, I weren't feeling heart-sad at being left behind. I was fretting for *her*.

'Mother and I thought we would give you a present,' she says brightly, fishing in her pocket. She pulls out a tiny stub of silver, worn and smooth. I take it from her and find that my thumb fits inside a groove in the silver – it's an old key. 'It unlocks the Opal Chamber, so you can visit the stones,'

Kes tells me, grinning.

'Let's go, then!' I put my head under the blankets and dig my fur-lined slippers from the bottom of my bed. A fool that climbs out of bed barefooted is a fool that loses toes to winter's jaws.

We step into the crooked corridor outside. Thaw glides by my shoulder, throwing the cloak of her shadow over the glittering stone floor.

As I glance sideways at Kes, her words buzz in my brain. *You can still make waves.* I can feel the seed of an idea throwing roots into my blood.

We wind our way up three stairways hewn into the mountain, past sputtering lanterns that cough up oily wreaths of smoke. We reach a small wooden door and fit the key into the lock.

Kestrel has to stoop to fit through, but inside, the space yawns wide into a cavernous antechamber. Another door, much bigger, is flanked by two guards with crossed spears. The Opal Chamber. Leopard waits with the guards. She smiles at me when I thank her for the key.

The warriors uncross their spears.

We step into the storm-restless feeling of the Opal Chamber. Kestrel gasps. Leo stands by my side, breathing fast. The walls are charred black, seeping fire-worms from tiny pits in the rock. The air tastes charred, too. The fire-worms thud against my heavy cloak like scraps of burning black silk.

A pulsing silver ghostway gloops through a crack in the wall, so the guards can hear if anyone is trying to get too close to the gems.

The Opals hang from the ceiling inside two round iron cages, etched with glowing protective runes. Even though there's no breath of wind, the cages sway and the chains creak and groan. As I watch them, my skin itches on the inside. The Opals pull on my spirit, and I wish I could free them from their cages. Thaw rockets high in the air and swoops wide circles around the cages, feathers spiking. *Shinystones! Glintofgreenbluesparkles!*

I step slowly closer to the cages, dragging my fingers across the rough wall. There's a sour smell in the chamber. 'Are you making stinks cos you hate being trapped?' I whisper. The smell in here reminds me of how my armpits get when I'm nerve-jangled.

In answer, the Sea-Opal glows bright green and weeps chips of ice. Gold flecks swirl in its depths. It throws shadows on the cavernous walls, shadows in the shape of seals that writhe and twist and float together, sliding sleek dark skins across the damp rock. Salt rides the air. I stick out my tongue to taste the tang.

The Sky-Opal's blue deepens like dusk, as it splutters puffs of smoke and flurries of blue sparks that print pictures of clouds and birds and bats and the night hunts of owls on my vision. Shadows shaped like feathers dance across the walls. The cages holding the jewels pull towards each other, creaking.

'They hate being separated,' I murmur. Leo stands close by my side.

'I am sorry for it,' she says. 'But we decided that together their power was too great.'

I chatter to the Opals, imagining they're listening to me. They throw a fire-spirit glow onto the wall and I try to read the pictures. They twine together in ribbons of silver, like a plume of hair caught in a sea-wind. Hair like Grandma's.

Thaw rasps a cry, wrenching me from my thoughts. A scuffling sound makes my skin twitch.

'Who's there?' demands Leo, face sharpening to full alert as her fingers wrap around her spear.

'Protector?' calls one of the guards, knocking on the door.

Thaw dives past our startled faces, hurtling towards the floor. I turn around and see a small furry creature wriggling away through a gap at the bottom of the wall. Thaw shrieks her anger, her claws scraping against the stone floor. 'Oh! It's just a lemming,' says Kes.

Leo's shoulders sag. 'It's nothing, we're fine,' she tells the guard. She and Kes begin to laugh.

But a chill spreads through me. I breathe, trying to work out why I'm getting the fear. *Notjustlemmingnotjustlemming*, croaks Thaw.

Slowly, the knowing trickles into my veins.

'I didn't hear that lemming's beast-chatter,' I tell them. *The beast had the same empty hole where beast-chatter should be that Crow has.* What if that lemming was a shape-changer?

'Perhaps you had no time to notice it?' suggests Leo.

I shake my head. 'I can tell when it ent there.'

'Right,' says Leo, eyes darkening. 'I will have a word with the Elders about this.' She nods to us and strides from the chamber.

Kestrel frowns at the place where the lemming vanished. Then she fixes me with troubled green eyes.

'I feel like something's changed, about the chatter,' I tell her slowly. 'Da's been fretting about it. He told me to keep it secret, and he's never said that before. It's like it's suddenly a thing of shame.' Thaw glides towards me and I hold out my arm for her to land. Then her head nuzzles my jaw. 'I've heard folk say mean things, too. Like Coati, and some of the older girls that hang round Lunda. I'm not telling tales – I can handle myself against them, I just—'

'Mouse,' she interrupts gently. 'I know you can. But you're right to ask about this – I know I would. And I know something about it. Now seems as fine a time as any for the telling.'

'Go on,' I whisper.

'Since I stepped into the great wide, I have heard many foolish opinions of beast-chatter. Some view it as a sickness. A disease of the mind. It is an idea that is spreading.'

I stare up at her. 'A *disease*? But I ent sick.' I touch the blade at my belt, and Thaw shrills a cry of outrage.

'Of course not,' she adds quickly. 'But in times like these, folk distrust anyone marked out as different. Especially those with a connection to things they can't understand.

Some powers are so ancient that they are feared. I remember my mother teaching me of the old ways. She said there were once other chatterings, kinned with the same power, but different strands of it. Green-chatter, wielded over the plants, and wind-chatter, which is sister to the weather-witch powers, but more potent.'

Other chatterings?

'It takes its toll on you, doesn't it?' she asks, brow puckering. 'Is that why you fainted on the Sneaking?'

'It don't normally, no. That's the point – I feel like it's different. Something's changing. But aye – my chatter's what knocked me out cold.' I nibble my lip. 'What about Stag, though?' The name feels like it's knocking around in the air, bruising my skin. 'He don't keep his beast-chatter secret.'

Kestrel considers. 'He's using his power for ill-doings. Maybe that protects him, somehow.' She takes my hand. 'Enough about him, though. Just be careful. Please?'

'I'm stuck here, ent I?' I pull my hand away and turn to stare at the Opals, pins pricking my eyes. 'Can't get much more careful than that.' My voice comes out more bitter than I expected.

'I know. I'm sorry – you must hate me, coming back here and telling you what to do.'

I offer her a small smile. 'It's alright.'

She links arms with me. 'Now, more importantly – shall we go and find some food?'

49

We step into the flickering torchlight of the long-hall. The place rings with the cries of babs, the bleating of goats and a score of mismatched tribe-tongues. Squidges have wedged themselves into clusters along the tops of the walls and on the chains of the lanterns. The round, feathered, squidlike creatures squeal about the cold, chubby tentacles quivering. They drip ink onto folks' heads and into their food.

Great oaken eating benches glitter with hollowed, hungry eyes. The benches are laden with piles of kids, thumping each other's arms, tumbling around, jostling for space. As we walk past, they nudge each other, staring at my scar. Their stares make me feel skinned. What I did for Leo's lost spirit is famed round here.

'There treads the sea-witch,' someone whispers behind our backs. Nervous laughter whistles around my head, and my shoulders tense.

'Ignore them,' whispers Kestrel.

Easy for her to say. *She's* getting out of here. We stand in line for shallow bowls of goats' milk porridge. Pangolin joins us. She's bundled in thick wool dyed the colour of flame, and a grey enamelled pin in the shape of a draggle holds her cloak close around her neck.

She greets us both, but Kestrel's manner is stiff and the two eye each other warily. Maybe Kes still ent forgiven Pang for the way she was under the old regime.

I'm so busy watching how they are with each other, the seed of my idea swelling in my bones, that I end up stepping on Pang's cloak and she trips, almost knocking a pot over.

Curses whip from the cooks' mouths.

'She never meant to!' I blurt.

'Make her words big to her elders, will she?' threatens a fat old waddler called Kid, with six chins and three mean looks she switches between. She raises a tarnished ladle like a fist and turns to Kestrel. 'Sawbones, you keep these filthy sea-roving folk out of my kettle-fires.' She turns her broad back on us. 'That's the last of the provisions. Protector says we've to hold back the pot-scrapings for the prisoner.'

Axe-Thrower. But she wasn't the only prisoner, before. Leo captured a mystik and locked him in the belly of Hackles, but one day the cell was empty 'cept for a dark stain on the floor. The mystik leaked through the cracks in the stone.

Kestrel's cheeks have reddened. 'If my mother finds out you spoke of Mouse in such a way, she will not be pleased!'

Kid rounds on us, eyes rolling in her head. 'You dare take a tone with the women who have kept watch over you since you were belly-swell?'

Lunda appears, holding a bowl of porridge scraped clean. 'Your mother won't be around much longer anyway. Oh – haven't you heard?' she asks innocently. 'She received a summons, just before the mid-meal bell. She'll be flying to the Frozen Wastes as soon as possible.'

As me and Kes hurry from the hall, Kid's words arrow into our backs. 'She and her kin pine for the sea like a pack of seals. I say, let them fish for their breakfast.'

We find Leo in her chamber. She tells us the summons came from the Fangtooth Chieftain. 'Stag has turned on the Fangtooths,' she tells us. 'My strongest warriors are making ready to fly as soon as we are able.'

'You cannot accept this summons!' begs Kestrel.

'That Chieftain chased me and Crow into the sea with a volley of fire arrows,' I add, curling my lip. But I swallow down the real reason I don't want her going. *You can't abandon us!*

Leopard smiles sadly. 'How can I not go? My help has been requested. Isn't unity what we fight for? We are trying to re-establish ourselves as a major Trianukkan Tribe. The time for hiding is over.'

'Then there's something I need to tell you,' I say quietly.

Kestrel turns startled eyes on me.

Leo nods. 'Go on.'

I gabble breathlessly about how I reckon the Land-Opal is at the Wastes – cos that's what Da's magyk map told us the last time we used it. The map unlocked when Sparrow sang the old song, and showed us the bright amber orb, far to the north.

Leo pockets the knowing like an ingot of gold, promising to look for the Opal. But she won't let me go with her, however hard I beg.

7
The Summons

Three morning bells later, Leopard orders the riders to keep me busy with milking the goats, polishing the moon-lamps and helping in the sawbones' nest. Then she and Kes take to the skies, bound on their separate missions, leaving me stuck here. And while I work, all I can think is that Kestrel's gone, Da's gone, Leo's gone, Stag's still got one of the Opals and here I am, washing out old medsin bottles.

I only remembered that lemming with no beast-chatter after they left.

Time slips past. And the faster it hurries, the stronger my idea grows. If full-growns won't let me *do* anything, then the kids are gonna have to stick together to get stuff done. I just have to watch folks for a bit longer first. I have to know, good and proper, who I can trust . . .

'When's Da coming back?' asks Sparrow, blundering into the midst of my thoughts.

We're cross-legged before the fire in my chamber and I'm smoothing fat into my longbow, Kin-Keeper, to seal the new runes I've carved into the yew – though I've not yet managed to bring them to life, like Egret Runesmith can. Folk reckon she's the most gifted rune-worker on the mountain, and many are bitter that she left. But I know there's no way she and Kes would be apart.

Before I can reply, Sparrow pipes up again. 'How long do we have to wait around here? When can we go home? The whales need us, you know.' A slug of blue gloop leaks from his nostril and he sniffs it back in. 'The ones that ran away from Stag and then got stuck under the ice.'

I feel sick at the mention of Stag. He's taken everything from us – our home, our grandma, the whales. He tried to kill Da, and Kestrel. He made Crow do his dark bidding.

'The only way we can help them is by getting the Opals to the Crown, wherever that is.' I stand and brush myself down, rubbing the fat into my hands.

'But how?'

'Leo's planning to look for the Land-Opal while she's at the Wastes. So if Da gets back first, my bet is he'll go too.'

'And then he'll have to get all three to the Crown?'

'Aye. So, we need to think over everything we already know about it. There must be clues we've missed.'

'Well, we know that the Sea-Opal and the Sky-Opal are here, at Hackles,' he says, firelight tickling his cheeks.

I roll my eyes. 'Aye, *course!*'

'And the Fangtooths got the Land-Opal.' Sparrow wrinkles his nose. 'But Leo's gonna snatch it off them!'

'Aye – but we've got to pray the Opal's still there . . .'

'Cos the map's broken.'

I nod again. The map got so broken, when Stag kept trying to unlock it, that all the runes on it died. None of the Runesmiths at Hackles could revive them – not even Egret. 'So, that leaves the Crown.'

'The Crown's in a whale's belly, ent it? That's why Stag was dredging all them whales.'

'That's what the legend says, aye. But the Skybrarian reckons it's a lie, that Rattlebones never hid the Crown in belly of a whale. And that whale that swallowed *me* said that *Glint-of-gold cannot adorn a man's head*, so we know there's more to the mystery than just finding some rusty old normal crown.'

Sparrow's mouth opens but before he can reply Thaw screeches, thumping down out of the darkness to peer under my bed.

Thaw?

Sneakythinglurks!

A *beast?* I listen past her chatter for what type of thing might be lurking under there – and slam against the same void as before. The void where beast-chatter should be.

A lemming shoots out from under the hanging blankets. Sparrow shrieks.

Thaw ducks low to grab it in her talons, but it changes into a slug, lengthens itself on a strand of slime and drops away into the darkness of the floor. I sink to my knees, waves of horror stroking up and down my spine.

That ent no natural creature. And I've never seen anyone

have a choice of shapes before. I try to find the thing and close my hand over a lump of hard, slimy flesh, but it shrinks suddenly down, and it's become a thick-legged spider. I lunge for it, both hands outstretched, but it scuttles through a wormhole in the wall. I rock back onto my heels, swallowing a mouthful of spew.

What is going on here? I whisper.

Baaaaaaaaad-featheredblunderings, breathes Thaw, landing on my arm and snuggling her head under my chin.

Me and Sparrow face each other, his eyes pinned to the air next to my head. He opens his mouth, but a horn bellows outside, smothering his voice. Then shouting echoes off the rocks. I press my eye to an arrow-slit in the wall and gasp as I see the black outline of a draggle, wobbling towards the stronghold, caught in the mouth of a storm. I run, ignoring Sparrow's questions.

Folk yell at me as I barrel past them. It feels like an age before I reach the lower levels.

I jump down the steep steps into the guts of the mountain and tear past a startled Lunda – then double back and catch her wrist.

'Is it Leo? Where is she?'

A look of disgust traces her features. 'It's "the Protector", to you.'

'Where is she?' I hiss again, through my teeth.

'She's not *here*,' says Lunda, wrenching back her wrist. 'Her draggle returned with a message, is all.'

I push past her and tear to the draggle caves. A few

snoozing draggles crack open their eyes to peer at me. Coati and Crow are trying to tether Leo's draggle. It's the one she always rides, with a stripe of silver fur through the orange. I step closer to the draggle to listen to her chatter.

She's so strongly frighted that I can feel her chatter pulling on my brain and crowding my bones. I try to breathe, putting out a hand to steady myself.

'Grab the other wing, boy,' gruffs Coati.

'I'm trying!' says Crow, eyes flashing. He's been helping with the draggles cos they're the closest things to horses, in a Sky-realm.

I take a deep breath and try to tune to the chatter again. It takes a few beats to untangle even a word of sense.

Fleefleefleebloodhandssilverflashmissingriderwhere?

I force my mind back from hers, then reel, leaning on the wall for support.

'Mouse?' says Crow, noticing me for the first time.

'I need your full attention here, lad!' commands Coati. Eventually they get the draggle tethered.

'She won't settle,' says Crow in concern, stroking the beast's muzzle. She knocks his hand away, eyes rolling back.

'Must've had a bad flight though the storms,' says Coati. 'Get her warm and watered, then keep watch over her until she settles – they always do. Strong of spirit, each one.' He turns towards the tack room and almost crashes into me.

'Watch where you're treading!' he says. His arms are full of saddle, but a crumpled piece of parchment pokes through the gaps in his fist.

I point at it. 'What does the message say?'

'Just that the Protector has reached the Wastes and started secret talks with the Chieftain,' says Crow, still trying to soothe the beast.

'Why didn't she send one of her warriors?' I ask doubtfully.

'Guard your own business and I'll guard mine,' says Coati, eyeing me stonily as he steps past.

Crow rolls his eyes behind the grumpy old man's back. 'She needs her warriors by her side, Mouse. Everything is fine.'

But that's not the message I'm getting from the draggle.

Tornfrombackdragawaychiefmangonegonegone – chief man gone!

Chief man? I whisper, stepping closer and putting a gentle hand on her flank. *The Fangtooth Chieftain? Gone where?*

Coati emerges from the tack room and starts to trundle around the caves, whistling as he feeds the draggles.

'How do you know that message is really from Leo?' I whisper to Crow.

'I read it,' he says, shrugging. 'It was signed by her, and stamped with her own mark. There's nothing to fret about.'

Doubt plagues me. I shake my head. 'I don't think so. That's not what the draggle is say–'

I've forgotten to keep my voice down. Before I can blink, Coati's looming over me. 'Child, I won't have you practising your dark jargonings in my draggle caves. Off with you to supper!'

He ushers me out of the cave.

8
Our Own Sneaking

I find the round tower room where Leo's commanders rule over Hackles in her absence. I tell them something's wrong, that Leo needs help, but they won't listen.

'How do you know?' they ask me, eyes too calm, too blank, looking right through me cos I'm *just a child*.

'I – the draggle was spooked. I mean good and proper, and I know it weren't just storms—'

'Draggles encounter many irregularities during a flight,' says one, glancing at me from under big bushy brows. 'There is no cause for concern.'

I bang through the door and run down the steps from the tower, back into the main web of passageways.

Da needs to get back here, *now*. He'd believe me, in half a heartbeat. But for all I know, his mission could take ages longer. I scrape my fingertips along the wall as I hurry towards my chamber. All these full-growns having secret meetings, making secret plans, getting stuff done . . .

You can still make waves.

A glow heats up my belly. What if I could assemble my own crew?

If Leo's in danger, and no one believes me, then I could be her only hope. And if I can get to the Frozen Wastes to search for her, then maybe I can find the Opal!

Sparrow edges round the corner, using the stick Da whittled for him to help him find his way. Thunderbolt hovers in front of his face and his filmy eyeballs scan the air for me, using her light. '*There* you are!' he huffs. 'The ghostway spat this out for you.' He hands me a tightly wrapped scroll sealed with a splodge of blood-red wax.

I blink at him, startled that I've found my way back to the door of my chamber without even noticing.

We slip inside the chamber and I snap open the seal. 'What's it say?' jabbers Sparrow impatiently.

'Gift me a chance!' Sitting on the edge of my bed, I smooth the letter flat on my knees. Before my eyes, the runes tremble and glow moon-silver. Sparrow scrambles closer.

There are only three words etched into the parchment. *Read in private!*

As soon as my eyes drink them, the bright silver runes disappear with a small cracking sound, leaving a faint trace of smoke.

Then others appear. 'It's from Yapok,' I whisper, realising how relieved I am to hear from the Skybrarian's apprentice after so long. Then I remember the lemming and look quickly around to make sure no slitherers are watching from the walls, before reading Yapok's scrawled silver runes.

The Skybrary stands strong, and we are safe enough for now. The Skybrarian and I have been travelling to seek out new manuscripts for the collection – he says we don't have to hide so much now that the Sky-Tribes are returning.

We've been tracking some names of people who are known to protect books – in crowded bazaars, secret libraries, back-alley bookshops and grand houses.

And I've made a new discovery. I wanted you to know because of your quest. Some of the war manuscripts I've been looking at – I think they have much older runes hidden underneath the text.

My mind reels. *Underneath?*

I think I could find something helpful if I can just see beneath the writing, long enough to reveal the truth. But every time I manage to scrape away the newer runes, a strange symbol, like a strangling vine, bleeds upwards through the parchment, throttling the old runes.

Anyway, it feels like progress. I'll write again if I discover any clues about the Crown.

A shiver ripples up my spine, as a picture of a strangling vine coils in my mind. I turn to Sparrow. 'We've got to take matters into our own hands.'

I make my way to the sawbones' nest and steal a pan of squidge ink and some brittle old scraps of goatskin and scratch my message into them.

61

Time's come for a Sneaking of our own. I call a secret youth's Tribe-Meet. Honour this law: no full-growns. Bone-crypts, after lamps out. Come if you're brave enough.

I slip into dormitories and stuff the notes under the pillows of the biggest blabbermouths on the mountain – the kids that can't turn down a challenge. Then I wait.

The day drags on for ever. I'm a bundle of nerves. My mind keeps straying to the seed I've sown. When it's time to bed down again, I pray to all the sea-gods that my note is enough.

Then down, down, down through the murk I slip, Thaw riding the air by my side.

I scurry down to the bone-crypts, until the crushing weight of Hackles hulks overhead. The crypts are deeper than even the draggle caves, but off in a different direction. I step through an archway sculpted from thighbones and stare around. Thousands on thousands of Sky-folk shoulder blades, collarbones, fingers and toes, and piles of staring skulls boom their chalky death into the tomb-chamber. They've been arranged in ornate patterns to honour the dead. I feel a grin melt across my face. If we have to plan for the end of the world, this is a proper place to do it.

I settle down to wait. Thaw stays close, and I try to stroke away her frights.

But soon, I'm praying for something to move. Cos no one comes, and the cold prods my bones. *Lamps must be out by now!* I chatter to Thaw. *Where are they? Sparrow ent even here – and he said he'd bring the kids from his dorm.*

Gods. He'd better not have broken his neck on the way down here. I said I'd help him find his way, but the stubborn too-soon just said *lemme be*!

My eyelids are growing heavy when slowly, one by one, ghoulish shadows wisp through the thighbone archway into the crypts. My gut turns hot and tight. Thaw shuffles her wings and puffs a belch of fright into the gloom.

'I could be at Hackles the rest of forever and still never learn all its secrets,' lisps a Wilderwitch girl called Ibex, with hair shaved to her skull and the stubble dyed bruise-blue.

Relief *whumps* through me.

'Quiet!' shushes someone from the gloom.

'Hope we *won't* be here forever,' mutters Ermine, from somewhere to the left of me.

'Don't fret,' I husk, making him startle halfway out of his skin. 'Soon, we rove.'

'Mouse!' whispers Hammer. 'Don't do that!'

'I was just *saying*,' says Erm, to cover his frights. 'Aren't you creeped out of your pelt down here?' He scowls. 'Just me then.' His gaze burrows under my skin. Then he tips back his head and stares at the underside of our world.

'I'm frighted, too,' says Sparrow.

'I never said I was *frighted*,' spits Erm, crossing his arms.

'This is the one who left the notes,' Lunda tells the kids that're trotting after her. She fixes her eyes on my scar. 'The pearl-fisher that talks to animals.' She stalks towards our group with a lantern raised in her hand.

My heart drums and my blood kicks for a fight. Part of me

wishes I never invited her – but she's gonna be useful.

'Oh, you're Sea-Tribe, aren't you?' asks Ibex. 'How fascinating! I've never even *seen* the sea!'

I gift her a grin.

But Lunda chuckles coldly. 'I'm not sure I'd call roving sea-creepers a *Tribe*! And I've no idea why we're giving them shelter-feather in our sky-fortress.' She's goading me for a brawl. A brawl I realise I've been thirsting for.

'Don't think this girl walks alone, will you?' snarls Hammer, who's got my back along with Ermine and Crow.

'Aye, and she's got more than little boys standing up for her,' says Crow. Someone snickers. Hammer's fine black brows quirk together in a frown as he rounds on Crow.

'Boys fighting over her, huh?' scorns Lunda.

'Your words are dust to me,' I say calmly. *And I am ready for the next battle.*

Thaw-Wielder chats straight into my head. *ArmLAND!*

For a beat I watch myself from above, through her eyes. It's the strangest feeling, like there's a wormy cord threading out of my belly and connecting me to my hawk. I unfurl my wrist and she drops onto it, out of the immense nothing yawning over and around us, like someone high up has dumped a bucket of feathers and claws and quickness into the air. Even Lunda gasps as Thaw resettles her feathers, twitching her head around at them all.

I smile. These kids are starting to know something about my fierce.

'I'm not fazed by your tricks,' says Lunda. 'Soon, you will

be dust, too. Only the strongest will survive this Withering.'
Her words wreath from her mouth like pale spekters.

I push my face into Lunda's. 'Either rest your jaws, or say
that again – if you dare.' I can feel my magyk pulsing in my
blood and in my gut and in my dark-gulping eyes. I could do
anything in this beat.

'Mama says that's not how girls should act,' quavers Ibex.

I reply to her, not taking my eyes off Lunda's. 'Your
mama needs to learn herself a thing or two.'

Lunda's eyes are like hard blue chips of ice. 'What are
you waiting for, sea-witch?'

'I didn't come here to fight, spear-flinger.'

She stares at me and spills two words that sharpen the
air. 'Didn't you?'

This night belongs to us.

I ent sure who moves first. But then all of a sudden the
crypts are one giant tangled sweaty brawl and all I know is

Fists

Feet

Eyelids

Ribs

And all we are is

Clawed

Punched

Pulled

Scrambled

Laughing

Yelling

Thaw roosts atop a skull and screams encouragement, making my foes shudder.

Fists to fists, we practise our fight for the end of the world, then someone steps on a lemming and it screams and we're all falling about in stitches of laughter. Breath-clouds puff all over the crypt.

The sharpness has been squeezed out of the air and it feels easier to breathe. Pangolin says something to Lunda and the Spearsister laughs, in a pure way I ent heard her do before. The sound gifts me heart-strength. She's here now, like it or not. And if Pang trusts her, maybe I can learn to.

Thaw, I chatter, while the others are still laughing and a few fights are still growling, *keep watch for any sneaky blighters that look like beasts but don't have chatter. I don't want any spies down here.*

She screeches, lifting up into the air to start her patrol. Everyone turns to stare at me.

I make my spine arrow-straight. 'I called this secret meet cos we need a crew.'

'What is a crew?' asks Pika.

I grin at him. 'It's *everything* – kinship, knowing how to weather storms together – storms in the world *and* storms in your heart. It's having each other's back, no matter what. It's – it's sharing heart-love for what matters most and gifting each other the heart-strength to fight.'

'Pretty speech,' snaps Lunda.

'Why do we need a crew?' asks a boy.

'Naught's going right round here. They tell us to let the

full-growns save Trianukka. But who's gonna save them?'

'What are you talking about?' demands Lunda. 'You're the one that endangered the whole Sneaking because of whatever's going on up there.' She gestures to the sides of her head and pulls a gruesome face.

Crow steps towards her but I hold up a hand. Da said not to reveal my chatter. But how can you make a real crew if you ent honest with them? 'It's true that I'm a beast-chatterer, and that my chatter can overpower me.' I pause, waiting for the whispers to fade. 'But it means the beasts can tell me things we wouldn't know elsewise. Like this now – something has happened to the Protector. Something bad.'

Gasps rattle through the spaces between the bones.

Pangolin steps forwards. 'What has happened?'

'I don't know. But her draggle was spooked—'

'So would you be if you flew through those storms,' says Lunda.

'It was more than the storms!' I yell. 'I *heard* her! She said *missing rider, torn from back*. Something happened to Leo. And now I've got to find a way to get to her, cos none of the full-growns believes me.'

Lunda snorts. 'Small wonder.'

'If you don't want to be crew, Lunda, that's no blubber off my blade. But if there's even a chance that something's gone wrong, don't you wanna be sure?'

Lunda slides down the wall until she's sitting cross-legged. She puts her face in her hands, saying nothing.

'So . . . what do we do?' whimpers Ibex.

I blow out my cheeks. 'First, I need to know who's in. Raise your fist and thump your heart if you're crewing up!'

Slowly, one by one, each kid in the crypt steps forwards and thumps their chest. My heart glows. Lunda stands, keeping her eyes on mine.

I swallow my pride though it snags in my throat. 'Be part of our crew. Help us, Lunda.' I hold my fist to my chest and she hesitates, big pale eyes wavering as the struggle under her surface rages.

Then she swears in, too. But not without another challenge. 'Who is leader of this *crew*?' Her accent clips the word and makes it whistle through her teeth like a birdcall.

Pride punches my chest and stings my cheeks.

'Oh, you?' She laughs.

'Course!'

'Why am I not surprised that the sea-creeper seeks attention?'

'You didn't even know what a crew *was*—'

'Hey, you two!' says Pangolin. We turn to face her. She's standing next to Pika and the two of them are chuckling into their hands. 'Settle your feathers. There is room – sure, there is *need* – for more than one leader. I vote for one from each Sky-Tribe plus Mouse to represent the Sea-Tribes.'

I study my boots. 'Grand idea, Pang.'

We cast votes and count them up. The three leaders are decided – me, Pika and Ibex.

Pika strides into the middle of the crypt. 'Our crew needs a plan. If the draggle spoke true, we have to get to the

Wastes and find Leopard.'

'How?' asks Pang.

Silence.

'Take the draggles?' suggests Hammer.

'A few of us have weather-work,' offers a Wilderwitch kid. 'We could try to push the storms away from you.'

'We can't all go out there riding draggles. Someone would see!' glooms Ermine.

I nod. *But one girl . . .*

Crow catches my eye and frowns. I smile at him, but it's a proper beam by accident. Too late, I try to wipe the look off my face but he scowls. Then he puts his mouth close to my ear. 'Gone and had a terrible idea, have you?'

I push him away, biting back my grin. *Aye. And I'll make you help me with it. I'll need a lookout. Who better than a boy who can take the shape of a harmless crow?*

I turn to Ermine. 'Not if one girl took the journey. Alone.' The thought makes fire stir behind my eyes and I have to breathe quick, my veins jumping with excitement.

'*Not* alone,' says Lunda impatiently.

We look at her in surprise.

'Haven't any of you realised it yet?' she says, voice bubbling with irritation. 'Even if you got as far as the Frozen Wastes, the Fangtooths would sniff out a sea-creeper. But there's one person at Hackles who'd be admitted into their territory, bold as daggers.'

I meet her eyes. 'Axe-Thrower!'

Lunda bites the skin around her thumb, nods briskly.

'But she's a prisoner,' says Pang. 'She won't be going anywhere.'

'No, she won't,' replies Lunda. 'Unless we break her out.'

Crow curses all over everyone's shock.

But the hooks of Lunda's idea dig into my skin. Cos what if the vision Sparrow had of me in a place of sleds and reindeer skin ent a destiny that will happen to me, but a destiny that I can choose for myself? 'That's a flaming *good* idea!'

'It's too dangerous,' warns Crow quickly. 'Your da would never let you do a foolish thing like that.'

And there they are. The words that decide it. 'Da's not here,' I whisper.

Lunda grins, eyes sparking. 'Good girl.'

The spark leaps into my chest and sets my heart drumming against my ribs.

9
Wandering Warriors

When a new day's been birthed by the lighting of the lamps and I'm standing in line to get my breakfast, Kid gifts me a flint-eyed stare. 'What've you been up to?' She gestures to my split lip and the bruises cluttering my forearms.

'Naught,' I mutter, allowing myself the ghost of a smirk. *Just planning how to save all your skins.*

We make our plans. We keep them secret. We watch the routines of the cell guards and try to choose when to make our move. Over the next few nights we fight some more, cos it helps us put our trapped energies to good use. When I get back with Leo, all the crew will be better at fighting off enemies – and if something happens in the meantime, we'll be prepared. I help them with their target practice, shooting arrows through the eye sockets of ancient skulls. Ibex teaches me handstands. I try it against a wall and Thaw settles on the soles of my feet, making me laugh upside down.

We plug as many gaps in the stone of the stronghold as we can find, to stop spies wriggling through the rock. Ibex

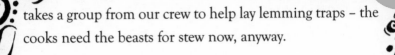

takes a group from our crew to help lay lemming traps – the cooks need the beasts for stew now, anyway.

At supper, I realise heart-sadness is rolling off Thaw's feathers. It prickles my eyes. *Thaw? What is it?*

Thawdon'tknowwhat'swhat. She shuffles her feathers. I know she's not been eating proper, cos everything's so topsy.

Poor beast. I reach for her and she bows her head like a queen, until I can reach her feathers to give them a stroke.

She looks down at me, tilting her head to one side. And I find myself pitching suddenly forwards, falling into her.

My spirit pushes across the oaken table, skimming through the broth-steam, and thumps into feathers, burrows into skin, muscle, innards, bone, and then I'm blinking in a sticky way, and my nose feels curved, cold and sharp.

I look down – and a squawk blows from my mouth. My feet are scaly, yellow and tipped with claws, one still snagged with fish-flesh from my hunt.

Then I shuffle my feet. Open my wings. Enjoy the long stretch, dip my head under the feathers and preen away a lump of grit, some specks of salt, some blood.

When I blink across the room, through vapours puffed out by wormsfishworms, I see a black-hair two-legs with her watching holes rolled back in her head.

Wait.

That's me.

How did I–

A small, silvery shape flits around the girl's head. Thaw's spirit!

I'm in her body! Somehow I must've pushed her out.

How do I dream-dance back again? I shut Thaw's eyes, feel for the edges of her body, then push forwards like an arrow. When I open my own eyes, Thaw spews a bellyful.

Ouchhurtsouchhurtswobblyspinheadfly!

She bolts in a cloud of silence.

What have I done?

Thaw disappears for the whole night. *She must be hunting. She won't have left me.* But I'm proper frighted, cos the other sea-hawks have gone on their winter migration. She only stuck around for me. And look what I've done. A tear nudges out of my eye but I scrub it away. In the back of my mind, there's a feeling that my beast-chatter is even odder than I thought.

I struggle to sleep. But I must've dropped into a restless doze, cos suddenly I'm woken by a rush of air on my face as Thaw swoops back through the arrow-slit into the chamber. I scramble onto my hands and knees in my bed. *Thaw,* I chatter. *Thaw-beast, I'm so so sorry!*

Her silence charges the air.

Thaw?

Finally, she glides down from her nest to land on my pillow. *Nevermore,* she croaks. *Never-do with no-warning.*

Never, Thaw! I promise. I'm so sorry. I didn't mean to do it – I don't know what's happening to me. Can we work it out together?

She inclines her head. *Heart-love-forgive, feather deep,* she says.

Heart-thanks, Thaw, I choke, through my streaming tears.

By morning bell, more folk have arrived at the stronghold. They straggle inside; hollow-eyed, some burned by black rain, half-starved and full-frightful. I'm squeezing past them, weaving between damp cloaks that cling to me, when I notice a ragged group standing near the doors, staring straight at me, their faces hidden by cavernous hoods.

I wrinkle my nose and turn, trying to push through another way. But I don't get far before a hand shoots free from the press of bodies and clamps onto my arm.

'Get off me!' I yell, kicking out. My boot makes contact with a shin.

Someone yelps. 'Mouse! Stop struggling, it's me!'

Then I look up into a pair of coppery eyes, and everything stops. The noise of the hall fades. Time stretches and slows.

'*Bear?*' The tall, brown-skinned oarsman I've known all my life wears a claw-gouged cloak and a few new lines on his face. He's thinner than I remember, and grey hairs pepper the black in his beard. But it's him – solid as oak, and sunbeam-warm.

Others squeeze through the crowd. First comes a curly-haired woman in bloodied skirts – Vole, the prentice who always used to scold me. The sea-sparkle has faded from her blue eyes, but a tiny bab is strapped to her chest in a cloth sling. Behind her steps a broad-shouldered almost-man with a mass of red hair and mossy green eyes. Frog! I gape at each member of the *Huntress*'s crew in turn, then my heart leaps into my mouth and I jump into Bear's arms.

'Bear?' I croak. 'Bear!' I shake my head in disbelief as he belly-laughs, gathering me close. Vole strokes my hair.

'Frog and Vole, too!' *Never thought I'd be so heart-glad to see you!* 'And – who is this scrap?' I stare at the top of the bab's head.

'This is our sweet daughter,' says Vole proudly, nodding at Bear.

'Mouse, dearest heart.' Bear pulls away and looks at me, at my scar. 'I thought of you every beat. I dreamed you were haunting me all the while I was chained to my oars.'

I chew my cheek. 'I did visit you, once or twice.'

'Where can I take him?' calls another voice I know, bones-deep.

It's Pipistrelle, the sandy-headed cook with a knife-stump for a hand. I wave as he breaks free from the crowd of homeless wanderers.

'Mouse,' says Bear, warning in his throat. 'Just be ready to calm your sails.'

There's a bundle in Pip's arms. A fair-haired man, too frail to be Da . . .

Oh, no.

'He's going to be alright, Mouse,' says Bear, holding me back.

Pip's eyes never leave my face. 'Praise the sea-gods,' he says. 'Gritty as a pearl, you are.'

'Aye. But is Da?'

Pip nods. 'Never doubt it, Bones. He's way-worn, and his leg is injured beyond bearing his weight. But he will heal.

So help me, after all this, he *will.*'

In the long-hall, we sit before one of the huge, crackling fires. Pip casts wary eyes around the clattering room. Vole rests back with her bab sleeping on her chest. 'Bear was freed by a member of Stag's own crew,' she tells me.

'*Why?*' I gasp.

'They needed my strength to help sail through the storms,' says the oarsman, huddled under a goatskin. 'Things have been going badly wrong at sea, Little-Bones. Stag has given up on his search for the Crown as the ice spreads. He is *furious.* But when he destroyed your grandma's medsin lab he lost her inventions – risking more lives. He lost crew to sickness when Captain Wren never would have. He sailed to the ship-breaking yards. But our ship stuck fast in the ice just before we got there.'

'Saved by the frozen sea . . .' I whisper.

'We tried to lead our own mutiny,' growls Pip, fingers wrapped around a tankard of spiced rum. 'Bear's leg was badly bitten by a polar dog. We fought Stag, during a bad storm. We each knocked out a few of his teeth.'

'Yes!' I punch the air. Pip grins.

'What happened after that?' I ask.

'When the storm shrank back, Stag and his cronies abandoned the icebound ship and took all supplies with them,' says Pip bitterly. I notice all of a sudden that the knife on his stump is missing, leaving just a blunt stick of rags. 'They took most of the crew to sell as slaves. They shot at Bear when he tried to go after them.'

Bear nods. 'We left with Vole—'

'I'd hidden,' she adds.

'—and tried to find somewhere to rest and write a note that we hoped might reach the Icy Marshes, but the lawlessness everywhere kept us running for our lives. Then the bab came, and we put all our heart-strength into keeping her warm. Your da searched for us. We owe him our lives.'

Pride swells in my chest, sharp and sweet.

I talk with Vole in the still hours and cradle her bab, a smooth-faced, wise-looking thing with masses of black curly hair and a tiny, puckered version of Bear's face that makes me smile. The firelight plays on her skin.

'I want you to know something, Mouse,' Vole says softly. 'I never wanted to make you feel disapproved of.'

'I know. I've done a lot of growing, since we last met.'

'I can see that.' She smiles. 'I need your help, Mouse.'

I stay silent, waiting.

'We need a name for the bab. We've looked to the fire spirits, but they hide away and give us no answer. I want your help to coax them.'

The fire spirits gift our Tribe visions of what our young ones' namesake animals should be. 'I've got a lot of learning to do, Vole,' I tell her.

'I know,' she says. 'We all of us do. But I believe in you, Mouse. I always have.'

77

After she's finished her telling and I've done mine, I creep to the sawbones' nest. Da's awake and I gift a silent thanks to all the gods of Sea, Sky and Land.

He spies me and struggles to sit, but I wave at him to rest his blubber.

His eyes are more troubled than I've ever seen and the vicious cord of the pain is throttling him worse than ever.

'Sparrow?'

'He's alright.'

He relaxes, but only for half a beat.

'Bones, I failed.'

I shake my head but anger crumples his face. 'I did. I was stupid. Now I can't follow Leo to help her win the Opal. What are we going to do?' He shakes his head and looks at me. 'Sorry, Bones. None of this is for you to worry about. Just promise me you'll stay close, and stay safe.'

I feel the lie claim my tongue before I speak, and I hate it. I've never lied to Da before. 'I promise,' I whisper.

A sawbones steps close and presses more pain medsins into Da's hand. He swallows them. Then he nods at me, his muscles relaxing as the pain is swept away for a few more beats of the drum.

'This is stupid,' says Crow, as we wait in the bone-crypts for the rest of the crew.

I shake my head. 'It's time to rescue the Protector and hunt that Opal.'

'Lunda's just setting you up with a dare. Do you have to

78

take the bait?'

'She ent. And anyway, nets don't mend themselves. I can't stay here.'

'Don't start spouting all them captain's sayings at me.'

'I'm right though, eh?' I nudge him.

Crow winces. 'Your da made me swear to watch out for you after you frighted everyone to death sneaking out!'

'I'm *sorry*, alright?' But a little spark flares in my belly. I don't want Da telling anyone to look after me.

Silence moulds around us. We watch each other, and I wonder if he's thinking the same thing as me. *How did I end up with you?*

But I'm heart-glad I did.

When the crew is assembled, I stare around at them all. 'My da and the Protector were going to make another plan when they returned to Hackles – to rescue an ancient stone of power. But Da can't go anywhere now, and Leo's in danger. So here's my new plan: save Leo, then find the Opal. Da's map told us the Opal is at the Wastes.' I tell them how we've already rescued the other two Opals, and that they're hidden here at Hackles. I make them swear to guard that secret with their lives.

But doubt crawls over Ibex's face. 'How is that our fight?'

'It's all linked with the Withering,' I explain slowly, chewing on the thoughts as they come. 'Until we get the Opals back together, winter will only tighten worse. How can I get to Axe-Thrower?'

'I have been pondering the same,' says Lunda. Her mouth is set in a grim line and her eyes spill white fire. 'At morning and evening gong, the cooks have to get food scraps to her cell. They hate doing it. One of us can offer to take the scraps – they'll never suspect anything.'

'That should work,' I tell her, grinning.

'You'll need a disguise, too,' says Pangolin. 'Ibex and I brought supplies to change your looks as best we can.'

A hunted child. I nod.

Pangolin crouches next to me. She combs out my tangles with oil and then weaves the strands into a braid so tight it pulls at my eyebrows. 'I am envy-stung,' she says, her voice buzzing painfully in my head.

Startlement nips me. 'Why?'

'So thick, your hair! And lustrous black. Very eye-pleasing.'

I grimace. 'What's the good of that?' *Especially with a scar long and twisted enough to make innkeeps and dockmasters weep.* 'By the time I'm your age I'll likely be as scarred as the moon!' *If any of us survive that long.*

She laughs, then makes me dunk my head in a basin of blue dye.

Lunda gifts me a scarf to cover my face. 'Raindrop mail may draw too many looks, or even trace you to Hackles.'

'We cannot disguise your eyes,' Pang says solemnly. 'So don't do that thing you do, where you look too closely at people. Cast your eyes low.'

'Oh, and you're a boy,' says Lunda. 'Remember that.'

Before leaving the crypt I scratch a message to Da, gifting him my heart-sadness, and begging him – *please* – to trust me. 'I need you to give this to Da,' I tell Sparrow, pulling my letter out of my pocket. The silver key Leo gifted me comes out with it and drops on the floor, so I gift him that, too. 'But not until he's feeling well enough to seek you out.'

'Why don't *you*?'

'Sparrow, can you just do what I'm asking for once in your life?'

My little brother lies on his bed, glaring up at me through the thin glow leaking from his moonsprite. 'Where you going?'

I lower my voice. 'I'm going away for a bit.' He bolts upright and opens his mouth to complain but I shush him. 'Sparrow! This is proper important!'

'Aye, so's Thunderbolt! She's not well, but *you* don't even care.'

I squint at the moonsprite lying stretched along his collarbone. She's grown fainter, and harder to see. I reach out to her in beast-chatter. *Thunderbolt. You alright, girl?*

The moonsprite moans faintly, then squirms. She don't answer me.

Rest yourself, Thunderbolt, brave girl, I tell her.

Cold, her faint voice chitters finally. *No fly-powers. Weak, no life-warmth.*

I know, I'm heart-sorry. Wetness blurs my eyes. Thunderbolt is part of our Tribe. A link to our home.

'Is she talking?' asks Sparrow. 'What did she say?'

'She's feeling cold and weak,' I tell him. 'That's why I have to go, too-soon. Cos I *do* care.'

'If you cared you wouldn't be leaving me,' he insists, rivet-stubborn.

'Please, just do as I say,' I beg. 'And I need you to watch over them Opals. Any sniff of trouble, let Da know.'

'Just cos you're famed round here, don't mean you can be bossing me around all the time,' he hisses. A smell of burning creeps into my nose.

'Oh, shut it, will you? And don't even think about threatening me with lightning just cos I've asked you to make yourself useful.'

There's a flash of purple. *Zap!*

'Argh!' I yell. When I look down, I see a tiny hole in my breeches, seeping smoke. He's flicked a bolt of lightning at me. 'Spar*row*! You can't *do* that!'

'It was only a little bit,' he says quietly, smiling. Then he starts to weep. 'Our kin's getting back together and now you want to leave me here.'

'You've got Da, and Bear, and even Vole!'

He peers up at me and grabs hold of my wrist.

I stand up, trying to prise his fingers off. 'Sparrow, I have to go. You have an important job to do here. You have to look after Da.' A thought strikes me, sudden as a hammer in the gut. 'Oh, Sparrow.'

'What?'

'You've got to look after someone else, too.'

My hawk puffs herself up and spits, flaps her wings into

a frenzy and thuds onto my shoulder, sending me sprawling to the floor under her weight. Then she ducks her head under my chin and coos and croaks. *I know, Thaw-beast. I know it hurts.*

It takes all my heart-strength to force Thaw-Wielder to stay in the chamber with Sparrow. The sobs rattle up and out of my chest from depths I never knew I had, scraping me hollow.

I can't take you with me, Thaw girl.

Nottake? She is proper outraged. *Stay feather-close, for ever times. MY two-legs.* She screeches wildly, like I've plucked out a feather.

The guilt smashes over me like a wave. *Thaw, please, PLEASE try to understand. I can't keep you hidden. The Fangtooths hunt sea-birds. They will rip you from the sky! It's for your own good.*

Thaw rip THEM. She huddles, bright-eyed with fury, on Sparrow's knee. He tries to stroke her but she nips his fingers, making him yell.

Thaw. I reach for her and she turns her back. *Thaw. Oh, please, Thaw love!*

But she won't talk to me. She's silent as a shape-changer.

'You should go,' says Sparrow.

I nod. When I shut the door behind me I hear Thaw's body smash into the wood as she throws herself against it. Then she *screams.*

I blunder away, through a veil made of tears.

I step into the long-hall, head still pounding. The cooks' backs are turned but I can hear them gabbing about the same thing as at breakfast – resentfully holding back scraps of the food at the bottom of the pans for the prisoner.

'What's wrong with a good old-fashioned sky-burial, eh?' demands Kid.

'Protector thinks her a valuable hostage, as you well know,' says a friendlier one.

But doubt slithers through me as I listen. For a hostage to be worth a stitch, someone has to *care*, and no one has tried to claim Axe-Thrower. It's like no one's missed the Fangtooth at all.

I move along the hall towards the kettle-fires, pulling my scarf away from my face. The cooks turn around, jaws slack enough to catch flies. 'We're busy, girl,' barks Kid.

'I'll take the scrapings to the prisoner for you,' I offer, casually.

Doubtful full-grown looks are swapped between them. '*You*? Why?'

'I'm never any use round here.'

'That's not why. I've seen your proud look.' Kid draws herself up. 'Why really?'

I sigh through my nose. 'Alright, I'll tell you, waddler.' Fire whips into my cheeks. 'I wanna taunt the Fangtooth. She helped drown my grandma.'

There's a pin-sharp pause. Then Kid begins to croak a thick laugh. '*There* it is. The truth's not such an ugly thing, is it?' She passes me the pot-scrapings in a clay bowl and a heavy iron key. Then she dips her head. 'Have fun.'

Have I gone and got that old cook to gift me some respect? I take the bowl with a grateful nod, and scarper. I feel Kid's eyes on my back.

As planned, Crow links up with me on the way to the cell. I squint into his eyes. I'd swear to all the sea-gods that they're more yellow. And has he grown more scrubby hairs on his chin, or are they the stubs of feathers? I lean onto tiptoe to look more closely, but he jerks away. 'Let's be gone if we're going,' he snaps, shaking his arms to make long, greasy black feathers sprout all over him; an extra layer against the cold.

I feel a quick stab of jealousy – wish I could control my powers as well as he can. Or *at all.*

On our way to the dungeon, he snaffles a pinch of old fat for the energy he'll need to shape-change.

'The time's come for this hunted child to become the Huntress,' I whisper.

'Don't be so ruddy dramatic,' he says, as our bodies blend into the gloom.

10

One Condition

A dark thrill bubbles in my blood. We wait at the end of the passageway until Pika's distracted the guards. Then we hurry forwards and I put the pot down outside the cell door.

I fumble the key out of my pocket and fit it into the lock. Then I stand there, struggling to breathe. My fingers tremble. Crow guards the door while I step inside, pulling my scarf tighter around my face.

As my eyes slowly widen to let in the threadbare light, I see her-- the Fangtooth first mate who helped Stag murder my grandma and claim our ship. But she's a husk of the muscled Tribeswoman she was. She's thin, and it looks like she's been pulling her hair out in clumps. As I watch, her fingers pull and twist one of the strands still clinging to her scalp.

'Axe-Thrower!' I blurt, the name burning my tongue. Crow lurks behind me, a shadow.

She glances at me. 'Who are you? What do you want from me?'

'I'm Rat,' I tell her, plucking the first name that pops into my mind. 'Son of one of the cooks.' She watches me and unbidden the memory rushes back, from the night she stalked me here. The dread as she folded her palm around my mouth.

With shaky hands I slide the bowl of pot scrapings – blackened onions and jellified bog-myrtle and rubbery clumps of flour – towards her.

Axe-Thrower scuttles over and snatches the bowl. Her thin face stretches into a grimace as she hurls the spoon across the floor. Then she tips up the bowl and the scraps plop out into her filthy straw. I think of how little there is to go around, and anger lurches in my belly.

'Ent you hungry?' I whisper.

'Oh, yes.' Her hollow laugh carves a chunk out of the darkness. 'But I don't know how long they plan to keep me alive, or what they'll do to me in the end.'

'Who? The draggle-riders?'

She laughs bitterly, shaking her head. 'Not them. The others.'

There's something terrible about the way she says *others*. It makes my skin crawl. 'What others?'

She just looks at me, with a strange, sad smile.

'Do you want to go home?' I hiss.

She spits. 'Cruel child.'

'I mean it – *do* you?'

Her head snaps up. 'Why do you taunt me?'

'No one has claimed you.'

She hisses through her teeth. 'Take your gloat, and—'

'Except me.' I stand arrow-straight. '*I* claim you. I will set you free.'

She stiffens.

'On one condition.' I breathe deep, steeling myself. 'You take me with you.'

We check the passageway and slip out of the cell, locking it behind us. I know the crew's working hard to make sure no one comes this way, but my heart's still kicking against my chest like a wild thing. I pass the Fangtooth a hooded cloak and a scarf for her face. Crow walks on the other side of her; a tall, shadowy form in the corner of my eye. He keeps his face covered, like mine.

'You know, your senses have deserted you,' she whispers, close to my ear. 'Don't you know what's out there, little one?'

I ignore her. Every door we need to pass is unlocked, thanks to the work of the crew.

We move through the passageways, sneaking past doorways where groups huddle together, telling stories, playing games, piping music or brewing spells against the weather.

In the draggle cave, there's no sign of the warden. Ibex must've lured her away as planned. I get Crow to wait with the Fangtooth just outside the main cave, so I can chatter without her hearing me.

I chattered to the draggles about our plan before, and

it seemed like they were willing to help. But now, none of them want to talk to me. I stare up at their sleeping forms, hanging from the roof of the cave. *We need to get back to the place where your leader is in trouble*, I beg. *I know it's dangerous, but we can't abandon her, and none of the full-grows believe me!*

A long pink snout pokes out from a mass of orangey fur. *Long flying. Wind-snap winds. Danger. Nest-mate quiver-frighted from time before.*

Aye, I admit, casting a quick look over my shoulder, half expecting to hear the pounding of boots as the riders realise what's happening. *But how can we leave the Protector of the Mountain stranded, with no way out?*

The snout disappears, and I'm faced with a wall of filthy, drool-soaked fur. A scream of frustration pushes up my throat. But then the draggle breaks away from the flock and drops heavily to the floor. I saddle up quickly, thanking the beast under my breath, and grab my longbow and a bag of supplies from the hiding place I agreed with Pika.

Crow leads Axe-Thrower into the cave. Her face dissolves into a mess of angry fright when she sees the draggle. She rounds on me. 'Why do you want to get to the north? Why are you risking so much?'

'I *have* to get there. Without you, I'll never get into Fangtooth territory. That's all you need to know.'

'Then why are you hiding your face?'

I tug the scarf tighter over my nose. 'You ent in charge, here! Without me, you'll never get home. So stop asking me questions.' I turn away, fitting a metal bit into the draggle's mouth and making sure the lantern works.

'Why should you want to get to my homeland?'

I bite my lips. I can feel the weight of all of Hackles sitting on my shoulders. 'Cos.'

'*Why?*'

I drop my voice lower and spill the first lie that pops onto my tongue. 'I want to join the Fangtooths,' I say, proper earnest. 'Work for them, learn from them, get as far from this mountain as I can. I can't stand these goat people.'

She glances around her as I speak, curling her lip at the sight of the cave. Then she nods. I hold onto the reins as she climbs into the saddle. The draggle sniffs her fright and I feel the creature's nerves grow as tense as the Fangtooth's.

Peace, I chatter softly, trying to calm her sails.

Then I guide the draggle to the mouth of the cave, climb up in front of the Fangtooth and squeeze the beast's sides with my heels. We soar into the air.

I'm sorry, Da. Forgive me.

PART 2

The Moonlands

11
The Inn Between

We teeter through the storm. I turn my head and glimpse Crow leaping into the void, shape-changing into a blur of tattered black feathers studded with two bright yellow eyes. Axe-Thrower presses her skull painfully hard between my shoulder blades. She warms my back with her screaming.

I loathe the sight of the Fangtooth's fingers laced around my middle, and the feel of her bones digging into my flesh. Hers are the fingers that once tore at my hair, to keep me from reaching Grandma. The hands that held me down while Stag cut antlers into my arm. The same ones that pressed down over my mouth when she hunted me to Hackles. The memories crowd so thick behind my eyes I have to shake my head to clear them.

We travel eastwards across the Iron Valley, towards Hearthstone, painful-slow against the wind. I chatter to the draggle, trying to help navigate, but I have to bellow against the wind.

Then Axe's grip loosens from my middle as she catches

my elbow and pulls, hard, twisting me around until she's able to thrust her face close to mine.

'Get off me, you loon!' I yell, fright bursting in my belly. *She's gonna throw me off.* In this beat, I'm heart-certain of it.

'Silver-grey eyes and a way of talking with beasts?' she purrs, almost gently. 'I know you, *girl.*' There's a gloat in her voice but I feel like it's covering something like shock. Now that she knows who I am, she's got to be wondering why I'd help her.

I jab with my elbow until she lets go. Then I clutch the reins tightly, hands shaking. 'You don't know nothing about me,' I bite. 'And anyway, what do you care? I got you out, didn't I? Ent like you're about to try and go back now.'

She clams her pipes, lacing her fingers around my waist again, and her touch makes me want to throw up. I'm sure she's squeezing extra hard just to hurt me. Then I catch snippets of her bitter muttering, as we weave through the winds. '*Tricked* . . . why help me?'

I have to bite my lip and swallow my fire-crackle to keep from challenging her about what she did on my ship. Just until we get into the Frozen Wastes. After that, there's no telling what I might say – or do – to avenge Grandma.

Crow's a black scrap of ruffled feathers in the corner of my eye, hunched against the wind. There's a gaping hole of nothing where the beast-chatter would be if he weren't really a boy.

Me and Crow pored over one of Leo's worn old maps before we left and now I try to keep it conjured in my mind's eye. We bear north, passing over the outermost tip of the Eastern Mountain Passes, then turn west towards the two rivers I know run between here and the southern shores of the Wildersea.

Soon enough, we're plagued by lightning slashes and hailstones that make sky-travel too perilous. I start to guide the draggle lower, my belly rolling as we dip through the sky.

'What are you doing?' screeches Axe-Thrower, clutching me even tighter.

'We've got to land!' I yell, bringing the draggle lower and lower. When we touch down in a snowy stretch of scrubland, I use my chatter to send the draggle home to Hackles. Then Axe-Thrower decides we need to shelter until the storm slackens. I nod, and from that beat we do everything in stony silence, shooting each other vicious glares. She scrapes together a hovel made out of packed snow, and we take shelter inside. Crow digs himself into a dip in the snow nearby, feathers fluffed against the wind. *He'll be warmer in crow-shape, anyway.*

We break a small loaf of bread apart and share the staling innards. I check myself over and find little crescent moons dug into my palms by my nails, from gripping the draggle reins so hard. When I look up, the Fangtooth is watching me, face opened into something like softness. But as our eyes meet, her face tightens again, and her eyes narrow to glinting slits of black. I force myself to stay facing her and not to fall asleep, in case the wretch chooses to wring my neck. *I'm watching you, Fangtooth.*

When the storm's grip loosens, I climb out into the open, check the compass Crow loaned me and trudge north-west towards the Wildersea, gesturing for Axe-Thrower to follow. She shoots me a look of scorn as she strides forwards to take the lead, like she thinks little of my navigating device. *Good. All the better to watch your movements, mutinous scum.*

Every few beats I stop and stare over my shoulder, skin tingling under all my warm layers. I keep thinking I've heard footsteps crunching behind us, but there's no one in sight, except a faint black blur that tells me Crow is still flying. I catch the Fangtooth doing the same, and our eyes meet uneasily. Then she jerks her head roughly. 'Come, keep up,' she gruffs, breaking the long silence. 'Someone is on our tail.' I stumble after her, sudden fright squeezing my ribs. If she finds a chance to leave me alone out here, and disappear . . . either the cold will claim me, or the hunger, or whoever's following us. This might be the stupidest plan I've ever had. But then I will myself heart-strong. She *ent* abandoned me, yet.

Unless that's just cos she's waiting to gift me right into Stag's clutches. Two words ring inside my skull, one for each footfall. *Hunted, child. Hunted, child.* Even my heart sings it.

My muscles are raw and screaming by the time we find a ramshackle inn on the edge of the Wildersea's Black Beach, built into an overhang of cracked grey rock. We crane our necks to stare up at a lightning-scorched sign that swings in the wind. The Inn Between. Crow settles amongst the thatch, fluffing up his oily black feathers. We agreed that if we had to stop on the way, he'd stay in crow shape for feather-warmth – that way, he can safe-keep his energy. 'Caw,' he utters. I wrinkle my nose at him.

'Come on,' I tell Axe, stepping towards the door. 'We'll stay here a night.'

She jumps, startled at my speaking. 'I have nothing for payment,' her voice stabs, nervously. Her face twitches as she chews her lip, flicking glances between me and the shadow of the Black Beach in the distance. Is she plotting something?

I clench my fists. *I'm* in control of this mission, and if she tries to move against me I'll flaming well see it coming. 'Lucky I brought silver, then, ent it?' I tap my pocket, and the handful of silver ingots inside clink against each other.

The raging of the wind means I have to knock hard enough to tear a nick in my eelskin gloves. But finally, the door's wrenched open.

The common room swarms with whispered trade-tongues and strange smells and hard looks. We buy two bowlfuls of a scummy brown stew and take them to two chairs in the corner. I watch the room from the depths of my hood. Travellers play cards and blow colourful smoke rings.

When I dip my cracked wooden spoon into the stew, it tastes like old bootlaces have been boiled in mud and a few stale grains have been thrown in, but at least it's hot. Wish I had a few of Pip's peppercorns to add flavour, though. A snuffling, slurping noise greets my ears, and I glance up.

Axe guzzles her bowlful with an urgency that gifts me a strange heart-sadness. To her, this ditch-swill must be a hundred times better than the burnt, claggy old scrapings she was getting before.

I push back my chair, ignoring her questioning eyes. I ent hungry, and I ent got time to feel sorry for the likes of her.

Upstairs, I step into the heaving sleeping room. There's just one huge straw bed, and a small hungry fire crackles in the hearth. Almost all the places in the bed are taken by snoring traders. I lie on the edge of the low, scratchy mattress and squeeze my eyes shut, my belly clanging with missing Thaw. Bed bugs scuttle across the bedding, *Gasprunrunrunnobloodleftnibble?*

I toss and turn for a while. Then Axe's shadow looms on the wall and hot, heart-stuttering panic clangs inside me. I tense my muscles to spring if she tries to attack me, but all she does is find a place in the bed, and soon her snore joins the others. But I can't sleep. What if she's just faking, and planning to steal away? The voices from the room downstairs have risen. A chair is scraped across the floor.

I roll out of bed and step lightly from the room. Then I hide on the stairs, watching the grizzled old men rambling below. I've almost dropped to sleep on the stairs when an urgent voice makes me jolt awake and listen keenly again.

'You've heard the tales, same as I,' grunts a man, heavily ringed hands wrapped around a tankard, like he's holding on for his life. 'A king amongst the ice, face of a wolf.

Loaning weather-witches to the Skadowan, in exchange for the safety of his own hide.' He slurps his ale and bangs the table.

'You daft old soak,' scolds a fisherman with thinning hair and ruddy cheeks. 'The Skadowan were stamped out – what? – *hundreds* of years ago.' He drums his fingers on his belly. 'If they ever existed at all. They're just a story, used to threaten badly behaved children.'

'Dark times bring dark tidings, and darker acts,' warns the ale-drinker, in a slurred voice. He goes to wipe his mouth with the back of his hand and misses, tweaking his own nose.

The room erupts in coarse laughter. I swallow, and it's like some careless stranger is knocking the inside of my throat with a stick.

The Skadowan? I remember when I was seal-pup young, and Grandma had to use threats to make me bed down. *Sleep, little demon-child,* she would scold, even as laughter bubbled in her pipes. *Or the Skadowan will come for your skin!*

'Someone stop him ranting on, won't you?' pleads the innkeep.

I turn and crawl back up the stairs.

'Where did you go?' whispers Axe. She's lying on the edge of the bed, staring at me.

'Mind your business,' I tell her. 'Why ent you asleep?'

She rubs her forehead. 'I cannot. I think too much of where we will go.'

'The Frozen Wastes? Your home?'

'*Girl.*' She croaks out a low chuckle. I wince, but no one stirs. 'That is not the name those lands are called by. Not by us that know them.' Her voice has filled with longing.

'Read a map,' I tell her, yawning.

'Map? *Hah.* Who made these maps? Not *my* people. My lands are wounded. But they have never been a *wasteland.*'

I frown. 'But I thought nothing lived or grew there,' I whisper. 'I thought—'

'What would you know? Why would you think anything?' she snaps. Then she breathes. 'My home is the Moonlands.'

I blink, unsure what to say to that.

'They used to be called the Moonlands.' She props herself up on an elbow. 'A place of brightly glowing snow, a place of rich dreams and richer stories. A place with many names for ice and many ways of knowing.'

'Shush your hole!' someone warns.

But it's the love and homesickness in Axe's throat that makes me step back. She's gone home, in her mind. And missing home is a thing we've got in common.

She turns over and budges up, making space for me. I don't want to sleep. Not next to her. But sleep thieves my strength anyway.

Next thing I know, Axe is wrenching me to my feet. 'I will not wait for you,' she growls, all traces of the heart-truth she showed last night withered and gone.

12
Dagger-tip Cold

Axe shoulders the door open and we step outside, into the blistering cold. Crow bolts from the thatched roof. *Fleeflyflyfree*, he jabbers.

I freeze. It sounded like a streak of beast-chatter flew from his beak.

Axe pushes me in the small of my back and my legs start trudging before I have to force them to. I watch Crow in the distance, as he wheels around to follow us again.

Even though we ent crossed the sea yet, these shore-lands have places to trade for polar dogs and sleds. Axe-Thrower stalks past packs of skinny dogs and heads into a squat wooden hut. I hang back. Then she bursts out of the hut.

'What is it?'

She eyes me, grinding her teeth. Then she lets out a rush of breath. 'That man in there! He will not loan me a dogsled – he violates the ancient code of helping stranded Moonlanders reach home. And he did not take my word that I would repay him!'

Her innocence startles me. 'You expected a favour, cos of some old honour code?'

She looks like she wants to deal me a slap. 'If you want to get there, you'll have to lend me the silver.' Pressing her lips thin, she stretches out her hand.

I put three silver ingots on her palm and she spins on her heel, back to the hut, trailing her shame and fury. I'm heart-glad the crew thought to send me on my way with some silver. Elsewise, we wouldn't have got far.

Axe haggles for a skinny pack of four dogs that're so tall they reach her ribs, and a roughshod sled, bristling with splinters and lined with the rags of old furs. I hang back, scenting the dogs' hunger on the wind.

Axe gets the dogs tethered to the sled. The din they make is desperate-eerie, a banshee wail stabbing into my ears. They growl whenever they catch a whiff of my scent.

I won't move closer to the sled. In the end, Axe-Thrower's rough hands bundle me onto it. 'Hold on,' she growls.

She lashes the dogs. The sled jerks to life and I fall back, then quickly grab the wooden sides. Axe whoops, and the dogs run faster. The sled bangs and swerves, jarring my spine and knocking a mouthful of shock up my pipes.

The cold carves me like a dagger-tip and thieves the strength from my bones. It grips my face in jaws of iron and shakes me dazed. I keep hold of who I am by watching the tattered black bundle in the sky, just behind us. The bundle of my friend, Crow.

After a while, the Fangtooth barks a command and the

sled *slishes* to a stop. Thirst to run fills the polar dogs until they wrench at their chains, jolting the sled. They snap at the diamond-dust that glitters in the air and then they snap at each other's necks.

Axe leans down and grabs my chin, shining her blubber-lantern into my face. Her lashes are baubled with ice crystals. 'Show me your nose,' she instructs, plucking at the cloth wrapped tightly over my face.

'Get off me!' I snarl.

'You want your nose gnawed black by the ice-bite?' She scowls. 'Do you?'

Eyeing her sullenly, I pull the cloth off my nose and let her check me for ice-bite.

She nods, satisfied. 'All is well for now.'

To our right, Crow thumps into the snow. He pecks at the ground, sidestepping and cawing. She looks towards him and I use the chance to wriggle out of her grip.

'At last!' she murmurs. '*Real* belly-filling.'

I jump onto her back as she lunges for my friend, toppling her, and he takes to the wing with a startled *thwawk*.

Axe rounds on me. 'Give me a reason not to leave you to die in the snow?' she threatens, eyes bulging. And suddenly the sight of her is more than my belly can hold.

'Because you *killed* my grandma!' My words echo in the emptiness, ringing off the heavy sky.

Axe-Thrower freezes. Then she curses, climbing back aboard and wrapping the reins tighter around her hands.

I scramble back to the sled and thump onto the seat, heart banging wildly. Then I twist to stare at her.

'No,' she says, simply. 'The killer is Stag.'

'You helped!'

'No,' she repeats. She cries a command and the dogs run again, their shaggy white backs lumbering faster and faster. 'You are wrong,' she shouts over the *slishing* of the sled. 'I had no choice. Believe me when I say – I had no choice *at all*.' The jolting, thumping sled knocks the wind out of me. I fold my body forwards, clinging on for my life, tears seeping from my eyes and turning to ice.

Now that the words are out, my head aches and my throat feels sore. I can't believe I kept it in for so long. 'Everyone's always got a choice,' I say. But my breath loosens. I feel light as the air after the breaking of a storm.

After a thickened, furious snow flurry, the sky clears. I blink, sunk in a fug of dreams. Wait – it *can't* be . . .

'The great dog of the sky has sent up her howl,' mutters the Fangtooth. 'The lights come.'

The fire spirits.

Their white flame wisps up out of the darkness, the only other creatures out here with us. At first they look like another puff of polar-dog breath, feathering into the sky. Then the flame spreads up and sweeps over our heads.

They're an untamed silver spill. One beat they're a twine of hair, then they're a flurry of fish, next a silver thread with a pale green tinge.

As the sled hurtles along, I think of Vole's fresh-baked, wise-faced little bab. *We need your help to find her namesake.*

I watch the shapes in the lights flicker and shift, focusing on the bab. Clumps of ice weigh my lashes down – I can see them when I blink. I watch the fire spirits for pictures of animals. *Fire spirits*, I pray. *Let there be a world left for the bab. Let her grow and learn and howl and dive and be joyful. I will fight to keep her safe if you'll just gift a name for her.*

My eyelids are gluing shut and this cold burns fiercer than any I've ever known. I thought I knew cold aboard the *Huntress*, and among the Sky-Tribes. I was wrong.

But I can see just enough to watch as the shapes in the sky turn spiky, like the spines of a snuffling creature of the undergrowth that I remember Grandma telling me is called a hedgehog. I store the name away at the back of my mind.

Axe-Thrower lashes the dogs again and the sled lurches forwards, throwing me hard against the side.

Soon, a shadowy bulk of wood hazes into view. Men with guns lounge atop a wooden gatepost. They swig from silver flasks, coarse laughter steaming from their mouths.

I twist in my seat. 'What's that?'

Axe growls under her breath. 'The checkpoint. Hide your weapon.'

I stash my longbow under some furs and pluck at the scarf on my face, trying to make sure it don't slip, but my hands are stiff and clumsy, and I snag the cloth. The wind claws my scar and I know I must've exposed it. Are the guards gonna know about the hunt for a scarred child?

'Slow down!' I hiss at Axe, but my voice is weak. I turn to look at her and flap my hand. We're almost underneath the checkpoint.

The guards train their guns on us. 'Who goes there?' one demands, swiping snow from his eyes.

Axe commands the sled to a sharp halt. Then she swings herself off it, catching my arm and pulling me roughly with her. I struggle in her grip. What've I done? How could I have been so stupid? She's gonna turn me in, and I'm leagues from Da, or anyone that can help me.

Crow soars above my head, his faint shadow blotting the snow. *Don't shape-change*, I pray, squeezing my eyes shut.

'I am the daughter of the Moonlands Chieftain,' she calls to them. 'This is one of my slave boys.'

'The *what?*' one says, nudging the other, a mean, mirthful look playing across his face.

'We don't honour that name', says the second guard, a portly, black-bearded man with unblinking eyes.

She hesitates. 'I do not unders—'

I tug her sleeve, heart punching my chest. 'Call him the Fangtooth Chieftain,' I hiss out of the corner of my mouth.

She glances down at me and brings her hand up as though to strike me in the face. 'Quiet, slave!' she yells, proper loud. But instead of hitting me, she yanks my scarf higher up my face, hiding my scar.

Then she turns to stare up at the guards again. 'I am the daughter of the Fangtooth Chieftain,' she calls. 'And a faithful servant of Stag.'

My head swims. Which of the two is a lie, and which a truth? Is she claiming to be a chief's daughter just to get us through the checkpoint? And oh, *gods*. I bet she is still a servant of Stag. What've I done?

They lower their guns, but they still don't let us pass. 'Prove it,' says one.

She pulls down her sleeve and flashes a glimpse of Stag's *Hunter* mark – it matches the one etched into my own skin. The guards spring into action, each one twitching their cloak aside to show Stag's mark printed on their necks.

'Forgive us, lady,' says one with a scar through his eyebrow. 'We did not know the Chieftain had a daughter. Welcome home.'

Axe returns to the sled. She salutes the guards and we race through. The gates swing closed behind us. 'You were right,' says Axe grimly. 'Everyone does have a choice.'

And I know she's made hers and that I've reached this place in one piece cos of her. I feel a flicker of trust, wriggling through my bones. But I don't know if I'm a fool for feeling it.

As we're moving I think about how Axe called me a slave and the guards didn't blink. Grandma used to spit nails about the trade in slaves. If she saw any ships she suspected, she'd scratch a quick-sharp letter to the nearest dockmaster. Sometimes she'd try to board slave ships. Once, we spent a winter huddled up with twenty child-slaves she rescued.

When we're close to the edge of the sea, the dogs blunder to a halt. However hard Axe lashes them, they won't run.

So we take the chance to rest. Together we make another shelter, by sculpting a wall of packed snow. We huddle on the sled behind our wall. Snotcicles crunch in my nose.

Axe-Thrower lifts a skope to her eyes and peers towards the rotting docks, where abandoned longboats lie clutched in the sea's frozen grasp. On a slime-blackened wooden post, the great ragged crow hunches, watching us through one yellow eye. He peels a shellfish off the wooden dock and smashes it over and over until he can stretch out the morsel inside. He opens his beak and gulps it down.

Later, when Axe snoozes, I tiptoe away from the shelter and push against the wind to reach him. 'Crow!' I hiss.

The bird startles and squawks, flapping inky wings.

'She's asleep! You should become a boy again for a bit!'

The bird cocks its head at me.

'Come on,' I mutter, shuffling from foot to foot with cold. I don't like how long he's been a crow this time. And I don't like seeing him *eat* in crow-form. It gifts me the fear.

When I listen hard, I can almost make out the fizzling, crackling whisper of a faint beast-chatter. I plead with him for a few more beats, but the cold is trying to saw my limbs off so I turn to go – and there's a groan behind me, then a smell of burning. I spin around and there he is – Crow, ashen-faced, curled at the foot of the docks. I fall to my knees and help him wolf down a few more shellfish and a strip of dried goat meat he's kept in his belt pouch.

'Mouse – I saw – something,' he says through rattling teeth.

'What?'

'Two cloaked figures – one pointing at you.'

'When?'

'Just after the checkpoint. But then the wind blew me off course and I lost sight of them. Keep your blade sharpened and your arrows ready. I think someone's following you.'

'Why won't they take us closer?' grumbles Axe, when she's rested. Crow's a bird again, keeping out of her eye line. Thunder threatens the snow dunes.

I watch the dog pack, see the way their gums are bared and their fur is raised in ridges.

Bad place, no home. Not go backbackback.

'Should we try another way?' I ask, careful not to show her that I understood them.

Run, husk the polar dog pack in turn. *Far, fast, run, hide. Not win fight here.*

'There is no other way.' She lifts the skope from her eye and takes a hollowed-out bone from her pocket, then unscrews a cork from its neck. She tips a handful of white cubes into my palm.

I gift her a quizzical look.

'This is moons-buried shark meat. It is too fine for you, but I won't see you starve. Even I do not have the stomach to watch your corpse pulled apart by the dogs.'

I push one of the soft, cold cubes of flesh between my chattering teeth. A salty, slimy tang explodes on my tongue. I force the sinewy pulp down, blinking against the pungent stink blocking my nose from the inside out. What kind of

Tribe takes good, fresh shark meat and *buries it* underground for moons, until it's half rotted?

Still, I'm heart-glad she's sharing with me. My belly's worse than desperate.

I stare up at the smooth slope of Axe's nose in the half-light. 'Why are you called Axe-Thrower?' I ask.

She glances down at me in surprise.

I fold my arms. 'I mean, I don't reckon any new ma looks at her bab and decides, "Aye, she looks like an axe-thrower, that little one".'

'Less of your foul-mouthery,' she says, but her eyes glimmer with a grin. 'My mother called me Little Moonlet,' she whispers, her mouth letting the words slip peacefully into the air. 'That was my true name. It was the Chieftain that forced a battle-name onto me, along with a set of fangs, after he ripped my own teeth out.'

I shiver, picturing the scene, almost tasting a mouthful of blood when I imagine the same fate befalling *me*.

She lashes the dogs again but they still won't go closer, so we approach the stagnant docks on foot. A clutter of Fangtooth longboats are tethered to a crumbling, rotting dock. But then a cloaked shape snags at the corner of my eye, and when I glance behind me, it darts out of sight.

Behind us, the polar dogs thrash and gift guttural whinings to the storm. I push my croaky voice into life. 'Someone's following us.'

'I know.' We watch each other. Our breath-frosts mingle. Behind us, in the distance, a fire glows into life. It's purple. A *mystik!*

I wade towards the fire, clutching my dagger tightly.

'*Wait!*' hisses Axe. But I press forwards and she curses at my back, before her footsteps begin to crunch in my wake.

I point my arrow down at a hooded figure seated by the fire. 'Show yourself!'

Suddenly, a hawk bolts from the black branches of a dead tree and barrels towards me. '*Thaw?*'

The cloaked figure pulls down their hood. I'm staring at a young boy with ice-nipped yellow hair. Most of his face is covered but I'd know them big brown eyes anywhere.

'*Sparrow.*' I take a step back. Inside, I'm screaming. He's got a little jar that's spilling light – I squint. Thunderbolt? But then I realise the light's tinged blue and see that it's a scrap of whale-song thudding about inside – gifting him the light he needs to thin the fog on his eyes.

'How did you—' I clutch uselessly for my words.

'Bribed a man to drive me on a sled,' he says.

My mouth flaps like I'm a stranded fish. 'But – but . . . what man? Where?'

'He's gone now – he didn't want to go over the frozen sea. He dropped me after the checkpoint. I hid under the furs to get through,' he finishes triumphantly.

'How could you be so slack-witted?' I groan.

'How could you leave us *behind?*' he counters.

I glare at my brother and my sea-hawk.

Thaw splutters her own outrage at me.

Thawnotsitwaitstupid! She shuffles her feathers, filling

them with fight. *Thaw be with two-legs girl! Home!*

'Me and Thaw reckoned you'd need us,' Sparrow says firmly. Then he reaches inside his cloak and lifts out a tiny tinderbox. His face is licked all over with the fiercest dark defiance I have ever seen in my life. He slides the box open and a purple flame springs up from his finger to gift enough light to show me what's inside. A smear of silver. 'Thunderbolt died!'

I stumble backwards, almost tripping in the snow. Oh, no. Not *this*. 'Sparrow, I'm sorry!' I reach for him but he twists away.

'I miss her too much.' His face crumples.

My gut feels slashed. Our moonsprite.

I'm about to try again to gift him comforts when a gleam of light spills from his cloak. 'What's that?'

'Naught.'

'Spar*row*.' I put all my warnings into the name.

Before he can stop me, I snatch open the edge of his cloak, and there they are, bulging inside his pocket. Two bright, round gems, spilling over with ancient power.

I pull the Opals free and cradle the bright stones in my palms. A tiny lightning bolt flickers inside the Sky-Opal, and a miniature sea tips up and down under the skin of the Opal of the Sea.

I lift my eyes to my brother's face. 'You disbelievably wretched slackwit!'

13
Disbelievably Wretched Slackwit

I lean forwards and grab him by the shoulder. 'How did you get these? Why did you bring them *here*?' The weight of carrying the gems and the death of Thunderbolt jolt thick tears into my throat.

'Get off me, fool-heart!' yells Sparrow. 'You told me to look after them!'

'Who you calling fool-heart? You ent got nine suns yet, so don't be squawking to me like that.'

Thaw hisses angrily.

No, Thaw-beast! I GET to be angry! You and my brother have done all the things I told you not to, and I didn't tell you not to for nothing!

Axe-Thrower trudges towards us. 'What is going on?'

Sparrow gulps a breath. 'The best friend I ever had is dead, and just like I thought, my sister don't even care,' he babbles, not even noticing who he's chatting to.

Axe-Thrower frowns as my brother turns his back on me. 'Best friend dead? You should show kind-heartedness.'

'I ent letting someone like *you* preach on at *me* about kindness.' I turn on my heel and stalk away from them, dropping the Sea-Opal in my left pocket and the Sky-Opal in my right. When I'm alone, the loss of Thunderbolt thumps me full in the gut and I sob silently into my fist. I can hardly remember a time without the sprite. I feel like every beat that passes, another piece of our home dies.

We're at the eastern end of the frozen Wildersea, and in the west, far to my left, I can just make out the looming sparkle of the giant Iceberg Forest. I stare, my breath frosting. Spooky-odd to think that not so long ago I was inside the Skybrary, in the very tip of one of the bergs. Thunderbolt was with us then, too. And she helped me when I had to find a way to tell Sparrow about Grandma. She guided him through life for so long. He's gonna feel so alone without her.

I walk right up to the rotten docks, kicking through filthy snow, and start poking around in the boats. The wind scrapes my eyeballs and plucks handfuls of black sand into the air, like swarms of sharp flies.

When I spin round and catch sight of Sparrow, he's clutching the tinderbox and shuddering with tears. I've got to show him I do care. But when I open my mouth to say something, a great claw of sadness scratches the words away.

The dock creaks and sways in the gale. The boats rock.

'Something foul treads *my* paths,' Axe whispers, behind

me. I flinch – I never heard her approaching.

Thunder booms overhead and she hisses like a cat. Her eyes stare across the stretch of sea greedily, like she's thirsting for the land on the other side.

'We have to hurry up and get to the Frozen Wastes,' says Sparrow, reaching for the stick Da made him and standing up.

'That ent their true name,' I tell him firmly, glancing at Axe. 'From now on, we should call them the Moonlands.'

He pulls a face and shrugs. But Axe gifts me a small proud nod. 'We cannot get the sled across in a boat,' she says. 'The dogs must run on frozen water.'

She unties the dogs and I help her drag the sled across the docks and on to the sea.

'Will it hold our weight?'

'Let us pray so.'

Get away get away get away! the dogs chatter desperately.

I weigh my choices, then spit onto the ice. I have to risk showing my beast-chatter in front of Axe. *You can get home, dogs!* I yell.

Water flow, water not hold dogs up. Dogs drown!

No, it's frozen solid. Look! I jump on the frozen sea to show them it's safe.

I coax them past the rotting docks and finally we board the sled and we're running again, the sled sliding smoothly across the ice. Sparrow plonks himself down in front of me and I make sure his hood stays up, elsewise he'll likely lose an ear. But it's proper hard to hold onto the sled and his hood at the same time. My body knocks against the wood. Thaw and Crow fly overhead, staying out of sight.

Axe calls the sea-paths the 'whale-ways', and it makes me feel strange. Cos it's like she – a *Fangtooth* – is gifting respect to the whales with that name. But then I remember her Tribe's true name and wonder if there might be more to them than I know.

Sparrow leans over the side of the sled and flicks purple patterns of lightning across the dark icy sea. Shallow dents melt in the ice where the lightning touches, like he's got a spark of life in his fingertips. I remember him saying how he zapped that dead frog at Hackles and made it move.

'I left your letter under Da's pillow,' he says quietly. 'I put my name on it, too, so he knows I've gone looking for you.'

I put an arm round him. 'Heart-strong you are,' I tell him. 'Feel sad for Da, though.' *His guts must be tied in knots, with both of us gone!* 'How did you even get out of Hackles?'

'After I nabbed the Opals I hid in the caves. Someone was down there saddling a draggle. When they went off to the tack room, I stole it!'

I splutter. 'You ent never even ridden a draggle on your own!'

He sticks out his lip. 'Leo took me out riding lots of times. I've always been a better rider than you – it's just like riding a *horse*.'

I raise my brows. 'Oh, *aye*,' I say, and he sniggers.

'I took that key you left behind to get to the Opals and

used my lightning to smash the cages!' His voice trails off and fright fills his eyes. 'Please don't send me back. No one else knows I did it.'

Gods gift me heart-strength. I've got no words.

I pull away from him and stare at his pleading face.

'Course I won't send you back!'

Sparrow beams up at me and goes back to fizzing with heart-pride at what he's done and I find I can't fight off a grin of my own.

We tear past a fatly heaped walrus herd, snoring on the ice.

Shuffleshufflesleepsnoozehungrygrumbledragsnooze.

One cracks open a bulbous eye and peers at us.

When we reach land, I wish we could turn back. Have we really sought the place I was always taught to dread, the folk I was always taught to hide from? Thieved warships bulk along the iced black sand, their rigging strung with dagger-long icicles. *Devil's Hag* is among them, red sails torn to tatters and hull sealed tight in the clutches of the ice. She's the warship me and Crow hid aboard to escape Weasel – when Stag sent the Fangtooth Chieftain to claim me. Axe guides the dogs through a gap between two ships. Their wooden flanks press close on either side, walls of deeper black in the grainy darkness. Then we jump off the sled and drag it across the beach, our boots squeaking as the sand changes into shiny, bone-white stones shaped like eggs. Lightning strikes the stones, and we dodge, shrieking, and the eggs hop high into the air, chattering back down to earth like teeth. When I glance over my shoulder, a sea-hawk and a ragged black crow flap across the frozen sea.

Then we're back on the sled again. We drive across vast plains of ice and snow, past strange herds of squat, dusky purple beasts, their mottled skin covered in pink lumps, huge lantern eyes swivelling in their small skulls. When we ride close to them, they flee, big feet slip-slapping on the ice. Sparrow gasps, shrinking back from the creatures.

I never reckoned I'd set foot in this place, and I *never* in a thousand moons would've guessed I'd do it out of choice. Now the land is opening up around me, I'm realising how I only knew it from the stories of an enemy Tribe – my own. I never knew it at all. I struggle to breathe. I feel my guts grow hot, and loosen. Then my mouth fills with spit as bile rushes from my belly to the back of my throat. The Frozen Wastes. The most dangerous, forbidden place my boots could ever tread. What am I doing here? And *gods* – now my brother's followed me!

We race faster and further across the hard-packed snow. The sled slides from side to side as Axe follows a path I can't even see. It feels like running down a dark grey tunnel. I feel speck-small.

An age passes before we meet another human. Then two appear through the murky snowscape – old women swaddled in furs, crouching next to a hole in the ice. They're using a curved bone covered with netting to clear loose ice from the hole. They call out to Axe-Thrower and she answers them in a tongue I don't know, shaking her head.

'What did you say?' asks Sparrow.

'I told them the fish have fled,' she replies, with a sigh.

We come to a skin tent that looks big enough for twenty full-growns, and Axe-Thrower stops the sled. I'm so stiff and sore it takes me a few beats until I can stand. I help Sparrow from the sled and Axe ushers us inside. 'A resting tent,' she tells us, looking half asleep on her feet. 'Leave your weapons.'

The tent is full of the stinks of smoking meat. The air sparkles with embers and the diamond-dust that sweeps in from the outside.

Axe shows us a place to sit by the fire. I stare at the hole in the roof, like a bitten-out moon. Even though we've stopped sledding, I still feel like we're shushing over the ice. I wrap my arms around my knees, bones sore and throbbing. The base of my spine feels proper bruised.

Sparrow sits close to me. I rest my cheek on top of his head. Will we ever get home? And if we do, will it ever be the same as it was?

'Wish Thunderbolt was here,' he murmurs. He draws his knees up to his chest.

'*Gods*, so do I, too-soon.' I sniff. The little sprite would be a welcome light in this unknown world.

Axe brings a purple egg for me and Sparrow to share. She whispers that even these folk are saying it's cold.

Crow hops sideways through the opening of the tent, pecks at an egg and gets his beak through its tough shell before someone chases him away. My palms turn hot. I can't let him stay a crow for much longer. I'm halfway certain Axe won't harm us, but something makes me feel like he should stay hidden, just in case. If anything goes wrong, he can fly back to Hackles and raise the alarm.

Folk string up a reindeer carcass trapped inside a block of ice, and set it thawing over a fire. I gift Axe a questioning look. 'Another storm-killed beast,' she mutters. 'They say many are being lost in this forever-winter.' Her eyes brim with startling tears.

'Do you all have fangs? Do you have to sharpen your teeth every day?' babbles Sparrow suddenly.

Axe laughs, wiping her eyes. 'Some of us have our teeth wrenched out and replaced with animal teeth when we're younglings, to make us look fearsome and to lend us the power of the animal-spirit. We don't file our teeth!'

She turns to the folk gathered round the fire and talks to them, gesturing at Sparrow, so I reckon she's telling them what he said. Her face looks open and unguarded for the first time since I met her. She looks as startled by her own laughter as I am.

'Can you ask if Leopard's been seen round here?' I say in a low voice.

'Leopard?' she asks blankly.

'The Protector of the Mountain.' I watch her expectantly.

Her look clouds over. But she asks all the same, listening while the traders confer. Then she turns back to me. 'These people do not recollect a woman of her description,' she says, and I feel my shoulders sag. *Leo, where are you?*

'If she answered a summons here, with things the way they are, there is no hope for her,' she tells me softly. 'Is that why you risked this journey?'

I nod. 'I won't give up hope, neither,' I fierce, warmth lashing my cheeks.

Axe raises an eyebrow, but a smile dances in her eyes.

After that, the talk is all about the Chieftain and how he ent been seen for ages. I catch a few words here and there. The rest of it Axe translates into the common trade-tongue. 'They fear the Chieftain's second in command – Stag. He drains terrodyl blood across their land, and sells their children as slaves to pay debts to the Stony Chieftains of the West.'

As they say all this, their jaws tense, and their eyes flick to the mouth of the tent as though they're frighted Stag's gonna barge through with his gun. I know that fright and I pity them for it.

The Tribesfolk say that Stag tries to make them feel primitive – that he wants them to stop using their native languages, and to dampen the old powers until they lie blackened and spitting stale smoke.

'He believes we are "in the midst of nowhere",' says Axe, 'but to us, this place is fattened with generations of dreams and blood. It is a sacred, wild place, teeming with life.'

I gaze into her face, willing my heart strong. 'He did the same thing to my Tribe, to our ship.'

Her eyes soften, and she nods.

Warmth makes us drowsy. Sparrow falls asleep with his head in my lap. His spine shows through his tunic, all nobbled bones, ridged like a dorsal fin. On the back of his neck is a smudge of silver moondust. Thunderbolt's final footsteps. I trace the silver with a fingertip, careful not to rub it away.

Axe-Thrower covers Sparrow with a reindeer skin and gifts me a Moonlands lesson. 'When Moonlanders put the back of their hand to their forehead and pull the hand along—'

'Like wiping sweat?'

She nods. 'While wiggling their fingers, that means: *quiet the mind, whale is near.*'

I squint. '*Whale is near.*' I make the movement, and she laughs.

'You said something else. Something – rude. Practise.'

I do, and the traders smile softly in the lamplight. They teach me how to make a loud rush of high-pitched air, like a whale-breath from deep within my belly, and teach me how it means *to surface from dreams*, or *my dream-self must breathe.*

I practise shushing out a bellyful of air like I'm winded, and the folk with fangs pull back their gums and whistle. They teach me to say I'm hungry by rubbing my belly while making a gargled glugging sound in the back of my throat.

Once the lesson is over, I look round at each of their worn, quiet faces and feel a surge of heart-thanks that they're sharing shelter with us so openly.

Then I realise a question has been brewing in my blood ever since we left the Inn Between, and I voice it. 'Who were the Skadowan?'

A woman makes a sign on her chest with her finger. Another murmurs something to the man next to her. Dark eyes rest on my face. None of these folk are laughing like the ones at the Inn.

Especially not Axe. 'Where did you hear about that?' she asks sharply.

I tell her about what I heard. 'But I thought they were a myth,' I add.

'Not a myth,' says a man with his little son tucked against his side. The boy stares at me with huge, long-lashed eyes. 'Our people have kept the old tales alive – telling of a thousand winters ago, when *they* first came to control Trianukka, claiming to speak for the people. They were defeated, but the shadow of evil forever lurks under power, waiting to rise again.'

The way he talks about the Skadowan makes me remember the strange symbol in Yapok's letter; the symbol he said was bleeding up from underneath the runes of his manuscripts.

'It is dangerous to speak of such things,' Axe snaps, face crawling with fright. 'Let us all seal our lips, for our own sakes.' She stands up. 'I will check on the dogs.' She ducks out of the tent.

Silence falls. The flames gobble the air.

Before sleep snatches me, Axe returns and the traders teach me the sound for travel – a sliding noise hissed between the teeth, made to sound like *a skin-hulled brown slider riding across ice*. I work out that *brown slider* must mean sled. Sparrow startles awake when they make the sound, then glares around him and curls back down into slumber.

'Why do you gush so many sounds instead of babbling words?' I ask, through a yawn.

Axe-Thrower pauses, pulling on her earlobe. 'Sounds to us bear greater weight than words. Pictures, too.' She scrapes a fingernail over the ice, drawing a likeness of a walrus.

'For trading we sometimes need letters, but not all-times, even then.'

I feel a pang of guilt when I think of what Grandma would say if she could see us now. Consorting with Fangtooths! But hare-skip-quick, the guilt deepens into missing her, like usual.

All night I listen to the scrape of Axe-Thrower's crescent-shaped knife as she etches her Tribe stories into a jawbone. As she works, I think of Thunderbolt.

'Can't sleep?' asks Axe.

I shake my head, heart-sadness tugging at my mouth.

'Try to rest,' she tells me, pulling an extra reindeer skin up and over my shoulders. 'Sleep helps.'

When dreams sniff me out they're *grey as storm clouds, merwraith tails, my eyes. They feel whale-skin cold and they taste like blood mixed into the sea. They smell of iron and hidden meanings.*

I claw into wakefulness, blood rushing in my ears, heart-wrenched. I was home; I felt it so strong. Someone snores, walrus-heavy, and I wish it was Grandma, just across the cabin from us. Howls and barks crack from the throats of

123

the polar dogs tethered to the sled that waits beyond the walls of this skin tent, inches from my face. My spine tingles.

A family have arrived while I slept and their little ones climb all over me like wolf pups, making me chuckle. I prop onto an elbow and watch them. Stag don't want folks to run or laugh or sing or play or climb or hug or greet each other like wolf pups. But that's what this Tribe are doing, anyway. Kestrel was right. There's no way one Tribe could ever all be bad-blubber.

A woman with a little kid hanging from her skirts holds out a platter to me, and I lift a soft piece of boiled meat from it. It's in my mouth before I know I've moved, sticking in my teeth, and the strength from the chewy meat seeps into my gums. I shut my eyes, breathing gratefully. 'What is it?'

'Boiled whale blubber,' she answers.

Sparrow whimpers.

I retch into my mouth. She crouches in front of me and presses underneath my chin, forcing me to swallow.

She watches me with a quiet face. 'The creature was trapped. Now some good has come of it. We will have meat and lamp fuel and ribs to paddle our boats. For us, this can be the difference betwixt life and death. If we leave a whale to rot, the meat is wasted and the stink fills our tents.'

I bow my head, shamed.

When we bundle onto the sled again I grit my teeth through the pain in my back and my eye sockets feel hollow and stretched. The dead day is fevered with storm-light.

14

Lucky Find

We pass a thinning of ice, where the snow lies brushed over like shorn fur, and I yell 'til Axe stops the sled. I point at the thin ice. 'Over there!'

A dark shape is pressed against it. A trapped whale.

Axe leaps from the sled. She stares down at the shape, curling and uncurling her fingers and whispering amazement under her breath.

When she bashes open a breathing hole, a calloused, barnacle-strewn snout shoves through and the V of the whale's breath grunt-*shushes* into the air, freezing as it goes, frayed ribbons of ice shattering over Axe-Thrower's boots. Sore-looking tracks from the sharp hooks of whale lice are scored around the whale's eyes and in wounds on its head.

At the sight of it, our shared knowing of the sea floods sharply behind my eyes. I fall to my knees and reach out to touch the dark grey skin but Axe-Thrower snatches my hand back. 'Show care! Their skin is too sensitive for dry-touch.'

Heat prickles my face.

Sparrow falls to his knees at the hole, wets his hand in the snow, stretches it out and rests it on the whale's head. Blue song-notes tumble from my brother's mouth.

You leap,
Wild,
Like blood,
Like joy,
You dive,
Deep,
Like roots,
Through soil,
You dance,
Free,
Like sparks,
In night-time air.

Soon his tears replace the song in his mouth. I rub his back until he feels ready to stand.

Axe-Thrower crunches back to the sled. I gape at her. 'You took part in Stag's whale hunt. You begged for *first cut*.' I spit into the snow.

Shame bites her hard in the face, twisting her features. 'I was so desperate to prove myself and save my skin, I closed my spirit to feelings. I let the darkness in. But below decks, in secret, I wept.'

As we race along the worn path to the Moonlander settlement, the sound of hollow rattling fills the air. Ropes of teeth are strung between creaking lanterns, and they clink against each other in the wind. 'When we get there,' says Axe, 'you must bow your heads and follow close behind me. We must show them what they expect to see.'

We pass Tribesfolk sewing skin tents with lengths of gut, and others lashing skin hulls to wooden frames, using strips of walrus hide. I peer at every face and into every doorway, scanning for signs of Leo. But I find none. And why's it so eerie calm? I reckoned there'd be fighting here – they said Stag had turned on the Chieftain.

Dead terrodyls sprawl across the land like tawny, ice-nipped mountains. We ride past them and I stare open-mouthed at the black blood dripping from slashes in their throats into buckets. The life-blood that's been turned into a weapon by Stag and his army, cos it eats through whatever it touches. Great deathly wells have been tunnelled by blood spills. Wounds in the landscape. Axe-Thrower scowls.

When we finally reach the Chieftain's dwelling the cold that slams off the snow-packed hut almost knocks me flat, like the edge of a giant's blade.

'They're the doors I saw,' stammers Sparrow, clutching his jar of whale-song. 'In my vision.'

Axe-Thower yanks us off the wooden seat and shoves us through the calf-deep snow. We pass burning branches that spill light to guzzle the darkness, but the light can't guzzle it fast enough.

I look back to the sled and see Thaw's bright eyes watching me. I hold up a hand to tell her to stay hidden, praying that no one sees her or finds my longbow.

'Remember what Axe said, Sparrow,' I warn. 'Head down, stick close to her.'

Axe-Thrower knocks on the fur-covered doors with her lantern-staff, bellowing to be let in. The doors inch open, and a pair of ice-chip eyes glint out, mantled by bristling brows. 'Declare yourself,' a voice grunts.

She sighs heavily. 'The Chieftain's daughter!'

I puzzle up at her. They won't believe her lie *here*, will they?

The doors creak open and we walk through, into a fug of incense and smoke and muffled singing. I can't resist glugging the sights and stinks of the place, but I do it with my chin tucked close to my chest.

There's a central fire-pit and more reindeer skins, and circles of antlers hanging from the rafters with candles dripping fat on the skins. Near the fire is a table with a map pinned on it, surrounded by ornately carved chairs. One is grand enough to be a throne. Hunks of dark red meat thaw near the fire. A woman leans close and uses a knife shaped like a crescent moon to slice off chunks to boil.

Hollow-eyed men lean against walls, hard eyes following Axe. I brush my eyes across their faces, mouth sticky-dry. There's no sign of Leo, or her warriors. I try to keep my heart buoyed, cos she could be anywhere in the settlement. I'll get my chance to find her.

Axe hesitates, then prowls forwards. We stick close. We approach a wall of walrus-helmed guards. They stare at Axe.

'Where is the Chieftain?' she asks. 'I seek audience.'

The crowd parts to let a glaring old woman through. Polar-dog sleds are tattooed down her arms – she's the old heartless that threatened me and Crow when we escaped Wrecker's Cove aboard *Devil's Hag*. Her bloodshot eyes snap onto Axe-Thrower. 'Girl! What took you so long?' She steps forward and grabs Axe's upper arm, making her curse.

'The journey was troublesome, Grandmother. I – I found myself imprisoned.'

'And whose fault was that? Did we not teach you better than to get caught?' she spits. 'Who are those children?' The old woman squints at me, wrinkled lips curled up.

'Slaves I paid for with my own gold,' says Axe, through gritted teeth.

The old grandmother nods, satisfied. 'Slaves cast their eyes down,' she snaps at me, pressing her fingertips into my eyelids, forcing them down. 'Look into a face again, and I'll gouge them out.'

Sparrow presses against my side and grips my hand.

'I seek vengeance on my gaoler, Grandmother,' pleads Axe. 'I heard the goat-woman of the mountain was on her way here, following a summons?'

'Vengeance is not yours to demand, this day.' The old grandmother wrenches Axe's arm until she stumbles forwards, between the guards.

'But, Grandmoth–'

The old woman rounds on her granddaughter, her fury flecking the younger's face with specks of saliva. 'You may

129

give thanks – that goat-woman is likely a slave by now. Just like her so-called warriors – no one would escape slavers with wounds as grievous as theirs. Now – pay your respects!' She turns around, dragging Axe by the wrist.

My mind reels. Leo's wounded – but she's escaped. Whatever this old windbag reckons, the Protector of the Mountain is strong enough to heal. She might still be alive, somewhere – she *has* to be!

We follow the old woman behind a curtain, towards a great oak-and-whalebone casket. Women circle the casket, singing and beating axes against shields.

Axe-Thrower stiffens. Shock punches me in the belly. *Chief gone*, that draggle said. I want to groan aloud. Now I know what the beast meant, and I wish I'd listened deeper.

Inside the casket lies the Fangtooth Chieftain, a snarling polar dog etched onto his chest and a great sword clasped in his stiff hands. Firelight plays amongst the pocks and pits of his face. Death's barely eased the knife-blade frown valleyed between his brows. Huge red jewels glint in his eye sockets, and in his hair, and on his fingers. His arm's been draped over his walrus-skull helm.

And in the hollow of his throat sits a jewel of amber, brighter than a wolf's eyes in the dark. A stone with tiny fire spirits glimmering beneath its skin. The Storm-Opal of the Land. My chest lurches and pulls.

Why has he got the Opal?

My thoughts are dragged to the Sea and Sky Opals in my pockets. I swear I can feel them squirming, or is it my imagination? Can they sense their kin?

'Sleep warm-blooded, war-man father,' Axe-Thrower says quietly.

My breath catches.

Axe glances down at me. 'When I bit my blade into that oak, never did I dream the casket would cradle my own father.' Triumph simmers in her throat. 'Never did I guess I would be so fortunate.'

It's the truth. My thoughts flip and race and scurry.

'What's that you're muttering, girl?' says her grandmother.

Anger clouds Axe's face, but it drifts away like smoke. 'I said I have *been so fortunate*, having this warrior for a father.'

'Whatever you're saying, show some respect and say it on your knees.'

Axe kneels before the casket and we do it, too. I will Sparrow not to look at anyone. Axe trembles with what I'd swear is swallowed laughter.

When we stand, I keep my eyes on my boots.

'Stag steps here, soon,' gruffs the old grandmother. 'You have much explaining to do. Make ready.'

Axe-Thrower turns on her heel, pulling me with her.

'Hold your dogs, child.' The old woman pulls herself to her feet and hobbles over to jab Axe-Thrower in the gut. 'He will need a cupbearer. Leave one boy here.'

'But Grandmother, these are way-wearied, both. Let them rest, use another slave.'

The old woman shakes her head. 'Leave this slave, *you* go and rest.' Her skinny fingers wrap around my arm.

Axe-Thrower's gaze drifts across my face helplessly. Then she grabs Sparrow and leads him away without another word.

My heart raps against my breastbone. The old woman snaps her fingers at me. 'Follow.' She walks back towards the open space of the tent, and the guards part to let her through.

I hurry after her, trying to ignore the way their eyes burn my face. She points to the corner, behind the map table. 'Wait there. A sound from you, and the dogs get your toes.'

I wait where she pointed, next to a gallon flagon standing on one of the huge knuckles from a whale's backbone. The sight of it makes my scalp pull. I can feel the cold throbbing off the bone.

My eyelids grow heavy in the smoky warmth. Sweat weaves down my back. I try to untangle my thoughts. The Chieftain was Axe-Thrower's father. That might explain how she ended up crewing with Stag.

The doors are flung open and a bulk of a man strides in, with oiled black hair and glaring grey eyes. A pipe hangs from the corner of his mouth.

Stag.

Even though he'd never reckon on me pitching up right under his nose, and I'm disguised the best I can be, I shrink deeper inside my hood.

He kneels at the feet of the old grandmother, and she strokes a wrinkled hand over his hair. Then he kisses her hands, rises and throws himself into a chair near the fire.

He swigs from a tankard, lines of berry wine trailing into his beard, and chews rags of meat off a bone as he surveys the room from under hooded eyelids. Hidden storms flicker the muscles of his face.

His eyes swim restlessly in his head.

Then he throws the bone to the dogs, launches himself upright again and starts talking and laughing with a group of Tribesmen. It's like he's forced his mood to change – he's holding court, charming them all. I wonder if I'm the only one seeing the craftiness of his look. Shudders lick through me like the fire of shame.

Stag slams the tankard down and yells for more, making me startle halfway out of my skin.

'Boy,' snarls the old grandmother, snapping her fingers at me.

Fangtooths don't take orders from men in brass buckles. I send the Chieftain's words up like a fierce prayer. Gods, I hope some of them remember that!

I pick up the flagon with trembling fingers and step to Stag's side. He plucks a long, black terrodyl fang from his pocket and uses it to pick his teeth. With the other hand, he holds out his tankard without even turning to look at me.

I'm so close I could blow on his cheek. His stuffy smell of cedar and soap and something metallic slips into my lungs. The way he lets his spirit crawl all over every inch of the room makes my belly ache. Did my ma love this man, once?

I stare a beat too long. Wine begins to overflow from the tankard, down his wrist. He blinks out of his thoughts and springs to his feet, rage-slapped. Even without all his teeth, he's all teeth.

I step back – but a polar dog snaps at my ankles, forcing me forwards again. I keep my head down and my eyes on the floor.

The old woman yanks the flagon away from me, sets it down and grabs me by the hand. She pushes me in the small of the back and sends me plunging out through the doors, into the saw-blade night. I fall into the snow. But fingers pinch the scruff of my neck, lifting me to my feet.

Axe-Thrower has been skulking around, waiting for me.

Someone steps from the tent, holding a whip. But Axe-Thrower tugs me away. 'My slave, *my* discipline,' she barks.

We hurry through the snow and howling winds. My questions are a flurry of arrows in my mind. 'Where's Sparrow?'

'I'll take you to him' she hisses, from the corner of her mouth.

When we're further away, I ask why her da's body is lying in the tent like that.

'His spirit will linger near his body, these early death-days. He must lie untouched and guarded for three sun and moon rises. Then his spirit will depart, and he can be buried.'

What if someone takes the Opal? Or – what if he's buried with it? Stag wouldn't let that happen, would he? 'Is he always guarded?' I risk the question, hoping she won't notice anything too keen about it.

But she only nods. 'Just as he was in life. And Grandmother would never risk grave-thieves.'

'Why don't the rest of Trianukka know about his dying?'

'It will not be revealed until a new Chieftain is named, to avoid power squabbles and unrest. After the burial, it will be decided by combat.'

'Will you fight to be the next Chieftain?'

'Me?' Mirth glimmers in her eyes. 'Women cannot be Chieftain here. And if they could, it would never be me. A little rebel lives in my heart.'

I hurry after her, slipping in the snow. 'Don't you want to know how he died?'

She stares. Blinks. Then smiles – and it catches me off guard, cos it's a smile of heart-sadness. 'I wish it were so that I cared enough. Perhaps I did, once. I do not remember.'

Her words make my throat ache. 'Why?'

'He tormented me, as a child.' Torchlight flickers in her eyes. 'He planted a hunger for war in my heart.'

I grimace. I can't imagine being treated like that by my own da, or not feeling safe in my own home. But if Stag had stuck around after my birth, maybe the same would've happened to me. 'I reckon you should know the truth.' I use my arms to balance as we move through the snow. 'Stag – he's my blood father.'

Her eyes sparkle with feeling. 'I suspected a thing of that nature – I saw for myself how you were always plaguing his mind, and then I saw those silvery grey eyes you share. I wonder, which is worse? Having a father like Stag, or a father who would sell you to Stag?'

I gape at her. 'What you on about?'

She squints into the distance. 'Stag carved an agreement with my father. Riches, trade, defence.' She swallows. 'As part of the exchange, my father traded me like a tub of fish-grease.' She stares into the distance, and I know in her head she's still looking down on that coffin. 'I was prised from my lands, from my sled, from my dogs. The sea-sickness was the least of my suffering, though it scraped the lining from my belly and burrowed into my bones like shipworm.' Her eyes rest on my face.

I turn away, remembering what she did aboard my ship. *This little one is spirited*, she said, when she held me back while Grandma drowned. *Aye. And I never want her forgetting it.*

But she touches my arm. 'After Stag first visited our lands, my father addressed the people. He said that Stag was a great leader, and that we should ally ourselves with him. But I learned too late what a true leader is. Stag will never know – he forgets that all leaders – kings, chieftains, captains – should serve their people, first and last.'

I resist pulling my arm away and force myself to look at her.

'I know you can't forgive the part I played. But know that I never *chose* to play it. And if I hadn't, I would have ended the same way your captain did. I swear I will defy your enemy. I will help you defeat him.'

I nod, mind whirring with all that she's said. Then I pull

my arm away and we walk on in silence, past bone-keeled walrus-skin boats hanging from wood-and-bone racks, and lounging packs of polar dogs, their dirty white fur swept into frozen ridges by the wind. They touch noses, grunt questions up through their throats to the sky. Their breath steams in the torchlight.

End-days, all-darkness, a pack-leader growls, eyeing me. *Frightfrightfright wrongness foul-stirrings.* The others join in, and their panic strikes deep into my chest, rattling my ribs. The beast-chatter swells in the back of my throat like spew. It's hard to swallow down but it's just as hard to stomach. It makes me dizzy. I gulp breaths of blade-edge air, trying to stave off a faint.

Axe ushers me through the opening in another tent, into a cocooned world of shadows. I stumble down a short slope and falter before a fire in the middle, surrounded by reindeer skins.

I fall to my knees, holding my palms before the warmth, and stare around the tent. The flames dance and smoke tickles the air on its way out through the moon-shaped hole in the roof. Sparrow lies curled asleep under a pile of furs, the tip of my longbow poking through next to him.

Then I scuttle backwards as one of the reindeer skins shudders itself upright into the shape of a stooped, ancient Tribeswoman, with rings of loose flesh hanging from her neck.

15

Bloodcakes

The Tribeswoman's head is almost bald. Her eyes are bright and sharp, nearly as black as my natural hair, and thick bone hooks swing from her ears. Her nose is long and bony, but her face is pudding-soft. Age has thieved the lines from her palms and pressed them into her face.

She shambles close, looking from me to Axe-Thrower. Then she jabs a quick stream of words at Axe-Thrower, the sounds gargling from the back of her throat. She ent got fangs. She's got no teeth at all. As she grows more furious, a whale tooth thuds against her breastbone, making a hollow tapping sound. It's hung from a length of sinew around her neck. She pushes up her cloak sleeves and her brown arms are strewn with tattoos of running polar dogs.

'Stay with this squawker,' hisses Axe-Thrower. 'She is Old One.' She turns on her heel and strides from the tent. I gape after her.

Old One hunches over two pails, beckoning me closer. One of her fingers is missing down to the knuckle. I don't move, and she tuts loudly. She fumbles on a low oaken table for a whale rib, one end of it chiselled into a scoop. She uses it to stir a pail of glaring redness. Blood.

While I stand there watching her with folded arms, she tips some of the blood into the second pail and mixes it with the rib. She adds milk from a stone flask, then she lifts out lumps of bloody dough and sets them cooking over the fire. Soon the cakes are sizzling in pools of butter.

I breathe the butter in a stupor. Sparrow wakes up and stretches his arms up over his head. Thaw pops out from under his cloak and sits on his belly.

'Who're you?' asks Sparrow sleepily.

Old One clucks over to him, sinking bony fingertips into his hair and gasping over the gold. He wriggles away.

I curl up on a skin and watch the fire. *I'll just calm my sails and wait for Axe.* I grow drowsy. Old One pushes a plate of bloodcakes towards me but I just bare my teeth at her.

She throws me a husky laugh, drumming on her big belly. I sigh through my teeth. I came to find Leo and get the Opal. I try asking after the Protector but Old One just chuckles at me.

My eyes keep straying to the platter of bloodcakes. I reach out and take one. Before I get it to my mouth, Old One rushes forwards and dollops a spoonful of red berry jam on the cake. I eat the whole thing in two bites. The rich, salty-sweet, doughy taste flows through me and I feel my skin relax and my breath loosen.

Sparrow scampers over and starts tucking in. 'Mmm,' he

says. He curls up again and falls into a doze.

Old One gruffs more unknown words to me and rips her whale-tooth pendant over her head, fixing me with her fierce black eyes. The white tooth is etched with runes I don't know, though I do know why they're there – to harness the whale-wisdom sleeping dormant in the tooth, like a winter root.

She puts her hand out above the flames, hanging the whale-tooth over them. She starts making a noise in the back of her throat. It's a grunt-growl-hacking sound. I reckon she's showing off, from the way she's watching me with a glowing challenge in her eyes, ablaze with life against all the years pressing on her.

'*What?*' I husk.

She shouts something and the polar dogs outside the tent utter a storm of swirling yips and human-sounding howls, as the flames plunge low like they're frighted of her.

The smoke turns black and oily. Old One rubs her fingertips together and sticks out her tongue.

A thrill stamps against the wall of my chest.

Old One catches my eye and gives me the slyest grin I've ever seen. Then she breathes a crackly breath, picks up a thread of smoke and drags it from the fire. She flings it up into the air, the thread snaps and she whacks it with her whale-rib scoop. The smoke breaks into a crowd of black shapes and every time she smacks one of them with her rib, it shows me a different picture on the wall of the tent.

She calls up a picture-telling of her long life. I watch

the times she lost fingers to dogs or cold, and I see how she birthed six babs and how only half of them lived and grew. Now the ones that lived have aged and died, while she herself still lives. I learn to see how she wears her pain proudly, like armour.

Old One bats more pictures through the air and I see

Screaming mouths

A black-haired man looming over a sleeping bab

A silver-haired captain falling into the sea and drifting down to the depths.

An armoured girl standing on a deck of a ship – but her sails are torn and her hull's locked in ice . . .

Axe-Thrower calls for Old One through the mouth of the tent. The black shapes splinter apart, drifting through the air like dust. I gasp, feeling dizzy.

Thaw emerges from under a pile of skins and gifts me an outraged look. *Whatthatwhatthatwhatthat?*

No idea, Thaw, I say wearily.

Old One flabbles outside, gruffing something at Axe.

I follow them to the mouth of the tent and rake deep breaths of air, listening as their voices move away.

A raggedy black crow soars past my face and through the tent flap. It settles on a log and shakes out its wings.

'Crow?' I splutter, ducking back inside. 'Thank the gods!'

Shiver-feather.

'No, no, no. You ent supposed to have beast-chatter!' I reach into the beast-world and feel for the edges of his spirit.

His feathers start to melt away, turning from real feathers

141

on the floor of the tent to slippery black shadows, swallowed by the fire.

'Gods of all that slither and crawl,' he pants finally, eyes circled by dark shadows. I pass him a bloodcake and he wolfs it down. 'This *place!*'

I fill him in on the Chieftain and Stag, and my plan to pose as a slave again to listen in on the talk in the Chieftain's tent. 'I need to keep an eye on that Opal and make sure Stag don't run off with it!'

'How do we get out when you've got the stone?' he asks.

I wince. 'I ent sure, but I'm starting to put my trust in Axe-Thrower.'

He cocks an eyebrow. 'And you reckon that wise, why?'

'What else can I do? We need her. And she told me her heart-truth.'

'She's coming back,' warns Sparrow.

Crow gulps down another cake and reaches his arms through the space between worlds, becoming feathered and winged again. When the mouth of the tent gapes, letting in a blast of painful, icy air, he barrels past the Tribeswomen, making Old One stagger back. She winks at me.

Axe-Thrower sets herself the task of strengthening my disguise. She draws fake tattoos on my cheeks. 'Your slave mark,' she explains. She rubs something into my skin to darken it and I tell her my plan to work as a cupbearer.

'Why?' she rasps, eyes scorching my skin. 'You heard what Grandmother said about your Protector of the Mountain. Now you must stay away from Stag while we work out which

142

slavers she might have been sold to.'

I shake my head, preparing to take a risk there's no return from. 'There's something else.'

Her eyes are solemn.

'The jewel in the hollow of your father's throat – we can't let Stag take it.'

'Why not?' Her eyes search my face.

I set my jaw. 'It's a wild thing. It shouldn't be trapped by the likes of him.'

'I saw that jewel, aglow with wildness, like your eyes. It's one of the Storm-stones, isn't it?'

I nod, and pulls the gems out of my pocket, cradling them in my palms to show her.

She hisses her sigh between her teeth. 'Very well. If this gem holds power Stag wants for himself, then I will do all in *my* power to help you claim it.'

Even inside the Chieftain's tent, the cold is maddening. But still the smell of decay has threaded into the air.

After what feels like hours, the line of haggard folk paying their respects tails off, and Stag orders everyone gone but for three frowning warriors – the Chieftain's appointed corpse-guards. The gold adornments shining on their cloaks speak loudly of their high rank. They take seats around the map table, Stag easing himself into the grandest chair, the one like a throne.

'The old Chieftain-mother will not return until all the trouble we have created has passed,' breathes a guard.

'Excellent,' purrs Stag.

'What about the cupbearer?' growls another, flinging spiteful looks at me.

'The slave boy?' says Stag in surprise. He claps the warrior on the back. 'Even if he can understand us, he won't betray us. Just imagine what we would do to him.' He smiles, eyes empty of light. Then he leans towards me and seizes my arm, yanking me roughly to his side.

They all laugh. I force myself statue-still, aware that my spirit wants to bolt from my body. Stag blows a ring of smoke into my face and grins when I burst into a fit of coughing. I feel like a blade is poking around in my gut. I've never felt less safe.

Suddenly Stag's coughing worse than me. He pulls a kerchief from his pocket and spits a mouthful of blood into it. Then he stares round at the men, voice ominous-quiet. 'The plan is tightening. The Stony Raiders march closer. We must satisfy the men with fighting until they arrive. I do not want them sensing trouble.'

The warriors shift uneasily in their seats. 'And they will honour the bargain?' asks one.

'Of course,' purrs Stag. He snaps his fingers for wine and I pour it, biting my cheek while praying not to spill a drop. Then I shrink back into the shadows.

'Now, gentlemen,' drawls Stag, puffing on his pipe. 'To the matter of the Opal.'

I press as far back against the wall of the tent as I can, thanking the gods I remembered to leave the other Opals in

Old One's tent with Sparrow to watch over them. A deathly silence settles over the room and the candles flicker as Stag steps towards the curtain that hangs between the main room and the death-chamber.

'He must not be touched—'

'You people!' declares Stag, rumbling a belly-laugh that chills my marrow. 'So superstitious. You do realise the treacherous beast stole the Opal from *me* in the first place? I should have had it back as soon as he died, but for the fact my servant *failed* so dismally.' He grimaces.

'If I may,' grumbles a grey-bearded corpse-guard.

Stag glances at him. 'Please.'

'I sense there may be riots if the sacred rituals are violated.' The grey-beard clears his throat.

Stag considers, eyes coldly sweeping the man. 'Go on.'

'Your power here depends on not disrupting the established order more than is needed. You must feign respect for our beliefs, even if you feel none.' He lifts his eyes to Stag, and the two stare at each other steadily.

'Sound advice,' declares Stag finally. 'It has been heeded. In light of these *beliefs*, the rancorous old mother will expect to see an amber jewel upon the body at the time of burial. If you can win me a moment alone in here, just before the ceremony, I will put another stone in its place. A beautiful piece of amber, very costly. No one will know any different.'

'Why not do it now?' asks a warrior.

'I have not yet received the amber,' he replies, face tightening with impatience.

One of the warriors nods, slowly. 'That might work. As long as the old grandmother believes the powerful stone is accompanying her son to the otherworld.'

'How do we know it is a Storm-Opal as you say?' says the grey-bearded man, suddenly.

Stag steps through the curtain, towards the Chieftain's casket. The guards shift uneasily, and one draws back his lips to show his fangs. Stag emerges, rubbing the Land-Opal tenderly with his thumbs.

Ugh! My palms grow sweaty.

'Now,' he says, looking round at the warriors. 'I suspect that you wouldn't truly like to learn what can be done with the stone, for the truth may frighten you and leave your tails twitching.'

'Try us,' barks grey-beard. The other guards glance warily between him and Stag.

Stag turns the Opal in the lamplight. Little bolts of amber crackle through the stone. Stag grins, hissing through the gaps in his teeth. My heart begins to pound.

The tent walls quake. The ground shakes beneath our feet. 'Don't!' I beg, in a sudden, broken yelp.

My voice is swallowed by the filthy air, unheeded. My hands make fists.

Stag mutters under his breath – words that hoop round and round like a spell.

The grey-bearded guard that doubted the stone clutches the arms of his chair. Amber light lashes from the Opal, and delves into the Fangtooth's chest, rummaging around inside his ribcage. Shock splays his face apart.

Stag's eyes shine. 'It's working! Oh, of course it is, of course it is,' he rants. 'Something this sacred has to make itself manifest. Don't you want to be part of this power?' he calls to the others.

A blood-shivering shriek tears from the doubter's mouth. Then he falls silent and the tentacles of light pull back from his chest, holding onto a wriggling slip of silver. The man slumps sideways, his eyes open but glazed.

When the light pulls back towards the stone, it's pulling the shape of a man, but the man is only a shadow.

Find the scattered Storm-Opals before an enemy finds them, and uses them to wield dark power.

The shadow is sucked inside the Opal.

'An elixiration is the proper name for a spirit-draining,' says Stag gently. 'This is what we shall be able to do to countless creatures. And when we recover the other jewels, the power shall swell to claim the world – there will be no limit to the size of our soulless armies.'

'Power untold,' mutters one of the dazed warriors.

Another wears a fixed look on his face, rubbing his arms like he can't get warm. 'Never,' he mutters to himself. 'Never in my long days have I . . .'

The drained Fangtooth shudders on the floor, gulping for breath like he's choking.

'Servant – rise,' commands Stag, watching him coldly. He snaps his fingers.

The man blinks, then stands in one fluid movement,

arms limp by his sides, face expressionless.

'Kill them,' breathes Stag, eyes glittering.

Shock skins my eyes.

The soulless Fangtooth's swords flash, one in each hand, as he steps swiftly towards the others.

'What are you doing?' demands one. The other shrieks, scrambling out of his chair.

'Stop,' commands Stag, and the swords still in an instant.

'What is the meaning of this?' asks the guard that's standing up. He raises a trembling finger to point at Stag.

I skirt around the edge of the room as Stag paces in front of them. 'We will elixirate great armies,' he says. 'A whole village at a time. Powerful warriors that will stop at nothing, feel nothing, be completely controllable.' He takes no notice of me. A wide grin stretches his face as he leans down and puts the Opal back on the Chieftain's body.

. . . before an enemy finds them, and uses them to wield dark power . . .

He's done it. He's worked out how to wield the dark power. I stay glued to the shadows as they gab long into the night about their plans. I've got no clue what I'm meant to do if the wine runs dry, and my hands shake when I pour it, but I manage not to spill any.

Finally, the warriors leave the tent. Stag sits alone by the fire, grinning as the light plays on his face. I edge towards the doors, squeeze through and start running through the snow.

16
By Tooth, by Nail

A drum begins to beat, waking me from a dead-heavy slumber. I raise my head, then groan softly as what happened last night floods into my brain. I feel sick to the marrow when I think about Stag leeching out that man's spirit.

The drum beats louder and the rhythm changes, jolting the thoughts right out of my head. I stand up, pulling on my boots, and take the cup of hot juice that Old One passes to me. 'What's going on out there?'

She grins at me, then scuttles over to where Sparrow's sitting. She starts brushing his hair; copper now that she's dyed it as part of his disguise.

I tut. Outside, feet crunch through the snow. Once Sparrow's brushed and cloaked, Old One straps snowshoes to her feet and hurries us outside.

I chatter over my shoulder to Thaw to stay out of sight, knowing she'll try and follow to protect me.

ThawknowThawknow, she grumbles.

Old One's haste and the drumming makes me think there must be some kind of Moonlands ritual or celebration. 'Where we going?' I ask, even though she don't understand me and I wouldn't be able to understand her reply.

Sparrow trots next to her, holding her hand. She clucks to him and he grins up at her – neither understanding the other. I roll my eyes. He *always* charms the full-growns. I hunch after them through the biting snow, towards a central fire-pit built in a space between strings of chattering teeth. A group of Tribesfolk bang drums painted with polar dogs.

A girl sits in the middle of a group of full-growns and kids. The Chieftain-mother's with them, and she's got a sliver of silver in her fist.

Pliers.

The Chieftain-mother grabs the girl's jaw and pulls her mouth open. Her wide eyes shine, making me think of some wild, frighted creature. Tears begin to roll down her face, and though the old woman commands her to stop crying, all she does is cry harder.

My feet flood with fire and I leap towards them – I'm gonna get her safe – but Old One grabs my scruff and hauls me backwards. She puts a finger to her neck and draws it across, keeping her eyes on mine, and I don't need to know her tribe-tongue to catch her meaning.

But before I can blink again the girl's bottom front teeth are wrenched out of her mouth, together with sky-splitting screams and a chinful of blood. Somewhere in the ghostly snowscape beyond the circle, polar dogs clamour into a frenzy. The Chieftain-mother towers over the girl.

A group of men lead a snarling polar dog towards her. The dog's still a pup, but he's already huge. Terror squeezes my chest.

But the loudest terror ripples from the dog, as he senses a threat.

Blood-stink fright-pup ripriprip. Girl-pup lost crunchers. Whywhy? Whatprowlinghere?

The group crouch by the dog. One holds his legs, another his body, another his head. They force his mouth open.

No! Noleavealonehelppackmateshelphelpfightbitedangerhurting touchfurdangerhelp!

The sickening fright lurches into me, desperate beast-chatter snagging hooks into my mind. Then I'm pitching forwards into the body of the polar dog. I put out my hands but they're spirit-silver and they push straight through the dog's neck and then I'm blinking, looking out through his eyes.

Bigtallroundjawsallaroundflappyjawsbitingeyeswantto hurtmewhywhywhy? I ask, thrashing in the two-legs' grip, trying to rip my muzzle free.

Old fierceness bends close, claw of silver in paw. Holding my head – snap, bite! Can't get away, not safe, not safe! Silver claw in my mouth. Cold, hard, hurting. Waves of pain smash into me, knocking me out

of the polar dog and back into my own body, in time to watch as the Chieftain-mother straightens up, a long, curved fang gripped in her pliers. The dog squirms and whimpers, and I press my hands over my ears but the beast-chatter rattles around my brain, too strong to do anything about 'cept curl my toes inside my boots and bite my lips. My head swims. Old One grips my arm, heart-worry scrawled across her face.

'Bone glue,' barks the Chieftain-mother, as the girl trembles in the snow, retching, wiping her mouth, whimpering. Some of the other kids call out to her, in throaty yelps and grunts that I can't understand. It's like they're yelling heart-strength to her. Their faces are etched with fear and jealousy and awe, all mixed up.

'You know the rules! Trade-tongue or nothing!' orders the old woman.

'Chieftain never this bad,' mutters someone.

'The Chieftain is dead,' she yelps, eyes shining with grief.

The kids fall silent, so the polar dog's terrified whimpers drift on the air.

She bends down and cups the girl's chin. Then she takes a wooden stick heaped with sticky clear jelly, shoves it in her mouth and then presses the fangs into her weeping sockets. The girl can't close her lips around the fangs, but the blood begins to slow.

Then a Tribesman lifts the polar dog pup into the air. His legs kick. He thrashes. Blood is clotted across his fur. *Outawayrunrunrunsnapgetoffoffoffnotmothernotmyscruff!*

The knife finds his throat before I can blink and *the*

punch of terror and snuffing out of beast-chatter floods my brain so painfully that my vision blackens and my hearing fades into a distant ringing and I lose grip of my body as it falls into the snow, a dead weight.

Floating, dark space. Hurttouchwhyriptearhelphurtsinmouth.
Loping through the black sky and sniffing the stars.

I gasp awake into a crinkled brown map that I realise is Old One's face, inches from my own. 'Aagh,' she grunts, squatting low, bracing her hands on her thighs.

I cover my face with my hands. 'Back off,' I croak groggily.

Sparrow's stubby fingers jab into my side. 'You awake, stinker? What happened to *you*?' In his other hand is a little stack of bloodcakes and he takes a huge bite while I shake my head, struggling to grasp words.

Old One shuffles off to poke the ashes of her fire. She starts up her singing, all warbly-throaty. I watch as Sparrow reaches for a heap of white fur lying by the fire.

It's the dead dog from the tooth-pulling ceremony. The memory floods back to me. 'Sparrow, that pup is dead,' I tell him softly.

He tuts at me. 'I know that, stupid!'

I crouch groggily next to him and trace the polar dog's spine with a fingertip. Sparrow's tears drip into its fur. A dusky purple glow is gathering in his palms – I can see it shining through the fur he's clutching.

I glare at the lightning and wrinkle my nose against the charred stink. I'm about to pull the pup away from him

153

when Old One rests her cool, soft hand on mine.

Sparrow's lightning brightens. The pup's body is stiff and his white tongue lolls from his mouth. The tent creaks around us in the wind. A spark ripples from Sparrow's left hand to his right, straight through the pup. And by all the gods, I swear the pup's leg twitches. Just like what he said happened with that frog.

'Sparr—'

'Shhhhhhushup!' growls Old One, startling me.

The purple spark zips onto the iced ends of the pup's fur, until every strand glitters. Then his front paw kicks out, as though from a dog-dream.

My hands dig into the thick reindeer skin under me.

Sparrow sniffles. 'You'll be alright, pup-pup.'

The same leg jerks, then another.

I can feel the magic, thrumming in the air. Feel like I could reach out and peel the edges of this world away, uncloaking the stew of the dream-world simmering underneath.

Under Sparrow's hand, the dog's ribcage rises, falls. Once, twice. Then the breath comes, regular as oar strokes, but I feel like my own has stopped. The lightning is a flow, like I've never seen before – a gentle shimmering as Sparrow whispers to the pup.

Shock scrapes my scalp backwards.

The beast's chest flickers again and again into a rhythm as Sparrow's lightning beats his heart back to life.

'Gods!' I stutter.

The pup's eyes clear of death and snowflakes, and he

blinks. The blood in his fur slurps back into his body and the ice starts to drip from him as his blood heats.

Sparrow falls backwards, his lightning fizzling out with a sharp, dry-sounding sputter. The polar dog pup limps towards him and licks his cheek, uttering a curious yip.

Knowyouknowyoumother?Sleeplongtoolongpackmatesfled dreamsofpainwheregone?

'He brought a dead thing back to life.' I turn to face Old One. She gifts me a face-splitting grin. I shake my head. 'But – he brought a dead thing back . . .' I trail off.

The polar dog pup limps around the tent, confusion bunching his fur into spines. Old One ushers him back towards Sparrow, who lets him smell his hand and then strokes him calm. 'It's alright, dog! You're safe with us. We won't let anyone hurt you.'

Wherewherewheream? He licks Sparrow's palm and turns to stare at me.

Old One's tent, I tell him, trying to push against the dizziness crashing over me. *She's a good two-legs.*

'Sparrow – what if dead things don't want to come back to life?' My voice is tight, clamped in the arms of fear.

He fixes me with raging eyes. 'Why wouldn't they?'

'I don't know!' I snap. 'I just – I mean, how do we know creatures that come back are gonna be the same as before?'

'Why've they got to be the same?' he asks, puzzled.

I sigh through my nose, watching the dog. It's already fallen asleep next to Sparrow, sides rising and falling gently. Its face looks peaceful enough.

Dream-slow, I feel an idea begin to stir.

Later, I spy in the Chieftain's tent again, trying to steal snippets from Stag and his plotters about their plans for the Opal and the Chieftain's burial, which I learn is coming after one more sleep. Stag has the amber to replace with the Opal, and he's gonna do it tonight.

My idea swirls behind my eyes, growing brighter and more fully shaped. We have to be ready. There will only be one chance.

Back in Old One's tent, the pup sleeps, curled under the hem of Sparrow's cloak. When it wakes it gets restless and whines in a way that churns my gut. It's not the same as it was before. And cos it don't have its teeth, it struggles to eat the meat Old One gives it. When it does, it throws up.

'Sparrow, I don't think the magyk worked too well this time,' I tell him.

He glares at me and the air around him threatens tears, so I shut up.

But by the time we've helped Old One lug food and firewood into the tent, the dog is stiff and its eyes are glazed. Sparrow cries and rages over it, zapping it again and again until Old One and me pull his arms away.

'Ent your fault it didn't work,' I tell him, but he won't be comforted.

My fledgling idea's been pressing against my lips. But he's so upset that I wonder if it stands a chance of working. If he's this tearful, will he ever want to try his death-magyk again? And is it alright to do it, or is it proper dark and

156

wicked – is death a thing that should never be touched?

Old One somehow calms his sails and gets him sitting on a reindeer skin with his legs crossed. When I ask what he's doing he mutters that she's helping him focus on his visions.

After that she makes us eat cubes of dug-up shark meat and slices of blubber that I'm so grateful for in this cold, I swallow them without questioning for once.

While I eat, I ponder my idea – the seed that's blooming in my bones. The only plan I've got. 'Sparrow, d'you want to try waking up another beast?' I ask slowly, curling my toes. 'Want to fright Stag good and rotten?'

In the thickest, most silent part of the night, we creep from the tent and head towards the Chieftain's. We blend our bodies with the deepest shadows, passing polar dogs with icicles hanging from their muzzles. I bundle my cloak more tightly round me and feel the weight of the Opals in my pocket again.

Thaw drops warnings into my skull, from her viewpoint high above the frozen clouds. *Hurry*, she squawks. *Brass-buckle bad-blubber on the move!*

Crow, in his bird form, waits outside the tent. He shifts back into a boy and I slip him a stack of bloodcakes that he gobbles quick-sharp. He nods at me and Sparrow. 'Ready?'

'Aye.'

Crow cups his hands around his mouth. Then he yells a stream of warning-words, in the Fangtooth tongue. I never knew he could speak it, and awe glows in my chest. We hide between two tents as the guards streak out of the tent, looking this way and that for the trouble Crow's warned of. Then they run past.

Crow shifts back into his bird shape.

Inside the tent, flames crackle. The stillness makes me feel uneasy. 'Quick, we don't have long.' We rush towards the casket and duck down behind it.

Can I risk a dream-dance to search for the Chieftain's spirit, leaving Sparrow alone here with Stag so close? 'I'm going to see if his spirit is still close by,' I whisper. 'Maybe I can find it in the dream-dance realm and ask him if we can wake him up.' *And if I don't find his spirit, but Sparrow's magyk works, I'll just have to pray he don't hate that we dredged him back into the waking world . . .*

Sparrow grabs my cloak but I gently prise his fingers off.

I sit on the floor and feel for the rune charm around my neck, the one that gifts me protection for dream-dancing. Then I shut my eyes and listen to my breath sigh in and out like a tide. I let Sparrow and the tent drift out of reach. I push forwards, lean out of my body and float up *into the air. I search, holding tightly to the cord between my spirit and my body. The Chieftain's presence fills the tent and I'm startled by the heaviness of it. He sits on his throne, staring stonily into the distance. On his belly, a wound oozes.*

He jumps when he sees me. 'What are you? What are you doing in my tent? Guards?' He glances around the empty tent. 'Guards!'

He don't even know he's dead.

'Chieftain,' I say, the dream-word slow and long and clumsy. 'Look at that wound on you – don't you know you're dead?'

He jolts, his spirit splintering into a hundred raging fragments before buzzing back together again. 'Treacherous creature! My guards will have your head on a spike!'

I only realise it as I say the words. 'I think Stag had you killed,' I tell him. 'What happened to gift you that wound?'

His gaping spirit-eyes roam the cold, black space around us. 'A walrus tusk,' he admits, hunching low in his seat. 'I was abandoned on the ice. The fog clouded my vision. Too late I realised the walrus was a mother with cubs. I felt the tusk before I saw it – then that man in brass-buckles came rushing to me, claiming to have lost sight of me in the fog . . .' He clutches the arms of his chair. Then he fixes me with glaring eyes. 'What do you want from me, ghoul? Are you here to drag me to the under-realms?'

I float above his head. 'No. I want to wake you, with your consent, so that you can avenge yourself. Stag comes soon, to lift the Opal from your throat, before your burial.'

'I stole that stone, so now it belongs to me! I will accept your offer. I will return to life.'

'Chieftain, I ent certain how long we can bring you back for. I–'

'Fear not, ghoul. I am strongest among men.'

'I will help you cross back into the waking world. But if I do, I want the Opal.'

Outrage pins his skin taut. Then he closes his eyes, and nods.

I stretch out my hand. I feel a tingle when our spirit-fingers touch. I help him out of his chair.

'Follow me!' We hover over the casket and I show him his body.

159

He howls and rages, grabbing fistfuls of his cloak and hair.

'I can help you,' I tell him. 'You need to lie down inside your bones and let me do the rest.'

I whisk back to my body.

'Sparrow,' my lungs wheeze. 'Quick, he needs your fire!'

The Chieftain's body lies still and cold. But I can sense his spirit drifting nearer.

My brother leans over him again and drips gloopy lines of purple lightning onto his chest and neck, singing under his breath as he does it. He presses his fingers to the Chieftain's ribs. His voice gets husky as his energy slows.

'Sparrow, that's enough!' I pull at his arm, panic pulsing through me.

'Just needs a bit more,' he mutters sleepily.

'No.' I climb to my feet. 'You'll bleed yourself dry!' I pull him back and he releases a burst of lightning that thumps into the Chieftain's chest.

At the same beat, the doors bang open. Slow, heavy boots approach the casket. We drop down behind it and squeeze into the shadows. I hold my breath.

We're too late. I dig my nails into my palms, swallowing a scream of fury.

Stag leans down over the casket. We watch as he lifts the Opal from the Chieftain's throat and replaces it with a polished lump of amber.

Then he turns around and stalks away, the Opal glowing between his fingers.

It didn't work, and now he's going to walk away with the Opal, easy as anything!

I bite my fingertips. Then there's a tattered gasping sound. I twist around and watch as the Fangtooth Chieftain sits upright in his casket, clutching his chest with one hand and his great sword with the other. The icicles on the Chieftain's eyebrows melt and run down his face like tears.

Stag halts. His shoulders spring upwards, tensing against his ears. Then, slowly, he turns around.

The Chieftain lets go of his sword and flexes stiff fingers. Then he stands, stumbles, curses thickly. He stares around through eye sockets stuffed with rubies. When he scrubs his eyes with his knuckles, the rubies fall out, and he peers blearily through scratched eyeballs. His chin drops to his chest, and he glares down at us.

Sparrow weeps and squirms, kicking deeper into the shadows. But I point at the shadowy shape of Stag, face frozen in confusion mingled with spreading horror. I force a dry whisper from my lungs. 'He took the Opal.'

The Chieftain climbs down in a shower of grave jewels, bones clicking.

He jerks towards the fright-frozen figure of Stag. His fingers reach out to touch him, but the wretch bats his hand away, eyes popping with dread, veins bulging. 'What evil trickery is this? You're – you're *dead!*'

'No longer,' croaks a voice as old as tree roots.

The Chieftain reaches out and plucks the Opal from Stag's trembling palm. Then he stalks out of the tent clutching the gem and I curse under my breath. 'I told him to give it to *me!*'

We creep out from behind the casket. Stag blunders towards the doors, fiddling at his belt. We hang back, out of sight at the edge of the tent.

Too late, I see the gun as Stag pulls it free. Then he runs, slips through the doors – we chase after, I try to hold Sparrow back – and we get outside in time to see Stag blast a hole in the Chieftain's chest.

Except folk have started gathering for the burial. There are screams. Hands pressed against mouths.

The Chieftain topples forwards. The Opal lands in the snow. It's too far away for me to reach. 'No!' I hiss. We run and hide behind another tent.

Stag stands over the Chieftain's body, panting. Then he vomits into the snow and the spew steams in the night. His hands shake as he turns the Chieftain's body over with his foot. Is he dead again? I will the Chief to stir, but he don't. And I could scream.

'Dead things walk,' booms Stag, voice loosening an icicle that smashes at his feet. He glares around the burial-gathering, into rows of shocked faces.

He shot the Chieftain, flurry the whispers.

'I saved you from an abomination of nature!' Stag roars. 'Why did a dead man walk this night? Who set him to walking?'

'There is a witch,' someone answers. 'Old One. If any will know, it is she.'

The Chieftain-mother barges through the crowd. She

stares at the scene, chin quivering. 'What evil lurks here? Why has my son been disturbed?'

Sparrow strains against my hold. 'I can get it!' he whispers. He breaks away and dashes out from our hiding place, grabs the Opal and hurries back to me.

But Stag's eyes catch a flurry of movement. He rushes after us. Crow blurs through the darkness with a rustle of feathers, straight into Stag's face. He yells, stumbling and falling in the snow.

We run, as he bellows into the darkness at our backs. He screams for guards. They come blundering between two rows of tents and I squeeze away but one of them grabs Sparrow and he squawks, voice piercing the night. When I turn around, the others are staring at the Chieftain's body.

'Don't look at him – get the *thief*!' screams Stag.

I race back the way I came, but the guard is pressing Sparrow's face down in the snow and ripping the Opal from his palm.

I open my pipes to yell at the guard but then Stag steps up behind us and I swallow my voice back down, terror clanging in my gut until it's hot and bubbling. 'So, even slave children are learning of this stone,' he murmurs, close to my ear. Startlement throbs in my bones. He ent recognised us. *The eyes see what they expect to see.* That's how invisible slaves are to powerful people. 'Chain them and leave them out in the snow.' He turns and stalks off, not realising that he was inches away from the Sea and the Sky-Opal. But the gems know. The Land-Opal glows in his fist, and inside my pocket the other two burn.

17
Burial

Axe finds us after he's left. 'What did you do?' she barks, wrapping extra cloaks around us to keep us from freezing to death.

'He woke up,' says Sparrow.

'He died again,' I say.

'Stag got the stone,' we say together.

'*What?*' hisses Axe. 'Why didn't you tell me you were plotting your own executions? I might've been able to knock some sense into your skulls!'

'We had to try something!' I grip her eyes hard in mine. 'I'm fretting for Old One. They reckon she's a witch, that she set the Chieftain walking. You have to protect her!'

Thaw-Wielder bursts through the night and lands on Sparrow's head, staring at me accusingly. *Peace, Thaw!* I chatter. *I never meant to get caught.*

The black crow wheels through the air and lands in the snow in front of us, cocking its head. But then nothing happens.

Two-legs slumped in snow . . . I know? I know?

Yes, you know! I gasp. *Your name is Crow and you are a boy, not a bird!*

But the crow flies away again without replying. My insides twist, hot and sharp. What's happening to him?

Thaw, I chatter desperately. *Whatever happens, you have to protect that crow! Remember, he's a two-legs friend, aye?*

She splutters a beakful of outrage into my face. *Thaw remember! Thaw not soft-shell-skull like two-legs girl!*

All night, we huddle in the snow. The chains bite my wrists. Axe keeps vigil by our sides, making sure our scarves are tied tight against the skin-flaying wind, until the guards circle back from their patrol and see her off. When the grainy light has thinned as much as it's going to, preparations are made for the Chieftain's burial.

Not far from where we're chained, Tribesfolk saw open a huge hole in the ice. From our left drones a mourning song, and footsteps crunch slowly through the snow. Flaming torches throw flickering light against the sides of the tents. Then a procession marches into view – the casket is being carried on the shoulders of warriors.

When they reach the hole in the ice, they attach the casket to a sled and a pack of four polar dogs. Everyone gathers, blocking our view, but there's no escaping the unholy *crash-smash* as the whole dog-sled is tipped through the ice, together with the casket and the dogs, and a piece of polished amber in place of the Opal. Stag watches, puffing on his pipe, shoulders hunched around his ears.

It was worth getting caught just to see him almost piddle his breeches in fear. Teeth knocked out, fright lodged in chest . . . we will keep unravelling you, *I swear it*. We will unravel you 'til there's naught left.

The spite in my own thought leaves a bitter taste in my mouth. I try to blow it away, remembering that I can't let the darkness in me swell. It comes from him and I have to fight it.

Sparrow sobs quietly. He tries to talk to me about the polar dogs, but I shush him urgently. No way do I want to draw any attention to us.

The Chieftain's barely sunk through the hole in the ice when a *boom* throbs in my chest.

A distant drum.

I was taught the different drum-sounds from a young age, to learn when an attack was near. And this drum belongs to a raider. A horn cleaves the air, and there's a heavy thudding under the drums – the sound of a creature's footsteps.

'Stony Chieftains!' someone yelps.

'Silence,' commands Stag. 'I called them here. You have nothing to fear. Now that the mourning has passed for your Chieftain, new leadership must be settled.' A group of warriors detach themselves from the crowd of mourners and step to flank him.

Tribesfolk exclaim in the language of the Moonlands, grasping onto their old ways like spears. They use their bellies like bellows, raking in great baggy breaths and

166

gushing the air out.

'How many times?' demands the grandmother viciously. 'Common trade-tongue only!'

'*You* called them?' challenges Axe-Thrower, rounding on Stag. 'Grandmother, did he seek your counsel on this?'

The old woman gifts Axe a warning look. 'I think it is right and good that we ally ourselves with such fine warriors.'

'But the Stony Chieftains are out of control! Even *Father* knew that.' Axe-Thrower points at her grandmother, then at the hole in the ice. 'And he was your son, and he's barely cold!'

'Close your hole,' warns Stag. 'Come. Slaves in chains, including that old witch in the hut on the edge of the settlement. She will fetch a decent price if the Stony are as superstitious as the Fanged.'

'She is our shaman,' screams Axe-Thrower. 'You cannot do this!'

'She is a witch who summons the dead to walking,' he snarls. 'Stay out of it!'

A group of Tribesfolk step forwards to stand behind Axe, drawing back their lips to show their fangs. 'Oh, you side with her, do you?' purrs Stag. When he pulls his gun from his cloak, they scatter.

I listen, sick-hearted, as Old One is forced from her tent, back crooked and stooped.

When she sees us she clucks forwards, but Stag drags her back by her cloak.

'I hear tales that the witch has been teaching the slave

children spells,' husks a guard.

Guilt spears me. For helping us, Old One is losing everything. It's only now that I realise how much she was risking.

They lead us in chains to meet the drums. I keep Sparrow's tangled copper-dyed hair in sight. Thaw hides in dead trees along the way. Crow does the same. I listen to Old One's piteous weeping.

When the steeds of the Stony thump into view, my heart crashes. They're riding great four-legged beasts that lumber along the icy plains, probing with long, wrinkled snouts, *sighing* and moaning and rolling their eyes back in their heads. They're gleaming black and armoured like beetles at first glance, but at the next their bodies don't seem solid – they tower upwards like columns of oily smoke, and every time they stamp their feet forwards, they pull themselves up again with a *sucking* sound.

'Phantoms!' gasps a voice.

On each phantom's back is strapped a wooden box, and faces peer from seats inside them.

At the narrowest part of the frozen Wildersea, a Chieftain stands atop her phantom's head. A man stands beside her, gripping a black staff. 'Far sight!' he cries, and a light like a beast's eyeshine blooms atop the black staff.

The phantom kneels, and the woman climbs from its back.

'There treads Storm-Bringer,' mutters Axe-Thrower. 'She with a face as stony as the walls of her stronghold.

Devils shudder each time she rises from her bed. *What has he done?'*

Storm-Bringer lifts her helm from her head, revealing a wildness of red hair. Her neck is heavy with blood-crusted jewels and her belly is heavy with bab, but two great scramasaxes – two-foot-long iron swords, inscribed with runes and inlaid with amethysts – swing from her hands, and her steely eyes glitter with warmongering. She holds a scramasax aloft, and it's crusted with a rusty stain – she ent bothered cleaning the old blood from her blade.

'Where prowls the man called Stag?' she bellows.

Stag steps towards her. 'Stony Chieftain!' His bow is so deep that his chin almost scrapes the ice. 'Welcome.'

She steps forwards, claps him on the back, then stares around her at the settlement. 'Our Tribes made laws here, long ago,' she declares, failing to fend off a grin. 'Now, we break them.'

Stag returns her grin.

Her warriors lurk close behind her and beat their shields. The air is danger-scented so sharply that the polar dogs burst into an endless frighted jangle of barking and straining and jumping.

She eyes the dogs, swinging her swords in spirals. When a dog snarls, she snarls right back, into its face.

Behind her, miserable faces peer from the boxes on the backs of the phantoms. There are so many of them, all packed close together and not moving or talking, that I know they must be slaves. Shipping slaves in *plain sight,* and she ent fretting about it a stitch.

If I live to grow up, storms a voice in my head, *I will stop at nothing to protect folks' freedom. Nothing!*

She whistles, and the phantom kneels again, and the young man who stood beside her steps onto the ice, wielding weapons like hers. 'Meet my eldest son – your soon-to-be Chieftain.'

'*What?*' blurts Axe. 'Only a Moonlander can rule here!

The Stony Raider fixes the crowd with glittering black eyes. Even her unborn bab must be fiercing us. 'Axe-Thrower?' She laughs, cruelly. 'You are barely a woman grown! Keep your lips sealed in the presence of your elders. And if I hear that old name again, I will question whether you have need of a tongue.'

Old One turns to look at me. Her weary eyes speak her fright for the loss of her old Tribe-ways.

'Come,' says Stag, extending an arm to Storm-Bringer and her son. 'We have prepared a feast in your honour, Chieftain.'

They leave us and the rest of the slaves chained to the hissing phantoms, loading us aboard one of the wooden boxes along with chests full of walrus tusks – we're as much the cargo as they are. When the phantoms fall asleep they grunt bone-shaking snores through their snouts.

I jolt awake half a hundred times, listening to the laughter echoing from the tent across the ice, as they feast and make merry. Each time, when I check on Sparrow, he answers me with shuddering sobs. But if he can answer me, that means his blood ent frozen, and he's alive.

Old One fidgets and shifts in her seat. Her cloak slips from her shoulder, revealing a jutting curve of dark brown wood. She's hooked my longbow over her shoulder and hidden it under her furs. Awe lights me up inside.

When the merrymaking quietens, and the winds get to howling, Axe treks out onto the ice. She approaches the phantoms warily, eyes searching the boxes on their backs. I wave down at her.

'I can't get you free!' she calls, wincing and glancing over her shoulder. 'She has the keys to your chains!'

My heart sinks. We failed to get the Opal, or find Leo. And now we're being shipped like herring.

'I'm sorry,' calls Axe, between cupped hands. 'But here is one thing I can give you: the *thing* you search for – he will bring it to the city of Nightfall.'

The Opal?

'Axe?' yells a voice, across the ice behind her.

She startles, then starts backing away. 'Safe passage, sea-sister,' she calls, before vanishing from sight.

What's our world come to if I'm heart-sad to see Axe-Thrower leave?

Finally, when pitch darkness smudges to the bleak, grainy grey of the Withering, the Stony Chieftain steps out into the snow. Stag follows, breathing deeply like he's mighty proud of himself.

171

Storm-Bringer yodels a command and the phantom whose box we're chained in unravels its wrinkly snout to the ground. She steps onto it and the beast lifts her high, until she can step off into the wooden box. There's a space at the front and she stands there, staring across the icescape at the other phantoms and pulling a coiled whip from her belt. Her warriors call the same command to their own steeds and then the whole battalion forms up in ranks, ready to move off. When the phantom moves, we slide around on our hard wooden seats, and I notice the splatters of sick on the floor.

Sparrow is on the other side, and I wrestle with the chains, wishing I could reach for his hand. He quakes with the sobs he's forcing down.

I stare hard at Stag, willing him to drop down dead.

As the phantoms begin to shuffle away, gradually gathering pace until we're moving at a brisk march, Stag steps close to the edge of the ice, eyes fixed on my face.

He shakes his head. 'No.' He rushes to the edge of the icy sea, where the eyeshine from the Stony staffs spills a sickly pool of light. Then his face is the size of a pin. Then he vanishes from sight.

18
You with the Fire

Storm-Bringer rides at the front of the box, driver's whip in hand. Behind her, twenty of us slaves are packed tight into the box, in two rows.

Opposite me, in the other row, hunches a girl of about ten birth-moons. Ice sits on each of her eyelashes and a pink birthmark is spread across one of her cheeks. I gift her a small smile but she just stares at me, lost to terrors.

Then we're loping, faster and faster through the ice, the footfalls of the phantoms sending avalanches crashing down from the hills. In the distance, two bird shapes plunge after us. Thaw and Crow. Storm-Bringer swings her weapons in her fingers and laughs raucously into the wind.

Soon enough I wish I could flush all the frighted whimpers out of my ears. My backside turns numb and my bones stiffen with cold and my legs need stretching and my belly is sore, partly from hunger, mostly from fright. But there's no sign the beasts are slowing, and on we race, leagues passing beneath the phantoms' feet.

The other phantoms lope ahead when ours stops for a drink. 'All well, Chieftain?' calls another driver.

'All well,' Storm-Bringer confirms. 'Press on, we will catch you up.'

Sometime later, after we've set off again but not yet caught up with the others, I'm almost too dazed to notice when Storm-Bringer drops her weapons and places her empty hands on her ripe belly.

'Your time is not now,' she says to the mound that is the bab, voice flaying her lips. I glance up and watch as she tips back her head and sighs a white plume of breath to the hiding stars. *'Not now!'*

We press on, Storm-Bringer lashing the phantom with her whip, but soon she's doubled over, clutching the side of the box with fingertips like claws. If Grandma was here she'd be helping the Chieftain's bab into the world safely, slave-trader or no slave-trader. She helped anyone who needed her. I bite my sore lips, racking my brains for Grandma's teachings. How we gonna keep the bab warm out here?

'Breathe,' I tell her, before I can stop myself. 'Keep breathing through it.'

Storm-Bringer flashes me a vengeful look between bab-pains. 'What do you know, boy?' she spits.

I hesitate. 'M— my grandma,' I mumble through frozen lips. *'Midwife.'*

'A gatekeeper grandmother.' She nods, face filled with startling respect. Then the Other realm snatches her away again. When the pain's grip loosens she frees me, and I crouch by her side. I rub the bottom of her back, firmly, like Grandma showed me.

Terror squeezes me. I don't know what to do. Not *really*. I can feel the veil between the worlds thinning as the bab creeps closer. *Most times, nothing is what you do,* says Grandma's voice in my memory. *Until you have to do something.* I try to relax.

Old One twists her whale-tooth pendulum in her fingers. It throws shadows onto the sides of the box. I pray she's coaxing friendly spirits.

'You labour well,' I tell the slaver, trying to encourage her like Grandma would have.

'I have birthed eight times, and I started long before you first squalled,' she seethes.

I stay silent. Then—

'So why won't this one come?' she sobs.

Grandma said most babs come easy enough. But now and then, they need a smidge of help. I summon my heart-strength and check to be sure, dredging Grandma's teaching from my depths. 'That one's stuck,' I tell her, panic rippling through me.

'No,' she breathes. 'I have seen such blood-battles.' Her frighted eyes quest for my face. 'Can you help me?'

I shudder under the weight of the task. But then she's bent forwards again, rocking, wailing, and I can't just sit here in this boat and be a kid. I've got to be a captain.

I steel my nerves, thinking of Thaw and my longbow and Grandma. Then I work.

Once I've helped unstick the bab and it's plopped into my arms, the slaves in the boat break into a gasping chaos of clapping, hooting, foot-stamping and bab-welcomings in what sounds like a mixture of a hundred different tribe-tongues. 'I need something to dry her with!' Between them, the group comes up with a few rags and a scrap of fur cut from the bottom of a cloak.

The Chief weeps freely, relief easing her face, and she stares at the slaves in wonderment.

I dry the bab briskly, praying under my breath until her solemn eyes stare up at me and she sets to testing out her lungs and limbs. 'Thank the gods,' I whisper.

Then I help Storm-Bringer get the bab fixed to her breast and watch as she starts to suckle. I stroke her cool cheek, tuck a fur around her, dry off her sleek dark head with the edge of my cloak. She's just the same as babs born to peaceful folk. She don't know her ma's a warmonger. 'Keep her warm against your skin,' I tell Storm-Bringer, and she nods. She watches me quietly, and her slaves watch us both. The ice crunches under the phantom's heavy feet.

'How did you know, as one so young?'

I swallow. 'Like I said. My grandma. She were midwife to my Tribe. I watched her, and she made me learn after what happened to my ma birthing that one.' I point at Sparrow.

She blinks her great smudged eyes. 'Thank you.' The bab wriggles and mewls. 'You with the fire in your eyes, fire in your cheeks and fire on your tongue. What can I do to repay the debt?'

19
Forest of Nightfall

I gulp a breath. 'I wish a twofold payment – a truth, and a deed.'

She inclines her head, watching her bab from under her lashes. 'Very well.'

'I need to know if you traded a slave by the name of Leopard, Protector of the Mountain – tall and skinny, with brown curly hair and a cloak of feathers.'

'Yes. I remember her. She was brought to our trading post. One of sunken cheeks, and lips that spewed ill-thought-out threats.'

'Where is she now?'

Storm-Bringer blows out her cheeks. 'I would not know. I took her to our fortress and sold her on to a trader from there. The price was poor, as she and her warriors were wounded.'

Sorrow squeezes me so hard that I struggle to open my lungs again.

'This news pains you.' Storm-Bringer gifts me a

bones-deep look. 'For that I am sorry. What is your second request?'

'Free us.'

She groans. Then she sighs. 'Alright, I will free you three.' She looks at me, Sparrow and Old One in turn.

'No. Free *all* of them – from your transport boxes, and from slavery. Then take us to Nightfall.'

If the Opal is bound for the great clanking city of smog, then so are we – and maybe we can find the camp Kes talked of, outside Nightfall.

Storm-Bringer's eyes flash. 'I'd sooner break their skulls – it would be the kinder thing. How will you feed them? Owning slaves is not for the thoughtless.'

I swallow back my disgust. 'I *won't* own them. They will have their rightful freedom.'

'Child,' she says through a laugh, gazing down at the top of her bab's head. 'These people *are* slaves, through and through. That's how they were born and how they will die.'

I shake my head, trying to brush away the heart-sadness clinging to me. 'You're wrong.'

She shakes her head for *no*.

'But I just saved both your lives!'

'Wait, you impatient wriggler!' She chuckles. 'I am not going to Nightfall this time. But I can get you close.' Then she starts to laugh. 'Birthing always turns me into the strongest warrior I've ever been, then softens my heart. Good luck to you. You will *need* it.'

The phantom marches south, down a frozen, wide-throated river. We sight the others in the distance, and by the time we catch up, the river has yawned into a glittering lake. A fog-shrouded city hulks to our right – that must be Nightfall, with the Colleges at its heart where no girls are allowed, but somewhere Kestrel and Egret are weaving secret revolution spells. The creature slows to a stop, and Storm-Bringer unchains us. 'Walk westwards,' says the Chieftain. 'You will come to the Forest, on the edge of the city.'

I only leave the box after Storm-Bringer lets me check her bleeding has settled. Then she waves me off. 'I'll sever the cord with my teeth when the time comes,' she says, flapping her hands. 'Go, before I reclaim my wits.'

The raggedy band of once-were-slaves straggle after me across the ice-glittered, hilly landscape. A frail old man stumbles. His fear-stink tangs my tongue. 'Careful!' I gripe at him, like it's his own fault. He flinches away from me, as though I'm his slaver now, and the horror of it wrings my belly like a rag.

I've got no food for them. No shelter. No weaponry except my longbow, as Crow helpfully reminds me, when he swoops out of the sky beside me, making the others yell and scatter. He only half turns back into a boy. His cloak is a skin of black feathers and his nose is curved and brittle and bony.

'We can't save everyone we meet!' he caws, stumbling as his boots punch out of the ends of his scaly yellow legs.

'Why not? If they need us, we've got to help them!'

'How?' he asks, tense. He flaps his feathered hands in my face. 'Tell me, if you've got all the answers. What are we gonna do with all your strays?'

Fill a deck. Make a crew. I keep my thoughts locked in my head cos I want them to come true so much it's painful.

But one of the former slaves, a kind-faced old man swamped in a patched cloak, has heard us. He steps close. 'With respect, younglings,' he says, 'we must part from you now that our freedom is won. We listened to the bargain you struck with the slaver – you said we do not belong to you. I am Okapi. I was once a leader of my village. I will help these people find their ways home.'

I underestimated them all. I took it for granted they would need more help from me. I acted like they weren't free at all. Humbled, I bow my head and Okapi clasps my hands in his worn ones. 'Your kindness blazes, child,' he tells me. 'Please – do not feel shamed.'

At a crossroads in the path, Okapi leads the freed slaves away from us, and I wave until they're out of sight, a lump swelling in my throat.

'Hang about,' says Crow. 'What's she still doing here?' He points out the girl with the birthmark, who's lingering next to Old One.

Her cheeks flush bright red, blurring the edges of the birthmark. She won't speak until I get close enough for her to whisper in my ear. 'I can show you the way to Nightfall.'

I look down at her, startled. 'How?'

180

'I live there, in the outer city.'

'But I thought no girls could go there?' says Crow.

'That's the heart of the city, where the learning's done,' she replies.

'How did you become a slave?' asks old big-ears-big-mouth Sparrow.

'My Pa sent me away.' She twists her hands together. 'But I know he'll be glad to see me again.'

Sparrow's mouth falls open under the weight of all his questions, but I shut him up with a look and pat the girl's shoulder. 'What's your name?'

'Bluebottle.' She gifts me a wobbly smile. 'But most people just call me Blue.'

My hawk glides ahead, scouting the path. Old One slips so I scoop her fat elbow in my palm. 'I can help a stuck bab but I can't mend a broken leg,' I hiss at her, but all she does is gift me a gummy grin.

We rest. We trudge. Hopelessness tries to cling in our hair. Sparrow cries himself hoarse and then struggles to breathe. I've been carrying him on my back so much that my legs tremble long after I put him down.

We walk until we reach a clot of trees thicker than night.

'The Forest of Nightfall,' says Blue, dropped-pin-quiet. One by one, we crane back our necks and stare up at the dense wall of evergreen.

20
Sneaky Trees

The trees on the edge of the forest are tall and tangled. Their branches are dusted with ice, like sugar. The girl shows us where we can squeeze through a gap between them. The needles scrape against our cloaks.

We step through the outer trees, into deeper forest. Crow carries Sparrow thrown over his shoulder, and with every step my brother's arms flap. The trees smudge out the grainy light. 'Wake Sparrow up,' I whisper. 'We need his light.'

Crow sets him on his feet and he mutters blearily. The only thing I can see is Thaw's pearly eyeshine.

The forest is oddly still.

Sparrow turns to each of us and coughs up a glob of whale-song. We each cup a strand between our palms, holding out our hands to see by the gentle blue light.

Old One grins in delight, stretching her sticky note between her fingers.

'What is this stuff?' asks Bluebottle, scrunching her nose. 'It's pretty,' she adds thoughtfully.

'Whale-song,' I tell her, as my own piece of it utters a low, heart-sad groan. A groan that should be knocking against the hull of a ship, not the lines of my palm.

We stumble forwards, tripping over the tree roots that twine through the mud. The trees seem to lean closer and closer, like they're bending to see Sparrow's whale-song.

We pass ancient tree stumps, felled in the spot where they grew from a tiny seed, hundreds – maybe thousands – of years ago. They've left heart-sad gaps in the forest. We slip in puddles of blood.

'Killing bears and felling trees is forbidden here,' whispers Blue. 'Someone's been breaking the Law of the Forest.'

Our feet crunch ice-crusted mud and leaves.

Soon the trees are crowding and their whispers trace cold fingers up and down my spine. Then I'm tripping over a lump on the ground. A lump of icy, bloodstained fur – a dead bear. Crow pulls me away from it.

Silence crawls over the forest. And the branches of the trees are patterned with whorls that look like eyes. Eyes hooded with wrinkled eyelids, like they belong to dolphins, or whales. A picture of my ship throbs at the back of my brain.

We slip in wet, mushy droppings the size of shields. 'What kind of thing makes droppings like that?' asks Crow, lip curled.

'Scuttle-spiders,' whispers Blue, grinning.

'Spiders?' repeats Crow, face turning grey. He twitches to stare at the trees around us, wrapping his arms around himself.

I can't rein in my mind, and it slip-slides ahead of me, picturing how big a spider's got to be to have dung like that . . . and then I gift myself a shake and stride on. 'Come on,' I tell Crow, pulling him forwards before the horror can rip him in two. 'I'm sick of being frighted all the time! The sooner we get through here, the better.'

I can feel my eyes straining and pulling in the dimness. When Old One strays from the path, I grab her arm and pull her back. I know she's bone-tired. But we have to keep on.

From the corner of my eye I watch strange shapes twist in and out of the trees.

'I think someone's watching us,' says Blue, rootsy brown tangles quivering. She turns to stare into my face.

'I reckon you're right.'

She steps close and links her arm through mine, and though I feel proper hampered walking like that I force myself not to push her away.

Inside my boots, blood squelches, but I can't take off my stockings unless I'm ready to lose a toe.

When we've walked so long and far through the forest that we can't stand any more, we settle down to rest. Old One crafts a tiny fire.

'No,' says Crow, eyes wild, desperate. 'They'll see it.'

'Look at them,' I say, pointing at Bluebottle and Old One and Sparrow. 'They're half frozen. We'll have to risk a fire, just for a bit.'

But once it's lit, no one can face dousing the flames.

I pull off my stocking and stare at my foot – one of my toenails has grown long enough to slice into the skin of the toe next to it. I bend my knee, lift my foot to my mouth and bite my toenails short, spitting the clippings into the pine needles.

'That really is disgusting, even for you,' mutters Crow.

'Ack, clam your pipes, land-lurker.' I press close to him, leaning on his arm.

He moves away, flashing a warning look at me. 'D'you always stick to folk like glue?'

'What? You're warm!' I scuttle closer again.

The fire dies low, and there's nothing else around to keep it going, so we curl tight together, like roots. Sparrow feels too bony. His belly creaks. We whisper the foods of our home.

'What would *you* have?' he asks.

'That's easy. Lobster claws.' I close my eyes and imagine them, fresh from Pip's pot. 'Then steaming hot bread with a side plate of cockles. What would you have?'

'I'd have the biggest plate of grilled monkfish,' he tells me, snuggling closer. 'Greasy battered squid tentacles – ten, all to myself, I ent sharing! – and a bowl of mussels too.'

'How about some butter-tender cod, so soft and fresh it just slips off the bone,' I whisper. 'Birch-smoked, in sauce, or plain—'

'Cinnamon buns!' Sparrow bursts out, too loud, and I shush him. But the taste of fresh-baked buns is already on my lips and I breathe deep, and the diamond-dust glittering in the air is almost sugar, dancing against the black. I remember the clouds of sugar and flour in Pip's kitchens, the pain in my fingers when I stole a bun before it got a chance to cool. How the pain was worth it, and so was burning my mouth.

'You two ain't helping,' grunts Crow. Guilt tightens around me. His eyes have no lids – they're just shiny circles of jet. I remember seeing him stuff dirty snow in his mouth. He's too weak to shape-shift now, and he's too weak to shift back proper. `

'How we ever gonna get back to our ship?' Sparrow whispers.

'I don't know. But we will.' I grab his hand and squeeze his fingers 'til he cries out. 'We will!'

When I wake up in the faint, sickly gloom, I press myself up onto an elbow, blinking in the light of the whale-song Sparrow strung in the lowest branches of the trees. Old One's curled up on her side next to me and for a beat I reckon she's glowing red. I look closer. Then my heart starts to hammer. There *is* red – clotted in her wisps of hair and smeared across her cheeks.

Old One is licked all over with blood.

I search around. Spatters of blood paint the faces of all the others, too. No one stirs.

The forest is silent. My breath's too loud and time's too slow.

'Gods swim close,' I whisper. I touch my face and it's

tight with dried blood. Why is there blood on me when I can't feel a scratch? Is everyone dead? I climb onto all fours and I'm about to crawl to Sparrow when Old One moves.

I yell. The crust of blood on my face snaps. The others wake up too, eyes wide in bloodied faces.

Old One's eyes open, her lashes pulling up strings of blood. Then she screams and I'm covering her mouth, in case whatever did this is still nearby. When I peel my hand away she yelps cos the blood's stuck to her lips and glued our skins together.

'Where's all this flaming blood come from, if we ent hurt?' I whisper.

The others look dazed.

'Are we hurt?' I mouth into Old One's startled face. 'Are we?'

'No,' says Blue, stretching. 'It's the trees.'

I pull a face. '*What*'s the trees?'

Old One shudders. She keeps shuddering, and I realise she's laughing.

'Up,' she gargles, testing out one of her new words, learnt from me. She jerks her head, her stretched earlobes wobbling under the weight of her hooks. I follow her gaze. Blood trickles down the trees' trunks, pooling at the bottom.

I scowl up at the branches. 'What is it?' I ask. 'Why are they bleeding?'

'It's just the sap these trees have,' says Blue. 'They're healing trees. Tree-Tribes use the blood-sap on wounds, because it clots bleeding.'

187

'You might've warned us,' spits Crow through a tight jaw.

I spread my fingers wide, making space for my beast-chatter in the back of my throat. *Thaw?*

Somewhere high above our heads comes a tiny, far-off grunting chatter. She's keeping her distance, and I can hardly blame her.

We lurch to our feet, watching each other from underneath blood-heavy brows. Wordlessly, we tramp on. Our lives become one endless trudge of roots underfoot, tripping us up, and branches overhead, scraping our scalps

Then I feel my spine prickle as I sense something else moving, close by. I squint into the trees surrounding us.

Dark figures are arranging themselves in the shadows.

As they pull free from thick tree trunks, I see them more clearly – tree-blood in their hair and heavy bear-cloaks around their shoulders. Vole used to tell us tales of Tree-Tribes, akin to bears – is that who these folk are?

When one of the figures steps towards us, Sparrow crackles a palmful of purple fire and holds it up.

The figures step back, blending into the trees.

'Hey,' says Crow. 'Hey – we won't hurt you!'

'Come,' drifts a voice from the trees.

Blue scrambles to her feet and hurries after them.

I hesitate, chewing my lip. Then I spew a curse and follow her, the others close behind me. *I'm leading them all into danger if this ent safe. I don't even know if we can trust Blue, let alone these strangers.* There's a rush of feathers as somewhere high above, Thaw tails the pack.

We follow Blue along a path that winds through the trees. The trees begin to whisper to each other. The route soon joins wider paths leading north. The white spires of a city loom ahead, dwarfing the trees.

My boots fill dips made by moons and moons of roving. It makes me feel heart-strong.

Songs spiral back to us, along the path.

Songs about bears. Songs about wolves. Songs for the vanished moon and the sun hidden behind her skirts. Sparrow hums along with them, quiet at first, then louder. Soon, he's full-throat warbling, and a *put-put-putter* of faltering blue notes spangle the air.

Old One squeezes my hand too tight. I gasp and prise her bony fingers off.

We follow the song-notes through a knot of twisted tree branches and suddenly Thaw swoops low out of the sky, brushing over the tops of our heads.

We stumble into a wide clearing. Half a hundred shelters have been crafted to blend with the trees and the earth; their frames are built from branches and leaves, and mud and animal skins have been used to lock the chill out.

A whispering peels away from the trees and rushes around the clearing. Dizziness makes me sway as a chattering crowds close. A chatter that's deep and raw like mine, but with different sounds.

'Mouse?' says Crow, his voice too loud in the silence. 'You alright?'

I step past him, turning around in a circle, listening

hard. Thaw drops out of the sky and I put out my gloved hand for her to land on.

The gloom thins. A woman in a red cloak crosses a blanket of pine needles towards us, a sleek white wolf padding in her wake. The wolf lifts a muzzle dripping with icicles. Curiosity tips full-pelt into her wild bright eyes. They pin me to the spot.

'You followed an ancient song-path,' says the woman. She's tall, with flushed cheeks and a tumble of long white hair. 'Few have succeeded. Welcome to the Glade of Sorrows.'

'Who're you?' I ask.

'My name is Toadflax,' she says. 'And this is Astralia.' she places a hand upon the head of the great white wolf. My breath catches as the beast's eyes rest on my mine.

Toadflax lifts her chin and chatters to the forest. The branches of the trees creak as they lean low, then weave and knot and lace their fingers together behind us, hiding the way out.

'*Green-chatter*,' I breathe, feeling my eyes widen.

'Yes. We work together with the forest. We are part of it.'

A third figure steps into the clearing behind her, face shrouded by her hood. 'Toadflax,' she calls out. 'Who have you found?' The hood shines – it's woven from eagle feathers.

'*Leo?*' I move towards her.

'Mouse!'

21
True Mystiks

The Tree-Tribesfolk help us brush the dried tree-blood from our cloaks and hair. I use my fingernail to scrape it from the grooves in Ma's dragonfly brooch. We learn that Leo escaped from the trader who bought her from Storm-Bringer, and managed to limp into the forest and hide. She recognised the Forest of Nightfall from her maps and hoped to find Kes still camping there.

'Where is she?' I ask.

'In the heart of Nightfall, at the College of Medsin. She and Egret are posing as young men and using false names – Kite and Boar.'

'And what's going on here?' asks Crow, peering around.

'The Tree-Tribes are gathering allies, ready to resist the forces tightening their control over our world.'

'What about the other riders, the ones you took with you?' I ask.

Her mouth tightens. 'Of the three, only one escaped with me. At the time I left, one remained at the Frozen

Wastes; another was borne westwards by the slave-trader. But I will find them.'

We learn about the camp – normally, the Tree-Tribes live amongst the branches, but so many other folk have come to join them that they've made a camp on the ground. It's organised like a village, with tents for storing food and a place to cook it, a tent where healers work and another for a blacksmith. There's a great stinking pit of a privy, too, that they call a latrine. 'I'll be holding it in as long as I can,' I whisper to Sparrow, and he nods, eyes like platters.

While we've been gabbing, tribesfolk have laid furs out over the forest floor and the trees have laced their branches together overhead, keeping out the wind and snow. A fire has been lit, and it crackles in the centre of the clearing. And a feast has appeared.

I press my fingers to my mouth as my eyes gobble the sight of all the pots and bowls. 'Is it – real?'

A woman with a long, curved nose, dark hair and bright blue eyes nods at me. 'It's real. Please, sit with us and eat.' Concern is carved starkly into her face. She asks us for our names, and tells us hers is Hoshi.

We stagger towards the food. Crow snatches up a dark green leaf-parcel and bites it in half. Meat and onions spill out into his lap and he picks up the chunks and crams them into his mouth. He sees me watching and looks away, eyes flashing.

'Why you wearing a mystik cloak?' asks Sparrow rudely, eyeing the red cloth Toadflax is draped in.

She laughs. 'Because I am a mystik.'

I scramble onto hands and knees and fiddle for an arrow.

'Don't panic so, Mouse,' says Leo. 'Toadflax is not like the mystiks you have met before!'

Hoshi nods. 'You may have witnessed mystiks working under forces of evil—'

'Aye,' I break in, confusion plucking threads from my mind. 'Mystiks captured my brother! They possessed Leo . . .' *And made her do proper foulsome things.*

'But true mystiks do not abuse their power,' says Toadflax gently. 'The name "mystik" has been stolen and twisted, misused. Sometimes, a group of people can be defined by the actions of a few. But you and your brother have the look of *true* mystiks. You are kin with the ancients.'

Me *and* my brother? I boggle at their faces until Leo laughs. Sparrow's purple lightning tangles in my mind. Part of me knew he must be something like a mystik, cos the mystiks at Castle Whalesbane had the lightning power, too. But I never would've thought I might be one . . .

'I thought mystiks were just banished scholars from Nightfall,' I say.

Hoshi shakes her head. 'The chief scholars of Nightfall are the Akhunds,' she says. 'They exploit mystiks for their powers – they don't have their own magyk.'

'Mystiks are folk with ancient power, which can manifest in many ways,' Toadflax explains.

My mind whirls, but I'm too hungry to think straight, let alone pipe up any more questions. Hoshi crouches next to me and Sparrow and puts warm bowls of pink porridge into our hands. Soon I'm shovelling spoonfuls into my mouth and swallowing it so fast it scalds my pipes. The grains are chewy and swirled with honey. My belly feels full too quickly.

Next come steaming wooden cups sloshing with hot sweet juice that warms my bones and tingles my gums.

'Cloudberry juice,' Toadflax says, smiling. 'Cures all ills.'

She hands a cup of juice to Bluebottle, then pauses, tracing the marks from her chains with a fingertip. Blue hangs her head, until her brown curls hide her face.

'She was sold as a slave,' I say for her, clenching my fists.

The woman nods grimly, standing and brushing down her skirts. 'Our healers will have a balm to help the skin mend.'

As I'm sipping my juice, I watch the people of the camp stride between their shelters, kindling fires, stirring stews, mending boots and weapons, or talking in a mixture of tribe-tongues. Toadflax points out folk from different Tree-Tribes, and tells us many have travelled from other parts of the forest, or even from other forests.

Many of the folk of the camp are young, and I wonder if they've been gathered together by Kestrel. Toadflax catches me watching and smiles. 'The youth are far better at bonding together regardless of Tribe. Your Kestrel knows that very well.'

Sparrow cocks his head. 'Why *are* there so many people camping here?'

'Some are displaced,' answers Hoshi. 'Others came to

help us when they heard our dire need – we won't give the powers of Nightfall what they want, so they let their scuttle-spiders run through the forest. They forbid us from entering the outer city. They fell ancient trees.'

'What does Nightfall want?' asks Blue.

'Our land, and our bear-kin,' she says, bright eyes ablaze in her brown face. 'But we are not sure why, yet.'

'I've heard Stag speak of making great, soulless armies,' I tell them, and their faces turn graver. 'I saw him use the Land-Opal to wrench a man's soul free from his body, like all he was doing were pulling a tooth.'

Leo clenches her fists. 'We must get it from him before he can do more harm.'

'He's planning to take it to Nightfall,' I add.

'Straight into the corrupt hands of power,' murmurs Toadflax.

Sparrow interrupts the solemn talk – and my praise – by gargling his juice, like Grandma used to make us do with saltwater when our pipes were sore. Hoshi laughs.

We explore the feast again, tasting hot baked roots, rich truffles and spiced bone broth, and heavy little cakes packed with nuts and dried fruit. A boy squeaks mushrooms round a fat-bellied pan. He serves them to us atop flat pieces of bread, with squashed garlic.

As I eat, strength drip, drip, drips into my veins. I lean against Sparrow and listen to the pine needles shivering. I watch, awestruck, as the green-chatterer speaks gently to the trees and mushrooms and winter plants, and their tendrils lean into each other, branches linking fingers, and then move away again. The forest sounds as creaky as my ship.

'We have to stop the Withering,' says Toadflax. 'Leopard has told us how the Legend of the Storm-Opals is true, and how the scattering of the stones has led to this vicious chaos. She also told us how two of the Opals are already safe at Hackles – we may all take great comfort from this.'

I sense Sparrow turn quickly to look at me but I hold still and breathe deep enough to keep the stain of guilt from my cheeks. The Opals weigh heavy in my pocket. But this has always been *my* mission, since before anyone else knew about the scattering. And maybe it's my fate to bring the Opals to the Crown – what if they're safer with me than at Hackles, anyway?

I don't like locking secrets away from Leo. But I've got to prove myself to her, and to Da.

'We've been exchanging letters with the Skybrarian,' continues Hoshi. 'We know that your ancestor, Captain Rattlebones, never hid the Crown away – that was a lie spread to keep the Tribes at war.'

Astraia's muzzle steams a deep growl, and I dig my nails into the soil. 'At Hackles I got a message from the Skybrarian's apprentice, Yapok. He said that some of the ancient sky-scripts have older runes hidden under the ones you can read. Like the truth's been painted over with lies.'

'We learned the same thing, here,' says Leo. 'We should see how he's getting on with revealing these true runes, alongside continuing to try to work out the truth about the Crown.'

'Leo, can we call on the draggle-riders?' I ask. 'My Tribe have pitched up at Hackles, too. I know they'll want to fight. We could rally them here, with Da if he's better.'

'I have already sent a raven to Hackles,' she says with a smile. 'But I will send another, to let your father know that you and your brother are safe.'

I wince, and she laughs. 'You are going to have to face him at some point!'

'I know. I just don't want to do it before I've proven myself to him.'

'What *do* you want, child of salt?' asks Toadflax.

I blink. I feel like I've barely ever been asked what I want. I've just known how things are. I stare at my lap, the food making me almost as slow and stupid as the cold did, before the fire. All I want is sleep, but when I crack my lips apart another answer spills.

'To survive. And for all living things to survive with me.'

Before I can take another breath, Sparrow stirs. 'That's not the real thing what she wants,' he pipes.

Leo chuckles.

My mouth drops open. I reach out and flick his arm. 'Ow!' he croaks. 'Well, it ent. That's just what *everyone* wants, ent it.'

'Oh?' The mystik's face creases into a weary smile. 'And what do *you* think she wants, young man?'

'Aye, go on then. Why don't *you* tell everyone what it is *I* want.' My arms sneak around myself before I tell them to.

Sparrow puffs up at being called a man. 'To be a captain. That's what it's always been, with that stinker.'

Even as the truth of his words touches me, sudden hot anger stabs my bones. '*You* don't know.' I look away from them all.

'It is not a thing of shame,' whispers the chatterer.

'It is!' I whip to face her. 'It's selfish.'

'No. Haven't you learned the truth of it, yet? A captain carries so much of the weight of life for her crew. To lead is to serve.' Before her words have faded, Toadflax grows pale and gasps in pain. Thin black lines pop under the green-chatterer's skin.

When a tree is cut, she feels it, chatters the wolf, padding to the woman's side. *She weakens.*

I swap fretful glances with Leo. 'We've tried the pain medsins I brought with me, as well as Forest remedies,' she says. 'Nothing is working.'

I stand. 'Then there's no time to waste. I have to get into the city, link up with Kes and search for the Opal.'

'Not alone,' says Leo firmly, struggling to her feet.

'Not with you, neither – you're injured still, and you need to be better when the others get here.'

'Another of us, then,' says Hoshi, looking over at Toadflax, who nods.

But I shake my head. 'You said Kestrel's in the College of Medsin. The only way to join her is to pretend to be a book-learner – if I go in there with a strange full-grown, they'll sniff trouble for sure.' I look down at Blue. The sallow-faced girl leans drowsily on Leo's shoulder. She needs to get home. 'But if I go with Blue, she can show me how to reach the inner city. Aye, girl?'

She rubs her eyes, sitting up. Then she grins, dimples creasing her birthmark. 'Course. And Pa can help you get the papers you need for entry into the College.'

'I don't know about this, Mouse.' Leo's face is pained. 'You are too young to be going off into the city, and you're a hunted child, after all, and—'

'We'll have Thaw with us,' I blurt desperately, my insides pulling and squeezing with fright. 'She can stay out of sight, and fly back to warn you if something goes wrong.' *You ent my ma*, whispers a sudden, treacherous voice inside my skull. *And I heart-bright know I ent too young for this. I can do it.*

'See what your hawk says to that, then,' sighs Leo.

I chatter to Thaw and she puffs up her feathers proudly. *ThawprotectThawprotect!*

'She'll do it,' I tell them.

Leo frowns. 'Forgive me, Tribesman Fox, for what may be my greatest folly.'

I'm going! I bite back my grin and sit on my hands to keep from punching the air.

PART 3

The Beasts are Coming

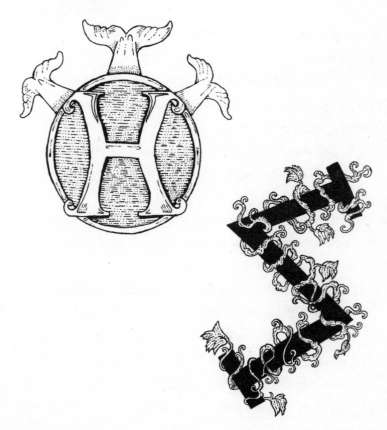

22
Nightfall

Astraia's voice wakes me from a deep, dreamless slumber. *Rise, girl-child.*

I stumble to my feet, yawning in the gloom of the forest. Then I stoop to wake Blue. Her eyes flick open before I can breathe her name.

Toadflax is curled by Astraia, her chin resting atop the white wolf's huge head. But she's awake already, calmly watching us.

Sparrow lies asleep next to Old One, quietly snoring. I feel a pang at the thought of leaving him, but I know this is the safest place for him until I return.

Crow cracks open one eye and peers blearily up at me. 'Really going then, are you?'

'You know I have to.' I kneel next to him. The skin on his face is pulled tight over the bones below, and his forehead is clammy. The feathers on his arms have worried the skin, giving it a sore, scaly look. His eyes are mostly those of a bird and so is his nose. He shivers.

'You ent well!'

'I just needed a sleep, and some grub,' he says, rolling onto his side and sitting up.

'You ent coming with us,' I tell him. 'You got to save your strength.'

He stands up, like he's about to argue with me, but then his face pales and he puts his head in his hands.

I gape at him. He straightens up, then sighs.

'It's just a dizzy spell. But you're right, I'll stay here.'

I sense that's the end of that, so I change tack.

'Can you guard this?' I say, passing him my longbow, and he nods. There's no way I can take Kin-Keeper into the city.

'Ready?' asks Toadflax, climbing to her feet.

I nod, swallowing down the lump in my throat. Thaw bolts from a tree branch to hover above our heads.

'Then travel this track to that other world of dust and smog.' Toadflax green-chatters until me and Blue are cocooned by branches and twigs, forming a pathway towards the city. 'Hunters will not detect you in here, and you will be safe from spiders and bears. Go!'

Branches lace together like fingers. The Glade of Sorrows fades from sight, along with my crew.

We walk through the hollowed pathway, steps muffled by the pine needles. Thaw glides ahead. The air thickens with smog. I can't see an end to the tunnel and we trudge on and one, stopping twice to rest. The third time Blue wants to rest I shush her and point to where the path is blocked by woven branches. 'There – that looks like the end!'

We push through the end of the tunnel and Thaw soars up into the air. Before us sprawls a clanking tangle of a city, with towers and funnels jutting upwards like filthy fingernails, everything shrouded in a festering yellow smog.

There's a slithering, creaking sound – the pathway to the forest has sealed shut. High overhead comes the heart-strong cry of my sea-hawk, so I know she's watching us.

The smog traces wet fingertips across my cheeks. It smells of graves and iron and ear wax. I can feel it painting my skin and clothes with a sticky layer of grease.

We trudge closer, joining a stream of people making for the city, churning icy mud into slippery tracks in their wake. Behind us, great damp trees dangle heavy boughs into the smog, and sometimes when the smog shifts I think I can see eyes among the trees, too. I wonder if the two Nightfalls – the forest and the city – are watching each other.

Soon we reach the outskirts of the city, where the poorest folks dwell. The small shapes of their bodies crawl across white ridges set into the hill rising ahead of us.

When we're closer, the hill towers over our heads.

'Welcome to the Backbone!' bellows a boy with tangled hair down to his waist, swinging from a walkway by his feet, like a monkey, twirling a lit torch in his hands.

The Giant's Backbone turns out to be named for exactly what it is – the huge spine and ribcage of a long-dead giant. It's a place of stinks and grime and shouted words so laced with filth they'd make an oarsman blush. Hovels are stacked ten-high along the ribs. Grot-streaked faces stare down, heckling travellers. They spill slops from buckets down to the ground, splattering whoever's passing.

We walk through a tunnel cut into the hill, feeling the weight of the Backbone pressing down on us.

We emerge outside the city gates, under a sky scabbed over with smog and spider webs. I keep bumping into shadowy figures, cos I can barely see a hand in front of my face. Folk loom suddenly through the smog, yelling at us to get out of their way.

The smudged outline of heavily guarded gates drifts in and out of sight as the smog crawls. A grime-streaked line of folk wait to get into the city. The guards point black-tipped spears down at their chests. Other guards patrol on the ground, sorting folk into different groups and searching them. They nod to some, letting them through the gates. But others are turned back.

The lamplight spills orange pools through the smog, showing frozen white spires at the heart of the great city.

A small group cloaked from head to heel in thick black bear pelts hurries past. 'Scholars,' whispers Blue.

The gates whine open and something huge and black scuttles out, tall as one of the townhouses I glimpsed when the *Huntress* docked at Haggle's Town. It's got long black legs, shiny like they've been ink-dipped. Its breath rasps as it passes by. Then another clacks past, and I strain back my neck and my gut clenches tight and hot as I catch sight of monstrous eyes, electric blue and big as dinner platters.

Scuttle-spiders! On their backs sit riders with whips,

wearing filthy silken hats that rise tall from their heads, like smaller versions of the city funnels. As I stare, one of the hats splutters open at the top, belching out smog.

'What's that?' I ask.

'What?'

'*That!*'

'Oh, that's a smog-filter!' She wrinkles her nose. 'Don't you know anything?'

The line bumps forwards. Soon, any exposed scrap of skin is stuck all over with specks of grot and grit.

Bluebottle presses her hand into mine. 'Get ready,' she tells me. 'I know how to get us inside the city. But we can't let anyone follow us.'

We stay in line until we're next to the wall of one of the towers. Strange, watchful creatures peer down from atop the gateposts, swivelling their bloodshot eyes. I listen into the beast-chatter space, and there's just a tear, a nothing, so I know they're hunched shape-changers, guards of the city in disguise as inky monkeys, vultures, cats, and other shapes that are trickier to make out.

Then a shadow drops over me.

'Watch out!' someone cries. I look up. A spider's eyes are fixed on me. Its breath rasps, too quick. Its inky black legs slither over the cobbles as it scuttles closer to me.

Oooohhhhhhmmmwarmbloodcrackneckgrindbonestopulp!

I'm under the belly of a brown, furred blot that's swallowed the smoggy city from sight. The whole thing twitches to the right and I duck, my fingertips squashing into the slimy cobbles. Then Blue's face appears up ahead, between the two arching pillars of its back legs. She beckons to me and I tear out from underneath it, skin shivering.

Thaw screams, darting through the air, but I send a quick bolt of chatter up to her. *Stay hidden, Thaw! I'm alright!*

But a shudder laps from my belly through my chest and into my mouth, along with a hot spurt of bile. The spider-rider's whip lashes at my feet, splashing filth into my face. 'Get out of it, 'fore I shuck the flesh from your bones!'

Blue pulls me out of the way.

'Get your skin home, Blue,' calls the spider-rider. 'Your pa's gonna spit sticks when he hears you've been out here!'

She takes my hand. We squeeze through a gap in the wall and race down a set of steps into the dark.

'Where are we going?' I pant.

'Shh!' she says. 'I know the spider-paths. Just keep up, don't slip, and don't slow down – don't want them weaving webs around you!'

Soon we're sploshing underground through freezing stone passageways. I keep tight hold of Blue's hand. Things brush past us – things covered in sharp, bristly hairs. I see their eyes, gleaming at me from corners.

We come to a crossroads and wade through muck towards a wide sewer. The stone passageway turns to a wooden one lit by lanterns. Spiders drop one by one out of the ceiling and scurry past. My skin tries to squirm off my bones.

'Here's my house!' calls Blue, voice echoing damply off the wooden boards.

She reaches up into the mouth of the darkness and hauls herself up where the spiders have been dropping from. Then her pale, spindly arm sticks back down and her hand flaps at me. 'Come on!'

I run towards it and jump, letting her help me up through the floor of a house built halfway between the upper world and the underworld of spiders. I straighten my spine inside a warm room painted red. The high ceiling is draped with the ropes of old cobwebs. Buckets are lined up along one wall – half full of dead birds, frogs, millipedes and woodlice. My skin itches.

On a wooden table a single tallow candle crackles in a green lantern, throwing twisted shadows across the walls. An old woman stands at the stove, pounding a lump of dough halfway into the next realm. A hairnet like a web covers her hair, and her chin quivers as she mutters to herself.

A tall man steps into the room, wearing one of those smog-filtering hats and a weary face full of long, deep lines. 'Is it flesh day, or fish day?' he asks the cook.

She twitches towards a bronze cauldron and dips a ladle inside, bringing up a clot of steaming, ragged meat. 'Flesh, master. Definitely something's flesh.'

The man turns his head, and startles so badly he thumps his head on the ceiling. '*Bluebottle?*'

The cook drops the ladle with a clang. Oily droplets splash onto her apron. She whirls to stare at us, floury hand covering her mouth. 'Oh, Missie Blue!'

'Pa!' shouts Blue. 'Nanny!'

'Who is this?' he barks, grey brows clamping together like the city gates.

'Pa, I escaped! Thanks to this gi—'

I hold my hand out to her pa. 'Name's Hog,' I tell him, in my deepest voice.

He clasps my hand and shakes it firmly, before turning back to his daughter. 'Blue, I sent you away because this place is no longer safe for you!' he says in a hushed voice. 'Children have been going missing all semester—'

'Out to fetch a pot of kaffy or the *City Bulletin* and they never come back!' wails Nanny, wringing her hands.

Blue's pa nods gravely. 'I didn't pay passage out of here for you to come running back again!'

Falteringly, between sobs, Blue tells him how the spider she was sent away on got killed by the Stony Chieftain's raiding party, and she was taken by the slaver.

He removes his hat and wiry grey curls spring free. He pulls her close in a hug. 'Oh, Blue!' His mouth twists.

A spider sweeps inside and clacks across the floor, bending its legs to fit under the ceiling. I gasp, shrinking back and squeezing my eyes into narrow slits. Blue's pa strokes it as it passes and the spider rocks on the spot, purring.

'*What* - why's it come in here?' I splutter.

'It's alright,' says Blue. 'He's just a little one.'

'It flaming ent alright - he's huge!'

'He won't hurt you,' she soothes. 'They all know us. Pa's the Spidermaster, he raises them himself, from hatchlings.'

'Each nychthemeron's turn, my beauties come home to

209

my lair,' he says. 'But with this maddening weather, they've been roaming wild. To put it another way, lad, we have lost track of them, and they seem to be growing ravenous. The food is running low, so they have been forced to begin their own, ah . . .' He trails off, searching for his words. 'Hunt.'

Oh. Hell's flaming teeth! I gulp.

'Do not fret. I work all hours trying to round them up.'

'What's a nickthem – whatever you said?'

'Nychthemeron?' He smiles. 'It's the time between each sunrise and the next. But of course, now that the weather's turned so bizarre . . .' He trails off, smile fading.

The sound of chanting seeps into the room. 'Oh, not those ranters and ravers,' says Nanny, looking disgusted. 'There's no use raving about the end of the world, say I. What are we to do about it, even if it *is* coming?' She pushes us into chairs and brings a fresh, steaming loaf of dark brown bread to the table. We cut slices and spread them with butter. She brings us small bowls of brown stew and I dunk my bread into it.

'So,' says the Spidermaster, pulling up a chair next to us. 'What brings you to my lair, young Hog?' He watches me with mild blue eyes.

I take my time swallowing the chewy bread. 'I was shipped as a slave along with your Blue,' I tell him truthfully. 'We escaped and found our way here. I've always wanted to try my luck in the city, at the College of Medsin. Can you tell me about this place?'

'The inner heart of the city is where pupils live and learn

under the guidance of the Akhunds,' he tells me, tearing off a piece of bread. 'They travel to classes on spiderback, so I am responsible for the transport timetable. I know all the paths.' He waggles his fingers and his eyebrows at the same time, grinning. 'Of course, that means I have to maintain them, all year round. When the mud is—'

Blue leans across to me, tumbling brown curls as wild as her pa's grey ones. 'You'll regret asking Pa about the city, especially the transport network,' she whispers. 'He *loves* it.'

'Spidermaster?' I ask.

He stops, looking surprised. 'Yes, lad?'

'How do I get to the College?'

He sits back, wiping his mouth with a rag. 'If you leave through my shop at the front of the house, where the pupils buy Spidertokens, you'll find a Spiderstop right outside. If you catch a number three Spiderbus you'll be taken straight into the inner sanctum – though at peak times, you could be waiting a while for a space, so please leave plenty of time to reach your destination.'

Blue rolls her eyes at me.

'Younglings start off at a general school, studying many subjects. But they specialise at age thirteen. Then, they must choose a college,' says the Spidermaster, messily mopping up his stew with a slice of bread. 'There's Medsin, Philosophy, Runelore and Ancient Lore. But you can't just walk in and enrol, I'm afraid.'

I nod, hooked on every word. 'I know that,' I lie. *Gods. Nightfall is proper controlled!* The grains from the bread are sticking in my teeth, so I reach my fingernail into my mouth to pick them out.

Blue jumps in her seat. 'Almost forgot!' She rummages in a box on the table and passes me a toothpick. 'The flies always stick in your teeth, eh, Pa?'

'Quite right,' he laughs, reaching for his own toothpick. 'What?'

Blue gestures towards the half-eaten loaf. 'That's fly pie.'

I do my best to breathe and still my roiling belly. I stare at the bread – now she's said it, I can see how black the grains are, and how there are shiny bits that look like wings . . .

'The look on your face!' Blue giggles. 'The spiders always catch more flies than they can eat, so we help them out. It'd be a waste not to, especially now food's running short.'

'Heart-thanks for the food,' I tell them, pushing back my chair. 'But I should go into the city, now.'

'Not tonight,' says Nanny firmly. 'You children need to rest, and I won't have you out after the night bell.'

'You will need robes and a bear pelt if you want to enrol as a Medsin pupil,' says the Spidermaster. 'Since you took such care of my daughter, I'll see what I can do. There is a trusted friend I think I would be wise to send you to – Akhund Olm.' He stands, thrusting his hands into his pockets. 'Nanny, I go out searching for my beauties again. See the children get to sleep.' He sweeps a black cloak around his neck and returns the smog-filtering hat to his head. Then he strides away.

By the time I wake up, my bones have thawed out and the deep ache in my muscles has eased. I feel like I've slept for an age. Across the room, Bluebottle still slumbers. There's no sign of Nanny or the Spidermaster, but a pot bubbles on the stove. A bear pelt has been draped over me, and on a chair nearby a scarlet robe is folded. A pair of shiny black boots wait underneath the chair. On top of the robe is a ribbon-tied scroll.

I get up, careful not to disturb Blue, and force down some more of the fly pie from last night. Then I wriggle into the robes and pelt. When I check the pockets, there's a small black book of tickets inside, each showing a picture of a spider. Heart soaring, I unwrap the scroll. A second piece of parchment drops out. I stoop to pick it up, holding onto it while I read the main scroll – I'm relieved to see that it's written in the common rune-script. My eyes drink the runes as I step from the room. Then I grin. The Spidermaster has found papers proclaiming me a new pupil of the College of Medsin. Next, I read the second note.

To reach the house of Akhund Olm, take a number three Spiderbus towards Dagger Lane. Then change for a number five, travelling west towards the house of Land.

'Heart-thanks, Spidermaster,' I whisper, stuffing the scrolls into my pockets. I hurry down a long corridor lined on each side with tall metal cages. Half the doors are hanging open – I remember what was said about the spiders starting their own hunt, and shudder. In the locked cages, a few giant spiders scuttle closer as I pass, platter-eyes gleaming.

The shop at the front of the house is jostling with boys trying to trade for the Spidertokens I heard about. Nanny stands behind the counter, calling for quiet. I slink towards the door, hoping she won't notice me.

'Ma's only gone and forgotten to send me enough silver for the week!' moans a boy. 'How will I get anywhere?'

I squeeze past and step outside, onto the busiest street I've ever seen. Figures lurch out of the smog, faces covered with stained masks that might've been white, once. Filthy streaks of old cobweb veil my face, hanging in the air. I reach up to brush them away and the webs stick to my fingers.

Filthy slush gnaws at my ankles. I tip back my head to stare at the towers that stretch so tall I can't see the top of them, and someone yells at me to mind where I tread.

The Spiderstop is a tall stake pierced through the cobbled street, wrapped thickly in white spider silk. Under the silk, moths, bats, birds and flies have been smothered. An old man sits in a rickety wooden seat atop it, wisps of cobweb caught in his beard, voice creaking. 'Next Spiderbus number three, number three next Spiderbus. Have your tickets ready.'

I step towards it, almost slipping in more of the shield-sized droppings we saw in the forest. I join a gaggle of boys waiting by the stop, hopping from foot to foot and complaining about the cold. One of them picks at the sticky silk on the Spiderstop. 'Snack, anyone?' he asks, poking the belly of a dead bird. I can just make out the shape of its beak under the webbing.

More boys hurry to the Spiderstop, lining up behind me, pushing and shoving. Then a giant spider click-clacks towards us, a man in a smog-belching hat sitting atop its head. 'Whoa,' he cries, and the creature jerks to a halt. The man tethers the spider to the Spiderstop and unrolls a rope ladder from its back. As we start to climb aboard, the spider tucks into one of the birds trapped beneath the silk.

At the top of the ladder, a circle of seats has been strapped to the spider's back. 'Move along, move along, use all available space!' yells the driver.

I hand him my ticket and take a seat. A cord hangs down in the middle of the circle, marked 'STOP'. When the last seat is filled, the driver untethers the spider and lashes it into a lurching scuttle that makes my belly feel hot and tight.

The spider hurtles to the end of the street. Then it shoots out into a busy main road, choked with a press of bodies, clanging bells and crowded stalls brewing vats of smoky black liquid. I grip the edge of my seat and stare down at the street. Everywhere I look, tall, pale spires brush the smoky, blackened sky. The place is full of sweeping stone steps and ornate lanterns and windows made of so many colours that rainbows play in the snow.

I find myself wondering what Da might be doing now, and if he'll ever forgive me for making this forbidden voyage.

A song and the sea are kin, says his rich, gentle voice in my memory. *Changeable kin, like you and your brother. For whenever you meet one or the other, neither is the same as the time before. Songs and seas are never the same twice.*

I smile. Bet he's gonna find us changed again, next time we meet.

A boy leans forwards and grabs the STOP cord, yanking it with two hands. The spider releases a bone-scraping squeal and slithers to a stop. I fall forwards, landing in a heap in the middle of the circle of seats. Boys laugh as they step over me and clamber down the ladder. I scramble back to my seat, cheeks on fire.

'*Kaffykaffykaffy!*' bellows a voice. 'Get yer kaffy!' I lean over the edge of the circle, peering down at a man selling cups of steaming black liquid.

'At *your* prices?' the driver yells. 'That kaffy might as well be molten gold!'

'These are lean times,' fires back the man. 'Stay warm or die, eh? Supplies running low. Get your kaffy while you can and keep yer bones warm!'

'That's nothing but old dishwater. Shame on you!' says a passing woman, cheeks threaded with fine red veins like webs.

The driver chuckles, and we set off again, dashing madly along the streets.

People shove through the crowds, carrying coffins on their shoulders. Others sit by the side of the road, faces empty of hope, like they're never gonna get up again.

'*Gods*,' I whisper under my breath. In Nightfall, death jostles with life for space in the crowded streets. And it looks like death is winning.

'New round here?' asks a boy next to me.

I hunker down in my bear cloak, shrugging. I'm trying to watch for my stop, I don't want him to distract me.

'Dagger Lane!' roars the driver. I propel myself forwards, grabbing the cord and pulling so hard that everyone tumbles out of their seats.

'Watch it, will you?' says the boy who tried to talk to me. The spider's squeal is loud enough to make the driver curse.

I avoid his eyes as he unrolls the ladder and I slither down it, jumping into the street below.

Giant woolly spiders click past, showering me in dirty slush as I stumble through the smog, searching for signs of a Spiderstop for a number five Spiderbus. Bloodshot eyes watch from the tops of walls and lampposts – more crouched shape-changing monkeys. The spiders that ent being driven lurk behind stone, spinnerets whirring, blue eyes flashing. Now and then when I turn my head, I glimpse one shrinking back behind a wall.

Your master's out looking for you! I hiss out of the corner of my mouth.

Ownbusinessminditminditmindit little morsel, it replies, inching a hairy foreleg out of the shadows. I hurry away. Is it the spiders making children go missing?

A puppet master stands on a stone bridge, using tricksy flicks of his fingers to work a tribe of puppets without strings, made in shapes of toothed beasts and brightly feathered birds. My mouth drops open as I watch him control a puppet of a girl my size, with long, snow-soaked

217

yellow hair tied in a red ribbon. Her face is blank and her limbs jerk stiffly, but otherwise I'd have thought she was real.

'Watch it!' a woman yells, when I blunder into her shoulder.

'Can you tell me where to catch a number five Spiderbus?' I ask. But she's already huffed and puffed away from me, disappearing into the murk.

As I cross the bridge, through hanging clots of smog like ghouls, I bang into a post but it's a guttering street-lantern with great yellow icicles hanging from it like rotten teeth. I must have gone too far – I can't even see the place where I got off the first Spiderbus.

Beyond the lantern, the bridge is lined with bent-backed old women wearing headscarves glittering with frost. They mould dumplings in their hands and set them frying by the side of the road. 'Tater dumplings?' they call mournfully.

'Is this the right way for a number five Spiderbus?' I ask one of them.

The dumpling woman shakes her head. 'Nearest stop's way back. Where are you trying to get to?'

'The College of Medsin,' I say.

'Take a left down that side street,' she tells me. 'Go all the way along and then take a right, another left, then a quick right and walk all the way to the end.'

I thank her, cross the bridge and slip into the side street. Then I stare doubtfully at the web of narrow streets spreading out before me, all drifting with thick yellow smog. I stand in the dark, snow stinging my eyes, wishing I could scream.

The backstreets are much quieter, but I'm aware of eyes peering from behind filthy curtains and from doorways.

I'm turning right down another side street when a rogue spider slithers out from a dark alleyway and looms over me, rasping heavily.

Feaaaasty . . . richfeastingsscuttlingcloser . . .

The chatter slips into my bones. I cover my ears, backing away, slipping in the slush. *The Spidermaster will get you, you're not meant to be loose!*

I fall. Roll onto hands and knees. Try to stand. But a sharp point holds me in place. When I look over my shoulder, the spider's hairy leg has pressed between my shoulder blades, pinning me to the ground.

There's a roaring of air as Thaw plunges through the sky.

No, Thaw, it's dangerous!

Suddenly a yell rings out. There's a loud thwacking noise, and the spider shrieks, before releasing the pressure on my back and hobbling away.

'Spidermaster?' I call. 'Was that you?'

Thaw don't land – she must've done as I asked. *Two-legs take more care,* she whistles mournfully, from somewhere high overhead.

I stand, trembling.

But instead of the tall, wiry-haired Spidermaster, a stooped old man walks towards me through the shifting smog.

23
Akhund Olm

The man walks with a staff – a smooth white stick, wide at the top and pointed at the bottom. It's a tooth, I realise. From the gum of some giant beast. A pair of eyeglasses rests on his nose and his pale, pink-rimmed eyes peer through them at me. 'You look lost,' he says, smiling.

'You saved my life!' I gasp.

He smiles gently. 'This city is a dangerous place, now that the spiders are ravening. Tales of missing children cut me to the quick. Would you like to come and get warm?'

I glance up and down the cold, dank street. 'I should really be on my way,' I tell him. 'I'm trying to get to the College of Medsin. Have you heard of someone called Akhund Olm?'

He laughs. 'Child, *I* am the one you seek. My dear friend the Spidermaster asked me to expect you. When you did not arrive on the number five, I came out to find you myself. We can go to the College together. Though even *I* still get lost, sometimes!'

My blood kicks. Finally I might have enough heart-luck to find Kestrel and Egret, and even the final Opal.

We walk through the narrow streets, the Akhund's staff tapping sharply against the cobbles. He buys two cups of kaffy at a roadside stall, and we take them with us to the Spiderstop, where another old man cries the numbers. 'Next Spiderbus number five, number five is the next Spiderbus!'

When the spider shrieks to a halt, we climb aboard and careen around breakneck bends. I've only got one hand free to hold on with, cos of the kaffy. The bitter, dark liquid sloshes in the cup and some spills from the lid on the top.

We pass a smog-blackened house, tall and leaning to one side. I crane back my neck to read what's written above the gate. '*Poorhouse*. What's a poorhouse?'

'It's a place for the poor to live, when they can't afford to pay their way,' he says. 'The poor I visit tell me they shall stay out of there no matter what! But sometimes they are forced to break that vow, when there is no choice left.'

'No choice left? Why don't they have Tribes, or families? Imagine having no way to be free!'

The Akhund blows on his kaffy, nodding sadly. 'I cannot imagine it, for I am too privileged.' The spider lurches, and he puts out a hand to stop himself falling. 'The Spidermaster tells me you're to be enrolled in the College – I must say, I am so glad you're going to be joining us, young Hog! The journey to reach our great city is perilous in these strange times, so you have already shown the strength of character needed in a future Nightfall Scholar.'

Relief punches through me. The Spidermaster ent breathed a word to the Akhund about my false papers – he's just told him I'm enrolled as a pupil.

'Heart-thanks! What's the College of Medsin like?' I ask.

'Oh!' he gasps, looking up at me. The kaffy has fogged his eyeglasses. 'It is most wonderful. You will have the best years of your life at the College, Hog. It's a big, busy place, and you've just missed the start of the Wakening's Dawn Semester, but you'll soon settle in, and learn to find your way around. I shall supply you with a map before we part.'

Gloriousness! 'I need to find some friends of mine there.'

'Who is it that you're looking for?' asks the Akhund,

'My friends, Kite and Boar. Do you know them? Kite's got coppery hair, and he's tall, with light brown skin and green eyes. Boar's got black hair, and he's shorter, and tattooed.'

'Tattooed . . .'

'On the face.'

'Ah, on the face.' He scrunches up his cheeks. 'Hm, it rings no bells, I'm afraid. But I will enquire around the college,' he vows. 'I could obtain a list of the latest scholars to enrol.'

'Aye, heart-thanks, Akhund Olm!' I feel my muscles beginning to relax for the first time in an age.

'A simple "Olm" will do, youngling.'

At the end of a bridge the spider passes a gateway on the left, and gets lashed to a stop by its smog-hatted rider. 'College of Medsin!'

When we climb down the ladder, my head's spinning from the ride.

Bear-pelted pupils head through an archway, clutching bags and armloads of books. They climb a sweep of red-brick steps towards the wide doors of a grand house.

Olm rummages inside his cloak pocket, brow furrowed. 'Ah! Here we are.' He presses two crumpled pieces of parchment into my hands and takes my cold, half empty cup of kaffy from me. 'One of these is a map of the College. The other is a Spiderbus timetable. On the back is my address – if you have need of me, you will find me there.'

I startle to see that the Spiderbus timetable is enchanted – black dots are crawling along the lanes etched into a map.

'That one's in real time,' he says proudly, grinning like a kid. 'Isn't it wonderful?'

I nod, grinning back at him. His excitement catches onto me like a flame.

'When you reach the College building,' says Olm, 'you'll need to check in at the desk and then find your way to the Junior Common Hall. Your fellow scholars can show you around once you're there. Do remember to enjoy yourself!'

24
The College of Medsin

I stand, blinking, inside a vast entrance hall with polished, wood-panelled walls. Candles sit inside huge round circles hung from the ceiling, sputtering the news of their fat.

Pupils hurry past, laughing and squabbling, steps echoing on the shiny floors. One drops a book with a loud *smack*.

I approach a stooped old man who's sitting behind a desk so tall that at first all I can see of him is the top of his head and a pair of half-moon eyeglasses. I hand over my papers. He nods, barely checking them. I stuff the papers in my pocket and head down the passageway, following the footsteps of the scholars.

The heads of beasts are mounted on the walls and they stare down at me through dead, misted eyes. I whisper heart-sadnesses to them. *May your gods roam close to you.*

At the end of the passageway I step through a door marked *Medsin Junior Common Hall*. Inside, everything is red velvet and wood panelling again. Bear-cloaked scholars sprawl into plush chairs, pulling off their smog masks.

The room is shrunk by a huge hearth and a long oak table scattered with books. Bookshelves stand around the walls. On either side of the hearth is a human skeleton, wearing a gown. The hands have been twisted into unnatural poses.

'Any of you seen a tall boy with red hair and green eyes round here? His name's Kite.'

A boy wearing smudged eyeglasses picks his teeth with a gold pick and then turns it round to pick his ears. He nudges his friend, a boy with his elbows propped on the table, reading a thick book. He slips, hitting his head on the book, and then whirls to glare at the first boy. 'I'm studying! D'you realise how hard it is to memorise all these potions?'

I step closer. 'Well, have you?'

'Listen to the rough way he speaks!' scorns toothpick-boy.

'*You* stink from the mouth,' I hiss at him. 'But you don't catch me harping on about it.'

Someone laughs, shocked. I regret my words straight away, but the boy blinks, turning the toothpick in his fingers. Then his pockmarked face ruptures into a grin. 'Respect! Are you one of the new intake?'

'Aye.' I gulp a breath. 'Fresh into the city.'

'Don't be minding any of these hooligans,' he says. 'But I've not met any red-haired boys this semester, I'm afraid.'

'What about a boy called Boar? Black hair, tattoos?'

He shakes his head.

My belly twists. Maybe Kes and Egret are staying out of

sight – I'll just have to search. 'Can you show me where I'll be sleeping?'

'I can show you around, sure. Semester's already started, so there's only one room left,' he says. 'Hope you like it!'

We step out of the Common Hall and across the hall into another passageway. He opens the door of a simple room with a polished floor and a soft bed with rich, clean linen and furs – the sort that would fetch high prices at market. Unbidden, my trader's fingers check the weight of the cloth.

'I'll let you settle in,' says the boy.

I look around the room, trying to calm my heart. There's nothing here, so I press my ear to the door, listening in case the boy's still lurking. But when I poke my head outside, the corridor's empty. He must've returned to the common hall. I sneak out of the room and try the door of the room opposite. It's unlocked, and empty. I slip through the door and search the room, but there's no sign of Kes or Egret.

I search three more rooms, my heart sinking lower. But when I check the last room, my boot bumps a squishy lump stuffed under the bed.

It's Kestrel's battered old medsin bag – the one she kept her tools in when she stitched the wound on my face. I kneel by the bag, pop the fastenings open and a small, round, feathered bundle flaps into my face – a squidge!

NonononononohelphelphelpnonoflyatyouEttlerwilltearyouhe willgetawayget–

Ettler! I whisper, catching Kestrel's squidge-assistant in my palms. *Will you calm your flaming sails? It's me, Mouse!*

Ettler's tentacles shiver. The little feathered squid-beast stares up at me with frighted black eyes.

Ettler? What's going on?

Ohhhhhdeardeardearnonono!

What?

Badverybadvery, noberries, badVERY!

Tell me. I gently stroke his tentacles until the shivering stops.

Girlslockeddeephallfaraway! Don'tknowEttlerwhenEttlerfind! Gonefaraway. He chokes out a little sob and wets my palm with ink.

Girls locked away, gone far away. *You mean Kestrel and Egret?* I husk.

Verybadawaylocked,KestrelKestrelKestrel!Snipingbitingflap pingbirdtoo!

Ettler, what can I do? Where can I find them?

Mantookmantook, he grumbles, in so much fright and heart-sadness that my chest feels carved in two. *ManNASTYmandeadeyes—*

Footsteps clatter along in the passageway outside, and boys' voices grow louder and closer.

Ettler, get in here! I hiss, opening one of my pockets. The squidge don't need telling twice – he thumps into the pocket like an arrow into a target. Swiftly, I kick the medsin bag back under the bed and hide behind the door. *Please walk past, please . . .*

But the door swings open, whacking me in the side. As

227

someone grabs the edge of the door to close it, I barrel out of my hiding place, straight into the boy with the toothpick.

'Hey! This isn't your room, I showed you—'

His words are shoved from his mouth as I barge past him and run breakneck down the corridor, back through the Common Hall and out of the College. Ettler bumps up and down in my pocket, squealing. I pull the Spiderbus timetable out of my pocket and run towards the closest black dot on the map. I don't stop running until I'm wedged into a seat aboard a Spiderbus, with folk peering at me strangely as I fight to catch my breath. On the ride, I stare down at the grey streets, wondering if I can risk asking Olm for help with the Opals. He's a friend of the Spidermaster and Bluebottle, he took me to the College, and he feels heart-sad for the folk in the poorhouse . . . and he saved me from that spider.

Once we've crossed the bridge, I ask someone how to get to the address scribbled on the back of the timetable and then catch another Spiderbus to Olm's house.

I stare up at a tower so high that the top is hidden by smog. At the top of a set of stone steps is a door in the middle of the tower. On the wall next to the door are bells marked with different names. When I press the one labelled Olm, the door clicks open and I step into a circular corridor cut into the stone like a worm-tunnel. The walls are a dark, gleaming wood.

Olm shows me into his set of rooms. 'Do make yourself at home!'

In the sitting room, a lamp stands on an old wooden table – inside the lamp, pink and green fire spirits flit and twist. The light spills across stacks of books, piles of blankets and a heap of stockings for mending. I pull my cloak off cos the room is proper toasty.

Olm busies himself with setting a small iron kettle over a flame. 'That's a nasty scar,' he comments. 'How did you get it?'

Hot panic *clangs* inside me. I forgot to keep my face covered! Though how can I, all the flaming time? 'A – kitchen accident.'

He nods. 'I am gladdened to see it healing nicely!' The fire-spirit lantern makes Olm's face glow with green light. 'How did you get on with your search for your friends?'

I shake my head. 'Not well,' I tell him. 'I'm frighted something's wrong.'

'Ah, not to worry! Many of the scholars would have been in class. There will be plenty of time to meet up with them.' He steps into a back room and reappears with a loaf of bread wrapped in wax paper and a lump of butter on a dish. 'I haven't much exciting fare to offer you, I'm afraid,' he says, carefully slicing and buttering thick slices of bread. 'In leaner times, we fall back on some of our favourite alternatives – grubs and bugs, ticks and lice, worms and slugs. We can make highly nutritious loaves from them.'

I watch him preparing the food, trying to put my fretting aside. 'That's the kind of thing my Tribe eats when times are tough. Bugs, and terrodyl meat – though it's tough as anything. I tried fly pie at the Spidermaster's house!'

The scholar laughs, eyes crinkling at the corners. 'Yes, that is a very particular *delicacy* of his.' He reaches into a cupboard for platters and turns away to stack the bread on them.

Inside my pocket, Ettler stays quiet. But I can feel him shivering, and my fright for Kes and Egret tumbles anew inside my belly. I put my hand in my pocket to lift him out but he bites my finger, making me gasp.

'I heard there's been trouble here,' I say, watching Olm's back for signs of wariness. 'They say a man called Stag controls this place now.'

'Stag?' he says, turning towards me in surprise. 'Not to worry, dear – he's not as powerful as he'd like to think.' He smiles brightly and passes me a platter with four thick slices of bread on.

'Heart-thanks,' I mutter, biting my cheeks. *Reckon I'll have to do the worrying for the both of us.*

'So, young Hog. Did the scholars show you where you'll be sleeping?'

I nod.

'That's good. I will keep my promise to find the names of those enrolled, so we may track your friends. Now,' he wheezes, taking a chair at the table in the middle of the room. 'How else may I help you?'

I take my time working out how much to say. I want to tell him about the Opals, proper bad, and part of me wonders if an Akhund like him might know about them anyway. 'Maybe you could write to let the Spidermaster and Blue know I'm with you?'

'Already done.'

'And – could I send another letter, outside Nightfall?'

He nods. 'I can lend you the ink and parchment. As for your letter, however, I cannot be certain it won't fall into the wrong hands.'

I nod. Then I realise – if I send it with Thaw, it can't go astray. 'I'll be careful.'

When he brings me the ink and parchment, I scratch a quick note to Leo, telling her I've found Ettler, but not what he chattered to me – I've barely made sense of it myself, yet, and I don't want her sending anyone after me in case we get discovered.

'Would you like me to send your letter on for you?' Olm asks.

I shake my head. 'I want to write a bit more,' I tell him, feeling guilty for lying.

He smiles. 'Just let me know when you are ready. And good luck at College tomorrow! Now I must put myself to bed. Help yourself to warm milk – there's a pan on the stove.' He creaks to his feet and takes the platters to the wash basin. The sight of his frailness and the thought of everything he's done to help me makes me realise I trust him enough to ask for more help.

As soon as I start talking about the Opals, it's a proper relief. 'There's something else, Akhund. A man is bringing an ancient jewel into the city. I need to get it from him.'

The old man slides pink-rimmed eyes over my face. 'I see! What sort of jewel is it?'

I take a deep breath, the risk I'm taking pounding against my skull. 'It's a Storm-Opal.'

He sits up straighter. 'From the legend?'

'Aye.'

'Goodness me!' He clears his throat, eyes shining with excitement. 'The last King of Trianukka had a golden crown, in which three powerful Storm-Opals were due to be set, uniting the Great Tribes of Sea, Sky and Land together in peace. But the Sea-Tribe captain, Rattlebones, hid the Crown in the belly of a whale . . .'

'Aye,' I say, smiling at how much energy he's giving the telling. 'But stories grow twisted over time . . .'

'What makes you say that?'

'Well, it's just – how do we know what bits of a story are truth, and what bits are lies?' I chew my cheek. 'What if Rattlebones never took the Crown?'

'What an extraordinary thing for so young a person to say!' he exclaims. 'I have a feeling you have the makings of a very fine thinker. Food for thought indeed,' he says.

'I heard that Stag is planning to bring the stone here. I need to find out where he'll take it.'

'Ah, what a web, what a web!' Olm declares. 'Alright, child. Let us see. Do you know which of the three Opals he is bringing here?'

I nod. 'He's got the Land-Opal.'

'And what is known of the others?' he muses.

I hesitate.

Olm's eyes dart around the room as his mind flickers. 'I am deeply surprised the Land-Opal is not heavily guarded, as the others must be. Otherwise anything could happen to them!'

I feel a burst of pride flush my veins. I'm keeping them safe, with no guarding at all! 'Well, the thing is . . .' I pull the Opals from my pocket and let the lamplight make them glimmer. Gold flecks shift under the green of the Sea-Opal, while sleek black shadows dance under the Sky-Opal's skin. Both jewels warm under my touch, and their crackle-power makes my eyebrows tingle. 'I found these two, and kept them safe.'

Startlement slackens Olm's mouth. 'Hog, you ought to feel most proud! What a thing to achieve, before you even begin your Nightfall training. May I?' he asks, holding out his hands, fingers laced together.

I nod, tipping the gems into his palms. He examines the Opals gently, lips forming silent exclamations. Then he looks to the window and sighs, before passing the Opals back to me. 'Might I suggest you leave these remarkable stones here, whilst you embark on your studies?'

I smile. 'Heart-thanks, Olm, but no – they stay with me.'

He nods, then rubs his neck. 'I am so sorry to spoil the fun of this conversation – it is the most interesting I have had in a long time! – but the hour grows almost as old as my bones.' When I follow his gaze to the window, I see that the street-lanterns have been doused. 'I shall have to put myself to bed, dear boy.' He takes my cloak and hangs it up in a cupboard, then starts to hobble away, staff tip-tapping. 'I suggest you do the same and resume your search in the morning.'

A yawn pulls at my throat. 'Can we talk about it again before I leave?'

'Certainly. He takes my cloak for me and hangs it up in a cupboard. 'Goodnight, Hog. Sleep soundly.'

I tuck myself into one of the fold-down beds and listen as the Akhund's tooth-staff taps away towards his bedchamber. Then I remember the letter I started and topple out of bed again, grabbing it from the table. I go to a window and open it. Thaw sits on a nearby chimney. *Thaw girl*, I chatter. *Can you take this to the Forest, to Leo?*

Thaw not leave two-legs girl, she utters fretfully. *Mountain two-legs say Thaw stay with—*

I know, Thaw! But this is the only way for my letter to reach her safely, and you'll be back in no time!

Her feathers tremble. But she flashes me a look of heart-strength, takes the letter in her beak and flaps towards the forest, quickly becoming a distant speck in the sullen sky.

When I turn back to face the room, Olm is standing by the stove, pouring a cup of milk. I startle halfway out of my skin.

'Sorry, child,' he says, flinching like he's proper vexed with himself, and leaning against the wall for support cos he doesn't have his staff. 'I didn't want to disturb you.'

Pity lurches in my chest. 'Here – let me help you.'

But he waves me away. 'No need, no need. Goodnight!'

It's only as I'm drifting to sleep that I remember Ettler is still in my cloak pocket. But I'm heart-certain he won't mind spending the night there, so I let myself fall asleep.

When I wake up, Olm is busy mending my boots. I feel a pang of guilt as I watch him hunching over them, scraping and stitching and polishing. He's so old and his hands are shaky. 'Good news,' he tells me cheerily.

I swing my legs out of bed. 'What is it?'

'I have received word of your friends!'

I stare at him. 'For real and true?'

He laughs. 'For real and true.'

'Let's go!'

'Breakfast first, child. And no rushing, if you please.'

I eat some bread and drink some kaffy, trying not to kick the table leg in all my itching to get going.

'Did you want me to send that letter for you?' he asks.

'Oh, no, I—' I pause, thinking.

His eyebrows shoot upwards. 'Yes?'

'I don't need to send it now.'

'Ah.' Olm pulls on a thick cloak and taps towards the door with his tooth-staff. 'Well, anything you need, let me know. Come on, dear,' he says, hobbling from the room.

I pull on my cloak and follow him outside.

25
Webs and Smog

'I sent a parchment to the other Akhunds,' Olm says, 'and I am told that your friends have been seen entering the Hall of Moans, to sit their examinations. Follow me. I'm sure they will be delighted to see you again, and then your mind can rest.'

I follow him through twisting, tangled, smog-choked streets, heart soaring, until we reach a grand old building behind wrought-iron gates.

We push open the heavy wooden doors and stand in the entrance hall. 'Where now?' I ask, bursting to find Kes and Egret.

'Just behind you is a classroom,' he tells me.

I turn, press the handle, push open the door, and . . . they're not here. There's just a dusty, empty room set up with rows of tables. I back away, legs trembling and a lump in my throat. 'What – where are they?'

'Oh, are they not in there?' asks Olm, coming and standing beside me. He places a soft hand on my shoulder.

'Oh dear. Do you think perhaps they climbed out of the window and ran away?'

I shake my head. 'There's no window.'

'Isn't there?' He cranes his pale neck and looks around the room like he's seeing it for the first time.

'*You're* the Akhund!' A spark of anger leaps into my voice. 'You're the one that's meant to know this place!' My voice dies. Shame nips me. How could I snap at this kindly old man?

He blinks calmly at me. 'Well, of course I am the Akhund, child.' He stares around the room again, breathing slowly through his turned-up nose. 'Of course I am.'

I turn to look around the classroom, trying to make sense of why he's brought me here. But then a man with greasy ropes of hair and greed-glittered eyes steps through the door and my words fade to a bitter taste in my mouth.

The man is Weasel – the ship-wrecker that helped Stag smuggle Sparrow to Castle Whalesbane.

What's *he* doing here? Is he leeching off this poor old man? 'Sunk your claws into someone else now, have you?' I bite out. 'The weaker the better, aye?'

Weasel glances at me, startled. Then his surprise melts into amusement that tugs his mouth and brows on end, pulling them upwards like the puppet masters with their strings. He clutches his sides, shoulders heaving with merriment.

'Weasel,' says Olm mildly. 'Control yourself.'

There's a sternness in the voice I ent heard before, and I

237

turn towards the old man in surprise.

'Where are—'

'Your friends?' he interrupts softly. 'Naughty girls, aren't they?'

An alarm bell jangles in my belly. 'What? No, I don't know any girls, they're – boys, they're . . .'

Olm lets out a little bubbling laugh and wipes his mouth. 'Like you are, I suppose?' His eyes narrow.

I shake my head. 'No.' My mouth turns dry. In a flash I realise what I've done. I've brought the Opals here. I told Olm about them, and all cos of my own stupid pride! My mistakes stab tears into my eyes.

'Oh *dear*,' whispers Olm.

'If I were you, Mouse,' says Weasel, 'I'd stop twisting on that hook you've caught yourself on.'

'She said her name was Hog,' says Olm gently, with a trace of his old kindness. He laughs. 'I'd say, that makes her a filthy liar.'

My skin prickles.

Then Weasel grabs me, turning me to face Olm. I wriggle, kick, lash out, try to bite – but the wrecker holds me in place with an iron grip. Olm's face is filled with hate, like his kindly look was a mask. 'The Skadowan dislike those who meddle in our business. And as their chief agent, I consider it *my* business to put a stop to you.'

I scream, fighting against Weasel's grip.

'You only have yourself to blame, you know.' Olm cocks his head at me. 'You chose to use that disgusting chatter

of yours to send that bird away with a letter, did you not?'
A smile plucks at his rubbery lips. 'Now no one knows
where you are!'

'No!' I scream 'til I'm hoarse and my throat feels
torn.

'You will exhaust yourself, child.' Olm smiles
blandly.

Weasel wears a grin like a knife-slash. He points
at the floor and a gleaming black puddle gloops
open there. I gape at him – the wrecker's got
magyk? Olm claps his hands gleefully.

The puddle makes a skin-tuggingly
gruesome *panting* sound. Panting, grunting,
huffing and whispering. It spreads, slowly,
gasping as it reaches for my ankles.

I thrash desperately, but Weasel's
arms never loosen. 'What you done
with my friends?'

'Do shut your silly mouth,
won't you?' Olm says sweetly.
Then the black puddle quests,
snuffles, leaches towards me.
I'm sucked in, then I tip
straight down its throat.

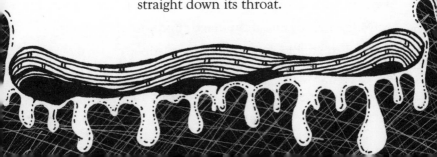

26
Beckoning the Spirits Out

I put out my arms to stop myself but it's no use – I'm falling down a slimy black tunnel through the floor. My sides are squeezed tight. I'm pulled down, down, down, and when I scrabble at the walls, the puddle suckers tighter onto me, pulling harder.

I fall out through the end of the tunnel and land on a hard, polished floor. I lift my head, gasping for breath as slime streams from my eyes and mouth in great wet clots. I've been dropped into a classroom – my pulse gallops. It's the same one I was just in, 'cept now, boys are hunched over every table, scratching quickly at rolls of parchment. '*What?*' I gasp.

Weasel thuds out of the black puddle on the ceiling and lands next to me, panting. 'Curse this place!' he mutters, grabbing hold of my arm.

Slime keeps catching in my throat and I bend double,

holding my stomach as I cough and retch. When I look up, there's a black stain on the ceiling, fading with every punch of my heart. I try to call out to the nearest boy, but the slime catches in my throat. Weasel tugs my arm. 'Quiet!'

I kick his shin and reach towards the boy, and pull on his arm. But the boy don't even look up. I try shouting to the others. When they don't react, I dodge Weasel, dancing around in front of the desks. But . . .

None of them can see me.

Then Weasel grabs my arm, pulls it painfully behind my back, hauls me to my feet and drags me out of the room.

I startle, heart thumping into my throat – something bellowed, underneath the earth, sending a buzzing up through the soles of my feet. 'What was that?' I ask, trying to twist to look at the wrecker.

'Keep it shut!' he barks.

Ettler whimpers inside my pocket.

Every time we take another step, the noise comes again.

It's like the same place, but different . . . like another Nightfall. I glance down at the slime on my cloak, to gift myself proof that I really was sucked through the floor.

Weasel pulls me through another door, into a passageway with shelves all over the walls. Glass bottles have been arranged on the shelves, all of them different shapes, lengths, sizes and colours. They're held in place between carvings of animals, or children. Now and then one of the bottles quivers.

A few paces away, a door squeals open. Weasel stops, but

he keeps his hand on my arm. Ettler is so frighted that my pocket is sagging under the weight of his ink, and drops of it plop through onto the floor.

A boy steps out of the doorway and starts walking slowly towards us. His limbs move stiffly and his eyes are blank, unblinking. I stare. Horror scratches and squirms through my marrow.

'Get back, ghoul!' whispers Weasel, hoarsely. It's almost like – he's *frighted* of him.

The boy reaches up to one of the shelves and takes a bottle neck between his fingers. Then he shakes it, puts it back, reaches for another bottle. The air crawls with dread.

'What are you looking for?' I ask.

The boy keeps on searching, arms moving stiffly. His face is set with determination.

'I – can't remember,' he replies, frowning, voice dull and flat. He keeps sorting through the bottles.

I try to back away, but Weasel keeps hold of my arm and my skin twists painfully in his grip. 'What—'

Weasel curses and mutters under his breath, dragging me along the passageway until we're level with the boy. Then, with a shudder, Weasel grabs the boy's arm in his other hand and pulls him along with us, through a set of double doors.

We're inside a great hall, three times the size of the long-hall at Hackles.

And at the other end, an army stands frozen.

There must be a hundred bears, standing on their hind

legs, faces fixed in twisted fury.

A hundred human children, faces glazed, mouths hanging open.

Weasel marches the boy towards them and shoves him into line. He clicks his fingers and the boy's face shuts down. The boy is lost in a sea of blank gazes.

'Welcome to the Hall of Moans!' Akhund Olm stands in the middle of the room, grinning. 'The heart of the New Order of the mighty Skadowan.'

My voice is krill-small. My heart stutters. 'What is this place?'

Olm looks at me, grin dying. 'I will show you.' The way the word *will* creeps from his mouth makes me shiver. There's too much force pressing on it.

Hands grab me. I'm bundled into a chair and leather straps are tightened over my wrists.

And hunters lead three chained brown bears into the room.

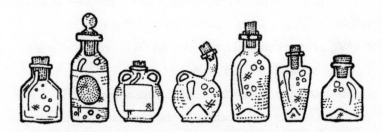

27
Rough as a Clam

Underneath Nightfall's City, its rotten heart beats. Being in a human dwelling with beasts fills me with horror. The bears are too wild-glorious to be here. Respect is their birth-right. Their frighted snorts of breath fill the room and their chatter clamours with *cubssleepwarm thmeatwherehomewhereforest?* The chatter swells inside my skull.

Olm's pale eyes rest on my face. He draws a glowing amber jewel from his pocket and grips it between thumb and forefinger. Then he steps closer, leans down and slips a hand into my cloak pocket. Ettler squeals proper loud and zooms out, bashing into Olm's chest and pinging off across the room. *Fly away, Ettler! Quick! Go to the forest, find Leo!*

The squidge sobs, flapping away, oozing ink when Weasel tries to grab him. He slips under a gap in the door.

'Where are they?' whispers Olm.

I glare up at him, and when he searches my other pockets I squirm, yell, try to bite, but before I can blink Olm's sneaked the Sea and Sky-Opals out of my tunic pocket. He wipes the squidge-ink off them, tongue stuck out between his lips, eyes burning in the Opals' light. He cradles the jewels in his palms. All three.

I should've told Leo I had them. I should've left them in the forest. What have I done?

When Olm finally rips his gaze from the Opals, the look he gives me oozes so much greedy glee that I shrink away, a whimper leaking from my lips. My feet scrabble uselessly against the floor and my nails dig into the arm rests. The salt of my snot tells my tongue what I've done.

Seek the scattered Storm-Opals of Sea, Sky and Land, before an enemy finds them and uses them to wield dark power.

One bear snaps her pain and fright into the iron muzzle clamped around her jaws. Another moans, brown eyes rolling back. The third snorts and paws the ground.

Olm clicks the bones in his neck. 'Hold them down.'

'No!' I scream.

The hunters tighten the chains on the bears, pulling until their spines are flattened to the floor.

'Mystik!' calls Olm.

A hunched figure in a red cloak pushes through the doors and hurries to Olm's side. Olm presses the Opals into the mystik's palm, and the mystik extends a forefinger, crooking it into a slow beckon. Whispering claws my ears.

'You don't have to do his bidding!' I shout at the mystik.

The bears growl, their fur jagging into spikes wrench against the chains, paws slipping on the polished floor. A smell weaves into the room, crackle-hot, decaying.

The noise of their fright is too painful. My beast-chatter rips out of my throat. I can't keep it hidden. *Fight it!* I scream to them. *Fight the pull! Lock into your bones and never let go!*

But three tendrils of light snake from the Opals and along the floor towards the trapped beasts. And out through the beasts' eyes drift soft black shadows, tall and pointed like pine trees, stealthy as the finest hunters. The shadows twine and tumble like cubs in spring, before slurping into Olm's finger. He drips the shadows into the end of a black tube, shaking his finger to get every last scrap and drop. The shadows roll along the tube and into a glass bowl. When they drip inside, they turn into a dark purple liquid.

'Fire,' says Olm.

One of the hunters lights a flame underneath the bowl and the liquid begins to steam. Soon it writhes, bubbles and jumps.

A howling wind rattles through the pipe. There's a trickling sound as a bright silver liquid is drawn off the purple, beads of it tapping against the glass.

The quietness makes me sick to my bones. The stealing of a soul should never be quiet.

It should roar.

'Distil,' chants Akhund Olm.

'Refine,' answer the hunters.

'Separate!' they declare, together.

Olm grimaces, showing small, sharp teeth and pale pink gums. '*Improve,*' he purrs.

The bears' strong bodies fall limp in their chains.

And when each pair of brown eyes blinks open, they're blank, dull and obedient.

Olm scuttles forwards, tips the silver liquid into a glass bottle and seals it with a bear-shaped stopper.

'Add this to my collection,' he commands, passing the bottle to a hunter.

'Success, Akhund!' declares one of the hunters. He falls to his knees, awe spilling off him.

Olm stoops by a bear's side and takes her muzzle in his hands. Her confused eyes reach for his face. I can feel her lost chatter, buried deep. Searching endlessly for something she can't remember. Her home. Her family. 'Oh, but you shall be so placid, now that your innate evil has been excised.'

Bile licks my tongue. 'Don't you *dare* touch her!' I thrash against the straps on my wrists.

Olm's giggle slithers into my ears. He turns to one of the hunters. 'Have you sorted the poorhouses? Have you found orphans to elixirate?'

The guards nod.

'You can't do that!' I scream. I remember when I asked him what the poorhouse was, and he sounded like he cared about the folk there . . .

'I do tire of you.' Akhund Olm turns to me, face changing, quick as a snake. Scorn lurks under his skin. 'Try to think beyond your own needs, for a moment,' he says. 'Try to imagine how much more *productive* this world would be, without common people able to feel, or to think. Imagine how much harder they would work. How much *faster.*' He rubs his papery hands together. 'And consider, if you will, the sheer misery these people endure. What kind of a life do they lead?' He shakes his head, a thing like twisted sadness plucking at his face. 'Not any kind of life you or I would wish upon them. No longer shall they feel such despair at their lot.' His pale fingers reach for my face.

I jerk away from him, but my head hits the back of the chair and he's still too close, much too close.

'And then we come to you, warrior queen.'

Fright digs bony fingertips into my eyes, trying to push my eyeballs back in my head. 'I'm no warrior queen! I'm just a kid, that's all!'

'But that's *not* all, is it?' He smiles gently. 'Stag was the most promising pupil I ever taught. And you are carved from a piece of him. You desire greatness as he does.'

'*You* taught him?'

He smiles brightly. 'Indeed, though he sought me as a man grown. He was rough as a clam, running from the people who had taken him in as a child, running from his second-born. Grieving. Out of control.' He clears his throat.

I wanted to shoot her gloating Hunter's Moon out of the sky. That's what Stag said to Crow about me.

'He was still so young, and – malleable. He became an asset to the Skadowan. He quickly learned to master his emotions, until it seemed that he had none at all.' Olm giggles and steps away, looking lost in thought.

The leather straps dig into my wrists.

'Do you know what this means?' Olm raves, clenching

his fists. For an odd beat I reckon he's asking me, but then I realise he's jabbering half to the hunters, half to himself. 'Our army currently numbers merely this precious first collection—' He gestures at the blank, silent figures standing in the room. 'As well as our allies – a few at the Western Wharves, the Hill-Tribe fortresses, Castle Whalesbane, Wrecker's Cove, the Northern Fluke, the Frozen Wastes – though time will tell how strong Stag's hold is there.'

I scowl. *Lost Hackles, though, ent you. Me and my crew saw to that.*

'Many more followers have been crawling from the woodwork, of late,' says one of the hunters, eagerly.

'Yes, yes,' says Olm, eyes feverish. 'All well and good. But their numbers are scant compared to what we will be able to achieve with these stones. Now, we will be ready to wage battle in a matter of days – the battle to *win* the war! The Marsh folk continue to bother our forces at what remains of the Icy Marshes – but now, we shall be able to elixirate them into obedience. We will crush the rebels in the forest, level it flat, and march on to conquer the lands not yet under our control. Assemble the other Akhunds, and the rest of those mad-dog mystiks. Tell them to prepare for war.'

The mystik's face twitches, but he stays silent under the slap of Olm's insult. The hunter salutes Olm and strides from the room.

I've got to warn the forest! The blank faces of Olm's army catch my eye again. There are so many of them, and something about the sad horror of the place starts the panic peaking and rolling through me, crown to toe, and my heart lollops in my chest like a dying fish and my breath comes too quick and ragged. I scan brown eyes, blue eyes, grey eyes. There's yellow hair, black, brown. Dark skin, light skin, brown skin, curly hair, coppery braids, bundled on top of the head . . . With a sickening jolt I realise one of the figures is oak-tall, with light brown skin and green eyes. Eyes with all the light drained from them.

Kestrel. *No!*

I grip the arms of the chair. If this is what they've done to her . . . I swallow, and my mouth's so dry my teeth stick to the inside of my lips. How will I *ever* get her back?

'In the name of the Skadowan, we will draw out the volatile parts,' Olm orders, pointing at me. 'Let the great shadow pierce her brain and heart. We will coax her evil spirit out. Then she will do no more harm.' He holds up his arm, pulls his sleeve up – and on his arm is a symbol, etched deep into his skin. It looks like the S rune for *Sol*, meaning sun, with a vine wrapped around it, like it's strangling the life from the rune. The corrupted rune from Yapok's manuscripts, blotting out the older, truer runes. The symbol of the Skadowan – the poisoned shadow spreading across Trianukka.

I fight until the last breath. I watch the mystik's finger. I sense the beat when he's about to bend his knuckle, to drag me from my body, and I do the only thing I can think to do.

My spirit *flees*.

28

Gather the Ghosts

In the dream-dance world, I watch the moment when Akhund Olm seethes with triumph. He barges the mystik out of his way and holds my jaw between his fingers.

But the triumph splinters into spitting rage, when he realises he can't drip me into a jar. He shakes me by the shoulders, and I watch my eyes rattle in my head like a doll's. 'Where are you?' he screams into the air, neck swivelling.

The mystik scans around with faraway eyes. 'Her spirit has flown,' he tells the Akhund. His eyes fix on me and sharpen, and I edge away from their piercing glare. He is seeing me. I can't let him.

Crank. Click. Shush. The blood-jangling noise of the door unlocking. They've pulled my body out of the chair and now they're dragging it from the room by the wrists. My eyes are sunken and my head lolls to one side.

I ping into the body of the nearest bear. I snarl, leap onto all fours, knock each hunter flying to a different corner of the room. Instinct pops all my claws out, and I thump Olm in the face, raking the claws through his skin. He screams, then falls backwards. He lies still.

Other robed two-legs race towards me. They're going to kill the bear – me – if I don't move out of her body right now.

I glance at Kestrel. I have to get her free, but my own body is being dragged further from me, so I snort a lungful of frustration and lope after it, swiping at the men until they let go of my wrists. Then I wade out of the bear's body, drop into my own and growl, my voice all spirit-glooped and beastlike. The men shrink back as I jump to my feet and throw myself at the door, running.

Olm sends a blood-thickened shriek delving between my shoulder blades like an arrow. 'Catch the vermin!'

I wrench open the door and charge the robed Akhund that enters, knocking him flat. Then I sprint down the shelf-lined passageway, but I know I won't get far before they follow. I slide onto the floor, scraping my knees, and wedge myself into a space under the lowest shelf. Lying flat, my chin on the ground, I glance back the way I've come.

Sickening thoughts of the Opals blunder into my mind, but I push them away.

Akhund Olm marches through the door behind me, blood from the wounds I made dribbling down his chin. He grimaces. Then he raises a hand, clicks his fingers and elixirated Skadowan soldiers mobilise behind him, like they're emerging from a dream. 'Form up. Hunt the chatterer!'

Human soldiers are followed by rows of bears standing

on their hind legs, armour glinting on their heads and around their muscled shoulders.

They prowl closer. I squeeze my eyes shut, but that's worse, so I open them again and stare at the feet as they march past. *Don't look down*, I pray.

Then a thin sliding sound rasps behind me. I flinch, spine shuddering. A hand shoots out from the shadows and grabs my cloak. I tumble backwards, into a fug of freezing air, and there's a soft thump as the light of the passageway is snuffed out by the closing of a small wooden hatchway. I push myself up to sitting, but the space is so cramped my head touches the ceiling. I'm in some kind of cupboard. 'Don't move,' whispers a voice, close to my ear.

I turn and meet the eyes of a girl with mountains tattooed across her cheeks, and dark, furious eyes.

'Egret,' I gasp, head churning.

A silver tongue juts between her knuckles – a throwing arrow, tucked almost out of sight. Her eyes flick between me and the hatchway in the wall. She presses a finger to her lips. We listen as the sound of the marching army grows quieter.

'What happened out there?' she demands.

I tell her everything from when that black puddle sucked me through the floor, to now. 'What are you doing here?' I ask.

'I was pretending to be part of their army,' she whispers. 'I couldn't leave Kes. But one of the hunters realised I hadn't been elixirated. I got away before they could do it to me.'

She tells me how they were posing as scholars when they were summoned by the Chief Akhund for Medsin – Olm – and knew they had been betrayed. They tried to flee into the forest, but were caught by guards at the city walls. Egret escaped again when they were being brought to the Hall of Moans, thinking Kestrel was right behind her – but they got separated. When she retraced her steps, Kestrel had already been elixirated. 'I've been waiting for a chance to get her out of there, but there are always Akhunds or mystiks in that room.'

As I listen, my sorrows carve my chest in two. I'm crowded with aches for Kestrel, for the bears, for the poor folk drained of their souls . . . and for losing all three Opals, after *everything*. 'Let's get out there and find her!'

'We have to be careful,' she mouths, breath tight and ragged. 'Olm will be lurking somewhere, waiting for us.'

I shake my head. 'He's leading his army into battle.'

'No, Mouse. *That's* partly why they elixirate – they don't want to do the dirty work themselves. The Akhunds haven't even a thread of magyk amongst them. They will stay safe behind their tower walls.' Disgust tars her words.

I bite my fingertips, struggling to untangle my thoughts. 'So – one of us needs to watch for Olm while we find Kes, and the bottle they're keeping her spirit in.' I sigh. 'Then I have to put my wrongs right. I have to get the Opals back.'

She clasps my wrist, looking into my eyes. 'You won't be doing it alone,' she says. 'We all make mistakes, girl. Even future sea-captains.'

My belly plunges, cos I've roved so far from that fate she don't even know.

Egret fits two blades to the knuckles of either hand, then presses them flat until they look like silver gloves. Then she peels open the small door and we squeeze out on our bellies, onto the polished marble floor of the passageway. The place is deserted, and proper eerie. When I listen hard, it's as if there's a high-pitched bell ringing at the edge of hearing.

We stare up at the bottles, lined neatly on the shelves. Egret bites her lip. 'Right. We have to find something about one of the bottles that reminds us of Kes.'

'There's hundreds of them,' I say, before I can stop myself. She silences my doubts with a look.

We search. There's a ladder that must be used by slaves to get to the higher shelves, and Egret climbs it, picking up bottle after bottle.

Then I hear a terrified, familiar beast-chatter.

Ettler?

The squidge pokes out from behind a row of bottles. He must've been too frighted to get away like I told him. One of his chubby tentacles is wrapped tightly around the neck of a glass bottle, and his black eyes shine with grief.

'Egret,' I whisper loudly. 'Come here, *now!*'

'What?' asks Egret breathlessly, jumping down from the ladder.

'Found her,' I gasp, pointing up at Ettler, who's too terrified to chatter back to me.

'And we've found you,' creaks the voice of Akhund Olm.

He slips out from behind a white marble pillar, followed by the mystik who elixirated the bear spirits.

Egret springs towards Olm, slashing wildly with the blades fixed to her knuckles. She moves warrior-fast and fierce, whispering to the runes in her blades and making trails of sparks and colours jump from their hidden meanings.

Olm covers his head with his arms. 'Help me, you fool!'

The mystik eyes Egret, as a smoky ball of fire brews on his palm.

'You don't have to do what he says!' I yell. 'He's got no magyk of his own. He's using yours for evil!'

But the mystik flicks a string of red lightning at Egret and it hits her in the ribs, sending her crashing to the floor.

Ettler, I chatter urgently, as I rush to Egret's side. *Be brave. Bring me that bottle, and please please please don't drop it!*

To my right, Olm groans. Bright drops of blood are pattering onto the floor from a long cut in his arm. Egret hauls herself up and clutches the wall, swaying with exhaustion. Then she pushes me away and flings herself at the mystik, roaring a battle-cry.

Now, Ettler! I shout.

The squidge weeps and grumbles, farting ink that trickles over the lip of the shelf, onto the bottles below. Gods – what if his grip's too slippery? *You can do it, Ettler! Come on, make your tentacles strong. You can–*

A body slams into me, strangling my chatter. 'Stop that hideous mewling!' whines Olm.

But Egret charges at him, blades poised for his throat.

Ettler lands in the crook of my arm, still gripping the spirit-bottle tightly. *Well done, little beast!* I scoop him and the bottle into my pocket and call for Egret. She detaches herself from the Akhund, who's lying on the floor, breathing raggedly.

We back away, into the room where they tried to drain my spirit. Kestrel stands frozen in her place among the ranks of the elixirated. Egret grabs her hand and pulls her away from the others, and I unstopper the spirit-bottle. Egret holds up a shaky hand. 'Wait – how do we know it's really hers? I know the squidge was holding the bottle, but . . .' She takes the bottle from me and holds it up to her face.

'Don't!' I warn. 'You might sniff her spirit up your nose.'

She frowns into the bottle. 'There's a silvery tangle in there,' she says sadly. 'It's beautiful, but it's hard to believe it could be enough to belong to that big-spirit girl.' Then she pushes Kes's head back, opening her mouth, and tips her spirit down her throat.

I press Kes's chin shut to make her swallow.

'Kes,' says Egret, voice iron-strong, but underneath I can sense a quiver of desperation. '*Kestrel.* It's time to wake up, now.' She reaches up to her shoulders and gives her a shake.

But Kestrel's face stays blank and her eyes stay dull.

No. This ent how it goes. It can't be.

'Kes,' hisses Egret, lip wobbling. '*Please.* I need you to wake up.' I can see how long she's been trying to stay strong.

'Let's get her to the Forest,' I whisper. 'We can't stay here.'

Egret don't answer.

'I need your help,' I beg, as I try to drag Kes towards the door.

We each take one of her arms and lead her out of the room.

Olm blocks the doorway, leaning on his tooth-staff. In the ceiling of the corridor, a black puddle drips slime.

Egret springs like a cat and presses her blades to his neck. 'Let us out now, or die.'

A soft laugh burbles from his lips. 'That is well and fine. Go, good children.'

Egret releases him, curling her lip. 'Why?'

Olm rocks with silent laughter. 'You think you matter.' He hugs himself gleefully. 'You think you can do anything, now? The Opals were the only reason that creature mattered.' He points at me. 'Now we have them, our mission is complete – as we speak, my hunters are gathering unsuspecting soldiers for our army. Thousands will be elixirated, all at the same moment – beauty untold! So please, do leave this place if you will, and wait your turn to die.'

'You're cracked!' I yell at him, as Egret tries to drag me away. She wraps her arms around Kestrel and pulls her along with us. 'Where are the Opals?' I scream.

'Just leave it,' Egret snaps, pulling on my arm. 'Let's go!'

We leap for the black puddle before it vanishes, and soon we're spat out into upper Nightfall.

29
The Shadows of Spiders

We lurk underneath the sill of one of the College windows, arguing about where to go next. Shutters bang closed, all along the street. Wild winds kick snow into our eyes. The lamplighters douse the street-lanterns with a sizzling, gassy hiss. 'I have friends we can go to,' I tell Egret, while Kestrel stares around blankly, not even rubbing the snow from her eyes.

'Who?' whispers Egret.

When I tell her, the runesmith's nostrils flare. 'The Spidermaster is one of the most important people in the city. How can we trust *him*?'

I hesitate. 'He's the one that sent me to Olm.' Egret's brows quirk into outraged arcs, but I let my thoughts flow. 'But I ent sure how many folk here know the truth about the Akhunds, or the Skadowan. And I rescued the Spidermaster's daughter from slavers. She smuggled me

into the city. Without them, we'll never get out again.'

Egret nods. 'Fine. What choice do we have, anyway?'

No Spiderbuses are running, so we trudge all the way back to the Spidermaster's shop using the map Olm gave me. We scuff around in the street, faces bitten blind by sleet-bladed wind, until there's no one else in the Spidertoken shop. Then we whisk inside.

Blue spots me and leads us down the passage to the back rooms. 'We were so worried when you didn't come back! Pa's been searching everywhere for you! He even stopped looking for his spiders,' she adds, in an awed tone.

She brings us to the kitchen, where a wild-haired Spidermaster and ashen-faced Nanny are clutching steaming cups of kaffy. They leap to their feet when they see us, Nanny's chair falling backwards with a clatter.

I tell them everything that's happened, and Nanny sits with her hand clapped to her mouth.

'Child, I am so sorry!' exclaims the Spidermaster. 'I hadn't the faintest notion of the true nature of the Akhund.'

He grabs his coat and hat and a whip.

'Pa, you're not going out spider-hunting again now, are you?' asks Blue, fret pinching her features.

'No.' His hat coughs out a splutter of old smog, and he takes it off to tap it against the table. 'I am taking my best beauties and going with you and your friends. They need our help. Nanny, close the shop, draw the shutters, and don't let anyone in. Olm will be sending people after you, so we must leave now.'

Nanny nods, clutching fistfuls of her skirts. Then she races through to the shop and the front door bangs shut. We listen to the snapping of the shutters.

The Spidermaster unlocks the cages in the passageway. He returns to the kitchen, spiders lining up behind him. 'I once had three thousand beauties in my fleet, living at a central Spiderbus station, serving both the inner and outer parts of the city. Now I can only offer you a hundred – some are here already, some we will collect on the way.' Heart-sadness clouds his face for a beat, before steely resolve toughens it. 'But they will follow me into any battle.'

One by one, we drop through the floor of the Spiders' Lair, into the sewers beneath. The Spidermaster whistles, and a spider pokes its legs through the hole, then sploshes after us. The others follow, plunking one by one into the sewer.

We flee underneath the city, through the spider-paths. The shadows of spiders flicker across the walls. We stick close behind the Spidermaster's flapping cloak. 'Keep pace with me,' he instructs.

'Won't they find us, down here?' demands Egret, struggling to keep Kestrel walking fast enough.

'The Akhunds shouldn't come down here – in all my years, this has been my domain. Others do not step here, for they fear my beauties.'

'And when we emerge?' she challenges.

'My position in this city is a long-trusted, powerful one,' he assures her firmly. 'We shouldn't be challenged. The

261

main thing is that we appear purposeful.'

Outside the city walls the Forest of Nightfall waits on the hill, seeping eerie silence. Terrodyls swirl above the treetops. The spiders balk at the sight of them, rearing and stepping backwards.

As the Spidermaster fights to regain control of his beasts, I stare at the dense wall of branches and needles. They seem to have coiled tighter, refusing us a way in.

'Toadflax?' I call softly. 'Leo? Astraia?' I watch over my shoulder for signs of the Skadowan. 'Come on!'

'We can't wait here,' says Egret, taking a silver throwing arrow and fitting it between her knuckles. 'Let's forge a way through.' She leans her shoulder into the branches and uses her other hand to hack at the brambles, twigs and vines.

'You shouldn't cut them,' says Blue, anxiously.

Egret ignores her. I hold onto the blank-faced Kestrel, who keeps trying to wander off.

Every time Egret cuts the foliage, it heals. Eventually, a branch snakes free and shoves her so she lands with a thump in the snow. She curses, wiping sweaty black hair from her forehead.

Then I spot a shape above the trees that sings joy into my veins. *Thaw!*

Two-legs girl of nest-home flew too long, Thaw fretting in skull!

Sorry, Thaw! Can you tell the green-chatterer, Toadflax, that we're back? Get her to let us in – quickly, Thaw-beast!

She hoots, soaring away and disappearing from sight.

Soon, a tunnel slowly unravels from the thickets, tall

enough for the spiders to squeeze into. When the last of us is through, the branches weave closed, and relief spreads through my belly. We follow the rootsy, musty smell of green-chatterers and wind-chatterers using their powers to hold the terrodyls back. Finally, the tunnel opens out into a clearing.

Two-legs nest-place girl! Home! Thaw swoops from the sky and lands on me so hard that my knees bend under her weight.

Thaw girl! You are one beautiful sight!

Thaw flew to two-legs but two-legs gone!

I'm sorry, Thaw. I went looking for Kestrel. I reckoned I knew what I was doing, but I didn't.

She hoots, showing forgiveness by nudging her smooth head under my chin.

As my eyes grow forest-focused, I notice the crowd that's assembled in the Glade of Sorrows. They turn to face us.

'Mouse?' Crow climbs shakily to his feet, still not fully changed back to a boy. Then he, Sparrow and Old One are climbing all over me, weeping, laughing, tugging at my cloak and hair. Frog and Bear sweep me into tight hugs, eyes sparkling. Even Lunda steps closer, gifting me a swift pat on the back.

A thin, golden-haired man paces back and forth. He startled when we first appeared, but now he strides towards us.

'Mouse!' Da folds me into his arms.

30
Back from the Brink

I pull away, squinting up at him. 'Am I in proper trouble?'

'If life's sails were calm, no doubt you would be.' He smiles, but heart-sadness dwells in his eyes. 'But enough trouble has gripped us already.'

Toadflax stares up at the scuttle-spiders.

'This is the Spidermaster.' I wave him forwards. 'He's a friend, here to help us.'

'Myself and my beauties are at your service,' he declares, sweeping a bow.

Toadflax takes his hand in both of hers and thanks him heartily.

Then Egret appears, leading Kestrel through the tunnel into the camp.

'Daughter!' cries Leo, rushing over and sweeping Kes into a hug. Kes's arms hang limply by her sides. Disgust crawls over her face. Leo pulls back and takes Kestrel's shoulders gently. 'You're so cold, child. And stiff as a board! Are you ill?' She utters a soft gasp. 'Kestrel, answer me!'

When Leo looks to me, my mouth is dry. 'She's . . .'

'Not herself,' finishes Egret bluntly. She and Leo settle Kestrel on the floor.

Kestrel's fingers touch the ground. She rolls pine needles, picking at them. 'Dirty,' she mutters. 'Work to do. Work—' She stares up and around the clearing. 'Not *here*!'

'What's wrong with her?' says Leo, fright-bitten.

'The Skadowan are in charge of Nightfall and they're using the Opals to suck out spirits and build a soulless army.' I steel myself to spill the next words. 'They leeched Kestrel's spirit out.'

As the crowd surrounds me, I tell them everything I learnt at Nightfall, and everything Olm said about the Skadowan. Everything except the thing that makes guilt grip me.

That I delivered the Sea and Sky Opals to them.

Curses swirl around the clearing, mingled with gasps of horror and fright.

'We found her spirit and made her drink it, but nothing happened,' continues Egret. 'Her body and soul are still – severed.'

Leo covers her mouth with her hand and shakes her head. 'No,' she whispers hoarsely.

Da puts a hand on Leo's shoulder, tears coursing freely down his cheeks.

'It's still her, somewhere in there,' I tell him. 'We have to do something.'

'Like what, Mouse?' says Egret. She stands at the edge of the group. Toadflax watches her with heart-sadness.

Egret presses a hand to her mouth, fury kicking up clouds in her eyes. I know that feeling, when you're on the edge but you can't show it, elsewise you'll fall to pieces.

I tip back my head and stare at the tops of the trees, spearing the sky. I have to hold myself proper still. Cos otherwise this fury building in my bones is gonna spill over.

'I feel like all that time we spent forging links with the youth has been wasted.' Egret's throat closes. She clears it. 'Maybe I could have convinced her to stay at Hackles, where she belongs. Then none of this would have happened.'

'But if you never rove, you never know what's possible,' I remind her, thinking of Kes's true spirit, her thirst for adventure.

Leo wipes her eyes. 'Seeing the world outside Hackles is what she wanted, more than anything, Egret.'

Egret looks up, eel-quick. 'So what? It's not like it was *worth* it.'

She's right. I look each one of them in the eye. 'I wasn't heart-truthful with you. I had two of the Opals with me when I went into Nightfall. Now the Skadowan have all three.' My vision blurs with tears. 'My pride clouded my choices. I'm sorry.'

There's a pause. Then Leo clasps my hands. 'What's done is done. You did what you thought was best.'

I leave the three of them alone and head back to the main group, heart-heavy.

More and more folk are emerging from the trees. There's not just the crew from Hackles, but others that I don't know.

Da sees me looking. 'They came when we spread the word about Mouse Arrow-Swift's rebellion against Stag,' he says proudly. 'Once, they were too oppressed to act. But the fact that one young girl escaped her ship after a vicious mutiny, saved her brother, then her da, and found two of the Storm-Opals, has given the people enormous hope for a future they feared dead.'

I swallow drily, my voice locked deep inside my pipes. *You're all wrong about me. I've lost the Opals. The future IS dead.*

Lunda steps forwards. 'We found out that the Wilder-King was imprisoning beast-chatterers in one of his icebergs. We rescued them and brought them here to help. The draggle-riders and the Marsh folk have taken the Iceberg Forest.' She allows herself a proud smile and I can't blame her. I nod my respect.

'I am sorry for how I was before,' she says, turning scarlet. 'Are we crew, still?'

'Course,' I tell the Spearsister. 'Didn't you know a crew's for life?'

She grins. 'That gladdens me.'

Then I hear the chatter of draggles beyond the trees' canopy of protection and stare upwards.

'What is it?' asks Da.

The chatterers cower on their haunches, eyes wild.

'Something's coming,' I say. Then, slowly, the trees' fingers begin to unlace, revealing a scrap of sky.

Two huge orange blots sweep towards our camp. Tiny figures are huddled on their backs. As they get closer, I see who they are – Yapok and the Skybrarian! They descend, getting closer, before finally landing in the glade. Everyone covers their faces against the stink stirred by the beasts' wings.

'The *Skybrarian*?' I breathe.

'He's the oldest book-wielder in the world,' says Da, face lit with awe. 'He knows what's at stake here.'

More draggles thud into view, bearing old men and women wearing eyeglasses and holding books close to their chests.

'I offer the anti-Skadowan movement the allegiance of the book-protectors of Trianukka,' croaks the Skybrarian triumphantly, long white hair wrapped around his neck like a shaggy scarf.

Once the draggles are settled and the newcomers fed and watered, we sit around the campfire making plans. 'How did you know the Skadowan had risen again?' Hoshi asks the Skybrarian.

'My apprentice showed me a symbol that he could not remove from the manuscripts – it was enchanted, and was suffocating the true runes written underneath,' he explains. 'He had unearthed the symbol of the great Shadow itself.'

Painful-looking red blotches creep up Yapok's neck and break out across his face. He fidgets, like he wants to fly right back to his Skybrary, and his books.

'Well done, mate,' says Crow, clapping him on the back and drawing even more attention to him. 'Praise where it's due!'

The Skybrarian clears his throat. 'I performed extensive historical investigation with the help of my colleagues, and we realised that certain patterns from the last time of the Skadowan were being repeated. I became convinced that the Skadowan were rising again.'

Sparrow curls into my side. He's told me that Old One's been helping him to work on his life-spark power, and learn to control it. But it looks to be tiring him out more than ever.

'Our spies inform us that the Nightfall army is assembled, and almost ready to march,' says Toadflax.

'This is confirmed by what Mouse and Egret witnessed inside the city,' says Leo, who's trying to stay heart-strong until we fight to the last.

I nod. 'The Skadowan is making ready to bring a battle to end all battles,' I tell them. 'Akhund Olm says he wants to crush the rebels in the forest, level it flat, then march beyond, snuffing every last flame against the dark. We have to be ready for them.' I swallow, realising that every pair of eyes in the glade is fixed on me. Sparks hurry from the fire, and the kindling *snaps*.

Then terrified whispers swarm around the clearing.

'We thank you for your report, Mouse,' says Toadflax. 'The Nightfall army is readying to quash any remaining resistance, until they hold all the power in the land. Sadly, they now possess all three Storm-Opals.'

'No!' someone cries.

'We're lost!' says another.

Leo chooses not to tell everyone how the Skadowan got the jewels, and I know I should be grateful for that, but shame still squeezes me, making my face burn.

While arguments rage, Da leans close. 'I am heart-proud of you, Mouse.'

I flinch away. 'Why?' I hiss. 'It's all gone proper wrong cos of me. I don't even know why I didn't tell Leo I had the Opals before I went into the city. I think I just – wanted to prove myself.'

He rubs his temples, taking a long breath. 'But you dared believe you could just – go in there, and take that last Opal. You believe in the possible more than any of us full-growns. I wish I'd been even halfway as brave as you when I was your age, daughter.'

I gift him a watery smile. 'Heart-thanks, Da,' I whisper. 'How is it you can always make me feel so much better?'

He pulls me into a hug. 'It's all part of a da's job.'

That night I try to sleep, but the beast-chatter of the draggles and the scuttle-spiders seeps into my veins, lacing my blood with hot, spiky panic.

I'm up and pacing before folk begin to stir, making breakfast. Sparrow pulls me to one side. 'I had a *vision*,' he tells me with solemn impatience, like I should've flaming guessed or something.

'Aye? What did you see?'

'Merwraiths.'

'How many?'

'*Lots.*' He rubs his eyes. 'But they was walking again, like they used to before they drowned. I think we've got to find them, so I can try to wake them up.'

'What?' I whisper, heart skipping. I notice the great white wolf, Astraia, watching us keenly. 'How do you know you even can?'

He shrugs, scowls. 'I woke up that dead Chieftain, dint I?'

Astraia pads across to us. *Your sea-people are many.*

I frown at her. *Sea-folk were many, once upon a sometime. But they ent nowadays.*

They only sleep, she replies softly. *In the realm of fog and pearls.* She nuzzles Sparrow's arm. *Let the boy try to wake them. The battle for the light will be lost if you do not find your people. In battles of old, Sea-Tribe armies were rarely defeated. Find your ice-clutched ship.* She looks right into me, down to my bones. *A great warrior of the sea haunts the waters there.*

I gasp. Rattlebones once told me how she trailed our ship to find me, how she watched over me when I was growing up. Maybe she's waiting in the water, ready to help us in our time of need. And if the Skadowan march as soon as I reckon they will, we ent got long to gather as many warriors as we can find.

I scramble to my feet and pick my way through the folk around the campfire, until I find my Tribe huddled together near the base of a tree. Away from the fire, the cold is sharp as the edge of a blade. 'Vole, Pip, Bear – can you remember where the *Huntress* ran aground?'

31

Realm of Fog and Pearls

'If the stories are true,' says Bear, 'merwraiths trail their ships. Most ships that weren't wrecked in the wild are at the ship-breaking yards. That's where we'll raise our army of the dead.'

I shudder at the thought of seeing my ship again, cos I don't know what state she'll be in.

'What of the Sea-Tribe folk who are still living?' Da asks. 'The Marsh-folk travelled with us from Hackles. But there must still be others.'

'Don't lots of them rove the waters around Fisherman's Flukes, and trade at Stonepoint?' I muse. I remember the first time I saw the mighty, heart-bright beacon of light spilling from the great lighthouse of Stonepoint. Many a Sea-Tribe life's been saved by the lighthouse-keepers there. 'If any trading's still going on, they'll head there, won't they?'

'Good thinking, Bones!' Da beams at me. 'Stonepoint and the Flukes are southerly enough that, with heart-luck, they might not have frozen solid yet. We can go there afterwards, if we've time enough.'

'I'll go ahead and suss the place out,' says Frog, mossy green eyes glinting.

'And I'll go with you, lad,' adds Bear, firmly.

While we're readying to leave, Thaw flies to the city to spy for us, and returns barely a breath later, feathers spun into ice-capped panic. *Nestsrippedapart, two-legs outoutout, into fighting!* she gabbles. *No free-flying, nosafetysafetysafety!*

I sift through her chatter until I can make sense of it. 'She says folk are being torn from their homes. The Skadowan army's got full control of the city. Everyone's being made to fight – there's no freedom left, and no safety.' Heart-sadness drags at the corners of my mouth. But then I gulp a deep breath, and force myself arrow-straight. 'We rove!'

We fly in pairs, on borrowed draggles. Da and Sparrow, me and Crow. Kin-keeper is flung over my shoulder, and Thaw flies by my side, ready to crush bones to dust if anyone threatens us.

As we soar over Nightfall, we see the army march through deserted streets. Elixirated bears walk on two legs, clutching spears hewn from their kin's thighbones.

I chatter to the draggles, begging them to fly faster.

Our faces are bundled tight beneath layers of fur. Draggle breath streams up our noses. I'm lulled to sleep and I dream of Stag. A terrible dark cloud leeches from his back, and he spits rivers of blood.

When I wake again I watch the world through ice-clumped lashes.

Somewhere far south of Nightfall and north of Riddler's Hollow, we find the ship-breaking yards. The pain of seeing a place where ships go to die bites away my breath.

Dead ships sit on blocks, chained, great gaping holes smashed in their sides, masts splintered, sails torn down. Giants with chained ankles swing their fists into the ships' flanks, crushing them. Others pull apart clinker planking, wrench free masts and oars, tossing them all into a towering heap of wood. They snack on sails.

'Enslaved giants,' mutters Da.

On the edge of the ship-breaking yards, the *Huntress* sleeps in a cradle spun from ice. Abandoned, but for one fretful polar dog.

'May the sea-gods swim close to you,' says Da.

Calmcalmcalm, I chatter to the polar dog desperately, as we tiptoe towards the ship, out of sight of the giants. The dog draws back its lips, revealing sore-riddled gums.

Then a flame of horror licks through my innards. *If I'd thieved the title of Captain, I'd never have left her here!*

Da shoots an arrow into the lock on the polar dog's chains, and she runs away, even though I tell her to wait with us. 'At least the dog's free now,' says Sparrow.

We begin digging in the shadow of my ship, at a soft spot in the ice where seals have been. When I look up, I'm eye to eye with one of the *Huntress*'s portholes. 'We're gonna get you free,' I swear to her.

Sparrow starts crying. I pull him to one side. 'Remember what Old One taught you. Ready to put that spark of yours to the test good and proper?'

He snuffles, wiping his nose on his wrist. Then he nods.

First we make a camp in one of the drier hulls of a dead ship. Crow gathers wood to build a small fire. Thaw goes hunting, and shares her spoils with us, clattering mussels onto the hard ground. We prise them open and eat them straight from the shells, salty and raw and crunchy with ice. The thunder is too loud to bother trying to talk so we share the food in silence. I heart-thank Thaw with my eyes.

'See how the rain's turned to ice, even this far south?' murmurs Da, in a little space between growls of thunder. He gestures towards the long, gleaming daggers that hang from the clouds hulking over the ship-breaking yards. Then he blinks. 'Wait – who was posted to keep watch for–?'

'*Giants!*' shouts Crow.

A stog's face swoops out of the sky, as he bends low to stare at us. Open sores leak sticky yellow liquid onto the ground around our camp. We scuttle backwards, yelling.

The stog's like a whorl of old wood, a twisted root scraping the sky, and his eyes are like the egg stones from the shores of the Moonlands. The musty stink of him weaves into the back of my throat, gagging me. Da snatches Sparrow behind him, and Crow does the same to me.

But Sparrow wriggles out from behind Da and jabs a

finger up at the giant, bold as bronze. 'And *who* are you?'

'Sparrow!' hisses Da, grabbing my brother's cloak.

'I am a listener of your chit-chattings,' the Stog grumbles, not understanding Sparrow's question. 'We stogs want to join you who resist the Shadow.'

Everyone stays in a stunned silence, except the too-soon. 'But don't you have a *name*?'

The giant sighs. 'I am Spear-Flinger, third inheritor of the rights of these yards,' he answers wearily. 'Free us from our chains, and we will fight with you.'

I chuckle suddenly through my nose, remembering when I called Lunda the same name, as an insult.

'How?' asks Da, forcing himself brave. 'Aren't there guards?'

'They have been called away by the Skadowan,' answers Spear-Flinger. 'They tried to force us with them but ran when we crushed a few underfoot.'

Crow gazes around at everyone, amazement shining in his eyes. 'That's a ruddy good start, eh?'

'Certainly is, lad,' says Da, ruffling his hair. Crow grins.

We get into the guards' abandoned dwellings and find the keys to the shackles. Then we go round unlocking chains until we've got five bubble-sore giants staring down at us, ready to follow us into battle.

After a heavy sleep, tucked in a bed roll, I stir and sit up.

Da and Crow are sitting with their backs turned, muttering in low voices.

'Are you really going to let her do this?' pleads Crow.

Da sighs. 'No one "lets" Mouse do anything. And she is the most skilled diver among us.' I smile to myself.

When I get up and go over to them, Da musses my hair and rummages in his medsin pouch. 'Here – I've still got half a vial of your grandma's wolf-fish blood left.'

I take it and squeeze a drop onto my tongue, feeling the familiar heat lick through my bones.

Once we've re-cut the seal-hole in the ice, Sparrow lies down on his front at the edge and drips strands of lightning from his fingertips into the thickening water. My head throbs. Salt coats my lips and whitens Crow's jawline.

I fill my pipes. And I jump.

Even with the wolf-fish blood, the icy water snips a marrow-deep wound up through my body to my crown. I am parted. Hacked by the cold.

I tuck into a dive. Pale anemones let their tentacles hang in the inky depths. They tangle with my hair, until I'm forced to rip free.

I plunge deeper.

Hands grasp for me out of the darkness. Hands that almost forgot what they were.

Merwraiths – half in this realm, half in the Other – weave through portholes and squirm from burrows in the mud, drifting between green tongues of kelp. They wait, witching in the underwater wind, watching me. The current pulses me closer.

Rattlebones! I call. *Are you there?* But the space once filled by her spirit pangs like an empty tooth socket. I can't find her.

Other wraiths drop words right into my head, like Rattlebones did, but there are too many of them to untangle.

Quiet! I think at them. The words buzz, fracture, drift away, and then I'm surrounded by pairs of blind, questioning eyes.

What ARE you? A frighted wraith slams the words at me.

I tell them about the war, about what we want to do. I tell them about the lie spread against the Sea-Tribes. I ask them – beg them – to gift us their heart-strength.

A swirl of them confer on the seabed, flashing dark looks at me with pearly-pale eyes.

When they swim towards me again, faces questing blindly in the freezing water, one of them pangs a message into the middle of my head. *We will allow you to bring us back to the living, to help with the fight.*

I direct them towards the surface.

Some move quick-sharp, and gulp Sparrow's lightning greedily, blind faces questing for light, though there's none – for air, though they're gilled. The lightning shows up under their skin, and quivers in their chests, waking their slumbering sea-hearts.

Others are seahorse-slow; moving forwards, shrinking back, frowning with faces salt-nibbled, parchmented with layer upon layer of deep green seaweed. I encourage them gently, guiding them to where purple worms of lightning wriggle in the water.

I help the merwraiths out through the seal-hole, then surface to breathe. I meet Crow's amber eyes, then stare past him at the sprawl of merwraiths gulping at the air. Must be ten of them already.

I take a new breath and keep going. The wraiths know we're here now. More and more of them slither towards me. Some swim with fierce determination. They grab Sparrow's lightning like a lifeline in the water. I guide them towards the waking world and Crow helps them through.

As I dive, I hear a crunch as Crow places a lantern by the seal-hole. A glow drips through the water, making a guiding searchlight as I dive lower, past underwater icicles trailing from the ice above my head.

My fingers brush a whale's skin, as it makes for the hole to breathe. I swim until we're eye to eye. *A waker*, he booms, making my teeth rattle. *A waker knows you.*

Knows me? His tail brushes past my eyes. Then, from a gnawed gap in the underside of the *Huntress's* hull, a silver chunk slips free and thuds into the muck on the sea floor. I dive down and close my fingers around the silver.

There's a flash of remembering deep inside me. Quick, strong hands. *You were born in the caul. I had to grab my hook to cut you free.*

I see movement from the corner of my eye – another wraith – one eye socket empty, and the other shining with pearl.

279

I blink.

The wraith is gone.

Snow-thick fog blots my eyes. I've let myself run out of air. A groan seeps from my lungs, and there's a dragging feeling, pulling at my chest. The gloom is swallowing me. A noise knocks into the top of my head and I look up to see fists pounding on the ice above me. A pair of arms plunges into the water, frantically waving. I kick towards them.

Crow hauls me out by the scruff, scoops me up and runs with me across the ice to the fire. Water trickles hot from my ears, and all the sound of the world crashes into them.

I do more than gasp. More than splutter. I expand, raking, hoarsing, hacking. I blink and one eye stays netherworld-dark. My lips are blubbery-numb and between my teeth are shreds of seaweed and the flesh-salty taste of scales, filtered through like I'm a whale.

I feel hands tugging at my garb. 'Get her dry!' commands Da. They work to dry me, almost rubbing off my skin. I'm in front of the fire, bare-blubbered, but I feel no shame.

I roll over and spew seawater onto the ice, studded with sand and globs of seaweed and a round, fat pearl. The thundering of the giants in the ship-breaking yard hurts my head. 'Too *loud*,' I croak.

'That's all you've got to say?' demands Sparrow. He pinches my arm. 'Why dint you come up for air?'

But I can't summon enough life-spark of my own to answer him. Crow paces and the terror ent drained yet from his face. Sparrow stays crouched by me.

'Wraithed, was I?'

'Almost.' Sparrow rocks back on his heels. His hands reach out and feel my face. 'Salt-sticky, ent you, stinker?'

They wrap me in dry furs, until I'm lying bundled by the fire like a seal. My brain ticks slowly and I remember. As Crow makes me eat, and Da holds me close, singing to me, I remember her.

Grandma.

I open my still-clenched fist.

In the dip of my palm rests a heavy silver ring. A ring in the shape of a merwraith, with a catch. I flip it, revealing the tiny hiding place inside. Grandma's poison ring.

A great warrior of the sea waits there. Astraia wasn't talking about Rattlebones. She was talking about *Grandma.*

32
Don't You Remember?

I stare around at my crew helplessly. 'But – Stag shot her!' I babble. 'How can she be . . . ?'

'Mouse, you need to rest,' says Da.

'No—' I steal a glance at Sparrow, lowering my voice. 'I think Grandma's there!'

Da pinches the bridge of his nose. 'No, Mouse. You know that only folk who drowned become wraiths. Your grandma was shot.'

I open my stiffened fingers to show him the silver ring. 'This fell through the hull of our ship just now. It's Grandma's ring. Stag must've left it behind. And the whale said . . . and I saw a wraith—'

'Sometimes, when folk are running out of air,' he says slowly, and I know what he's gonna say and I hate it, 'they see things – things that ent there.' He gifts me a gentle smile. 'Don't set your hopes alight. They will only be doused.'

But later, when everyone's asleep, I beg Sparrow for help. I watch as he coaxes out a little purple breath of flame from his fingertip. He pokes it into the ring's poison cubby and I swiftly shut it tight.

I sneak past the former merwraiths, who are lying pressed together for warmth, tails entwined. Slowly, Sparrow's purple fire has been restoring them to life. The ones with intact tongues have started a clumsy kind of talking. *Some are so old that they don't speak our tribe-tongue, or anything like the common trade-tongue, unless they've just forgotten.*

Normally, if a wraith is dredged, the sea-change reverses when they touch air – that means they dissolve, except for their scales. But Da reckons Sparrow's life-spark has re-started their hearts, so their bodies will stay in one piece.

So far, their tails ent reversed back into legs – Da's been thinking on that, too. He reckons that'll take longer, so he's shared out bottles of purple fire between them and told them to keep drinking it to help stay alive.

I pull the heavy merwraith ring out of my boot and stagger towards the half-healed hole in the ice, dodging huge craters made by skull-sized hailstones. I kiss the silver and drop it into the water.

'*Don't you remember?*' I whisper, staring into the murky depths.

My net is cast. I can feel it weaving its shadow down, down, down, spelling towards the sea floor.

Before everyone's awake, I take another drop of Da's wolf-fish blood and dive again. My fingers plunge into the seabed and I cast around desperately, searching for a cloud of silvery weed-hair, or a fierce, pale face.

But there's no sign of a wraith, here. *Gods*, I pray, as I twist in the water, eyes straining. *Please let her be here. Don't let it be that I imagined her.*

Suddenly, iron-strong fingers grip mine. I squeeze my eyes shut, and pray to all the sea-gods. I pull, kicking hard, not daring to look back at who – or what – I've got clinging to me. Cos what if it ent her – and what if it *is?*

I reach the hole and haul myself through, then lie on my front and lean down to pull the wraith out. Her fingers dig deep into my palms with a grip like now-or-never, all-or-nothing.

I stagger backwards, wrenching her free of the ice. Then I crouch, panting, in the stillness of the ships' graveyard. Dead and dying ships look on, all broken masts and wounded hulls and torn sails. The place echoes with the snores of giants.

An old woman sprawls across the ground. A relic of a former sea-captain. Straggling, ice-sparkled silver seaweed is slapped wet against grey-blue skin and thick globs of fish-egg gunge cover the body. The eye in her upturned face is a faintly glowing, filmy pearl, like a moon behind cloud. Where the other eye should be, there gapes an empty black cave; a withered socket. Her fleshy earlobes are fish-nibbled.

I fall to my knees.

There's an opening below the bony ridge of nose, a thing like a blue-lipped mouth. It opens and closes, sagging and squeezing, like a gill. But the shape it keeps making is an M.

'Sparrow,' I whisper stupidly. Then my voice rips painfully from my mouth. 'Sparrow!' I howl. 'Help us!'

Someone yells. There are footsteps, running.

Da crouches next to me. He stares at the wraith in disbelief. '*Wren?*'

'I need Sparrow, *now*.' I look around desperately.

'I'm here,' my brother says, stepping forwards.

'Can you wake her?' I beg. My blood jumps in my veins. I can hear my heart beating like a drum.

'I'll try my best,' he whispers.

'Her sea-heart won't wake for always,' says Da, face sorrowful. 'You will have to say goodbye again.'

'I never said goodbye in the first place!' squeaks Sparrow, outraged.

'Truth be told,' I tell him, gritting my teeth, 'nor did I.'

Sparrow bends over the wraith, brow puckered, and in this beat I feel like he's so far away from me, so full-grown, that he's leaving me behind. He rubs his fingertips together until his purple sparks are rolled into a glittering, sticky thread. Then he pulses it – fast – into the middle of her chest. There's a smell of burning. Thunder grumbles and I ent even sure if it's storms in the sky or in the heart of our grandma.

I shake my head, thunderstruck. I'm half aware of the rest of the crew grouped around me, hands pressed against mouths.

'Is that—' whispers Crow.

'Aye,' whispers Da, squeezing my shoulders.

I nod, trying to smile. But I can't breathe and I'm at risk of being swept away by the crashing shock beating down over my head.

Then the wraith's lungs wheeze open. Everyone flinches. Sparrow scrabbles away.

A voice squelches out of her wet lungs. '*Mouse.*'

I breathe a lungful of sour air, but as I start to speak, it comes again.

'*Mouse?*' the earthy throat booms. Close by, snow murmurs.

Fright wraps around my throat and limbs, sticking me to the spot.

Everyone watches me.

The cavernous yelp scratches my insides again. '*Mouse!*' cracks the voice, like a sea-mountain if it could talk – ragged, rocky, caked-blood-raw. She claws the ice with blue fingertips, nails edged with ice, hands cluttered with limpets and fish eggs.

Sparrow sits in the snow, sucking his fingers and weeping quietly.

I step forwards. The wraith spits a slimy length of seaweed onto the ice, thickened with blood and oyster-pearls and chips of broken shell.

The eye swivels onto me as I crouch next to her. She grabs my hands with startling strength and cries out for me again. The voice carries scorched thunder. The breath is worse than fierce. The wave of knowing and loving her stronger than an oar over the head.

286

Her grip is like a lifeline to another world, a great sinewy cord. I know in my bones that's why she's saying my name and not Sparrow's. I was there in the beat that Stag wrenched her into the Other realm. Our spirits leapt for each other. Sobs judder through my ribs, cleave my body in two, hunch, aching, in my throat.

She lifts her barnacled hands to my face like she's checking me for hurts. Then she grabs my shoulders and pulls herself up to sitting. She is heavier than I can believe. Iron-tipped. Axe-skinned. She grunts like a landed thing of the sea.

The wraith glares blindly at us. 'Mouse,' she brittles out again. 'Get your blade, girl. Ye're to cut me, and do it quick.'

33
The Belly for the Work

'By the gods,' mutters Crow. Lightning flickers in the north. 'She can't mean—'

'And what would you know about it, sproglet?' clack the damp lungs of my grandmother.

'Aye, she means it alright.' I fish my blade from inside my goatskin cloak and kneel by Grandma's almost-tail. My hands shake. Snowflakes settle in my lashes.

'I know ye've the belly for the work, child,' scritches the voice, a beat closer to one of Grandma's stern old kindnesses.

I nod. When I press the tip of the blade gently to the tail, she spits onto the ice, waking beat-by-beat into a thing more like my grandma. 'For the sea-gods' sakes, do it, Mouse. I want to be a *walker* again, not some flail-by-blubber stuck on this sorry scrap of frozen land.' She spits *land* like a curse.

She's still got legs, I tell myself, haggling for time. *They're*

there, only partly sealed together. I can see the seam. I breathe. Shut my eyes. When I open them again, my hand's already moving, cos Grandma's sat forwards and she's helping me press the tip of the blade deep into her and then I'm pulling it, arrow-straight for all the stretch down her legs, to where the sea-change has flattened her feet and splayed them into a V shape. The scream she utters makes the snow groan.

But when it's done, she flexes each foot and sticks out her furred tongue and bends her knees. She's still got merwraith scales. Dark old blood oozes between them.

Crow wraps one arm around his belly and bends forwards, shuddering with dry tears, dry heavings and strange, panicked laughter. But Grandma dazzles. She digs her tattered feet into the ice and wrenches herself upright. 'Lend me your arms,' she commands, in a voice to make the mountains cower.

Da bows to her as she passes. Sparrow capers in her wake.

We hobble together, back to the fireside on the edge of the sea, in the shadow of the mountains.

Our crew has swelled by one.

'You left them like *that?*' Grandma eyes the other once-were-wraiths, hands on hips. They're huddled together for warmth, and their tails clank restlessly against the ground. When they move, it's like they're still below-worlds.

But it's Grandma I can't keep my shield-wide eyes off, so I just gape at her stupidly.

'What a flaming state,' she mutters, breaking the spell on me.

'Well–' I growl. 'I didn't know I had to *cut* them!'

She scoffs. 'Don't cut them, Mouse, and what then? How're they meant to *walk*?' She tuts.

'Da reckoned they'd change back eventually!' I whine. 'We ent stupid!'

'*Eventually* is no good to man nor beast,' she scolds. 'You could at least have sped things up for the poor blighters.'

'We only just woke them!' I shoot her a stormy look.

She shoots one back.

Then we're both laughing, painful hard. We cough up the seawater in our lungs. We check the other wraiths over, and then the proper grimness begins. She shows us how to slice the tails back into legs, then how to stitch the wounds. Then she gets tired and grows distant, like a turning tide.

Her hands can't hold a cup, so Da brings broth to her lips. The wind lifts locks of her hair and carries it about. I prod the sagging skin of her arm to prove she's real. Her roots are still in the seabed, so she barely looks at me, and I refuse to let it hurt.

'I have been dwelling in the kelp forest, among sea-spiders and stars, my memories circling like sharks, with teeth just as sharp,' she murmurs, eyes filled with fire. 'But some stitch of me always knew I had to endure such a fate as this.'

I watch her, even as my eyes cross with exhaustion.

Sleep sneaks like a thief in the dark, to knock us all over the head. I sink dreamlessly into the deep.

*

When we wake, there are so many unasked questions crowding the air.

Grandma must've summoned strength again – she's squatting at the tent mouth, frying fish caught by my hawk. Thaw perches by her side, devouring a raw fish. The wind pushes her feathers into frozen spikes.

'What happened after . . .' says Da.

'How did you become a wraith . . .' I ask.

Grandma cranes round to look at us all and snorts. Then she points at the underside of her chin with fish-gut-smeared fingers. There's a small clean hole through the tip of her chin. 'Threw myself backwards as the wretch fired at me.'

'You jumped?' I croak.

'Aye. Still managed to hit me in the undercurrents, he did, and it gouged a chunk from the bone of my chin. But if I hadn't jumped, I would never have turned to wraith. And salt water is the best for all wounds, eh, Bones?' She grins, showing ragged sockets in place of teeth.

I'm remembering the same heartbeat that she is. When I crouched in the shadow of sails raised by a mutineer. *'You've got to let my grandma go!'* I yelled, stupid-bold enough to believe my word had power on that ship, not knowing how scrap-young I must've sounded.

'No.' Stag said the word like such cheap talk could be

enough to trade for a whole life. He jerked his gun towards Grandma. *Fired*. And she disappeared into the sea.

Grandma squeezes me tight. 'We don't go quiet, do we, Bones?'

I smirk. 'No way!'

'When someone threaten us, we drum up a hellish hullaballoo, don't we?'

'Aye!' A proper howl steams from my jaws.

Grandma slaps her thigh.

I eat tucked neatly under her arm, same as when I was a bab, gratefully tearing fish-flesh in my trembling fingers.

'Wren,' says Da sorrowfully. 'I am heart-sad I was not there to defend our home at your bleakest hour.'

She reaches over and squeezes his arm fondly. Then she looks around the tent and down at me, frowning.

I lift my brows. 'What?'

'Where's the seal-pup? Young what's-his-name?' She snaps her brittle fingers, questing for the name she wants with growing annoyance. 'The child!' Her face crumples in concentration.

'Sparrow?' say me and Da together.

Her face relaxes. 'Aye. *Sparrow*.' She shakes her head, calls herself rude names.

'S'alright, Grandma! Some things must take longer to come back, I reckon.'

She gifts my forehead a cold, rough kiss. I can smell the salt and damp rolling off her.

'He's safe, um – Captain?' says Crow, proper awkward.

'He's asleep over there,' I tell her, stepping over to my brother and peeling back his cloak to show her his crazed stacks of hair. He moans in his sleep.

She smiles tenderly. 'My little chick.' She gasps suddenly. 'I swallowed a spark, a purple worm of fire. Was it – oh gods, was it from this one?'

I nod.

'Aye, well,' she says, shrugging. 'We always knew his powers would be quite the thing to behold.'

Next she turns to Crow. 'Lad! Lanky ne'er-do-well, over there!'

'Aye, he knows you're talking to him, Grandma.' I cast my eyes skywards.

She sniffs. 'Where's he from? He ent just any land-lurker.'

'Nowhere! Never you mind that now. He–' I feel myself reddening, for no reason. 'He treats us well.'

She laughs. 'Alright, lad from Nowhere. You must not call me by my former title. That one is to befall another.'

'Captain?' asks Crow.

'Aye,' she smiles down at me, pearl-eye shining. 'That's the one.'

'Others are waking,' whispers Sparrow, wriggling upright. He hiccups, and a purple flame pops into life on the tip of his thumb. 'Mouse, you're gonna have a proper old sea-army soon, if they keep waking up.'

His words make me shiver. The little fire Grandma kindled crackles. One of Sparrow's songs floats into my head. *Stare into the fire, see battles of yore . . .*

293

Grandma scuttles out into the open like a crab. Her cackling slices wounds in the dark.

We follow her, gathering more wraiths and helping them out of the ice. Grandma's hands are feeling stronger so she performs the cutting and stitching.

We keep going until Sparrow's fire sputters, weak and smoky at the ends of his fingers. He looks proper drained.

I stare at the wraiths. None of them is Rattlebones, and I can't sense her anywhere near.

'I don't know where Rattlebones is,' I tell the crew. 'I can't feel her any more.'

'Captain Rattlebones, dredged,' says one of the wraiths, her nostrils fish-nibbled into odd lumps of flesh.

Cold fingers twist inside my hollow gut. Da beseeches the heavens, muttering a prayer. But Grandma sweeps me into a salty embrace. 'We were lucky to have her watch over us as long as she did,' she tells me.

While Thaw hunts more food for the wraiths, I ask her more about Stag. 'Was he there at my birth?' I glance at Da and he looks away.

'Aye.' She clears her throat and spits out more sea-muck. 'But – ack, you might as well know – he didn't take well to you not being a boy.'

'*Another* boy.'

She looks surprised. 'You found that out, too, did you? Aye. My first grandson lived but seven sunrises.'

'Did you know about that, Da?'

'Aye. Hare told me all about it.'

'Why did Ma ever gather a wretch like that one?' I jab the asking like a spear.

Da turns away to start collecting the fish Thaw has dropped from the sky.

Grandma sticks out her lip. 'Folk make many bold-step, unwise choices when they're young, and Hare was awed by Stag the moment she met him. He had charm, back then. Good looks, too.' I wrinkle my nose and Grandma laughs. 'He had proper *passion* for new ways of thinking and he sparked up a dull room just by walking in. But none of us knew how broken he was, child. Stag suffered greatly at the hands of his own ma and pa – and when I say suffered, I mean they tortured the boy half out of his wits. He locked away his heart and forgot where he left the key – and Hare was the one to help him find it. But he chose not to unlock it. And the death of their firstborn made him throw the key away forever.'

A drum starts to pulse, muffling her words. She frowns. The drum is louder than the beat of a blue whale's heart, louder than any oarsman's drum, louder than thunder. I cast around and see the giants, striding towards us.

'It's the stogs,' I tell her, clutching her arm. 'They're coming to help us, Grandma. They ent just a story!'

Her mouth falls open. 'Never in my nights or days!'

34
Breaking the Chains

We march back towards the Forest. The draggles were so spooked by the wraiths that we had to send them back ahead. Sparrow rides on the shoulder of a giant, cos he's still so wiped. But he sings, and the wraiths follow him, the blue of his song-notes lighting their eyes. The giants stamp breathing holes for whales, and whale-breath shoots into the air.

Grandma and the other wraiths move stiffly, but the fog on her eye thins with every step, and life oils her creaking joints. Sometimes she runs a few steps, throwing out her arms and spinning in circles. 'Ent the air the sweetest thing you've tasted?' she asks me, bundling me close.

On, on, on through the gritty gloom we prowl, a Sea-Tribe army grown from fathoms across time.

'So, we're to fight the last battle on land, eh?' Grandma utters a throaty chortle. 'Well, now. It'll have to do.' She claps her hands together and rubs them briskly.

But my heart feels suddenly heavy, cos I don't want to fly straight into the fight. I got my grandma back. All those times I wondered what I'd say to her if I could, and now all I've got is a lumpy throat and a dry mouth. No words.

Crow watches the wraiths in awe. We meet eyes and he grins so widely it's like his thin face is gonna crack. I return the grin and I know the reason for it. With Captain Wren by our side, we feel like anything is possible. And it's cos of us and Sparrow that she's here in the land of the living, walking again. We made this wildness happen.

But somewhere along the way, Grandma signals for us to stop. 'We must have taken a wrong turn,' she mutters, as the storm-winds snicker, breathing snow into her eyes.

I look around, but thick fog has crept so close it's hard to make out my hand in front of my face.

'How'd you know, Grandma?' asks Sparrow.

'Use your fire and have a squint into the snow over there,' she tells him, ducking to his height. 'We've approached Nightfall from the wrong angle, dear-heart. We wanted the forest, but we must've veered east. Them spindles ent tree trunks. They're towers.'

Goosebumps prickle across my skin. I turn in a slow circle. The dark shadows of the city walls loom up ahead. I remember how them walls crawled with eyes. We're exposed as a bone out here.

Da groans. 'I thought something might be wrong when we crossed that field of icier ground. But it wasn't frozen ground, was it? It was a lake!'

Grandma nods. 'We need to double back and make

south-west towards the forest before we're spotted out here.'

'Arrows could be trained on us right now,' I add grimly.

We turn back the way we've come, into the full force of the wind. But before we've taken twenty paces I feel a stirring of wings. A scream *throbs* suddenly, out of nowhere.

A tawny shape plunges through the sky. It dives fast – huge, reeking, eyes gleaming. A terrodyl.

Da bundles me and Sparrow out of its path. 'Run!'

But I pull back. 'I can help!' I press my chatter into the air, reaching out for the beast's mind. *We ent your enemy!* I tell it. *We mean peace!*

But the beast is hate-filled. It tosses its head, like it's shaking off my words. *Warmbloodseekfindhuntgirlbeast findkilldeadripdraindrinkdry* and I'm covering my ears but the chatter's broken through my skin and *I'm rising up, up, up, and staring down at a grey-eyed child and a screaming full-grown standing over her in the snow. Get that bab. Get her or lose nest-home. Lose life-blood. Hungryhungryhungrysupbloodbewarmmmmmm!*

Someone grabs my shoulder and shakes me, hard. I wrench my eyes away and thump back into my body and use my chatter to force the beast off us. I've almost got it turned around when the chatter sears my brain so violently that I double over, retching, letting go.

The crew shoot arrows and hurl spears but the terrodyl wobbles out of shot and then comes at us again. I empty my lungs into the sky. '*Hell's teeth!*'

The stogs form a ring around us, raising huge fists.

The terrodyl dodges them and barrels through the air.

I use the last burst of chatter in me to shove it to one side. Its jaws open, but they fasten on air instead of flesh.

'Halt, trespassers!' commands a voice.

We turn to see Stag and Weasel advancing on us through the fog. They're draped in red cloaks and flanked by a hunting pack of terrodyls, swirling in the sky. More terrodyls than I've ever seen clumped together in my life. Stag cracks open his throat and spits hateful beast-chatter.

Attack, he growls.

Two terrodyls cut through the mist, making for the giants. They collide, snapping and ripping and tearing. The stogs stumble backwards and one falls to the ground, rippling the earth under our feet. Sparrow begins to wail.

Stag sends another terrodyl. But I push my chatter against his, searching for the beast's own mind buried under Stag's control, and the terrodyl gets snagged in the air between us.

Blood slugs from the corner of Stag's mouth. His eyes are glassy and his fingers clench stiffly. Is he sick, or is the chatter overwhelming him, too? But whenever my eyes sneak to his face, I lose my grip on the terrodyls, and he pushes them forwards another inch.

I feel someone brush past me. Grandma strides out from the protection of the giants. She stands there in the gloom, facing Stag. 'What's wrong with you, then?' Mirth bubbles in her throat. 'Still hurling all your toys out of your cradle?'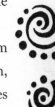

The scream Stag howls when his eyes fix on Grandma could stop the heart.

35
Not Too Clever

Da and Crow try to step in front of Grandma but she taps her chest. 'I've clawed back from the dead, lads. I ent afraid of them.' She thumps an arrow into Weasel before Stag can blink.

Stag starts up a sloppy, desperate beast-chatter. But Crow tears forwards and barges him to the ground, knocking the chatter from his pipes. He tries to roar, but coughs and splutters snotty blood into the snow. Crow pins him down.

The terrodyls wheel and tumble through the air, shaking their heads in confusion. Two snap at each other and a third lunges at us. Da chases it off with a volley of arrows. Before the merwraiths can launch their spears I yell for them to wait and use my chatter to calm the beasts.

Get away from Nightfall – find your home, I tell them, and they streak away, heading south.

Grandma plants her boots in front of Stag's face and he whimpers with rage. 'Hush up,' commands Grandma, and he does. But then he kicks Crow away and tries to run. Da catches up with him easily, and sends him sprawling.

I laugh.

'Well that weren't too clever,' says Grandma, squatting next to him. She draws her rusted silver blade from her belt. 'Form a circle around us,' she commands the crew.

'What you doing?' I ask.

She frowns. 'What d'you think, Bones?'

'No.' I'm shocked into quiet, but my blood clangs.

Her reply is danger-quiet. 'Mouse, turn your back like the others if you can't watch.'

'That's not it,' I wail. 'We *need* the wretch, don't we?' My own words gift me a quease in the belly.

Stag goggles at Grandma, eyes stark in his face. 'H— how – how can you—'

'Ack, *stay* hushed, will you? Button up,' says Grandma.

I step close to Grandma and she lets me whisper in her ear while she frights Stag with her look. 'Can't we force him to help us defeat the Skadowan? He's *been* one of them,' I tell her. 'He knows things.'

She twists her mouth. 'Pains me to say it, but you're right, Bones.' She sheaths her blade and drags the murderer to his feet. To my shock, he trembles when she touches him, and screws up his eyes, pleading under his breath. For the first time, it makes me see how he's just some man. And naught but a coward, at that.

Every bedraggled member of my crew looks him right in the face, until he hangs his head. Then Da sets to binding his wrists.

'I'm outnumbered,' he says. 'I will not do anything rash.'

Da snorts. 'I'm still binding you, fool.'

Grandma shoves him in the back to get him walking.

'Look how the table's turned,' sings Sparrow cheerily.

Grandma stalks away, pulling me with her.

'Wait,' stammers Stag.

Grandma keeps walking.

I hurry after her, triumph punching in my marrow.

But when we're approaching the Forest, dread hangs heavy on my bones. Cos from the shoulder of the giant I'm riding with Crow, I watch the Skadowan's army massing at the city gates. And it has *swelled*.

Back in the Glade, the Forest army is readying. Bear and Frog have returned from Stonepoint with a crowd of Sea-Tribes – fisherfolk, lighthouse keepers and traders from the Southern Flukes. Folk are clad in armour and forming up in ranks. Last minute repairs are being made to weaponry and a man rushes past, yelling for someone to help find a lost boot. Once I'd have called this crowd huge – but now I know it ent, compared with what's waiting for us out there.

Toadflax stares at the straggling merwraiths. Then she cranes her neck and goggles at the giants ducked underneath the frozen clouds, beyond the trees.

'Where are the others?'

'What others?'

'How many more did you bring?' asks Hoshi. 'The battle will soon come knocking.'

Disappointment drags at my edges. I reckoned we'd done alright. Irritation spikes across my skin. 'I almost drowned raising these warriors!'

'Sorry,' says Hoshi quickly. 'You've done well. We'll just have to hope it's enough.'

I search out Egret and Kestrel. The runesmith is trying to keep Kes settled on a fur blanket at the edge of the clearing. She tries to feed a bowl of stew to her, but Kes knocks her hand away.

'Let me go!' she growls, in a horrifying voice that don't belong to her. 'I am needed in the city. I serve the Shadow.'

Egret's face is smudged with tree-blood and tears. Her hands and neck are covered in scratches. 'Mouse! She's worse than when you left. I can barely keep her from gouging out her own eyes. She won't take food. She won't keep warm. All she wants is to work for the Skadowan.'

When I sit next to Kes, she hisses at me, eyes burning my face. 'Kestrel,' I beg. 'Don't you know us?'

She gifts me the most withering, empty, bones-scouring stare I've ever seen. One that looks so wrong on her once kind, soul-beautiful face.

I try to gift Egret a break from the looking-after, but she won't leave Kes's side.

Hoshi passes me a brass skope and I put it to my eye, shinning up a tree like it's a mast.

'Not enough,' I tell them breathlessly, when I've climbed back down. 'We ent brought enough fighters to cope with what's coming.'

Toadflax watches the beast-chatterers. They're cowering under the lowest branches, fingers dug into the soil, sticking together like a pan of boiling, gluey bones.

Fear scratches a fingernail through the pit of my guts.

Before I have to answer, Sparrow hurls a glowing glob of lightning to the ground. 'After all that! Why did we even bother if all's what's gonna happen is we're gonna lose?'

'We can't lose,' I tell him. 'We just can't.'

Grandma steps close and closes her iron fingers over my shoulder. She whispers into my ear. 'Tell them, Mouse. They will heed you. They will follow you.'

Her heart-strength catches my own, kindling a raging fire in my bones. With her by my side, I can't believe we won't win, cos not even the sky would defy her.

I jump into a yew tree and stare down at them all. 'Listen up!' Murmurs die as faces turn towards me. 'The Skadowan are a bunch of heartless cowards, with no soul, no rawness, no feelings between the lot of them. They reckon they're better – with their book-learning, their grand dwellings, their machines.' I notice Stag blink slowly, shaking his head, so I thump my chest and keep going. 'But they're proper stupid, cos they don't know that every living thing is made equal. They don't know that beasts have feelings and kids' minds are needle-bright. They are dull and stupid and evil and we gonna fight them, aye? With *everything we got!*'

Folk crowd around my tree, craning their necks to listen.

'Cos all we can do is our best for what's right. It's that, or idle by as the world ends! Answer me – who of you is gonna let that happen, to your friends, your kids, your crews?'

The roar that answers me almost knocks me out of the tree.

'Merwraiths!' I yell. They crank their ancient necks to look up at me. 'The Sea-Tribes almost died out when the last King spread a lie across the world – that Rattlebones stole the Crown and hid it in the belly of a whale. That never happened! He used our captain to start a war! We have to end it, now!'

They beat their chests and roar up at me.

'This is the fight for the end of the world!' I yell at the top of my lungs. I yell it again, until I feel like I've cracked a rib. I feel Stag's eyes burning my face, but I don't care. 'The Skadowan have been stamped down before – we can do it again!'

'Aye!' they boom.

'This is the fight for *freedom*!'

I gasp, as scores of fists punch the air, people cheering me. My eyes drift to Egret and Kestrel, huddled on the ground. The sawbones girl has turned her head to stare at me. Her fingers twist her skirts in her lap.

'Kestrel?' pleads Egret. 'Are you in there? Can you hear me? Were you listening to Mouse?'

But Kestrel just turns her head to stare coldly at Egret. Then she spits in her face.

36

Wherever We Rest Our Bones

After my speech, folk prepare for battle with a fresh burst of battle-spirit, and the sight gladdens my heart. Toadflax asks the giants to form up in a circle around the Forest. Yapok finds me to say that while we were away, he and the Skybrarian found a clue about the mystery of the Crown. 'I found an obscure reference in a book of stories for children, which seems to have escaped the Skadowan's choking symbol,' says the Wilderwitch boy. 'And it really intrigues me. It tells of a lost citadel in the clouds, where a giant rested his head for many thousands of suns and moons. I believe it could relate to the location of the Storm-Opal Crown. I believe that giant may have been the guardian of the Opals.'

As soon as the word *Opals* leaves his lips, shame squirms inside me. I want to stay and babble with him for longer, but instead I find myself hurrying away, promising to come back soon. Cos what good is finding a clue about the Crown when I've lost all three Opals?

In readiness for battle, we sharpen our weapons, nibble our rations of food and take it in turns to sleep. But my bones won't settle.

I turn over in my bed roll and meet eyes with Crow. 'Can't sleep?'

He shakes his head, making the bedding rustle. He utters a crow-squawk, then hides his face, ashamed.

'Crow, it's alright, it's just me!'

He clears his throat until his voice births human. 'Thank you, Mouse.' He reaches out of his furs and grabs my upper arm. 'I mean it. Before this fight, I want you to know how grateful I am.'

'What you thanking *me* for?'

In the low lamplight, I watch fire burn in his eyes and in his cheeks. 'Whatever happens, I – I won't ever forget that you gave me a home in this world, for the first time in my life.'

'But I never gifted you a *home!*'

'You did,' he says, smiling gentle-sad. 'My home is with *you*. Wherever we rest our bones. It's with you.'

I flush fiercely. I know Grandma's snoozing nearby, wrapped in bearskins with Sparrow, and I pray neither of them is listening. Then I lean across the space between me and the boy and press my forehead to his. We stay like that for beats and beats, gripping onto each other's hands. I feel like the whole world is spinning and he's all I've got to keep me anchored. When I pull away, we lie face to face. 'Crow,' I whisper. Our lips almost graze when I talk.

'What?' I can hear the smile in his voice.

'We ent gonna be resting our bones any time soon. We're gonna *live* – just so you know.'

I hear him wheeze a thin, cold-achy breath, but before he can say anything there's a swishing movement of stirring air. Thaw thumps to the ground next to us. *Comingnowcomingnowcomingnownownow!*

Small yellow mushrooms bunched around the feet of the trees begin to crackle and glow, like tiny lanterns. They quiver, making a damp popping sound that pulses between them.

Crow's eyes glint. 'The trees use the mushrooms to warn each other of danger, Toadflax says.'

I crane my neck and watch countless dark blurs thudding to land in the trees all around us.

'No . . . they can't—'

Sparrow stirs. 'What's going on?'

'For the gods' sake, Mouse!' hisses Grandma nearby, drawing her blade and staring around her. The gold threads in her sea-spun tunic glitter in the half-light. 'What've you sensed?' Gods. What if she heard us, before? She always did keep one ear propped open while she slept.

I push the thought away and tune my ears into the treetops. But the shapes that hulk in the branches ent got a trace of beast-chatter. Which can only mean one thing.

The shapes in the trees begin to stir. 'I need light!'

Sparrow answers me with a sticky burst of purple light on the ends of his fingers.

And we watch, open-mouthed, as huge, ragged eagles shift into red-eyed monkeys that leap from branch to branch, lower and lower through the trees. When they hit the ground, they shift again into scores of red-cloaked mystiks, carrying books and holding cracking balls of lightning.

'Who comes to battle with books?' scorns Crow, swinging his sword, Blood-singer, from hand to hand.

One of the mystiks grimaces.

'Don't let him open that book!' shouts the Skybrarian.

'Yeah, yeah,' mocks Crow.

'Why—' I feel the word shrivel on my lips.

The mystik flips the book open to a page showing a snarling polar dog. Then he sucks at the picture with his fingertips and mutters a spell, shifting into the dog. The book disappears and I run, pulling Sparrow with me. *The Akhunds have sent their mad dogs after us.*

I twist to shoot an arrow over my shoulder but miss, and it twangs into a tree trunk. I draw another arrow but the dog swipes a paw out under my leg and trips me head over feet until I'm slumped, dizzy, against the foot of a tree.

Nearby, a giant hand reaches through the evergreens and plucks a screaming mystik from the ground, carrying him up and out through the canopy. But the next beat, there's a zapping sound and the deafening crash of a giant falling.

Grandma swirls through the battle, arrows dancing through the dark. One pierces the polar dog and then she's hauling me to my feet. I let her pull me away from the tree and then dodge as the Spidermaster rides a giant scuttle-spider between the trees, charging the mystiks. Other spiders follow.

Kestrel thrashes in the ropes she's been tied in. Egret's fighting off an attacking eagle, so I run towards Kes, to make sure someone's defending her. But before I reach her, two mystiks corner me. Toadflax and Hoshi green-chatter webs of branches and pine needles over the mystiks, until they're smothered by the trees. 'It's an ambush! They're trying to weaken us before their main attack!' yells Toadflax. 'Pull back into the trees!'

Branches swoop down and knock mystiks flying. The fighters on our side hurry towards Toadflax. The branches drop in front of us until we're cocooned deeper inside the tree cover, leaving our camp abandoned. We're trapped in a smaller clearing, in the heart of the forest.

We hold a gasping, straggled war council to try to find a way out of disaster's jaws.

Toadflax turns to us. 'The ambush is over, but they now have control of part of the Forest, and the worst is yet to come. How many fighters have we lost?'

A leader from each group of fighters does a count. Hoshi speaks to them and reports back. 'Two Marsh-folk, a draggle-rider, one merwraith and three Tree-Tribe warriors fell,' she says sadly.

Sparrow tries to bring them back, but it don't work.

I watch how he stumbles, half asleep on his feet – hair lank and eyes ringed with black circles.

And that's when I realise it – anyone we lose in this battle ain't coming back.

'This is madness,' says Crow, mouth and nose gruesomely conjoined into an almost-beak. 'So, what – we just wait here for the next attack, like sitting targets?'

'No,' I tell them, my mind whirring. 'There's someone else we can call on for help.'

'Who?' croaks a merwraith.

'Axe-Thrower, daughter of the Moonlander – Fangtooth – Chieftain.'

Grandma scowls. 'Why would *she* help us?'

'The Fangtooths were once called the Moonlanders. Their tribe ent what it sometimes seems. And they're just as strangled by all the bloodshed storms as the rest of us. Plenty of them remember who they really are – Axe included.'

Grandma stares at me strangely. 'Much and more happened while I was sea-dreaming, eh, Bones?' She scrunches her nose. 'But if you say she's to be trusted, who am I to say otherwise?'

'You won't regret it!' I vow. Then I turn to Hoshi and Toadflax. 'I need to get a message to Axe.'

37
Brew an Uprising

Hoshi gifts me a soft piece of parchment made from dried bark to scratch my runes into.

Axe-Thrower, please answer this call for help. We are under attack from Skadowan forces, at the Forest of Nightfall. We have captured Stag. The Skadowan are building a soulless army, thousands strong. If we don't stop them, they will devour everything in their path. Tell your people I know the Moonlands ent just some barren wasteland to be used and chewed up. Their lands are by rights the Moonlands, ancient and proud and singing their stories. Tell them that the girl who freed the slaves – some their own kids – from the stony Chieftains, needs their help. Tell them I'm just a girl of thirteen moons, but I am swollen with fire. The man called Stag stole my ship and killed my grandma and killed the whales in the sea. Then he tore up your lands, planted his own flag, killed and tortured there.

Axe, please come. You can defy your grandmother.
You've got to! You can brew an uprising. They will
follow you over that Stony Chieftain.

Mouse

I tie the message to Thaw's outstretched foot and check she's heart-certain she wants to make the journey. I'm filled with terror that she'll be shot down, but she screeches a battle-cry. *ThawhelpThawhelp! Thaw stay hidden over solid-cloud.*

Alright. Stay heart-strong, brave girl. Safe roving!

After my hawk has disappeared through a parting in the Forest canopy, I mill around the cramped clearing, my gut twisted into knots. But it's not just Thaw that's gifting me bellyache. It's wondering what we're gonna do if the Moonlanders don't answer my call.

When my hawk returns a day later, the full attack from Nightfall ent come. Thaw says she dropped the message at Axe's feet. I can hardly keep still, so put my restlessness into trying to help folk recover from the ambush.

Time drags by.

I find Grandma helping the wounded, washing wounds and binding them with poultices of tree-blood. 'Good stuff,' she says, sniffing it. 'I traded for this whenever I could.'

'What can I do, Grandma?'

She glances up at me. 'Use your best weapon, dear-heart. Your voice. These folk want rallying again. Their battle-spirits were dented in that attack – and the spirits of the chatterers were already smashed by the Wilder-King.'

I find them cowering at the edge of the clearing, in a black-cloaked tangle. Must be three dozen of them – more than I ever knew existed.

'You ent mad,' I tell them. 'Beast-chatter don't have to be a sickness, it can be a strength.' One of them, a woman of Vole's age with filth-streaked light brown hair, stares up at me. I get to her level and touch her arm. She shrinks back.

'This is what happens when chatterers grow up getting told they're mad,' says Da, appearing at my side. 'They don't learn how to cope with the endless noise of it, and they end up believing there's something wrong with them.'

'Well, there ent,' I hiss, tears blurring my sight. 'I'm a chatterer, too. I grew up knowing it made me different, but that being different weren't no bad thing. Everyone has special things about them that can be used as strengths. We can chatter all the terrodyls out of the Skadowan's control!'

A man pulls away from the group and stands, shivering. 'You – a chatterer?'

'Aye. Watch.' I chatter out for Ettler, and the little squidge huffs and puffs over to me, before dropping to land on my outstretched palm.

'How do you live with the noise?' asks a young girl.

I think. 'Lately I've been feeling like the chatter's been changing. Like it's been sending me mad. But I reckon it's cos the world's in chaos. And at the root of it the chatter just shows our deep bond with nature – a power we can use for good.'

The girl scurries forward and jumps up, wrapping her arms around my waist. 'So I'm going to be alright? she says.

'Aye, you'll be fine,' I tell her, resting my chin on the top of her head and watching the others. Some look hopeful. Some don't look sure. I just have to pray they'll believe me in time.

I watch as Ettler grunts his way back towards Egret and Kestrel. 'Will you help me?' I ask the chatterers. 'I believe in you. You should never have been locked up in the Wilder-King's iceberg just for being different.' *Or cos the Skadowan was hunting for me.*

One by one, each with more certainty than the last, they vow to help us.

I grow aware of a presence behind me. I turn. Hundreds of our fighters are watching, curiosity brightening their faces.

I stare around me, at faces known and unknown. There's Da, and Pike, Frog, Crow and Bear, Grandma and the merwraiths we raised, Yapok, and the Skybrarian. Leopard watches me proudly, with Lunda and Pangolin and Pika and other draggle-riders I've glimpsed before in passing. Old One and Sparrow kneel at the foot of a tree gathering tree-blood to help heal the wounded.

There's many, many more, to boot – folk of the mountains, folk of the marshes, folk of the east, south, west and north, united here, steeling their blood for the biggest battle of their lives. Their eyes are on me.

I thump my chest. I pull down my scarf, exposing my

scar. 'I've been branded, scarred, hunted, imprisoned.' Leo looks away. Stag don't. 'I've faced down murderous false-captains and raging Chieftains and the mystiks that almost killed my kin. I've come too far and lost too much to lose the fight now, and I know you all have too! Who's ready to fight?'

The cheer almost knocks me backwards.

Crow sucks in his lower lip, watching me with sparkling eyes, and I feel a flush prickle up my neck.

A voice echoes from outside the clearing. It belongs to Akhund Olm. 'Rebels! Show yourselves now, and fight! Or our army will drag you out and crush your forest!'

I leap upright. 'Everyone, to your weapons! The battle's right here, right *now*!'

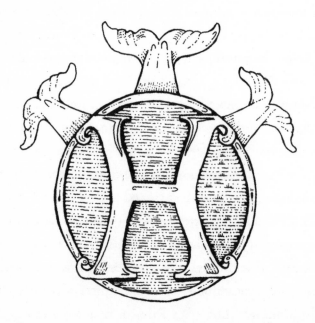

38

Battle

Jaw set and cheeks burning, Toadflax gifts us all one last look of fierceness. Then she nods. The fighters form up in ranks, clutching weapons. Toadflax chatters to the trees, until they unlace their branches, revealing us.

Beyond our hiding place lies a mess of felled trees and dead mystiks, as well as a wounded giant. But beyond the mayhem is a sight that slaps a sickly wave of dread through me.

The Skadowan's army is a wall of armour. Thousands of elixirated soldiers, formed up in lines and clutching weapons. Some are bears, some are youngsters, some are full-growns. All have the same emptiness about them. On the walls of the outer city, robed Akhunds and mystiks stand, Olm in the centre. As one, they snap their fingers. And the soulless army advances on us.

Bears march through the darkness. More and more of them come, cloaked and helmed and swathed in armour. Teeth flashing.

Between the territories of Nightfall, the battle crashes together.

'These soldiers don't know they're soldiers,' I yell to remind everyone. We vowed to capture them where we could and only harm them if we had no choice.

The merwraiths bend and slash, leap and hack, faces grey and eyes blazing. Marsh-folk charge, wielding shimmering fish-spears. Spiders stab enemy soldiers and wrap them in cocoons of silk. The giants stomp towards the enemy lines, crushing soldiers underfoot or sweeping them into the distance with their fists. But more and more and more advance.

The Tree-Tribes whisper bear-powers out of the bones they've etched with bear stories. Then they're loping on all fours, slashing with sharp claws.

My arrows fly as I whirl in a circle, fingers swift, bowstring twanging. A mystik swipes out, hitting me with lightning that crashes pain into my head.

Hands grab me, pulling me out of the way. Then a voice somewhere to my right bellows in fright. 'Terrodyls!'

They swoop over the tops of the trees, shrieking. On the edge of the battle, me and the group of chatterers band together and work to sever the terrodyls from the Skadowan's grip. But I feel the threads of Stag's mind, too, tendrils he sends slithering out of him, snapping like the pink threads of flesh that tether loose teeth.

'Stop!' I scream at him. He ignores me, still trying to help the Skadowan. So I send an arrow slamming into his shoulder and the chatter flies from his mouth as he screams in pain.

Soon we're surrounded by a thicket of terrodyls. The chatterers and me push them back, sweat trickling down our faces, but one breaks free and then out of the blackness swoops low, jaw clamping onto a screaming Tree-Tribesman. He's lifted up, legs waggling, and carried away.

Toadflax trembles with fear and fury. She green-chatters to one of the trees until it rips its roots from the ground and stalks towards the assembled mystiks, flinging them aside with long, sweeping branches.

Chatterers cower, terrorised mouths and eyes agape. I throw up my hands, chattering so desperately I can almost feel my words slipping over my lips, like warm blood.

I will help you claim your rightful freedom! I splurt, lips cracking open with the force. *But you have to help me first!*

A huge, ancient-looking terrodyl drops in the sky until her eyes burn into mine. Her breath steams hot into my body, stinking but thawing my bones. Powerful enough to send me sprawling backwards, pain slamming up my wrists.

Dareorderancient? she demands, sniffing my fright deep into her lungs and grinning at what she tastes.

I'm not ordering you, I plead. *But they are, and you don't have to do what they say any more. They kill terrodyls just to use the blood as a weapon. I hate them for it! We just want you to fly far away from here. Far away from the Skadowan!*

She roars. I ball my fists, feel the slime underneath my nails. Feel the fury of the smothered moon.

When she don't back off, I try reaching out like I did at Castle Whalesbane, pushing forcefully with my beast-chatter. But when I push the beast too far, the taste of blood plummets into my chest and I feel a painful tearing in my lungs. Then I spit a glob of foamy blood into the snow. 'No!' I won't be like him. I won't show the beasts disrespect and try to control them.

I pull my chatter into myself and the terrodyl shakes free. I rack my brains. I've got to help the beasts understand that the Skadowan ent to be trusted, despite all the food and castles they've given them.

I chatter to the terrodyl. *I'll do all in my power to stop the bad-blubbers, and free you and your kin!*

But then the Skadowan forces shoot the beast down, scarring the forest with a raging river of black slime. Fighters shriek, flesh being eaten by sizzling black blood.

'Chatterers!' I scream. 'They've done it now! Come on – this is *your* fight! You can own it!'

They press forward, skin and bones, black, tattered cloaks snapping in the wind. They conjoin their chatter and raise it *up, up, up* and back, against the terrodyls, making them halt in the air and begin to turn.

I join my chatter to theirs, dimly aware of the battle swirling around me. The next time the Skadowan shoot a terrodyl, we get it turned around and wheeling towards the city where it crashes into one of the white towers, crumbling it to the ground with a shattering crash.

'Keep going!' I tell the chatterers, and we push the

terrodyls back beyond the north of the forest.

But I know none of what we're doing is nearly enough against the ranks of wreckers and slavers, so-called mystiks and the elixirated soldiers that stream endlessly into the forest.

Axe, where are you?

Terrodyls dodge storms as they're flung at us. A draggle and her rider charge at them but one catches the orange-furred beast with the edge of a wing and the draggle crashes.

Gods. We've already lost. How long can this go on?

Crow hurries past, wielding his sword. 'Mouse, watch out!' he hisses.

I whirl, nocking an arrow to my bow, but a blank-faced girl knocks me flying. Kin-Keeper is flung from my hands. My fingertips brush it but the girl kicks it away, standing over me.

Suddenly there's a streaking blur of feathers and Thaw swoops out of the sky, claws and beak attacking the elixirated girl that was about to press a blade to my throat.

Thaw!

She wheels back to me, landing near my feet. *Two-legs home girl ThawbringThawbringThawbring!*

My breath catches. *Where?*

Before she can reply, Moonlanders push through the trees into the clearing, led by Axe-Thrower. They circle bolas made of sinew and runestones in the air, chanting battle songs. I whoop, tears streaming. Axe hauls me to my feet and wraps an arm around me. Seeing the Tribeswoman's fierce, sleek face again gifts me sorely-needed heart-strength.

'My people are remembering who they are, and soon everyone in Trianukka will know. And it's thanks to you. If we perish in this fight, at least we'll have died standing true to our ancestors.' Then she and her tribe launch into battle.

The battle swells to a peak. The mystiks are brewing great storms. Tendrils of lightning wrap around the giant's ankles, bringing them lurching heart-stoppingly to the ground.

And however many of the elixirated army fall, there are countless more that march to replace them. The Akhunds must be elixirating more and more, leaving the fighting to the soulless. I realise Olm has disappeared from his position on the city walls, no doubt to oversee the thieving of souls.

Then a scream pierces my heart.

It sounded like Egret. I'm running, searching – then I watch as Egret uses her bodyweight to shove Kestrel sideways, away from one of the mystiks.

Kestrel scrambles onto hands and knees. How did she escape the ropes we tied her in? She's meant to be staying out of harm's way!

The mystik's blade misses Kestrel and pierces Egret's belly. She stumbles, shock carving open her mouth.

I know I'm screaming, but my voice is muffled, like I'm underwater.

The Akhund stands over Egret, his long, tapering fingernails toying with the handle of the blade stuck into her.

'Get away from her!' I bellow, thumping an arrow into his back. He falls and I kick him away from my friend.

Kestrel sinks to her knees, hands covering her mouth, whole body shaking. 'Egret!' she screams, pressing her hands to the wound in her love's belly.

But the runesmith's spirit has slipped away, and her eyes are glassy.

I gently pull Kestrel away from the dead runesmith. Leo comes to help me, sobbing with her daughter. Together we lift Egret's body and step backwards, away from the battle.

Grandma and the wraiths cover us as we blend into the trees.

39
False Crown

Kestrel curls into a ball at the foot of a tree, great, beastlike moans shuddering up and out of her throat. I go to her. 'Oh, Mouse!' she whispers, pressing shaky fingers against her mouth. 'What have I done?'

'You couldn't have helped her, I swear to you,' I say through gritted teeth. 'They thieved your soul, Kes!'

But nothing can comfort her and she's lost to me, swept away on the tide of her grief.

'We'll never hold them off,' Leo whispers to me. 'Too many have been elixirated.' She turns back to Kes and scooping her daughter into her arms.

Yapok – who ent a fighter – comes tearing through the trees towards me. He presses a page from a manuscript into my hands. When I look at the parchment, the runes are red, over a sea of blue. They're the hidden truth!

The Storm-Opal Crown can be found at the highest mountain peak in the Citadel of Sky, above the breath of the first sea-god.

The highest point in Sky? That's Whale-Jaw Rock.

. . . Witches call to me, atop the Wildersea,
The hearth-stones treasure their memory.
You must remember
What waits there,
You'll find it at the point high in the air.

The Old Song was spilling the truth all along – but not about the Opals. It was the final piece of the mystery.

I feel a fleeting stab of triumph, but it's scuttled quick-sharp when I think how I don't even know where the Opals are, let alone where there's a citadel on Whale-Jaw Rock.

I stare at Yapok. 'You did it! Now we have to find the Opals and get them home.'

'How?' he asks.

Kes takes a shuddery breath. 'Mouse?' she calls.

'Aye, I'm here!' I sit by her and Leo, holding the sawbones' hand.

'I'll go with you,' she says, struggling to catch her breath through the tears.

I frown. 'Are you heart-certain?'

She throws me a look of fierceness. 'I won't have her death be for nothing.'

Leo agrees to let Da know where I've gone. Then me and Kes hike to the edge of the encampment. We search around, but it seems like all the draggles are working in the battle. I march off in the other direction, not giving up, but then Kes grabs my arm.

'Mouse,' she whispers urgently.

A terrodyl is hunched on the ground, watching the city and muttering to herself.

Onix not go back notgoback Onixnotgobacknever Notbespikedwithsharpenedsticks OnixnotfightWAR.

Onix? I ask. She swivels her head towards us and I feel Kestrel tense. 'It's alright,' I whisper, prising Kestrel's fingers off. 'I'll talk to her.'

I hold up my hands. *We mean no harm. Can you take us to the city? We need to find three gems there, and if we go on foot, we'll be found. You could fly silently, hidden, and get us there?*

The terrodyl blinks. *Fight back at city??*

I nod and she chuckles. *Fierce little scrapper, you. Onix will help.* She extends a wing and me and Kes scramble onto her back. 'This is for Egret,' says Kestrel. She passes me a raindrop cowl and I pull it on, eyes stinging with tears.

'Aye,' I tell her, thumping my chest. We lay flat, cos a terrodyl near Nightfall won't cause suspicion – but two girls on its back will.

Onix rushes right up to the city walls and turns in the air, swooping low enough for us to jump onto the wall and sway there, trying to get our balance. Then she pulls away, soars into the air and disappears. We climb down and crouch in a filthy gutter, panting.

Oily, spitting lanterns line the streets. Holding onto each other, me and Kes edge deeper into the city, brushing past hurrying figures half hidden by the smog.

'Watch out for spies,' I whisper. 'They could come in any shape.'

She nods. Tears have made tracks through the grime on her face. 'Are you ready for this?' I ask.

'I will smash them for what they did to us,' she spits.

We make our slippery way towards the Hall of Moans.

Kes presses a finger to her lips. High overhead, black and grey storms lurk, desperate to feast on the city. They're being held back by weather-witches. But where are they?

When we reach the the hall the front doors are open. I drag Kes behind an abandoned Spiderstop and we watch as blank-eyed, blank-faced soldiers pour through. We're about to sneak out from behind the Spiderstop when a stooped figure emerges. We hang back and I see the pointed white staff and pale darting eyes of Akhund Olm. I gasp as I realise he's wearing a crown, with the three Opals set in it.

'Let's go,' hisses Kes, and we follow him into the murk.

We hide outside Olm's house for what feels like an age after he disappears inside, working out how to get around the guards. Eventually we find an upper window at the back of the building and Kes boosts me to the ledge. I heave, the wood groans and rattles upwards, and then I'm tumbling into an upstairs room – I stare around, not recognising it. Then I turn back and help hoist Kes inside.

I freeze. When nothing stirs, I nock an arrow to my bow and advance slowly. Creeping unease tightens over my skin.

We prowl through the room. On the back wall hangs a tapestry like the ones I saw at Hackles and the Iceberg Forest. Chests and cabinets spill with jewel encrusted chalices and goblets and everything coated in the thickest grey dust.

We push open the door and it squeals loudly. We pause, wincing. Then we head down a passageway and I open another door.

The air in the room is thick and cloying. I step further in and turn to my left and feel my guts plummet into my boots. The room is full of people tied to chairs, mouths gagged, hands bound, eyes screaming.

Olm stands in front of them. He twists round to goggle at us. I see is more clearly this time – the brilliant band of gold, set with three jewels, one green, another blue, and the third amber. He was about to elixirate again.

I choke out a laugh, my bow shaking in my hands. 'You fool,' I whisper, feeling older than thirteen, and wiser than greedy full-growns like this one.

Kestrel waits in the shadows. *Olm don't know she's with me*, I realise.

The Opals in the false crown begin to spill a yellow light. 'How so?' Olm asks softly, tilting his head.

I keep my arrow trained on his chest.

'That ent a crown,' I spit. 'It can't be, when you don't deserve to wear one, and the Opals don't want to sit in it.'

'Peculiar child,' he comments mildly. 'Aren't you feeling tired? Wouldn't you like to lie down?' Tendrils of light twine from the Opals, towards me. They braid together, blue, green and amber.

Then I see the Opals' light billowing around my longbow. The skin on my hands looks like it's lifting off, fraying, bleeding into the air. It's happening. *He's elixirating me.*

'I am in possession of the most powerful objects ever cut from the womb of the world, and you come here calling *me* a fool?'

Just then, as I feel myself growing weaker, a silver shimmer streaks through the gloom, hitting Olm in the shoulder.

Kestrel!

Olm cowers on the floor, pressing his fingers to the puncture in his skin. My skin settles as my spirit eases back inside where it belongs. Then I step close to Olm, reach down and snatch the crown off his head, ripping out oily strands of grey hair with it.

I turn away but Olm snatches at my ankle, making me crash to the floor.

But Kestrel flings another dagger, and it spears his upper arm, making him scream in a frenzy of pain and fury.

I untie the ropes on the wrists of the folk he was about to drain, and they flee, too petrified to even thank us.

'Go!' I scream to Kes.

We tear back the way we came, towards the window. I sling my longbow over my back and shove the crown onto my head. Kestrel hooks her legs over the ledge and then pulls me out the window. I yelp as my leg scratches along the brick, tearing another rip in my breeches. Then we're scrambling down the side of the house and running through the sickly, greasy light of the empty street. We run, boots slipping, hoods bobbing over our faces. My face grows sticky-hot under the tight raindrop cowl.

We turn down alleys, losing ourselves in the maze of the city. Something stirs, high over our heads. I glance up – and watch the underside of a huge beast glide over us.

You waited for us, I chatter. The terrodyl swoops closer, muscles rippling under her tawny flesh, eyes glowing.

As we're climbing onto Onix's back, a boy creeps out of the shadows. 'Kestrel?'

Kes stares at him and cries a greeting. 'This is Mudskipper,' she tells me. 'Another scholar of Medsin.'

'We've been searching for you!' he whispers. 'We are ready to join your movement.'

I start asking if he could convince the others to ride terrodyls back to the Forest when Kes interrupts. 'Oh! But what about something even better – could you find a way into the Hall of Moans underneath the College and rescue all the bottles you can find there?'

We explain about the souls in the bottles and the army. 'We think we know a way to mend all this chaos, and we need them bottles to stay safe until then,' I say.

'Mission accepted,' says Mudskipper, melting back into the smog crawling through the streets.

Back in the Forest, I rip the crown from my head and use my dagger to prise the gems out, careful not to scrape them. I put them in my pocket and hurl Olm's false crown away. Then I tell Kestrel the plan that's been thumping at the back of my brain. But now we're back the grief is painted vivid on her face again, and she shakes her head.

'No,' she breathes. 'Don't leave me!' Then she flushes. 'I'm sorry, I just—'

'I know,' I tell her. 'But I have to go, Kes. I have to find the Crown.'

I leave Kestrel curled into Leo, sobbing again. Then I dart back into the fighting and try to find Toadflax. I yell to her about the Opals. 'The Skadowan supply of souls is cut off now!'

Toadflax nods. 'Finally, I can see a chance of winning. Morale is low – the troops will be cheered by this.'

Da and Grandma run up to me and I tell them what happened in the city. Da's so overcome with pride that all he can do is open and close his mouth.

'Now I've got the Opals, I have to keep going and get them to the Crown. Once Leo and Toadflax have decided who should stay and fight, others can follow me.'

Before they can argue, I chatter to Onix, who's waiting nearby, leap onto her back and she lifts up and away.

Moonlight trickles through the clouds. I stare down at the city walls as we streak back past Nightfall.

Fright like I've never known rattles up and down my spine. I'm alone, now. This is it. Might be a new beginning. Might be the end of everything I've ever known. I howl to the hidden moon.

40
The Crown

I glide high over the world, hunched on Onix's back, longbow slung across my shoulder.

I pull an arrow from my quiver. *I need to find Whale-Jaw Rock*, I tell the terrodyl. I flatten along her back, until my belly presses against one of her massive spines.

You bear the stones home, seethes the old terrodyl.

I wrap my cloak closer around me, adjust the raindrop cowl on my face and tighten my hood. The cold licks my eyeballs. I ent glugged a drop to drink for beats and beats, and my belly's clamped with a low-down stabbing pain.

In the east, above the scarred land between the Stone Circle and the Eastern Mountain Passes, we halt, flapping in the air. I scan the ground. There are many geysers here, spurting whale-breath high into the sky, and the whale-breath has frozen solid. But there ent one that points to a great rock crowned with the jaw of a whale. Have I remembered it wrong?

I turn full circle on the terrodyl's icicled back, half

sobbing under my breath.

We're turning in the air, the beast's wings wheeling against the wind, when the shadow of a mountain looms to one side. I stare up at it. The breath of a geyser has frozen all the way up to its peak. And right at the summit a whale-jaw stands, proudly rooted into the stone.

You bear the stones . . . you wicked, evil child, chatters Onix suddenly, and all the hairs along my spine rise, prickling my skin. The beast slows and starts to wheel around. Someone's controlling her.

'No!' I put my face in my hands and groan. Then I grunt a desperate beast-chatter as I try to wrestle back control.

Through the stark sky Stag rides, clutching the back of another terrodyl. As he gets closer, I see the mad look slapped across his face, and the way his lip twitches, so it pulls up into a sneer.

Oh, gods! He's following me!

Onix wrenches her mind free and snorts hot air out through her nostrils and thrashes her spearpoint head around. *Not for long!* She cranks her wings and pushes on, faster, faster, faster . . .

I twist. Stag lunges out of the murk, a dagger clutched in his hand. He slices a deep wound in Onix's skin, erupting a jagged wound that seeps black rain.

The beast screams.

'Get back! Leave her *alone*, you filthy flaming *savage*!' I grab for my longbow but the terrodyl booms at me.

Jump, now! Blood eat away whale-breath!

I stare down. She's right. The black rain is dissolving the bridge of frozen whale-breath that leads to the rock – and I need to climb it.

I'm so sorry! I jump. She shelters me with her wings until the last beat before she's forced to pull away.

I tuck into a ball and land, shockingly winded, on the bridge from the geyser below to the mountain above.

I gulp for breath.

'Mouse!' yells a cut-blubber voice.

Stag zooms closer on his terrodyl. I aim an arrow at him. He curses and the beast dodges. He guides it closer, closer. Then Onix shrieks her last breath and barrels at Stag's terrodyl, driving it away from me.

I stare up at the bridge passing up the mountain and through a hole in the cloud above.

And I start to climb.

Frozen Breath

With every laboured step, the Opals in my pocket clink together, making an oddly musical noise. The only other sound is the crunch of my boots, shush, shush, shush, in the ice.

To keep my spirits up, I start chattering to the Opals. *I am a vanquisher of monsters*, I tell them. *I am. I swear it. But now I know what the real monsters look like. They walk on two legs.*

My breath swells loud in my ears. I keep looking back, fearing Stag's murderous fingers on my neck. Are Kestrel and the others on their way?

There's darkness. I'm more alone than I knew I could be, ever. But a tiny sliver of hope pulses in my chest, like a moonsprite. I am here. I am trying. Whatever happens, I tried everything.

I hike. I can't believe I'm walking on the first sea-gods' breath – in the past I've watched it gush and babble, with folk crowded round to see it burst out of the ground, and

I've placed offerings by it along with the others.

I trudge. I rest. Repeat. I stare out across a vast, smoking field of ice. I feel the wind reach into my hood and trace my scar. I shudder inside my furs. Bite my lip. Turn around.

Stag's terrodyl drops him onto the ice below me. My nerves startle and I summon all my strength, hurrying as fast as I can without slipping.

At the top the air's so thin I can barely fill my lungs. I breathe quicker and quicker. Then I wait to see if Stag survives the climb. Cos I won't be hunted any more. I will face that lumbering man, not be chased.

Time for the hunted to become the Huntress.

When his head finally appears above the ice he blinks at me. Then he grabs for my ankle and I scuttle back. I stand, nock an arrow and train it on his neck. 'Ent you ever gonna learn?' I hiss. 'You've lost. I'm bringing the Opals home.'

His face tightens with rage. But when I gesture roughly with my bow to make him move, he does it.

Then, while I'm staring at him along the length of my arrow, my boot slips and plunges through a weak point in the ice. My hands flail for balance, and my longbow flies from my grip. I'm falling. I fall into the ice up to my chest.

Stag squats above me, panting quietly, red frothing in the corners of his lips. 'You will never be able to hold a ship against disaster or mutiny. I've already proved that a woman cannot. Why risk repeating history?'

'Just pull me out!'

He smiles. His hand tightens on my cloak.

'What makes you think I wanna be a captain now, anyway?'

He pulls a false-sorry face. 'Come, now,' he says, pouting. 'I know you.'

'You flaming don't!' I spit, right into his face.

He wipes it away. 'Charming, as ever.'

Something inside me snaps. I'm gonna set him straight. 'No, *you're* the one that ent charming! You've never been a captain, y'know,' I tell him. 'Cos you thieve dignity from everything, and you don't even know what it really means. I didn't use to, either. Now I know it's being a spirit guide.' He laughs but I keep trying to tell him. 'Why don't you know things? You think you do, but you don't. Like why don't you know that animals are folks, too? And why can't you see the life pulsing in all things?' I'm full, now. Brimming over with feeling. 'And why don't you know how much it *matters*?'

And still, here at the end of the world, after everything, he cocks his head and looks at me like I'm spouting stupids. And he just can't understand. He don't have it *in him* to understand. And I feel something new pop into my belly and swish there. I feel heart-sad for him, that he can't feel a stitch of joy at being in this world, that he can't feel the wonder of sharing it with all the beasts that fly, swim or crawl. He's got beast-chatter and all it is to him is a curse and a thing of terrible shame. And that's what lost him Ma, and me. And that's what's killing him.

Blood clogs the corners of his mouth. Gruesomeness cracks his face into a grimace.

337

I throw myself forwards and sink my teeth into his wrist and he yells and flicks his wild gaze into my face. He yanks my hair back so hard I feel like my neck's gonna snap.

Behind him, another terrodyl rears suddenly over the mountain. Akhund Olm slithers off its back, wearing bloodied bandages from Kestrel's blade. 'Well tracked, Stag. You can leave her to me, now.'

'She's my daughter.'

'What did you say, boy?'

'I said she's *my* daughter,' calls Stag, face creasing with annoyance. 'I will deal with her.' He reaches down and drags me up and out of the ice.

'Water must run in your veins, and *not* seawater, neither! I got my fire-crackle from my ma. *You* ent no part of me!' I wrench away from him.

'This is all particularly endearing,' says Olm, sneering. 'But I am afraid I can no longer find any use for you. Leave her to me.'

Stag stares at him. 'But—'

'You are nothing to me, boy. You have only failed the Skadowan.'

'After everything I've done?'

'Weakness is dangerous, intolerable,' Olm says. 'I cast you out.'

'You can't mean that.' The surprise tears his voice and slackens his mouth. Then he sinks to his knees, wringing his hands in a beg.

His stupidity stings me like a slap.

'They've used you up!' Sudden traitor tears spark in my eyes. 'If you're *gonna* steal ships and lives, you might as well make it count for something! How could you *let* them? Why did you ever let them in?' I never expected this muddle of feelings. But the man loved my ma, once, and she loved him. And they brought me into this world.

He turns to look at me. 'I know you're thinking of her,' he says, voice bubbling with blood. 'Hare saved me, Mouse. And I threw it away.' A haggard, heavy shadow crosses his face, betraying his broken spirit and the hugeness of his regret. 'And she never loved me like she loved her own blood. Her parents. Her child.' He drops his head into his hands. 'I never knew *love* like your kin does.'

Love sits on his tongue, hot and fat, like some poisonous toad.

'You could've *been* our kin, though, couldn't you? If you'd only learned to let the light in.'

He snorts. 'Light? It was crushed out of me when I was many moons younger than you are now.'

'Aren't you tired of listening to him whine so, youngling?' pants Olm. 'Wouldn't you like to put a stop to his words once and for all?'

'But – after everything–' mumbles Stag.

'Did you really think I would admit you to our order?' laughs Olm.

'I know I am a *mystik*.' Stag pushes the word through his teeth like a glob of poison. 'But I thought that if I proved my loyalty to the Shadow, pledging my powers to our – your

339

– cause, then the mysticism would be scrubbed from my veins, that the—'

'Tedious, isn't he?' says Olm, turning to me. 'Shall we put a stop to him?'

Stag laughs bitterly. 'I am already dying.'

Olm passes a thin silver blade to me.

I reach my fingers towards the weapon, to take it from him. Then I hesitate. Grandma's voice rattles inside my skull. *For the gods' sake do it, girl!*

But then I'm blinking, and breathing, and pulling my hand back in disgust. 'Leave me alone, both of you!' I turn and blunder away from them.

'Stop her!' shrieks Olm.

Stag mumbles something lost in the wind.

'You dare disobey me, when this is your final chance to redeem yourself?' spits Olm, advancing closer.

'Oh, I can prove I am ruthless, old teacher.' Stag pulls a sleek black handgun out of his cloak.

'You threaten me?'

'Not you, Olm. I said she's my daughter, didn't I? I said I would deal with her, did I not?'

He points the gun at me. He presses a lever on it, and there's a sickly *clicking* sound. I knew I was gonna die out here, alone, with no one who cares about me near. This is where the voyage ends. Biting like a ray, stinking like a draggle, swallowing hope like a gulper. There's naught left of me for fighting.

42
My Daughter

'No,' booms a rich voice. 'She is *my* daughter.' A draggle swoops towards us, and Da leaps onto the ice, Thaw-Wielder riding on his shoulder.

'Da!'

Thaw bolts towards us, scratching deep gouges in Stag's face. She sings her feather-truth. *Fledgling, no strength!* she calls, dragging her claws down Stag's face again, making him answer her with a wretched scream.

Flew anyway, life-not-death. Dredge strong wings from deep-heart places. FLYFLYFLY!

Her chatter gifts me heart-strength. But Stag roars. Thaw wheels away, and he follows her with the gun and—

'*No!*' My voice throbs off the mountain.

Crack.

Thaw screams, giving a last burst of strength, scrabbling in pain with her claws. She soars higher and higher in the air, until she reaches a frozen cloud. She plucks at the silver edge of it, clipping it away to let a dimmed ray of winter sun puddle on the peak of Whale-Jaw Rock.

Da charges at Stag, wrestles the gun from him and throws it off the mountain. Stag collapses into the snow.

Almost without thinking, I take out the Opals. Their light weaves together into a strong, glowing, multicoloured vine. The vine reaches out for the pale ray of sun, and the sunlight weaves into the braid. The light bursts upwards, hitting the frozen cloud and punching through the hole Thaw made. The hole widens, letting even more light through. Around me, the storms hold back like they can't touch the stones. Lightning withers and dies in the air, filling my mouth with the taste of burning.

Thaw plunges off the edge of the mountain. I storm the rocks with my tears.

'Mouse!' says Da urgently.

'But Thaw!'

'Hurry!' yells Da. Then Olm runs at him, snarling, and Da turns away to fight. Another draggle zooms into view and Kes leaps from its back, throating a fearsome battle cry.

I think of how Grandma dragged herself back into this realm I summon the fierceness I need to keep moving. I stow the Opals back in my pocket.

I stare at the little puddle of light Thaw scraped out of the frozen cloud. Then I fire arrow after arrow into the cloud, whispering to the runes buried in Kin-Keeper's wood. They burn bright. More golden light trickles through the hole.

I stagger to my knees, letting the light bless my skin. I gulp a breath and fire another arrow – more light spills down.

Ghosts begin to mill around me. An ancient citadel flickers behind the here-and-now – a village defended by a fortress, with arrow-slits along its walls and flags waving from its battlements. Ghostly Tribesfolk are garbed in celebration clothes, and gathering for a great feast.

More light spills onto the rock and finally, I know the full truth of the Crown – cos above me, the sunlight has cast a gold band atop the mountain and touched three gaping sockets, etched all around with deeply-scratched runes. The gold is the finest I've ever seen, and now I understand the whale's words, about how it can't adorn any man's head. The Crown ent a thing or place hidden up here. The Crown visits, forged by nature when the sun rises and sets. Like a gift from the tide. It can't be owned by anyone but nature.

I shoulder my longbow and climb towards the Crown.

Ghosts brush close to me, cloaks cobwebbing my eyes. I brush them away. I hear a yell. *Da?* I sob as I climb, but I know I can't stop to help Da or find Thaw. If I don't keep going, before the sunlight moves, I'll never get the Opals home and everyone else I love will suffer, too. Grandma. Sparrow. Crow. The thought startles me, but my bones sing its truth. I *do* love Crow. I love him like he's kin. Like I've always known him.

When I'm standing, breathless, underneath the golden crown that's grazing the ancient rock, I pull the Opals from my pocket. They feel lifeless in my hand. As cold as Sparrow when I thought he was dead from a shaking fit – waxen. Am I too late? I breathe over them. I want to lick them to life like a wolf mother. I want to kick out at the clammy paws of death, padding closer. *Not now! Not yet! Come on, you're almost there!*

I scream the words of the old song into the clouds. Liquid gold spreads across the top of the world, falling into my eyes and kissing the backs of my hands.

'*Open your eyes,*' croaks Sparrow, from somewhere near my elbow.

'I am, too-soon!' Then I blink, a shiver spreading across my skin. 'How did you get here?' I glance down at Sparrow. Shimmering, he floats. Cross-legged, in flaming mid-air.

'*I'm having a vision.*'

I release a great sigh. Thank the gods he's here.

Sparrow points skywards at the Crown. '*Mouse!*' he splutters. '*Do it, now!*'

I stumble, the three lifeless Opals tumbling and clinking together in my cupped hands. My cold-flayed hands, cradling ancient wildness, skin on skin. I'm dead tired.

I can hear sounds of a horrifying struggle. Olm begging and shrieking.

I glance back and see Stag chasing after me, clutching his bleeding face. He lurches to his feet and I stumble on, calf-deep in snow, breathing animal dreams.

Then I stop, sway and almost topple backwards. Terrodyls are circling like sky-sharks. Has he called them?

Stag chatters low in his throat, and a terrodyl with hailstone wounds cratering its body and wings like ragged bites lunges for me.

'*Roll right!*' says Sparrow.

I do it, sobbing, forehead touching the snow. 'So tired!'

'*Keep going!*'

I climb up, holding onto the ledge of rock, fingertips bleeding. 'I *can't!*' My voice emerges stupid, young, weak. The very sound of it makes me roar from the pit of my belly, up through my chest, through my throat, between my teeth.

I feel the heat of a terrodyl zooming towards my back and I hurl beast-chatter out around myself like a huge shield, and the beast pulls away from me, seething.

I growl and shriek my wriggling way up, hauling myself by trembling arms, and when a hand clutches at my boot, I kick out viciously, hearing the snap of a bone and a trickle of blood. 'Little devil!' bubbles Stag.

I stand panting beneath the Crown. I read the runes etched around each socket in the rock, then I lean forward and push each Opal into its burrow.

Then I collapse into the snow, breath ragged, muscles screaming.

A smell of sunlight on fur weaves into my nose, and I taste old blood on my teeth. I watch a flash of some ancient ceremony play out across my eyelids.

I close my eyes. My heart is a drum. It booms. I think my lungs are still gilling open and closed.

'*Mouse?*' asks Sparrow's voice, clear as a bell.

And in my bones I feel a deep stitching together of the cloth of the world – like the opposite of tearing. The storm-stink of the Withering clears, bringing fresh, clean air.

Another gap chinks open in the frozen clouds and light streams through.

I mutter words from the Captain's Oath. 'I'll read the pictures in the lights, the gifts that tell us future Sights.'

Stag creeps closer.

'My hawk soars strong, of heart and claw!' I yell down at him. 'From summer's freeze to winter's thaw! I heed the pulsing, the blue whale's call, that every ship has a soul!'

Inside the crown, the Opals chink into a bright dance of light, each one glowing. The fire spirits begin to play overhead and I fall, panting into the snow.

I watch the fire spirits twist into a picture of me, striding the length of my deck.

Stag reaches me, craning his neck to stare at the Crown with a look of wonder. 'I can still get them, before the light changes,' he mutters to himself. But then he collapses in the snow. 'Beautiful,' he whispers, with a nod, watching the lights. 'Not as beautiful as your mother was, though. Nothing ever could be.'

I keep my face blank and my arms crossed. But I listen.

He taps his chest, then points at me. 'I gave her that brooch. The dragonfly.'

'That's why you put it under your pillow!'

He nods, then bursts into a fit of bloody coughing.

The Crown disappears as the sun climbs higher in the sky. When I search the rock for the Opals, they've gone. Finally, they're safe from human hands.

'I'm proud of you, Mouse,' says Stag.

I scowl. 'You don't get to be proud of me!'

'Join with me, Mouse,' he says. 'Together we could be so powerful. I know your potential like no one else can. We can turn the tide against them.'

He watches me as doubt slithers under my skin. And suddenly I feel like running. I feel like a small creature caught in the claws of a cunning beast.

'And then we can make this world a purer place,' he gabbles urgently, wiping the blood from his mouth.

'No!' I turn away. I plug my ears to his ranting.

'What hope can there be otherwise?'

'There is so much hope!' I roar, defiance blooming in my chest like a rose of blood.

He sighs, heavily. 'Leave me,' he bubbles, blood spilling down his chin. 'I am dying. Leave me here.'

'No one,' I say, eyes fixed on his, 'deserves to die alone.'

He smiles. 'No. But I want to. Grant me that mercy?'

Before I turn to go, I reach down and pin Ma's dragonfly brooch onto his cloak. 'I want you to know that I forgive you.' I straighten up. I force myself to look right at him, and let all the rage and hate drift away.

He puzzles up at me. 'Why?'

I sigh. 'Cos your bad blood ent my burden,' I explain, slowly so his stupid can soak it in. 'I ent taking it on.'

Then I walk away.

'Sleep, you black-heart,' I whisper, remembering Grandma's old lullabies. 'Fall down a dream-well brimming with ghosts.'

43
Thaw

'Hurry, Mouse!' shouts Da. 'The thaw is starting!' He runs to me, and he sweeps me up in his arms, pressing a kiss onto my cheek. 'You did it!'

'What happened to Olm?' I ask.

'Kes and I disarmed him,' says Da grimly. 'But he chose to throw himself off the mountain rather than face justice.'

We jump onto the back of a draggle and lift up and away from the melting geyser. 'I've got to find Thaw!' I yell.

'She's gone, Mouse,' says Da, holding onto me.

I shrug him off. 'No.' I shake my head, shivering. '*No.*'

I scan the ground below and spot a tall figure. 'Look!'

We swoop low and find Bear, holding Thaw in his strong arms. 'I fought off Skadowan fool-hearts while your da flew up to find you,' he explains. 'Then I saw this poor girl plummet to the ground. I'm so sorry, Mouse.'

His care and heart-sad look wrench a raw cry up my throat and it cracks into the air, steaming.

He puts Thaw in my arms. She's limp, and heavier than

I'd have thought possible. Her love's flown, but mine aches in my chest, and what am I meant to do with my love for her if she can't feel it? What is a captain, without her sea-hawk?

My tears thump loudly on her blood-smeared crest. A howl brews thick in my lungs.

'We've got to go, before we're swept into a flood,' warns Da, eyeing the melting whale's breath.

I let my howl fly, and it clangs off the geyser ice.

'We have to go,' says Da, still gentle, but frighted-urgent.

'Hang on, please, just a beat.' I find a scrap of tree-blood poultice in my pocket. I squat on the ground, with Thaw stretched along my thighs, and search among her feathers for the wound. Then I press the poultice against her skin and let Da help me onto the waiting draggle.

Bear and Da exchange troubled glances, thinking I'm blind as well as grieving.

'Mouse, Thaw has no need for that,' Da says.

Bear wraps an arm around me, holding onto the draggle with one hand. 'She helped you save the world,' he tells me proudly. 'Never was a finer hawk. She'll have the finest sea-burial to match.'

But I block out their worry, even their praise. I'm sensing out for the death-sea. I'm gonna find Thaw there, and bring her home.

When we land in the Forest of Nightfall, smoke billows from the city. The gates are open and people move freely in and out, helping each other to shelter.

'The souls of the Skadowan's army have returned!' says Hoshi joyfully, when we return to the Glade. 'The battle ended and the bears turned on their masters.'

Crow bursts from the trees in crow shape, spilling long into a boy again as his feet touch the ground. His amber eyes sparkle. All the feathers retreat into his skin, like normal. He grabs me and musses up my hair. I push him away, laughing, forgetting my heartache for a tiny beat.

'The Akhunds have fled,' says Toadflax, running to greet us. 'But we caught some of them. There will be trials.'

'Where's my brother?' I ask,

'Here,' he says at my elbow, making me leap a hundred feet in the air.

'Stop doing that!' I scold.

His eyes glow bright white. His scraggy yellow hair tips his collar bones. I grab him and pull him towards a bed of pine needles under one of the trees. 'Please, help her,' I beg, peeling Thaw's limp body from inside my cloak where I've been hugging her to me.

He touches Thaw and a purple light glows on the ends of his fingers. He frowns and a bead of sweat drops down from his lips to his furs.

'I can't do it no more,' whimpers Sparrow, cradling Thaw in his arms. His tears plop into her feathers.

'What?' I take a step backwards.

'The power,' says Sparrow miserably. 'It's – going.'

'Mouse, I tried to warn you,' says Da. 'As much as it scalds our marrow, death is something we must accept . . .'

'No! Not *this* death, not *her!*'

THAW! I thunder my voice *across the worlds, through the water, popping into the dream-world and seeing her fluttering spirit, small and lost and alone. When she sees me she smiles with her eyes. She is an ancient. A sky-goddess visiting in hawk form.*

There two-legs girl! Thaw knew she would come. Thaw wait to say feather-farewell. *She jostles her silvery spirit-feathers.*

Come home, Thaw! *swim my words.*

Thaw goes home, to feather-nest. Thaw loves two-legs home-girl. But Thaw flies far, now.

She vanishes.

'Mouse!' Da's voice *smacks* into my ear, like water against a hull. For a few beats, my hearing is trapped underwater, unless it's just the blood in my ears. Da stares, ashen-faced. 'What just happened?'

But I can't answer him. I cradle Thaw's body close to me and rock, fingers deep in feathers, throat gouged by wailing. When Da scoops me into his arms I fold into him, tumbling into the darkest place I've known.

44
Sea, Sky, Land

There comes a time when the sun considers his return. It's as though he's waiting to be heart-certain that peace is here to stay. The dusk skies are brittle blue and the moon fresher than milk, and the day struggles to throw off the heavy cloak of night. But it's happening.

The first time I see another dawn, the sea is a spill of silver that reaches into my chest and pulls at me, *hard*. She's restless again. So am I.

The merwraiths return to their sea-mother's arms and I spend all my waking beats with Grandma, and at night I sleep curled against her back. Cos sometimes it feels like she's pulling away from us again, into some shadow-world. On the bad days, I beg her to tell me her name, but she's grown vague, prone to muttering and sitting alone, face closed up. And she don't know who she is.

'Let her be, Mouse,' says Da, touching my elbow.

But a seed of doubt has settled inside my belly. She was dead a long while. Now the fight's won, I reckon she don't know what to do with herself.

But on a better day we sit together and I watch her weave me a shawl from Thaw's feathers, and at some point, after falling into a void so deep and dark I thought I'd never find my way out, I feel ready to wear it.

Me and my crew travel back to the ship-breaking yards, to find the *Huntress*.

'I don't know if we can repair her, Mouse,' says Da doubtfully, running his hand along the rotting wreck of her hull. We stand on the thawing ground of the breaking yards. The *Huntress* sits in a cup of loudly cracking ice, steam smoking out of all the cracks forming around her. She looks gruesome. I mean *proper* wretched. There's a great iron spike sticking out her front in place of a bowsprit, like a narwhal's tooth, for cutting the ice. The merwraith dredging claw has weighted her down on one side, and the cannons have slipped out, bashing holes in her hull. Her sails hang like strips of torn flesh. The plank's snapped and so have the oars, and the storm-deck has rotted right through.

I suck my teeth. 'We'll flaming *try*, with every stitch of us!' I vow.

Crow nods. 'Aye. You all heard her!'

I chatter to ask terrodyls for help and they let us attach cords to their feet. Then they lift off for Haggle's Town, bringing our ship with them. The ship-builders will be able to help us. I pray they will.

The Hagglers always did say we brought the terrodyls to their shores. This time, they'd be right. But they won't do any harm. They swore me a promise.

When we get to Haggle's Town, the air bristles with the stinks of seaweed and sulphur and the droppings of all kinds of sea-birds. Folks burn oyster shells to make lime to repair buildings. Boats are heaved into the water again, and fisherwomen and men stand in them, jaws set, eyes sparkling with new hope. Coopers bash nails into barrels, the air rings with the hammering of the blacksmiths and chimneys cough up little puffs of steam as ovens are lit. Food's been shared out from the stores of the former Wilder-King and the Skadowan, so until crops regrow there'll be enough for the poorer folk to survive.

Somehow, even here, folk know who I am. They call out to me as I pass. 'Greetings, Mouse Arrow-Swift!'

'Try one of my cinnamon buns!'

Da whistles. 'You are famed, Bones!'

I punch his arm. 'Leave it out!'

We meet Pip, Vole, Frog and the little 'uns at the Star Inn. They toast me, making me flush. Pip musses my hair roughly, trying to cover the tears in his eyes. Bear grabs me and swings me up onto his shoulders like he ent seen me in a whole moon-cycle. His laugh rumbles deep in his chest.

While we're lodging at the Star, waiting in painful hope for news of the repairs, Leopard flies in to meet with me and my crew.

'Mouse!' she hurries to greet me. 'I've brought news. Is your grandmother here, too? I think she'd be most interested!'

'No,' I tell her, flicking my eyes to the ceiling, where in an upstairs chamber Grandma sleeps all day and night, babbling under her breath. A spear of pain pierces my insides.

'Oh. Well, you can tell her about it when she's awake.'

We take a table in the common room of the inn, next to the fire. The flames throw shadows over Leo's face.

'A king once found a way to steal the Opals for himself,' she begins, staring into the surface of the wine in her pewter goblet. 'It should have been impossible. The Opals were guarded. But the King bided his time and found a way.' She clears her throat. The inn's so quiet you could hear a needle drop. 'Stag was like the old King in the legend. He wanted to rule over all that lived. This is why it is vital that traders trade stories and songs. We must never let a Trianukkan forget what happened, how history can circle back round. Also,' she pauses, reaching out to cover my hands in hers. 'We must look to the old ways to protect the Crown, once more. Each jewel in the Crown keeps us unified. Differences bind us; they should not drive us apart. We must elect one king or queen from every great Tribe to rule for peace and people.' Her eyes are unwavering.

My heart squirms out of my chest and drops, quivering, into my boots. It lies there, like a dead fish, gills flickering.

No. Not this.

'Mouse, you—'

I push my chair back with a loud *scrape*. My heart bounds into my throat. Every head in the inn that weren't already

355

looking at me and whispering turns to me now. My cheeks burn. I try to speak but my mouth just flaps like a gill, so I blunder out of the inn and into the street. Ignoring the greetings that follow me, I run to the docks where my ship's being repaired.

I wish I could raise anchor, right now! I didn't do everything I did just to end up further from my home than ever. I stare out to sea. Then, walking fast, I skirt the hulls of all the docked ships, my boots crunching mussel shells.

The *Huntress* is rolled on her back, and carpenters swarm over her, hammering away at the clinker planking. I recognise one of them, who survived the mutiny against Stag. 'Mouse!' she shouts. She straightens, wiping sweat from her brow. Then she slithers off the ship onto the dockside, the little silver hammer at her belt tinkling.

We press our foreheads together in a Tribe-Kiss. 'Ent she ready, yet?'

The carpenter shakes her head. 'But it's more hopeful than I'd thought. The *Huntress* is a proper fighter.'

Despite my trapped, panicked feeling, I grin.

'What is it, Mouse?'

I scuff my toe. 'I need to get out of here,' I whisper.

The carpenter's eyes widen. 'You will,' she says, sweeping her eyes quickly over our ship and then back to my face.

'No. Leo's there, at the Star.' I jerk my thumb in the inn's direction. 'She says they're to crown three kings and queens. One for each of Sea, Sky and Land.'

'Oh.' The carpenter looks about as sickened by the news

as I feel. 'But no one from Sea can do a thing like that – if you're a queen you'd have to sit around listening to the people's gripes all day. We rove!'

'Aye, don't I know it!'

'How could they expect one of us to stay still?'

I shake my head, struck dumb by the stupids throbbing off it.

She blows out her cheeks. 'Alright, kid. Leave it with us. If we have to sneak you off these docks before the crowning, that's just what we'll have to do.' She stalks back to the side of the ship and heaves herself up onto the hull, picks up her tools and gets back to work with a fresh burst of fury.

I stagger backwards like she's slapped me. Her words confirmed my frights and made them bite harder. *If we have to sneak you off these docks . . .*

She *knows* they're gonna pick me. I double over and throw up into the water lapping the harbour. I ent no queen. I'm just me. And that's what I wanna get on with being.

When I get back to the inn, Crow's searching for me. His face is thunderous. 'I won't let them, don't you worry.'

So *he* knows what's coming, too.

'Mouse?' calls Vole. She rushes outside, her bab strapped to her chest, its head bobbing. 'We need you, upstairs!'

'Grandma?'

Vole's face is pale and the corners of her mouth are turned down and her eyes are ringed by black bags. When I ask after Grandma, two stark spots of colour burn in her cheeks. I should never have left her side, even for a heartbeat!

I take the stairs two at a time.

Either side of Grandma's bed sit Da and Sparrow, each holding one of her hands.

'Bones?' she whispers. 'Is that you?'

Da moves out of the way and I sink to my knees, taking her hand.

'Child. We had some *adventures*, aye?'

I nod, but my voice is locked underneath a lump like a rock in my throat. Not again. Not again. I can't lose her again.

'At least this time, we have a chance to say farewell,' whispers Da.

I bite down on my tongue, hard. I know he's right. But it don't make any of this a stitch easier.

'Take your lessons from bottlenose dolphins,' Grandma mutters. 'Be joyful, like them. For the gods' sake be joyful every now and then!'

Beyond the small window in her room, a twist of silver light begins to dance. Grandma turns her head on the pillow to watch the fire spirits. She stays silent for a long beat, then nods slowly. 'Mouse,' she says, turning to me. 'Will you join me in a reading?'

I gape at her. 'Aye, course.' What I don't say is that I don't know if I'm any good at reading the spirits.

I tuck in next to her in bed, and Sparrow gets in with us too. It's a clear night and soon the fire spirits have kicked into a joyous riot, twisting and arcing in white ribbons and green jags and purple flickerings.

'Open the window, child,' rasps Grandma.

She takes my hand and starts pointing out shapes. We look for signs. We mutter to each other. Sparrow's snuffled breathing soon tells us he's fallen asleep. I feel the fire spirits playing at the edge of the in-between, alive beyond the rules of time. Before dawn, we know who the crowns of Sky and Land are going to. As for the Sea, I can't tell and Grandma won't say. She asks for a scrap of parchment to write on. My heart feels heavy.

After breakfast, I hurry back to her room. She ent breathing often enough. I watch her chest. It barely moves, and when it does, the breaths are shallow. But she's smiling. 'I can feel her calling me, Mouse.'

'*Who?*' I gasp, against the iron-heavy sadness tugging at the corners of my mouth.

Her smile broadens. 'The sea.'

I twist my neck to look behind me for Da. He steps closer and puts a hand on my shoulder. 'I'm here.' His voice is torn to rags.

I close my eyes and let the shuddering, sorrowful wave roll up through me.

I press my forehead to her withered hand and let the aching in me gouge out tears that spill onto her skin.

In my dream, I fly to our ship, but the Huntress *is changed again. She's not wrecked, but she don't look the same. The guns are gone,* the dredger vanished. But I don't recognise the crew.

A hatch opens, and a girl strides out. 'Stop messing with me, Owl!' she shouts. 'I always know when Huntress changes course, even by a whisker!' Determination and fierceness and a spark of mayhem, shifting like the sea, set her mouth into a grim line and make her blazing eyes dance. She fights down laughter as she strides away from the hatch, her mess of wild, matted brown hair hanging down, curved silver blade at her hip. Hail drums against the sea, punching the waves flat.

Grandma?

Echoes pulse through me, from my own time.

Jump, witch.

My spirit rushes after her.

The girl – my fifteen-moons-old Grandma – prowls along the storm-deck, hiding behind barrels. Then she pounces, wrestling a yellow-haired boy with a sea-hawk on his shoulder to the boards. The hawk bursts into the rigging with a hiss.

Storm-Tamer no-sit, stupid two-leg brawlings!

Storm-Tamer? He was Grandpa's hawk – this boy must be Grandpa!

'Get off me, Wren!' He grins broadly, freckled face dimpling.

They look so heart-glad. Peacefulness fills me. I let the dream-currents pull me away from them, until their words are lost somewhere in the long-ago.

When I wake up, I realise I must've fallen asleep holding Grandma's hand. I lift my head. 'Grandma?' I murmur. But she's slipped away.

45

A Crowning

Spring warms our skins and makes the sea sparkle and shiver. The gods lay down green blankets for the beasts to birth their babs on. Sparrow patrols the harbour, singing with the whales that seek him. We celebrate his ninth birth-sun, and he makes us call it his nine-and-a-*halfth* cos the Withering froze the seasons, and so we're late marking it.

The Hoodwink sea-hawks return from the south. Watching them makes me feel like I've swallowed a rock.

A hawk who calls herself Bone-Breaker builds a nest in my chamber, and I can't chase her away. So in the end I shrug, like, *so what?* And I take to ignoring her.

But before I can blink, there are large, smooth eggs in the nest. Soon, Breaker's got hatchlings of her own. And they make a proper noisy racket in my room, with their constant shriekings for food.

Bone-Breaker! You sneak!

She chortles at me.

One of the fledglings makes a home in the hood of my

cloak and won't leave me alone. She chitters and chatters, zooming round my head, begging for scraps and games.

Worms, she whispers, proper husky-bab-soft.

And before I know it, I'm giggling and playing peek-a-boo with her and feeding her worms and tearing off bits of fish for her eager, gulping beak.

The guilt stings. No hawk could *ever* replace Thaw. But I've missed having a hawk by my side. And telling tales of Thaw's bravery to this little hawk will help keep her memory pulsing with life.

The ship repairs are slow but steady. Talking to the carpenters and ship-builders about our crew's needs distracts me for a while from the thought of Leo's return to Haggle's Town.

I've got one leg out the window of my chamber when Da steps into the room and hauls me back inside. 'You have to hear her,' he says, firmly. He's as fretted as I am, I realise. But he's right.

Folk have been calling at the inn to bring 'gifts for the Sea-Queen'. But I stay locked in my room. I've had robes stitched with golden sea-silk, flagons of spiced kaffy, wooden carved whale shapes and clay pots of lobster stew and necklaces of coral and amber and fat jars of priceless honey – I've eaten most of *that* straight from the jar, heart-thanks very much – and a litter of sleek white kittens wearing silk bows that I had to give straight back before Bone-Breaker could swallow them whole or feed them to her squalling fledglings. Of all the stupid gift-givings!

I almost trip over a pile of gifts as I stomp my way down the rickety wooden stairs to meet Leo. Outside, more folk are pressed against the windows, arms laden with gifts for me. When they catch sight of me, they send up a great cheer that rattles the windows and sends smoke belching out of the fireplace. Before I can gift them all my rudest gesture, Da pins my arms by my sides. 'Calm your sails,' he whispers in my ear.

'Right, I will!' I declare, marching over to sit by Leo. She turns to me in surprise. 'So, d'you wanna tear my sails down now, or later?' I hold out my hands. 'Why don't you bind my wrists and have done with it?'

'I'm sorry, Mouse,' she says, eyes round. 'I am unsure of what you mean.'

I fall silent, hide my face in the steam of a cup of wish-tea that the innkeep brings me. The tea tastes like a salty fish broth. Yapok and the Skybrarian sent a recipe here, as a heart-thanks for saving their iceberg from the storms. At least *their* gift is simple and of some flaming use to me.

'I came to talk to you on the matter of the kings and

queens,' says Leo, pulling a piece of parchment from her pocket. It's Grandma's letter – the one she wrote after we read the fire spirits.

My gut twists so sharply that I catch my breath. 'Well, I *know* that!'

'Mouse,' warns Da, drawing up a chair next to us. 'You are being frightful rude to our friend.'

I whip to face him, feeling fire lick my cheeks. 'What choice I got? You're not the one that's gonna end up strapped down to the land! I'd rather be fed to the scuttle-spiders! It's *my* life,' I finish lamely, sounding like Sparrow.

'Mouse, I think you have misunderstood,' says Leopard, sipping her tea. Her lips twitch with a buried smile. 'Your grandmother did not glimpse queenship as your destiny.'

'She wrote to you, though?' I whisper, hardly daring to breathe. 'She wouldn't tell me who would get the crown for the Sea, and I thought—'

She smiles at me. 'I and the other Tribe leaders would like to make you the Sea-leader at the stone circle, for every Tribe-Meet. But not the Sea-Queen.'

'*Gloriousness!*' I fling up my arms, knocking my tea across the table. I push back my chair and lean over, wrapping my arms around Leo. '*Heart*-thanks!'

The folk in the inn mutter amongst themselves. *Not queen? Why not? Who, then? She'd better give me back my sea-silk!*

'I never wanted it anyway, slackwits!' I yell joyfully over my shoulder. I can't wipe the grin off my mouth. It clings like honey and tastes just as sweet.

Leo casts her eyes across Grandma's letter, and swallows. 'Wren wrote that the Sea-*King* is to be your brother, Sparrow.'

'What?' hisses Da.

My mouth falls open. '*What?*' I echo. A laugh bursts from my lips. 'Sparrow, a flaming king?'

'This is not funny, Mouse,' scolds Da, like I'm the one that said it. His hands fidget like they always do when he's tense, and he twists his gold hair into a knot atop his head. Then he turns to Leo. 'My son is far too young and ill of health, and he needs his family.'

'Wren did express similar concerns,' explains Leo, gifting Da a sympathetic look. 'Nonetheless, she saw what she saw.'

Sparrow taps into the room using his stick, a moonsprite buzzing round his head.

They tell him the fate Grandma glimpsed, and that kingship would involve learning at Nightfall, and his face lights up.

'I don't think it's a wise step, though,' starts Da. But Sparrow's got other ideas.

'Da,' he whines, in his get-what-he-wants voice. 'I want to be a skoller at Nightfall.'

'Why you wanna do that?' I say, wrinkling my nose.

'That's where they've got the best healings in Trynka, *stupid*.' He pushes his loose tooth. 'I'll get more better there.'

'He's right,' I say in surprise.

'Button up, you,' Da orders, colour flaring in his cheeks Sparrow smirks.

Huh. Whenever there's kin-trouble I'm always the one to

suffer, whether or not I've caused it.

'You'll have to give me time to mull all this over, and talk in private with my child,' says Da.

'But,' pipes Sparrow. 'But it's *my* li—'

'If I hear that again from either one of you today, it'll be bed with no suppings,' Da declares. He looks tired and old. This must all have taken such a bite out of him.

By sunset, Sparrow's worn Da down. 'I'm the King,' he hisses close by my ear. 'You'd better bow!'

I hit out at him but he dodges. '*Bow*, my backside!'

When Leo returns, Da signs a golden parchment with a quill, proclaiming Sparrow the first King of the Sea for hundreds of years. *Hah*. What a lark.

We send letters for the other two the fire spirits chose to crown. Then we wait. The scroll Da signs splutters out clouds of impatient dust.

Crow's taken to watching me from the edges of rooms, and scuffing away when I approach him. I find him sitting on the dockside, swinging his legs over the side.

'S'pose this is it, then,' he mutters when I sit down.

'What you on about?'

'All this Sea, Sky and Land,' he says, looking at me sidelong. 'I'm from the land, ain't I. S'pose I'll see you at the next Tribe-Meet.'

I grab his hand. 'Would you stop spouting stupids? There's no crew without you.'

He gifts me a weak grin. 'You do know I'm gonna spew

all over your shiny new timbers?'

'Wouldn't expect anything less of a stinking *land-lurker*.'

He punches me on the arm and I kick out at his shin and then we're hugging and laughing and chattering ten to the dozen about everything that's happened and everything we're gonna do on our first voyage. 'Most of all, I'm gonna crush anyone I find trading slaves,' I vow.

He nods. 'Sounds like a ruddy plan.'

Kestrel arrives at Haggle's Town early the next morning, and quick as you like she gets to stealing everyone's breath with her jaw-drop beauty. It's stark-glaring-obvious how tall and rare she is, in this stooped little fishing town.

Kes finds me in my chamber and we hug rib-crack tight. 'Have you heard?' she asks, voice quaking with nerves.

'Course,' I tell her. 'I helped read the spirits.'

Her freckles glow. 'I hardly know what to think!'

I grin. 'You'll have to meet with the Sea-King – that's Sparrow, would you believe – at Nightfall. You could do some library learning while you're there.' I watch her face. 'You do *want* to be Sky-Queen, don't you?'

'Oh, well – yes, *desperately*,' she confesses, making me laugh. 'Is that terrible?'

'Never!'

'It's just – such a huge thing. I don't know if I'll do it right.'

'I know that feeling,' I tell her, thinking of my own fate. 'You'll be flaming thunderous, though.'

We spend time talking about Egret, and the strength of the love she had for Kes – the love that saved Kes's life and healed her soul.

At sundown, Axe-Thrower steps out of a Moonlands long-boat, onto the harbour. Me and Grandma saw the proud, fierce, loyal fighter in the fire spirits, and we saw how right it was that the power should go to a woman that's known the horror of slavery for herself.

Axe finds me and sweeps me into a fierce, one-armed embrace. She licks her fangs. 'Girl,' she says, eyes sweeping the docks. 'In my life, I never felt worth anything. You have shown me my worth, and helped me see that others find me of value – and not to trade, as my warring father did. I will always fight by your side.'

We leave for Whale-Jaw Rock and the next day, as the sun touches the sea, Sparrow, Kestrel and Axe-Thrower are crowned the new Queens and King of Trianukka, in front of hundreds of cheering folk. Some of them are proper important – lords, ladies, chieftains, true mystiks. Toadflax, Hoshi, Bluebottle and the Spidermaster are there, too, along with an overwrought Old One who keeps fussing over Sparrow. The Skybrarian is there – though Yapok chose to stay with his books – and the new Wilderwitch leader accompanied the old man.

Torches are set in crevices in the rock. Moonsprites swarm around our heads. One tickles my ear as it brushes past. I walk over hard lumps in the ground with puffs of steam rising from them. 'Mind the eggs, mind the eggs!' warns a woman. 'We'll be celebrating with these afterwards!' I stop moving and glance down at my boots. I'm standing on a dip in the ground where a pool of water bubbles – a miniature geyser. Inside the pool, an egg is poaching.

'One each of Sea, Sky and Land!' calls Leopard. She beckons each one forwards.

'Sparrow Sea-King!'

He stumbles forwards, almost tripping on the edge of his fancy-breeches cloak. He bows and she places a crown on his head, set with tiny bright green emeralds.

Da squeezes my shoulder and whoops loudly.

'Kestrel Sky-Queen!'

Kes walks forwards, elegant as anything, and to my shock Lunda lets the tears drip freely down her chin and claps the loudest of anyone. Kes's crown is set with blue sapphires.

'Axe-Thrower Land-Queen!'

Axe stalks forwards, chin lifted high. She accepts her amber-studded crown and then her eyes seek me out. We nod to each other.

After the ceremony, we eat the geyser-poached eggs nestled inside lumps of bread that's threaded with baked seaweed.

It hurts that I so badly wanted Kes for crew, and now she never will be. But she's found something she needs to do, and folk want her to do, so I push away my disappointment. Crow catches my eye and grins. I can read him like runes on parchment, along with all his hidden meanings. He's itching to rove as much as I am. Excitement pops in my belly.

46

Sea Voyages, for the Living and the Dead

I stand at the base of the plank and stare up at the towering flank of the *Huntress*. My fledgling sits on my hand, peering at me. *Nest-homenest-homenest-home!*

Aye, you're right, it's your new nest-home! Soon I'll have to get telling you some hero-tales of a hawk who once lived here, too. She was called Thaw-Wielder.

Bone-Breaker and the rest of her nestlings are already in the Hoodwink.

'Is there any of our blood left in The *Huntress*'s veins?' I ask the carpenters.

'Aye,' says one. 'The boards from the cabin where you were born have been sanded down and made into the new Hoodwink, so your blood and your ma's protects the hawks. But, other than that, much of her is new timber, Captain. I'm sorry.'

I think of what Crow said. Our home is together.

A *cabin's wooden walls, is all.* 'You've got naught to be sorry for! It's time to let the past set sail.' Then I realise what she said and flush furiously. *Captain?* Not yet!

Cheered by my crew, I walk up the plank onto the storm-deck. 'Crow?' I call behind me.

'Here!' He bounds onto the deck and stands there with his hands on his hips, surveying the ship like he's sailed a hundred times before.

'Keep your mitts off the raw eels – they're for bait, remember? – and you'll be fine.'

He guffaws, pinching me under the ribs. 'Yeah, yeah, Miss Big-for-boots. Don't forget us little folks when yer captain, eh?'

When everyone's aboard, we load an oaken casket onto the deck. Grandma. Raising anchor with us one last time. *And after that I'll be raising hell on her behalf.*

Then I stare down the plank. Sparrow stands there, wearing his kingly cloak spun from golden sea-silk and looking krill-small. His pearly eyes gleam with mischief, and his fingertips glow. 'Go on then, if you're going!' he yells rudely.

'Sparrow,' chides Da. I watch as he bites back tears. 'You're *heart-certain* you're going through with this?'

'Course,' calls Sparrow. 'You're the ones that ent brave about it, not me. Kes is waiting for me back at the inn. She said she couldn't do goodbyes and she'll see you at the Tribe-Meet for Dread's Eve, Mouse.'

I nod, trying to smile.

'Anyway,' says Sparrow. 'I'm the King, and kings can't stand around all day chattering to you lot!'

Da laughs, and his laugh splutters into a cry. Which makes me think it might be a good idea to get on with it before he can change his mind and grab Sparrow.

Plenty of the oarsmen and women were slaves, once, homeless stragglers looking for work that I wanted to gift a chance to. Some were living inside the wrecked hulls at the breaking yards and I hadn't got the heart to chuck them out. All of them assemble on deck with the crew I've known all my life, my Tribe, and I get them to gather round.

'Navigator,' I call.

'Present,' says Da, smiling.

'Chief oarsman!'

Bear steps forwards, thumping his fist to his broad chest, gifting me a broad grin to match.

I list the rest. 'Helmswoman, prentices, Whale-Singer—' I falter.

Vole steps forwards. 'I have song-spells and your brother's voice in staff-crystals, enough to guide us until we meet him next.'

I swallow, nod. Then I fill my pipes, ready to roar. '*We rove!*'

The whole crew boom the old Tribe-words back to me.

'*We rove to trade, to meet, for the restlessness in our bones, we rove at one with the sea!*'

Sparrow yells along with the crew. I watch their faces, proper awestruck.

There's a cranking sound as the anchor lifts from the seabed. Sparrow takes a step back from the ship, sudden uncertainty scrawled over his face.

I run to the rail and stare down at him. 'Sparrow! You're gonna be the best king ever!' We pull away from him. My belly drops. I can't leave him. What was I thinking?

'Sparrow!' I scream.

'Mouse!' he calls, but he's grinning. He flaps his hands. 'You'll do alright!' he yells, cupping his hands round his mouth. And I realise it's me who's doubting, not him.

'I'll miss you!' I shout. 'And I love you!'

'Love you too, stinker!' There's no trace of scorn in his voice. His face is open and keen. I clutch the rail, throat aching. I want to fix this picture of him in my mind, press a forever-memory there. Cos who knows how much he'll have changed, next time I see him?

The crew surround me, grinning and hooting and howling. Sparrow waves to them as the ship moves away. *Don't you dare weep*, I tell myself. *Don't be such a stupid bab. Shed your tears in private, like a real captain.* I catch my sea-hawk's eye as the sunlight plays in her feathers and on the waves. She lends me heart-strength.

The oarsman's drum, *Huntress*'s life-pulse, begins to beat.

The world boils down to the sickening lurch in my stomach as I watch Sparrow grow smaller and smaller on the dock. And oh, the song-notes. The notes are everything. Scores of blue jewels pouring from his lips, sending us on our way. He's singing at the top of his lungs. Da waves frantically to him, and I know he's fighting to look brave. Then Sparrow turns back towards the Star Inn.

Soon my world is as it should be – salty, damp, sweaty, rocking, stinking tallow-rich and gusting with birch smoke. I help with tarring the ropes so I can smell it again, and to take my mind off Sparrow.

When the stars spark in the sky, we finally gift Grandma her rightful sea-burial. Tears flood my face as crew shoot fire-arrows into the night, after the hunting boat cradling her casket has been pushed out to sea. Her gnarled fingers grasp her longbow. I smeared her cheeks in hawk droppings and made her a crown of feathers. Nestled close to her side is my heart-bright hawk, Thaw-Wielder. Pots of medsin made by Vole nestle in the casket, together with a map for navigating the death-sea. At the last beat I remembered Sparrow's asking and put the box that held Thunderbolt's moon-dust in the casket, too.

I don't know if Grandma will ever be a wraith again. But I know she'll always be the captain of my heart, guiding me.

I'm in the captain's cabin, changing for bed – but leaving my boots on, in case I'm needed on deck – when light flickers in the corner of my eye. I jump onto my bunk and fling open the porthole.

In the sky, the fire-spirits dance and ripple. Grandma used to say they told her I'd be a captain, before I was even born.

I used to think being a captain was about giving orders. It's only now I've roved with my crew, for the sake of saving what matters, that I know it's *so much* more, and that there's still so much I ent yet earned the right to claim. The bones-deep heart-truth of the teachings Wren gifted me ring through my marrow.

A skilful captain learns to weather stormy seas, but only once she's learned to weather her crew.

I turn as heavy footsteps thud into my cabin. Da and Bear duck into the room, grinning. I bite my lip, eyes filling.

'We just wanted to let you know, we'll be by your side *every* last beat,' says Bear, tapping his fingers on the drum slung over his shoulder. 'You don't have to captain this fine she-beast alone – though we know you could, girl.'

Da winks. 'You've got the belly for the work.'

47
Hunter's Moon

The morning of my fourteenth Hunter's Moon, I jolt awake, in a cabin again for the first time in so long. The lantern by my bed squeals on its hook as the ship rolls. I bury my face in my pillow, smiling at memories of when Vole showed me how to gather moonlight to make fresh moonlamps now that the moon's returned. But I was so clumsy I dripped enough scraps of moonlight to make a moonsprite army. I'll have to send a few to Sparrow at Nightfall, not that we could ever replace Thunderbolt. Tonight, I will have swelled with the extra moon I've gathered. I hold up my arms, looking at all the goose pimples and fine hairs, and the muscles I'm so heart-proud of. Am I different, somehow?

There's a knock at my door. 'Captain?' calls Crow.

'Would you stop calling me that?' I bellow. 'I ent captain yet!'

He barges into the cabin, carrying a platter of moon-day cinnamon buns.

'Thank the gods.' I prop myself onto an elbow. 'It were

getting lonely in here!'

He grins weakly. His face is green. 'Don't throw up in here,' I tell him. Then I remember I've still got some of Kes's sky-sickness petals in my pockets and rummage to get them. I roll out of bed in my smallclothes and Crow shields his eyes.

I laugh at him. 'What's your gripe? You seen me bone-naked, when I almost froze down that wraith-hole.'

'He *what*?' demands Bear, clomping down the stairs into the cabin.

'Er, nothing,' says Crow quickly, cheeks stained red.

'Better be nothing, boy,' grunts Bear

Even though it's my moon-day and Bear reckons I can take time off, I don't. I've found that I love the work of a captain, that I hardly find it work, though it's hard. I make my rounds, talking to the carpenters, checking on the oarsfolk, chattering to the sea-hawks and bringing broth to the helmswoman. I check folk for injuries and visit the medsin lab, where Vole and her little bab, who the fire spirits named Hedgehog, are busy working. Hog mostly gurgles and plays with roots and petals, but we forgive her for that, cos she's proper bonny. Bear's always fussing over her.

We dock to greet the Moonlanders and trade amber and jet for walrus hides. Then we grill herring and while the Tribes feast, I skim stones with Da. Each stone is a piece of land, passing through the sky before falling into the sea.

We speak of one day sailing beyond Trianukka, and I can hardly imagine it – but my blood thirsts for the adventure.

When we sail again, I scan the skies and the waves and try to stay aware of the workings of my ship. And then the sun sinks, and my moon rises, and it's time to swear my oath.

'Please be with me this night, Grandma.' *I need your guidance. We will rove, and we will trade. But we will guard folks' freedoms fiercely, and we will rescue, too.*

Vole comes to my cabin and brushes my tangles – the only bits of blue left at the very tips. She threads moonstones into my hair and drapes a gleaming white fur around my shoulders. I practise my vows under my breath until she slips cool fingers beneath my chin, making me look at her.

'Mouse. You will be fine. You are your grandmother's granddaughter. And – how wondrous – you will be a captain with the beast-chatter! A *true* captain,' she adds, when she sees my look. For a beat, I remembered Stag.

I haul my longbow over my shoulder, and breathe. 'I'm ready.'

'We all know it,' says Vole. Hedgehog gurgles at me from her sling on Vole's chest, and I kiss her head.

Above decks, I take the wrapped scroll from Bear. It's a map. The first map of my own. I face my crew. Crow's eyes shine bright in the darkness. The wind grabs fistfuls of my hair. 'Across the seas, by oar, by sail, no wind nor storm will see me fail!' I shout.

'The drum will beat, let no blood seep, down into the

water!' they answer.

'My heart, my life, my strength won't rest, until I've passed my True-Tribe's test!'

'Aye!' they boom, as one. 'Stand arrow-straight, stay heart-strong!

'I *swear* you'll find no truer form, to guide you through from dusk 'til dawn. Your captain fierce and swift and fair, who stands for all you do not dare.'

'Not us! 'Tis a captain's place!'

'For long since you've all gone to rest, according to the day's bequest . . .'

'With gripes and growls and belly-swells!' they roar, falling about with laughing.

I laugh with them. '*I'll* linger long into the night, in case some shade brings forth a fight.'

'Is that who you declare to be? Standing straight in front of me? Look inside, down to your bones, and swear above all else to rove!'

I lift my chin and thump my chest. 'I'll read the pictures in the lights, the gifts that tell us future Sights. My hawk soars strong of heart and claw, from summer's freeze to winter's thaw.' My hawk lifts from my arm and soars above everyone, making them gasp. She comes to rest on Crow's shoulder.

For the final part of the oath, the crew chant the words like a spell, voices rising louder and louder, and joyful enough to touch the stars.

'Kiss your bow and wrap your scroll, heed the drum

and glimpse the shoal, through the veil to a darker time, knowing no cabin can forever be thine!' In the black sky, a long, pale fire spirit, like a plume of silver hair, begins to dance.

'I heed the pulsing, the blue whale's call, that *every ship has a soul!*' I tip back my head, and I howl.

Cos our song is more than fight and fire. It's peace. It's hope.

It's home.

Huntress

Epilogue

The little 'uns want another story, so below decks I go. The sea's song fades as I descend into the gut of my ship. Every cabin door I pass gifts me a different ghost.

Oarsman Bear when he turned sixty, three moons before he passed into the Other Realm, white-haired and chuckling, clutching his birth-sun gifts to his chest.

Da chasing Hog through the passageways, when the child had six or seven birth-moons under her belt. Da again, after he wed Leopard, telling me he wanted to live with her at Hackles. Gods, how I teased him for choosing to dwell as a land-lurker!

Next comes a memory of Crow, barging out of his cabin to tell me to make anchor at the nearest dock so he could 'eat something without gills or scales for once.' He never quite conquered his sea-sickness.

My greatest friend. Lost so long, now. My knees creak and I wipe my hands on my breeches, bone-tired. My hands can't hold a bow like they used to.

'Tell us a story, Captain Mouse!'

'Tell us about how you became the greatest captain what ever lived!'

'Suck-up!'

'Am *not*! She *is* the greatest – she stopped the slave trade in Trianukka, single-handed! Without her, your grandma would've died in chains, *dolt*.'

Single-handed? Not a jot. I grip the locket around my neck, thinking of the lock of red hair tucked inside. *Kestrel made it look as if the defeat of the slavers was all my work. But without her, it could never have been done. Gods. Much missed, that one is!*

'You're still a suck-up, though. How old *are* you, Captain Mouse? My sister says you're a hundred and three!'

'You *can't* ask Captain that!'

'And *how* is your sea-hawk still alive? Is it magyk?'

'*Shhh!*'

'Tell us about Captain Rattlebones!'

'Nah, tell us about Captain Wren, when she death-walked back into battle!'

'Tell us about your brother, the great Sea-King scholar of Nightfall!'

Sparrow. I feel a smile flood my eyes. It's been many moons since I last shared a flagon with my brother, and I know I must see him and hear his song again before I settle my bones for the final voyage. *That decides it.* I will call him home one last time.

I whisper to my cragged old sea-hawk, and she swoops over, landing on my arm.

Come home, too-soon, I beast-chatter. The words scratch themselves into a piece of parchment as I speak them. *Come and sing with the whales and paint hidden maps on my sails.* My hawk soars away through a port-hole, the parchment scrolled around her leg. She'll ride the sky to where my brother the Sea-King keeps order over the scholars of Nightfall.

After telling the fireside tales, I'm just laying my head down to catch a few winks when the ringing of the alarm bell shatters the silence. 'Hell's flaming teeth!' I curse, bolting upright again. 'No rest for the wicked, eh?'

I prowl from my cabin, drumming my hands against my ship's walls. 'To arms! Bows and bills! Come *on*, you belching babble of layabouts!'

'Aye, Captain!' boom the crew.

Acknowledgements

Heart-thanks to the unstoppable Liz Bankes, for making Storm scrub up so nicely – you are a total hero. To magical Ali Dougal and everyone at Egmont for believing in me and for helping to bring this trilogy to life. Special mention to Laura Bird, Ray Tierney, Joe Mclaren and Janene Spencer for more gorgeous artwork and another epic cover. To Siobhan McDermott for being the best accomplice on the Sky Tour (and for always providing enormous slabs of post-event cake.)

To Ruth, for the road trip to the Sedlec Ossuary at Kutna Hora, which inspired the Bone Crypts of Hackles. I love adventuring with you.

To Becca for introducing me to old Icelandic lullabies.

To Alyssa for your amazing feedback on early drafts (especially the beat-by-beat reactions in gif form. You rock.)

To the Offenders crew for critiquing (what was then) chapter one of Storm and for always being there when I need you. Your support means the world.

To Abi Elphinstone for reading the almost-final

manuscript and being so enthused about it, and providing such lovely quotes.

To the Wellcome Collection for your exhibition 'Electricity: The spark of life,' which inspired the development of Sparrow's powers.

To Head Falconer Gerard at East Sussex Falconry, for a brilliant falconry experience at Herstmonceux castle. Your passion and respect for raptors made Sky's book birthday a more than memorable one.

To the wonderful folk at Ofelaš, northern Sweden, for the most magical time in the forest, under the northern lights. It was amazing to talk with you about Sámi culture, indigenous rights and Icelandic horses!

To the woman who held my hat on while we were riding the husky sled in -37 degrees. I owe you my ears and wish I could remember your name!

To my readers, including Juliette for sending me my first letter, Harry for building the extraordinary Lego model of the Huntress (and for the amazing feat of reading while tying your shoelaces), Ellen for reading along from *Sky* during a school visit, Eliza for going as Kestrel for World Book Day (complete with feathers, moons and stars), John for going as Mouse (complete with dragonfly brooch and amber amulet), Millie who told me she'd read *Sea* thirteen times . . . and every reader who has sent a letter or asked a question or waited to get a book signed or just generally been brilliant. You are the best readers an author could wish for and you all kept me going when the going got tough.

To Jay Griffiths for giving the world your phenomenal work *Wild: An Elemental Journey.* The book made for electrifying reading while lying on my bunk aboard the Arctic Circle Train.

It should be noted that while aspects of this trilogy have been influenced by various real life cultures, the Tribes and settings in my book are entirely fictional. If anyone would like to find out more about indigenous peoples and their ongoing battle to protect their rights and their land against oppression, I would recommend the following sources:

- Sofia Jannok, a singer-songwriter, environmental/ indigenous activist and 'yoiker' (a traditional Sámi vocal style) born and raised in Sápmi, the ancestral lands of the Sámi peoples. *sofiajannok.com*

- Survival International – the only human rights organisation dedicated to helping tribal peoples 'defend their lives, protect their lands and determine their own futures.' *survivalinternational.org*